P9-DEY-424

Praise for
Demons Are a Girl's Best Friend

"Step into Linda Wisdom's world of wonder and infinite possibilities, sexy demons and clever witches, laughter, danger, and a surprise on every page."

—Annette Blair, national bestselling
author of *Bedeviled Angel*

"Smart, sexy, and a hell of a ride. Linda Wisdom turns up the heat in this fast-paced adventure—a sizzling, irresistible read."

—Laura Bickle, national bestselling
author of *Embers*

"A wild ride of hexy fun. Maggie and Declan are smokin' together. The Hex just gets better! Wisdom delivers another hexy winner!"

—Nancy Haddock, national bestselling
author of *Last Vampire Standing*

"Humor, danger, and steamy sex make for an exciting read."

—*RT Book Reviews*, 4 stars

"Demons who are hotter than Hades… a story that will keep you captivated to the end."

—*Romance Fiction on Suite101*

"Plenty of romance and passion woven through a well-built and fascinating world."

—*Fresh Fiction*

Praise for *Hex in High Heels*

"Hold on to your broomsticks! Sassy, smart, and so much fun!"

—Terri Garey, bestselling author
of *You're The One That I Haunt*

"Wisdom does a truly wonderful job mixing passion, danger, and outrageous antics into a tasty blend that's sure to satisfy."

—*RT Book Reviews*, 4.5 Stars

"It's fun, it's sassy, it's sexy, and it's oh-so well-written."
—*Long and Short Reviews*

Praise for *Wicked by Any Other Name*

"Fan-fave Wisdom delivers a new tale from her clever magical universe and continues to delight with clearly defined—if somewhat offbeat—characters who face danger with pizzazz."

—*RT Book Reviews*

"As wildly entertaining as the first two with more plot and story line, it's great. A magickal romp you'll love."
—*Fang-tastic Books*

"*Wicked by Any Other Name* by Linda Wisdom is a wickedly fun and magical read!"

—*Cheryl's Book Nook*

Praise for *Hex Appeal*

"Jazz is as irascible, high-maintenance, and quick-tempered as ever, and Nick is the kind of vampire who loves her just the way she is… The main tale is an intriguing look beneath the bravado of Wisdom's characters to their inner fears and vulnerabilities."

—*Booklist*

"Prepare to be entertained as Linda Wisdom pulls out all the stops and tickles the funny bone in this second installment of her often wildly amusing paranormal series."

—*BookLoons*

"A spectacular supernatural story that is full of love, laughter, and plenty of magic in and out of the bedroom!"

—*Night Owl Romance*

Praise for *50 Ways to Hex Your Lover*

"Do not miss this wickedly entertaining treat!"

—Annette Blair, author of *Sex and the Psychic Witch*

"Linda Wisdom's imagination rocks."

—Elysa Hendricks, author of *Star Crash*

"Wisdom's work is a 'one-of' original—funny, sly, charming, and an all-around good time."

—Terese Ramin, author of *Bewitched, Bothered, & BeVampyred*

Also By Linda Wisdom

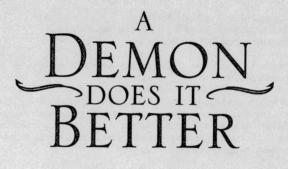

A
DEMON
DOES IT
BETTER

LINDA WISDOM

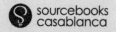

sourcebooks
casablanca

Copyright © 2012 by Linda Wisdom
Cover and internal design © 2012 by Sourcebooks, Inc.
Cover illustration by Tony Mauro

Sourcebooks and the colophon are registered trademarks of
Sourcebooks, Inc.

All rights reserved. No part of this book may be reproduced in any form
or by any electronic or mechanical means including information storage
and retrieval systems—except in the case of brief quotations embodied
in critical articles or reviews—without permission in writing from its
publisher, Sourcebooks, Inc.

The characters and events portrayed in this book are fictitious or are
used fictitiously. Any similarity to real persons, living or dead, is
purely coincidental and not intended by the author.

Published by Sourcebooks Casablanca, an imprint of Sourcebooks, Inc.
P.O. Box 4410, Naperville, Illinois 60567-4410
(630) 961-3900
FAX: (630) 961-2168
www.sourcebooks.com

Printed and bound in the United States of America
QW 10 9 8 7 6 5 4 3 2 1

In memory of my mom,
Thelma Randall, 1923-2011
You taught me a lot over the years, Mom.
I love you, miss you, and I hope
I will always do you proud.

In memory of Beverly Barton,
who departed this earth on April 21, 2011.
Your Champagne smile and infectious laugh
will never be forgotten, just as you yourself won't.
We miss you so much.

Chapter 1

"YOU'RE ALL GOING TO DIE!" A VULTURE, PERCHED ON a granite gargoyle guarding the double doors, flapped his large wings.

Dr. Lili Carter, witch-healer extraordinaire, rolled her eyes at the death scavenger as she walked down the stone steps. "You wish."

She trudged wearily through the parking lot toward her dark purple Mazda CX-7. Early morning fog caressed her ankles with frosty, whispery fingers and slid through her clothing. She shivered from the damp cold that permeated her heavy coat.

Lili tossed the oversize bag holding her scrubs into the backseat and climbed behind the wheel. She wasted no time starting up the engine and cranking up the heater to push back the night chill. She sat there, staring through the windshield, waiting for the interior to warm up.

The towering edifice known to the supernatural world as Crying Souls Hospital loomed before her.

The building hadn't changed over the years. Crafted of dark gray stone in a style popular in the 1700s, it sported squat windows, and old-fashioned carriage lamps dotted the front. She recalled her last time working here, when centaur-drawn ambulances pulled around back to the ambulance bay and dropped off patients unable to fly or materialize in.

The centuries-old hospital might have still boasted

an antiquated exterior but the interior was ultramodern and well-known for its excellent care for all creatures in need of healing.

After an exhausting full moon night in the ER, she should have been thinking about going home and crawling into bed for some much-needed sleep, but Lili knew, after that tiring shift, that any form of rest would be a long time off.

She smiled to herself. "If I'm going to stay awake, I may as well go do some shopping and visit old friends."

"She is back! My much-loved healer has returned! And so beautiful is she!" A portly wizard garbed in brilliant blue silk robes embroidered with gold and silver sigils waddled out of a shop. He smiled broadly as he threw his arms around Lili. Although he was a good five inches shorter than she, he used his magick to ensure he could properly embrace her and kiss each cheek. "Ah, Cleo, my lovely feline. You have also come to visit me." He smiled down at the cat that poked her head out of the cayenne-colored leather tote bag. The fluffy feline inclined her head, accepting her due.

The witch laughed as his salt-and-pepper bushy beard tickled her cheeks while she hugged him back. "You look wonderful, Asmeth. How are you?"

"I am blessed, but only because you knew how to cure those rasthe scales that tormented me." His round body jiggled like Jell-O as he laughed heartily. "Is it true you returned to Crying Souls?" His dark eyes showed curiosity. "And did I hear correctly that while you have been away you even treated mundanes in your last hospital?" He tsked and shook his head in wonder. "Ah, but then you do not have an aversion to working in mundane hospitals, do you?" His tone indicated he couldn't understand why she would do such a thing.

Lili laughed. "Even mundanes need a good healer, Asmeth. Plus, it's good experience. I've missed visiting Inderman," she said lightly, even as she made a quick visual examination to make sure her old friend was speaking the truth about his health. Rasthe scales were nasty as they changed the skin to a rapidly hardening surface until the victim suffocated. Even worse, they didn't always completely disappear after treatment. She was pleased to see he was still scale-free. "Now you won't have to travel as far when you need my skills," she teased.

"But I enjoy traveling to the odd lands of the mundanes to see you. Although I must say I was not very fond of that place you called Minneapolis," he declared, with the drama he was well-known for—one more reason why the wizard was considered larger than life. "Will you stay in Inderman? I know of a few cottages to let." He referred to the magickal plane that offered up everything a preternatural creature would require. Such as his shop, which displayed a wide variety of clothing for the discriminating sorcerer.

Lili shook her head, her high ponytail of curly black hair swinging between her shoulder blades. "I still have my house. I moved back in a couple days ago, although I still have a lot of unpacking to do. I just finished my first shift at the hospital tonight. Since I wasn't tired, I thought I'd come here and do a little shopping." She knew she didn't need to worry about the late hour. The Inderman plane was always open.

"You have come here to see what has changed and what has not changed. Alas, there have been few changes in Inderman." He waved his hands outward. "Reacquaint yourself, but then return to me. We will have wine and talk. I will give you all the gossip," he said with a twinkle in his dark eyes.

She nodded and moved on.

The color, sights, and sounds of Inderman's magickal plane assaulted Lili like a maniacal carnival. It was a place that was more energizing than tiring. There was no need for electricity when globes filled with faery light were much more reliable. She knew she would find everything supernatural she might need and even more she wouldn't. From her first visit, years ago, she'd loved the community that catered to every creature known to the magickal world. She was convinced she could even smell magick in the air like a variety of rare spices, tickling her palate. She watched wraiths weave in and out among the corporeal as they had their own gathering places.

"Some things never change," Cleo said, hopping out of the tote bag and walking beside the witch, her plumed tail held high. The chinchilla-colored Persian feline walked with the dignity that denoted her full name. "It was loud and insane the first time we came here in 1782, and it still is." She sniffed with typical disdain.

"I call it more alive and filled with energy," Lili corrected her. "Something I doubt I'll see that all that much at Crying Souls." Not when she thought about the real reason for her seeking a position there. She looked at the cat who shared the house with her. It was a fact that you couldn't own a cat. They were too arrogant to belong to anyone. Even if Lili was a gifted witch in the healing arts, Cleo was by no means her familiar. She had rescued the arrogant feline from a goblin who thought Cleo would make a tasty meal. Cleo had stayed with her since.

"It is a depressing place, but then, someone has to heal the sick, so it may as well be you, I guess." Cleo looked from right to left. "Is the gourmet fish store nearby? I'd love having some salmon or perhaps some lovely caviar."

"Salmon I can afford, for caviar you need to find someone with a larger bank account." Lili stopped at the fish-and-fowl shop to pick up Cleo's food.

"Ooh, take a look at the hottie," Cleo purred, perking up. Her malachite eyes widened in appreciation as she practically levitated with excitement. "You should go talk to him."

"Not interested," Lili sang under her breath.

"Look to your right and say that again, because he's seriously checking you out. Just don't look like you're looking. You tend to be too direct or talk too much about your work, which only scares them off," the feline advised. "This is why your sex life is nonexistent. A female cannot live by battery-operated instruments alone."

Lili winced. "Is not." The witch whispered a spell under her breath that allowed her to have a better view of who could be spying on her. "I had a date recently."

"That was three years ago."

Lili ignored her cat's snark while she did her best not to drool at the sight of the male standing a short distance away.

Hubba hubba!

Lili's sharp eye figured he was a couple inches over six feet, with black hair in need of a trim, but it didn't detract from his dangerous good looks. If she wasn't mistaken, he had a pair of blue eyes she could happily swim in. She also couldn't miss the shadowy fingers that wrapped around his legs as if they were there to protect him.

"Go over and say hi," Cleo instructed. "Tell him you're new in town and you would just love to know the best places to check out. And ask if he'd like to show them to you." She batted her paw at her very own private witch. "You can't let such a prime specimen get away."

"Are you sure your nagging didn't push Marc Antony into killing himself?" she murmured, smiling as she heard the cat's angry hisses.

Score one for Lili!

The arrogant feline glared at her even as she raised her head and sniffed the air. "Something's off," she muttered.

Lili ignored her furry companion's murmurs as she made her way stealthily in the direction of sexy guy. She knew she should listen to Cleo. After all, who else knew more about the male sex than the sultry queen of the Nile, Cleopatra?

"Subtle, my dear. Be subtle. Not like one of those galloping wolfhounds," Cleo suggested in her usual warm purr that just managed to border on sarcasm.

As always, Lili ignored her and continued window-shopping while edging her way closer to her prey. She mentally rehearsed opening dialogue if they had just "happened" to bump into each other.

Oh, hello. Do you happen to know where Rangel's Harvest Foods might be? Excuse me, but don't I know you from somewhere? Actually, I know I'd remember you if you had been a patient of mine. No forgetting a body like that.

"I said *subtle*." The arrogant feline hissed the last word, easily reading her mind. "No wonder the Greek empire fell." She was fond of making disparaging remarks about Lili's ancestry.

"That was the Roman Empire, and if anyone should know that, it would be you." Lili shook her head. Arguing with a cat in Inderman was nothing unusual. Of course, if mundanes saw her actions, they'd haul her off to a nice quiet cell with extremely soft walls.

There, now she was close enough to *casually* turn and speak to the man. Except he was gone. She didn't care about subtlety now and looked around, but it was as if he had disappeared into thin air. Considering the magick in the air, it was easy enough to believe.

"You'll see him again," Cleo said.

"How do you know?" Lili knew the moment she asked the question that whatever her feline sidekick said would come true. Cleo saw things so many others, even those with precognition, didn't see.

"It's so obvious it's not funny. I saw the way he looked at you." The cat hopped back into the bag and circled the bottom. She curled up in a fluffy ball and waved her tail like a feather duster. "No male looks at a female like that unless he intends to do more than look." She stretched her mouth into a kitty smile and purred. "Plus, he's demon. You know how focused they can be."

Lili smothered her sigh. She knew better than to argue with the feline. She always said the cat should have been a lawyer.

She took her time exploring some of the shops while keeping her senses open. Every so often she was positive the mysterious male was in the vicinity. Except every time she turned around, he was gone.

Cleo sneezed as Lili stepped inside the Shop of Scents.

"My allergies," she complained.

"Then don't breathe." The witch had no sympathy as she examined the many-colored bottles, some labeled, others a mystery.

"You wish something special?" The silver-haired woman at the counter greeted her with a broad smile. "Fragrance to tempt your lover? Something to give you luck perhaps?" Her pale eyes peered at her closely. "Ah, you are the healer. Something soothing, then?"

Lili picked up a bottle and pulled the stopper out. She smelled spring flowers and fresh greenery. Another bottle yielded a winter of sharp ice while the third had her thinking of an ancient bazaar of spices and heat.

"You have not been here in many years," the crone named Sameka said. "You chose a scent that was light and carefree." She gestured toward a delicate pink glass bottle. "No longer is it you. You require a fragrance that holds a hint of darkness and mystery." She held up a finger. "Wait here." She moved with the ease of someone much younger—Lili gauged her years to be past nine hundred. She parted the amethyst silk curtains and disappeared into the back of the shop. She returned a moment later carrying a gilt-trimmed bottle that looked as if it had been owned by royalty. She set it on the counter and carefully eased the stopper out.

Lili didn't need to lift the bottle to inhale the contents. They lifted their way to her. Images of silk, moans in a dark night, and a sensuality that warmed her bones were only parts of what she sensed in the perfume oil. She feared to ask the price. She only had to look at the shopkeeper to know it was very old and very rare.

"This is truly what you are now, and even more so as each day passes," the old woman told her with a knowing smile.

"Huh. She must see something we don't," Cleo muttered.

"Quiet, you." She wanted to try it on her skin. There were no worries it wouldn't smell right with her personal chemistry. Sameka never forgot a customer or what suited them.

"Try it." The male voice near her ear was as intoxicating as the perfume.

She looked up to see her mystery man standing next to her. Dark hair, eyes that rivaled a cobalt ring she had, and so good-looking her senses immediately kicked into overdrive.

He picked up the bottle and carefully tipped it against his fingertip. Turning toward her, he gently traced a path down her throat, then repeated the touch on each wrist. The oil turned to liquid heat, creating thoughts of wearing the perfume and nothing else.

Lili couldn't take her eyes off his hands. Strong, capable, yet gentle. She was positive they would feel the same everywhere else on her.

Get your mind back where it belongs!

Easier said than done.

He lifted her hand, palm up, and bent down to sniff her wrist. His breath drifted over the surface. When he lifted his head, his eyes blazed a vivid blue.

"She's right," he murmured. "This is meant for you."

"Oh my," Cleo said in a hushed whisper.

Lili silently repeated the words, not even realizing that little stunned the jaded cat. For a moment she forgot they had an avid audience.

"I shall wrap it up." The crone swept the bottle away and soon had it nestled in a velvet-covered box.

The witch didn't wince at the high price.

"Who are you?" she asked the man.

"Someone who knows what scent a woman should wear," the crone cackled.

He lifted Lili's hand and pressed a light kiss in the center of her palm. She felt the burn of his lips all the way to her core.

"Someone skilled in the blending of perfume oils?" she asked with a husky tone in her voice she couldn't hide.

This time his lips hovered near her ear. "No. Just a demon who knows what he likes."

As quickly as he appeared he was gone from the dimly lit shop.

"Many years ago, I would have tempted such as he," the shopkeeper sighed, her wide mouth displaying blackened teeth. Her faded eyes twinkled with mischief. "If you wear the perfume of desire, you will see him again."

"I'm not sure my senses could take it," Lili admitted as she gathered up her purchases. She walked outside, now ready to return to Asmeth's shop. She wanted to sit with the garrulous wizard and drink wine and listen to his gossip. If she was lucky, he might even know the demon's name once she described him. For now, she had the memory of his touch. She had a feeling his kiss, still embedded in her palm, would keep her warm that night.

———∿∿∿———

He shouldn't have approached her that way. Spoken to her, touched her. Felt the silken touch of her skin against his lips. The golden light surrounding her told him she was a witch, but there was something more about her he couldn't read. And it wasn't anything to do with her feline cohort who looked at him with a little too much curiosity. Not that an inquisitive cat was anything new.

A witch with a cat familiar. No surprise there.

Jared used the shadows so he wouldn't be easily seen when he was free from the hospital. They allowed him to roam through Inderman and the surrounding area like one of the many specters that inhabited the supernatural community. He was seen, but always managed to ensure he wasn't remembered. Females were drawn to him like moths to a flame. There were even times he didn't mind singeing their wings in a purely carnal way. But no longer. He preferred conserving his power, so he could indulge in trips away from his cell. The trouble was that while the shadows were his friends, they were also his enemies. While they gave him a chance to believe he could have a semblance of a normal life, they also took away that feeling when they decided it was time to return him to his cell.

He felt the painful hitch in his body that meant he would soon be pulled back to the prison he'd called home for so long. The place where he was known as the most monstrous of all fiends.

Jared hoped he would see the exotic-looking witch

again. He knew Inderman would be his best bet to do so. It might be a large community, thanks to the strong magick that kept it animated, but it also had the feel of a small town. He sensed she would return here for shopping and perhaps grab a bite in one of the many taverns and restaurants Inderman offered.

He hungered for the chance to learn her name. He already knew her voice was as striking as her beauty. The old crone had struck just the right note with the perfume oil she offered her. He'd filled his lungs with the fragrance, committing it to memory for the dark hours he would spend in his cell.

For now, his body wanted her. The need grew so strong he didn't feel the pain the shadows inflicted as they pulled him back to his prison.

Chapter 2

Lili sat on the floor with her back resting against the couch. She had a cup of chamomile tea resting by her bare feet. She bent over and touched each nail with a fingertip, watching a dark purple color shimmer on the surface. She next tried a neutral beige/pink on her fingernails. Classical music poured from the speakers that she had arranged around the family room, and pillar candles wafted the soft scent of sandalwood.

She hadn't been able to sleep, so she finally abandoned her bed and came out here to indulge in some girlie pampering. She used her jar of The Body Bakery body cream, a gift from Jazz that smelled like snickerdoodle cookies. She felt the cinnamon and vanilla were a perfect blend with the sandalwood-scented candles. Pretty soon her arms and legs were soft and sweet-smelling and her nails manicured. To top off her girlie night, she pulled a container of Ben and Jerry's Magic Brownies ice cream out of the freezer. The black raspberry ice cream swirled with fudgy brownies was the perfect finishing touch for a night of self-indulgence. Her mindless tasks also helped keep her from thinking too much. Except that now her nails were done and the empty ice cream carton sat on the coffee table, so there was nothing to keep the worries at bay. She leaned back against the couch, the cushion firm against her neck.

The image of the dark-haired male appeared behind her closed eyelids as she drifted in a soft mellow haze. It had been three days, and he hadn't left her thoughts, even if he was nothing more than a faint mist in her memory.

"Why are you haunting me?" The words were a bare murmur. "What exactly are you?"

A tingle of magick prickling along the surface of her skin was her first warning she wasn't alone. Her eyes popped open, and she saw the mysterious man seated on a nearby chair.

"How did you get in here?" she demanded, starting to jump to her feet, but she fell back before she could gain her balance. She chose to ignore her awkwardness.

"Hades if I know," he said, looking around. "You have a nice place. Do you have the sports channels?" He picked up the television remote control.

Lili pushed herself off the floor again and this time managed to remain upright. A wave of her hand sent the remote flying out of his hand and into hers. "This house is heavily warded against unwanted intrusions," she ground out. She tamped down the traitorous lower part of her body that felt all too warm and gooey at the moment. Cleo was right. It had been way too long between dates, not to mention her pretty much nonexistent sex life.

His grin flashed white with a hint of feral. "Let me tell you, I wouldn't be here, in this room, unless you'd been thinking about me." His intense gaze started at the top of her head with its messy topknot down to her bare, freshly polished toes. She resisted the urge to curl her toes.

She backed up until her knees hit the couch cushion.

At least she had something soft to land on when she fell backward. *Damn! She* had *been thinking of him!*

No way she could miss the darkness slithering around his ankles with an intention all its own. She didn't know a lot about demons, but she had no doubt those shadows doubled as reliable transportation.

"It's you!" Not one of her better moments, since she was usually a lot more coherent, but what did one say when a demon suddenly appeared in your family room?

He nodded. "Don't worry. I'm just as surprised as you are. This hasn't happened before."

"Stalking is a crime among the preternatural too." Magick sparked at her fingertips as she readied her defensive power.

"I was invited."

Lili frowned. "Were not."

"Was so." He grinned again, settling back in the chair. "You don't happen to have any wine around, do you? Perhaps a nice Burgundy or Bordeaux?"

She gestured toward her teacup. Plus, she preferred white wine. "So sorry you don't have time to stay." She lifted her hands, fully prepared to give him a good push out the door. Or through it.

He cocked his head to one side. "Why did you call for me?"

"I didn't call for anyone." Lili only hoped Cleo would remain asleep in the bedroom. No telling what the cat would say if she saw Mr. Cute Hottie sitting here.

He stared at her, his dark eyes intense and probing. His mouth twisted as if in pain.

Then Lili noticed the shadows wrapping tighter around his legs.

"I'm sorry, I guess this will be a short visit," he told her. "I'd hoped to stay longer."

"And I hope to strengthen my wards to prevent this," she said.

He flashed that bone-melting smile again. "It won't work, my Greek beauty. Witches are gifted, but a demon does it better."

Lili barely blinked her eyes, and her surprise company was gone from her sight. Only the slightest hint of sulfur in the air told her it hadn't been her imagination.

An hour later, Lili had the wards surrounding her house humming stronger than ever. But she still checked all the corners as she reheated her cup of tea and settled back on the floor. As she sat down, she glanced at the picture lying on the coffee table. Her heart hurt as she viewed her friend.

"Where are you, Sera?" she whispered. Her eyes closed and her senses flared, but to no avail. Not that she expected to pick up anything, since her friend had never set foot in her cottage. "What happened to you? Why can't anyone sense you?"

She picked up the photograph and flattened her palm against the glossy surface. While she wasn't a Seer, she could sometimes pick up a sensation when it was a close friend. This time she felt nothing but a dark void. It was as if the object of the photo never existed.

Lili stared at the image of her friend laughing at the camera. She refused to believe Sera could disappear from everywhere like that.

Sera's pale blond, pixie-cut hair was feathered around

her face, and her blue eyes sparkled as she mocked a high-fashion model's pose.

Lili's eyes glistened with tears as she thought of the day the picture was taken. They had attended a Medieval Faire. Lili joked that her memories of the time period were very different than what they experienced that day.

They drank mead, munched on turkey legs, and visited the many booths offering a variety of crafts. Lili still had a beautiful glass ball, filled with a rainbow of colors, that sat in her bedroom.

Sera hadn't been one of the witches who attended the Witches Academy with her, but she had become a close friend when they both worked in Chicago.

The nurse's magick empathy with her patients, understanding their pain and fear, and being able to ease it for them, was a valuable skill.

After Sera's bad breakup with Chad, the stockbroker—may he suffer in Hades for a thousand years—she decided she needed to leave Chicago. When she told Lili she was considering a nurse's job at Crying Souls, Lili offered her the use of her cottage. Except Sera decided she wanted something all her own.

At first, there were almost daily wallmails and phone calls. Sera loved her work and urged Lili to come out also.

The silence was abrupt. After three days of hearing nothing from her, Lili tried contacting Sera. The news that she no longer worked at the hospital was unsettling. Her cell phone voice mail box was full as was her text in-box, and wallmails to her were ignored. It was as if the witch had disappeared into thin air. Except Lili knew better. It wasn't in Sera's responsible nature to just go away without a word to anyone.

Lili picked up her cup and sipped her tea as she carefully placed the photograph onto the coffee table in front of her. "I'll find out what happened to you, Sera. I swear it."

"Wow, who did you piss off that you're now banished to the dungeon of horrors?"

Lili turned around to find Deisphe catching up to her with a ground-eating stride. "The dungeon of horrors?" There was no question what the nurse was talking about. She was curious about Deisphe's take on the underground ward set aside for the insane.

The Wereleopard's expression was serious, her golden eyes dark with concern. "Sorry, I know I shouldn't call it that. If Dragon Lady caught me saying it I'd be washing out bedpans for six months. Word all over the place is that Dr. M. wants you working below a few days a week," she said softly, touching her arm. "It's not a nice place, Lili."

Lili felt a hint of unease in the pit of her stomach. "Dr. Mortimer mentioned at my initial interview that he wanted someone who was able to work with the insane patients, but he didn't say anything definite." *Or to me*.

Deisphe nodded. "He gets absentminded at times. He always thinks he's told you something when he hasn't."

The two walked side by side down the wide hallway. Lili thought she detected a tall, dark-haired figure when she glanced in one of the office reception areas. She frowned as she realized all she could see were shadows.

A demon does it better.

Lili stopped so fast her heels skidded on the floor.

"Careful." The nurse grabbed her arm before she ended up on her ass. "Are you okay?" She looked closer at the doctor.

"Yes, thanks." She turned around and headed for the empty office. Just as she thought, nothing was there except a few tendrils of shadows that looked pretty suspicious to her eyes. "Who has this office?" *Someone like the cute guy I saw at Inderman, who popped into my house last night? But remember the last guy you dated, Lili? Not a good memory at all.*

"No one." Deisphe looked at her curiously. "Are you sure you're all right?"

"Just curious." She moved off with a faster gait as they headed for the locker room. "So the rumors are I'll be working in the dungeon, as you call it?"

The nurse nodded. "Good thing, since we've been desperate for some new gossip. Not all that surprising, since Dr. Mortimer spends more time down there than in his office or even treating patients up here. He set up the psych ward once he took over the hospital. Still, as long as he's working with the patients below, he's not looking over anyone's shoulder. Bad enough we have Director of Nursing Garrish for that. Still, I wish you luck, Lili," she said quietly as she pushed open the door. They entered the large locker room, Deisphe heading for a tall locker decorated with shiny stickers of fluffy kittens.

"Kittens?" Lili laughed, tracing one fuzzy sticker.

"My five-year-old niece thought my locker needed some decorations," she explained, placing her palm against the metal, waiting until the lock clicked open. "She gave stickers to everyone last Yule. My brother got Captain Jack Sparrow stickers, since she thinks Tyler looks like Johnny Depp. I tried trading with him, but he wouldn't do it." She frowned as a growling sound emitted from Lili's tote bag that the witch had left on a bench. "Is that what I think it is?" Hackles rose, and her eyes slitted pure gold.

"Back off, kitty cat," Cleo popped her head out of the bag and wrinkled her nose at the nurse. "I may be small, but even on my worst day, I can still take you down."

"No cat fights," Lili ordered the two, before Deisphe could respond. "You told me you don't have problems with Weres during Full Moon," she reminded Cleo as she unwound the hot pink cashmere scarf from her neck and draped it inside her locker. She was pleased to obtain a locker here. She had a tiny office, but there wasn't much storage space there. The locker gave her what she needed.

"*That* is not a Were." Deisphe glared at Cleo, who issued a nonkitty snarl. "The Dragon Lady will toss her furry ass right out of the building."

"I'm a therapy cat and have privileges in this forsaken place that even she can't revoke," Cleo informed her with her typical feline arrogance even as she hummed "Welcome to the Jungle."

"Cleo, I brought you in today because you said you'd behave," Lili warned her cat. She made sure to stay out of claw range. Been there, done that, treated the scratches.

"And Dragon Lady allowed it?" Deisphe pulled a pair of dark green scrubs out of her locker and quickly changed clothes.

"Cleo's presence is always written into my contract."

Lili also wasted no time changing into her scrubs. As the soft cotton fabric settled against her skin she felt the protective sigils power up. It increased when she slipped her lab coat over them.

"What do you know about the asylum?"

Deisphe glanced at the wall clock. Since she had time before her shift started she dropped down onto the bench by Lili. She reached into her bra and pulled out a cigarette, blowing magick on the tip to light it up.

The witch arched an eyebrow.

"Like my kind worries about their lungs." The Wereleopard waved it around. She dipped her head a bit and lowered her voice. "I guess you can tell that Dr. Mortimer is an old-fashioned guy. He dresses and acts like he's still in Victorian London. I think he'd be happier if the entire hospital was back in that time period."

"When was the new ward constructed?" Lili sat beside her.

Deisphe thought about it for a minute. "Dr. M. opened the dungeon not long after he took over. I guess about thirty years. He wasted no time putting the word out that he would take care of the 'troubled ones.'" She sketched air quotes. "The first patient appeared almost immediately, and we've had full occupancy since then. He has one down there he considers a true prize. I'm sorry, but I don't see it as something to be proud of." She shook her head. "I was sent down there to help out when one of the patients was badly injured. It's not a nice place. You're the doctor. Tell me why many of us who are immortal or even close to it can be felled by the common cold or a disease of the mind."

Lili didn't miss the desperation in the female's voice and eyes. "Family member?" she asked softly.

Deisphe pinched the end of her cigarette and tossed it over her shoulder, the white stick landing neatly in the trash can.

"Sixty years ago my brother was poisoned by cursed meat left out by a sorcerer who hated our Pack. It attacked his brain and turned him uncontrollable," she murmured. "My kind has been called wild animals for centuries, but Worifa turned into something..." she searched for the right word, "worse."

"He gave fully into his animal nature and couldn't return?" Lili probed.

Deisphe's fingers trembled. Her eyes turned a dark gold filled with sorrow. "It was much more than that. Worifa became a creature straight out of ancient times. Even our most powerful healers couldn't bring him back. Our Alpha had no choice but to destroy him. Although Pack law requires family members to watch the death, the Alpha ordered that my mother and my brother's mate not be present. He wanted to spare them that grief, and I was grateful he did. As it was, Worifa's illness almost killed my mother."

Lili knew Deisphe's mother must have been highly revered for the Alpha to excuse her from watching her son put to death. Emotion wasn't something found among the Weres. Even the females were expected to be strong. She wanted to reach out and touch her new friend, to offer any sort of comfort she could. She knew that Weres didn't accept physical consolation as easily as some others did. However, Cleo didn't believe in personal space except for her own. She climbed out of the tote and languidly stretched out along Deisphe's thigh. The Were smiled and stroked the feline's fluffy back in long grooming strokes.

"Is that why you became a nurse?" Lili asked.

Deisphe nodded. "I had my Alpha's permission to work in a Were healing center in New Orleans for a couple years, then I returned here when there was an opening." She wrinkled her nose. The nurse glanced at the clock, winced, and jumped up. "Good luck," she called over her shoulder as she left the locker room.

Lili nudged Cleo back into the tote bag and carried it into her office, which was a bit larger than a broom closet but held what she needed, including a small couch.

"Not very elegant for such a revered physician as yourself," Cleo said with typical disdain. "Not to mention *moi*, who requires a silk pillow. I hope you'll remember to bring one tomorrow." She hopped up onto the couch and kneaded the upholstery with her claws as she finally settled down. "I suppose I have to stay here while you're off doing your healing." She released a long-suffering sigh.

"I'll talk to the head of pediatrics as soon as possible, so you can make the rounds up there." Lili set out food and water in the Limoges bowls her furry roommate insisted upon.

"Be careful."

The witch stopped at the door and looked over her shoulder. A warning from the cat wasn't normal. Not one with concern layered over the words.

"What do you sense?" Lili asked, aware Cleo could ferret out things she couldn't.

"A strange power in the air. Something that doesn't belong here," Cleo replied. "Or perhaps it's because of the asylum. They never give off a good aura. Just like there was something odd in the house from last night." She stared long and hard at Lili who conveniently ignored her.

"No, they don't." The witch remembered working in London's Bethlem Hospital, also known as the infamous Bedlam, in 1633. She'd done her best to hide her magickal skills during the months she was there as one of the matrons, since the idea of a woman doctor was unthinkable. They considered nurses little more than maids. In their eyes, a patient who was insane didn't require medical treatment. The fear they'd label her mad and find a way to incarcerate her was a nightmare that still haunted her.

"Off with you." Cleo raised a paw in farewell. "I have a nap to savor." She curled up and closed her eyes.

Lili learned no elevator descended to the lower depths of the building and finally found the stone steps that did. She felt as if she were transported back in time as she ran her hand along the damp stone walls and felt the sense of hopelessness that pervaded the place.

She knew something was very wrong the moment she reached the last step.

The screams rending the air were filled with anger and fear.

Lili wasted no time running toward the large iron door. A wave of her hand opened it as if it were made of paper.

And the sight before her was one she thought she'd left behind hundreds of years ago.

Two ogres, the size of eighteen-wheelers, held a wild-eyed male who twisted and turned in their bone-crushing grips that left dents in his dirty flesh.

"Get the fuck outta here," one of the ogres growled at her. The name Turtifo was etched on a pendant circling his tree-trunk-size neck. His tan leather shirt showed food stains down the front, and she didn't even want to think about what the discolorations on his ankle-length pants meant. She doubted he'd bathed in the past few months.

"I'm Dr. Carter, and I belong down here," she told him, easily staring him down even if he was a few feet taller than she was. "What in Hades is going on here?"

"Nothin' you need to think about, sweetheart." Even with one on each side, their prisoner refused to go easily.

"*Stop.*" She projected her authority into her voice. It was enough to halt them in their tracks. Both creatures glared at her as she moved toward them.

"This asswipe has to be returned to his cell," the second ogre whose pendant stated he was Coing informed her in a voice that grated on her ears. Even standing a few feet away, he tried to loom over Lili, using his great size for intimidation. She noticed he didn't smell any better than his cohort.

He had no clue that terrorization wasn't even in her vocabulary.

She stared at the trio, not missing the fresh black blood streaming down their charge's face. *It's him!* She kept her features schooled, so she wouldn't reveal she had already met the patient. Except at the time, he'd been cleaned up and incredibly... *no, don't go there, Lili*.

"This patient needs treatment." She knew the cuts and

bruises would heal, but she wanted the blood cleaned from his skin.

"Dr. Mortimer will take care of it when he finally gets down here." They struggled vainly against her magickal order that she knew would hold until she released them. "Demon asshole needs to be back in his cell."

She narrowed her eyes at them. "He's not here, and I am. Where's the treatment room?" She looked around.

"They're taken care of in their cells," Turtifo snickered. "Can't afford for them to be too comfortable, ya know."

"Then take him there," she informed him before turning to his cohort. "One of you will bring me supplies to treat his wounds. *Now*." There was no doubt she'd just made two enemies. It didn't matter. She wasn't about to allow anyone go without prompt healing.

"He'll kill you as soon as look at you," came the grumbling as the male was dragged to an end cell.

Lili was almost rocked back by the stench in the rock-lined cubicle that seemed to be swamped in suffocating shadows.

"When was this room last cleaned?" she demanded.

"There's a drain. We try to hose it down every so often." Turtifo tossed his captive onto a bundle of straw that doubled as a bed. "His kind don't need much."

"Here." Coing returned, pushing a metal tray into the room. "Don't know why you're bothering. He'll heal eventually."

Lili glared at the two ogres. "You can go about your duties."

Turtifo crossed arms the size of a cow across his massive chest. "Dr. Mortimer wouldn't be happy if we left you here alone." He leered in the direction of her breasts.

"I'll make sure he knows I insisted." Her fingers tingled with the idea of dropping the ceiling on their heads. Even if only the rocks would break. The battle of glares eventually broke when the ogres looked away.

"We'll be right outside," Turtifo growled, leaving the cell but keeping the door open.

Lili turned back to her patient. "It's all right," she said softly. "I won't hurt you." She gently pushed back the filthy strands of shoulder-length coal-black hair that hung loosely around his dirt-streaked face. The large tear in his shirt revealed the brand marring his shoulder. Her lips tightened as she looked at it, knowing it declared to all that the bearer of the mark was nothing more than an insane animal.

Her skin burned with awareness the moment she touched him.

Protective runes kicked into gear while she stared into blazing cobalt eyes.

"What in Hades is going on here?" she asked once she regained her voice. She kept her voice low so her *guards* couldn't eavesdrop. She knew most ogres didn't have excellent hearing, but for all she knew, those two had been enhanced. "How can you be here when you were in my house last night?" *And how come you looked all clean and gorgeous then? Now you look as if you just rolled out of a county dump. All this filth isn't recent, either. Not to mention I don't sense one shred of insanity in your blood. So what is going on here?*

Then she remembered the shadows that lingered around him. That he'd disappeared in the blink of an eye.

Lili picked up a packet of wet wipes and began cleaning the black blood from the wicked gash marring his forehead. She could see the torn skin was already knitting together, but not as quickly as it should. She carefully touched her fingertips to the wound to speed up the healing. Her skin warmed with her power. Her lips tightened at the sight of raw abraded skin and jagged scars on his wrists and ankles. Iron shackles took power away from supernatural creatures and created as much pain as silver did. She didn't care how qualified Dr. Mortimer was; she was going to make sure that kind of treatment didn't happen again.

Her patient uttered guttural words that hurt her ears and caused her to wince as the painful sound bounced around inside her head.

"Oh puleeze." She rolled her eyes as she tossed the bloody wipes in the air and torched them. She knew that blood was a priceless commodity for many spells, especially the darker ones. A demon's blood was considered extremely valuable for baneful charms. She always made sure anything bearing blood was promptly destroyed by fire to protect the patient. "I may not be fluent in your language, but I know enough demon profanity to know it when I hear it. Do me a favor. Translation spells are a royal pain in the ass and hurt my head like Hades. But if that's the way you want it, I'll fire one up. Just be prepared for a mega-migraine, because I'll make sure you get it instead of me. So why don't you cut the shit and tell me how you can be in here and yet get outside without anyone knowing about it." She wiped away the last of the blood and now saw nothing more than a faint pink mark that soon disappeared entirely, not even leaving a scar. That cloth likewise went up in flames.

"Dr. Carter."

Lili looked over her shoulder to find her superior standing in the open doorway. Two gleeful-looking ogres stood behind him. The expression on the wizard's face wasn't good.

I can see we won't be friends. She didn't glare at them because she didn't want to give away her feelings too soon.

"Good morning, Dr. Mortimer. It appears one of the patients suffered an accident. I was making sure he was all right." She didn't move away from the demon.

Dr. Mortimer's normally genial features were twisted in a frown. "You shouldn't be in here alone with Patient 1172," he stated.

"We told the witch that, Doctor," Turtifo piped up with a smirk. Lili's hand itched to smack it off his face.

"That's Dr. Witch to you," she snapped. She reined in her fury a bit as she turned to her superior. "I came down here and discovered that one of the subjects had been badly hurt."

"Demons are remarkably fast healers," he needlessly reminded her.

"That doesn't mean he should be covered in blood when he's returned to his room." It took every ounce of willpower not to throw some anger his way. He was a doctor, for Fate's sake!

"Please come with me, Dr. Carter." He consulted his old-fashioned gold pocket watch before tucking it in his vest. As usual, he was dressed in a black frock coat and neatly tied cravat along with narrow black trousers.

Gold-rimmed spectacles were perched on his angular nose. "We have much to do."

Lili looked at her patient. "We'll speak again," she said, sotto voce, after hastily throwing up a privacy shield so no one else would hear her words. "You have a lot of explaining to do."

His lips barely stretched in a smile. "Like I told you, Doc. A demon does it better."

She heard the heavy thud of the cell door closing as she caught up with Dr. Mortimer.

"Patient 1172 is very dangerous," he informed her, not even bothering to look at her. "You should not have gone in there alone."

"He was out of his cell when I arrived." She didn't care if she was throwing the two aides under the bus. Damn ogres deserved it and more.

"He tried to escape when we took his meal to him," Coing hastily explained when the wizard showed his displeasure.

"Then we must ensure that doesn't happen again," Dr. Mortimer murmured. He directed her down a curving hallway that was as dark and dank as the first one, with torches lining the walls.

"How many patients are you presently treating down here?" she asked, hoping to bypass a lecture. She was tempted to witch up a few candles to shed some light on their surroundings.

"At this time I have seven," he replied, seeming to momentarily forget her transgression. "Three males and four females. This is why I wanted additional help down here. Each patient has their own unique problem that I know with time and care can be restored to full health.

Although 1172, the one you tried to help," his visage darkened, "well, let us just say he is more dangerous than all of them put together. He is a demon who slaughtered more than one clan because of his insanity. Even his kind did not want to deal with him."

"Why would you have someone so hazardous housed here?" Lili asked, curious, since she didn't sense any of the treacherous peril her superior hinted at. "Demons have always been very insular. I would think they would have preferred taking care of their own, or he would have been instantly destroyed for his crimes." It was because they stayed so much to themselves that most of her knowledge of demonkind came from books and scrolls.

"Normally it would be that way, but I was given the golden opportunity not only to treat one of their kind a few hundred years ago, but bring her back to a full, useful life. The woman's sire is on the Demon Council and suggested that I work with Patient 1172," he replied stiffly, apparently disliking her disbelief. "It appeared even their healers did not want to deal with this particular demon. Patient 1172's mother is also a member of the Council and was willing to allow me to work with her son. Naturally, I could not refuse their request to see if there was a chance in rehabilitating the creature. It was a challenge I could not refuse," he replied. "One hundred and eighty years ago, he destroyed an entire vampire clan deep in the Carpathian Mountains. During the battle, one of the vampires managed to force him to ingest some of his blood. It left him seriously deranged. Sad to say, I do not think he will ever leave, and the Demon Council need not fear he will escape from here.

The asylum is heavily shielded to prevent anything of that sort happening."

Lili thought about seeing said "deranged" patient in Inderman, but she silent. She preferred to find out on her own what was going on. "Considering his crimes, why wasn't he immediately destroyed?" She might not know a lot about demons, but she did know that they preferred to kill first and forget about asking any questions.

"As I explained, his mother is a high-level demon. She interceded on his behalf. She believes that I can find a way to counteract the insanity the vampire blood ingestion caused."

Lili felt the abrupt drop in temperature. A heaviness in the air indicated a strong magick that raised uneasy prickles across the surface of her skin. She tucked her hands in her lab coat's pockets and felt relief from the magickal protection her clothing provided her.

He wants to keep this place as a true Bedlam. A madhouse of old. His own kingdom.

She sensed a noxious miasma of sorrow and pain in a place she could only call a dungeon.

Upstairs was modern, healing magick at its finest. Down here was a return to the dark past. She was grateful Dr. Mortimer hadn't tried turning the rest of the hospital back to an earlier time.

"Dr. Carter, is there something wrong?" Dr. Mortimer asked, frowning at her inattention.

Lili quickly snapped herself back to the present. "No, sir. I just realized that this place reminds me of a hospital I worked at in London years ago."

He nodded with a smile, taking her statement as a compliment instead of dismay at the gloomy surrounding. "I was very lucky to find a sorcerer who could create just the right receptacle for the inmates. All of the wards here are set very high. How Patient 1172 left his cell is a mystery I intend to solve." His expression momentarily darkened then shifted to his usual bland face. "Since I was given free rein, I thought I would create a place that reminded me of the hospitals I presided over in Europe. They were all excellent institutions that kept the patients safe."

Lili's nose twitched at the musty scent of old tobacco that lingered on the wizard's coat along with something else she couldn't detect. She wanted to ask more questions about the demon. She refused to refer to him as 1172. She needed to learn his name. She had a good idea the only way she could do that was to go to the source.

"What afflicts the other patients held here?" she asked. As they passed each iron slab that doubled for a door, she felt the mental infection leach out of the metal and the walls. She knew it wasn't just from the present patients but also from those who'd been here in the past. She wasn't an empath, but her healing power meant she sensed all kinds of sickness. Sometimes even illness that had happened in the past lingered. This kind was strong and skittered over her nerve endings.

Her first inclination was to open the doors and bring the ones incarcerated there to the main floors. They needed heavy waves of healing and calming magick that could help them more than anything down here. Luckily, she knew better, since some distressed patients didn't do well unless they were cocooned in a comforting darkness.

As she turned her head, she caught sight of a wisp of pink smoke swirl in the air before the form of a little girl wearing an old-fashioned blue print ankle-length dress materialized.

Lili glanced at Dr. Mortimer and realized he either didn't see the tiny wraith or preferred to ignore her presence.

The little girl stood there, her small face upturned, staring at the witch with a sad expression in her eyes.

He never sees me, the ghostly girl told her in a breathy voice that echoed softly inside Lili's head. *I don't think he wants to talk to me.* She clutched a tattered teddy bear in her hands. *Will you talk to me?* she asked plaintively. *I'm very lonely and afraid. I can't find my mommy. Can you find her for me?*

Lili hung back just enough to nod her head and smile at the girl and communicate wordlessly that she'd speak to the girl later, and then ran to catch up with Dr. Mortimer.

Her steps faltered when she passed one cell door, where a pair of blazing orange eyes suddenly appeared behind the iron bars set in the heavy wood. A sharp hiss told her the occupant had come in contact with the metal that burned preternatural flesh. She swiveled her head and stared momentarily at the darkness before moving on.

The wizard doctor directed her into a room furnished with a square table and four chairs. A counter along one wall held a coffeemaker and a row of mugs along with a small refrigerator. The faint coppery tang of blood hung in the air.

Dr. Mortimer pulled a small stack of manila folders from a cart stationed under the counter and set them on the table. He picked up the top file and opened it.

She wondered why he hadn't bothered digitizing the files and privately vowed to scan them into her computer tablet as soon as she could. She might have been born in the thirteenth century, but she enjoyed keeping up with all modern conveniences.

"I am afraid I must insist that you not be alone with the demon again," he told her with a hint of regret in his voice that she really didn't believe. "I am aware you are extremely gifted in the healing arts. You must always realize I feel Patient 1172 is still much too dangerous for a lone female to deal with."

"Even with Turtifo and Coing standing guard?" she asked, determined to change his mind on that score. She needed to find out how the demon escaped the hospital and why he returned.

The wizard pursed his lips. "Patient 1172 is from a very strong and dangerous demon clan known for their dark hungers. Even clan healers weren't able to break through the fury eating its way through his brain." He tapped the file folders in front of him. "As for some of the others we house..." He took a deep breath before he continued.

"Panabell is a pixie with an addiction to rose dust that has rendered her incapable of living a normal existence outside of these walls," he explained. "She has been with us for seventy years and has worked very hard to battle this cursed dependence. She had a setback a few years ago, and it has been difficult for her to move forward. Perhaps you will be able to help her seek the correct path." He set the file to one side and picked up another. "Dermod was stricken with a baneful magickal brain fever that attacked his impulses and left him with terrible fears. Orkey has been in one madhouse or another for the past six hundred years, and sadly, he will never be cured. Then we have Pepta, who I feel will also deal better with a female healer. She has gone through a great deal of trauma that badly damaged her psyche."

Lili deliberately kept her gaze off the file that interested her most and on her superior's face. She didn't miss that Dr. Mortimer referred to his other patients by name and only the demon was referred to by his intake number. She wondered his reason for maintaining his distance from that one particular patient and not the others. "I understand and greatly appreciate your concern for my well-being, Dr. Mortimer, but I have worked with dangerous patients in the past. I'm sure you know the emergency room isn't always a safe place to work. I am eager to study the treatments you use. Hopefully, I can offer something that will further help," she said softly, offering the smile that usually calmed the most recalcitrant patients. She subtly pushed a little power into her smile.

She didn't like secrets. Dr. Mortimer holding back the demon's chart meant there could be something in it he didn't want her to see. For all she knew, something in the files could have something to do with Sera.

Her friend had disappeared from Crying Souls ten months ago. Her apartment was found emptied of all her belongings, and no Seer could find any hint of her spirit in the ether. Then it was discovered that others vanished the same way.

Lili needed to find out what happened to Sera and the others. It hadn't been easy to convince anyone she could do this. Luckily, her stubborn nature won out, and she returned to San Francisco.

She continued to keep the magickal push as subtle as possible. She knew Dr. Mortimer wasn't clueless and would pick up on too much power. She shifted her body in her chair. She kept his attention on her so he wouldn't be aware what she was doing. She knew from painful personal experience that wizards didn't appreciate being manipulated.

"You are well-known in this field. I'm sure you can understand the best way for me to work down here is to make my own observations and share them with you to see if I am on the right path." She sifted through the files, feeling tingles travel up her fingers as she touched each surface. Her "accidental" contact with Patient 1172's folder provided a jolt to her system that would have started a nonbeating human heart. Thanks to her wards, she didn't feel as much distress from the lightning zap through her body, but it was still alarming. Especially after that burning awareness she'd experienced when she touched the demon. "After that, I hope we can sit down and discuss each case." She continued smiling. "I look forward to learning from you."

Just as she hoped, the elder doctor fell under her spell, pun intended.

"Now I am positive I made the right decision in choosing you to assist me here, Dr. Carter." He beamed. "I do so enjoy colleagues who believe in going the extra mile, as you more modern witches say." His fingers slowly slid away from the folder, and he nudged it in her direction.

Lili waited until the file touched her fingertips. She picked it up and opened it.

Her mind whirred furiously as she read the remarkably scant information about their reputedly most hazardous occupant. Dr. Mortimer's old-fashioned copperplate penmanship recited Patient 1172's usual intake details, the doctor's visits with the demon, and his impressions of a dangerous creature, but she noted something was still missing. His name.

Dr. Mortimer pulled out his gold pocket watch and studied the crystal face.

Lili chose that moment to add an extra push but this time with words. "I'm sure you have matters to attend to," she said. She knew that normally the presiding doctor would introduce the new doctor to the patients. She had a feeling Dr. Mortimer didn't hold with that school of thought and would just leave her with the patients he'd assigned to her. "I thank you for giving me as much time as you have. I understand your unease in my treating Patient 1172, but I assure you, I was perfectly safe with the orderlies present." She continued to smile.

"I'll have the orderlies take you to the therapy room while I attend to my appointments upstairs," he announced. As he stood, he momentarily faltered and gripped the table. His knuckles turned white.

"Dr. Mortimer, are you all right?" she asked.

"Yes." He smiled then grew serious. "I still have reservations about you seeing Patient 1172."

"I promise to be very careful." She followed him out of the room. "And I will make sure that the aides are nearby at all times."

Lili reared back when the ogres stood motionless outside the room. She was positive just one of them could easily bench press the Golden Gate Bridge.

"Escort 1172 to the therapy room," Dr. Mortimer instructed with a briskness Lili hadn't seen before.

She watched him walk down the hallway toward the stairs, leaving her alone with what she privately called two cement blocks.

Her first day in the asylum was under way.

Chapter 3

THE WITCH HEALER SMELLED CLEAN. HE BREATHED IN deeply, savoring the fresh scent of a mature woman. He could even tell her fertility cycle was coming nigh.

He knew she wouldn't be allowed down here during that time unless she used spells and charms to mask it. Not unless the strong protections woven into the fabric of her clothing would take care of that.

Whoever designed the healer's wardrobe was making sure anyone who tried to hurt her would end up in a world of pain.

His lips peeled back a fraction in a smile meant to scare the shit out of whoever showed up. He had no doubt the *good* Dr. Mortimer would arrange some additional *therapy* for him. Something that involved pain and wanting to hear him scream. Dr. Mortimer insisted it would help *Patient 1172* with his illness.

Shows what the so-called skilled wizard didn't know.

The large door swung open, and Turtifo loomed in the opening.

The ogre's brown, jagged teeth flashed in a wicked mockery of a smile.

"The witch doc wants to see you, shitbag." Rusty brown eyes glinted with malice, and his stance warned the demon he was just waiting for him to do something wrong. "And no opening your mouth. This might be the time I decide to tear out your tongue."

Jared. My name is Jared. Not 1172. Not shitbag. My name is Jared.

The mantra he kept going in his head was the only thing that allowed him a sliver of sanity.

Past experience told Jared all it took was for him to breathe for them to accuse him of doing something wrong and beat him to a pulp. There was nothing ogres loved better than turning someone into raw meat. These two were experts at it.

He took his time standing up, not making even the smallest move that could be construed as a threat. Past experience had him learning that if he wasn't careful, he'd end up with a variety of cuts and bruises.

He'd barely straightened up when he found himself kissing the filthy stone floor.

"You need to watch that." Coing chuckled from his spot behind Turtifo's shoulder, the sound like razors across Jared's skin.

"Yeah, I do," he muttered, refusing to show any sign of pain. *Your turn will come, asshole, and I'm going to enjoy returning the favor.* He wiped his face of all expression and walked out of the cell with Turtifo leading the way and Coing taking up the rear.

His insides knotted up at the thought of going to Dr. Mortimer's Therapy Room, something that was straight out of the Spanish Inquisition but even more inventive. He had no clue how the "treatments" were supposed to help anyone get well.

The clean female scent filled his nostrils again. He lifted his head enough to see Dr. Carter standing in the doorway of a room he'd never been in before.

"Bring 1172 in here," she instructed crisply. Her

eyes looked him over and apparently didn't like what she saw.

He hid his smile. Seemed she wasn't too fond of the ogres, either.

This time the push into the room wasn't as forceful as usual. He figured that was due to the witch's keen-eyed observation. He didn't miss the magick sparking from her fingertips. He wouldn't have been surprised if she used it on his guards when she felt they got out of hand. Or even on him.

He had desired her from the first moment he had spied her at Inderman. That attraction grew each time he saw her. But she was a witch, an enemy of his kind. Besides, even if she wasn't a magick user, he had been raised to stay within the circles of his own kind.

Dr. Carter inclined her head toward a chair. "Sit there," she told him. Her head snapped up when she saw the ogres pull up iron manacles that were attached to the chair. "Not necessary," she snapped the two words.

"We need to—" Turtifo started, but she cut him off.

"No, you don't. And close the door on your way out." To guarantee they understood exactly what she meant, she swept her hand out, forcing them out the door, which slammed shut after they crossed the threshold. She muttered a few words. Jared easily heard the *snick* of a magickal lock that he bet would even keep out two cranky ogres.

This could prove real interesting.

She conjured up two mugs of coffee and handed one of them to him.

He inhaled the hot steam with an appreciative nose. "Handy trick," he said, sipping it slowly so as not to burn his tongue. He didn't have a fire demon's tolerance for scalding liquids.

"It got me through four medical schools," she replied, taking the chair across from him. "Well, well, well, Patient 1172. I fully expected you to ignore me and speak only in your birth language. Unlike the other night, when you broke into my house and was coherent for someone who didn't appear to have a cohesive thought in his head. Thank you for having the good manners not to continue the deranged act."

"There are times I can be polite," he continued, savoring his coffee. "Any chance you could hex up something to go with this? Cookies, sweet roll, ham and cheese sandwich? Maybe some steak fries?"

He realized her smile was the kind to entrance anyone with enough testosterone.

"Look, buster, I'm no kitchen witch. Lunch. Party of one." She snapped her fingers.

He wasted no time digging into the ham-and-cheese sandwich, pleased to see she'd chosen sharp cheddar cheese and Black Forest ham along with crispy fries topped with seasoned salt.

"You're a great cook."

She settled back in her chair and watched him. "Don't you eat when you're away from here?" she asked mildly.

The sandwich hovered at his open lips.

"I see that Greeks have stubborn streaks too," he said. He eyed her curly hair, swept up in a high ponytail that teased her shoulder blades, coffee-brown eyes, and the slight olive cast to her skin. "I eat sometimes."

"So why are you pretending to be a homicidal demon when it's clear you aren't? And, especially, how do you manage to fool Dr. Mortimer when he's one of the foremost practitioners in this field?" She pulled her computer tablet out of her pocket and sat back in her chair.

He gestured to his sandwich. "Think I can eat first?"

"I won't forget what I'm asking," she reminded him.

"I didn't think so, but I'd hate to see what looks like an awesome sandwich and fries get cold. Room service tends to be erratic around here." He popped a fry in his mouth. "Doesn't do much good to complain to the management, either."

"When was the last time they allowed you to bathe down here?" She wrinkled her nose.

Jared chewed and swallowed. "Hosed down with icy water is more like it. I heard you talking to Dr. Mortimer on how all this reminded you of the older hospitals in Europe. I guess you can already tell his idea of running this hellhole goes back to the Dark Ages."

"We're not talking about Dr. Mortimer, we're talking about you." She tapped away on her tablet, her fingers flying at the speed of light.

He watched her with fascination. He might have been a virtual prisoner for too long, but he'd managed to get out and about enough to know about modern conveniences. And missed them when he was pulled back here. Computers intrigued him, but since Dr. Mortimer was happier using quill and ink, he hadn't seen one in use the way Dr. Carter used hers.

"It seems your kind have abandoned you."

He winced at her blunt words. "You don't believe in soft and fuzzy words, do you?" Now that his stomach was full, and lo and behold, so was his coffee mug, he felt a lot better. All he needed was a long hot shower and a lot of soap to make him feel like a whole new demon.

"Not when getting to the point moves things along a lot faster." Lili looked up from her tablet.

"Are you going to tell Dr. Mortimer about my going AWOL?"

"I'll keep quiet—for now." Her lips curved in a smile, letting him know she now held all the cards. "And I'll make sure those two do the same."

Jared draped an arm over the back of his chair, content to study the lovely doctor.

He might not be able to see the protective sigils woven into the fabric of her clothing, but he could feel them pulsing around her like an extra heartbeat. For a brief moment, he wondered if she would taste as exotic as she looked. Temptation rolled along his muscles, but he ignored the lure. No use getting on her bad side too fast. Not when she was willing to feed him.

"Your boyfriend must really love you to provide you with clothing guaranteed to keep you safe from us crazies," he commented, stretching his long legs out in front of him.

Lili smiled as if she knew what he was doing.

"Do you participate in any group therapy with the other patients?"

"The inmates, you mean? Crazies? Loony tunes?" he mocked. "The ones who need a lot of help and don't get it."

She leaned forward. "Why are you so open with me about your complaints? Or are you yanking my chain to see how close I am to Dr. Mortimer, Patient 1172?"

She noted a slight flinch. *So he doesn't like being called that.* "Do you want to see if I mention any of this to him?"

His dark eyes bored into her with a chill she felt all the way through to her bones. "You smiled at the little girl."

That stopped her cold. "What little girl?" She could play coy too.

Jared smirked. "Give me a break, Doc. The wraith that haunts our gloomy hallowed halls." His grin suddenly morphed into something dark and not so friendly. "A child that doesn't belong down here among the monsters." His words sliced across her skin like icy razor blades. "You're the expert. You wanna tell me how an innocent could land down here in the house of horrors when it's obvious she belongs in the land of fuzzy bunnies and playful puppies?"

"I don't know," she said honestly. "I will have to talk to her and see if I can find out how it happened. It won't be easy, since she's so young and might not have any idea how she came to be here. Has she been around as long as you have?"

He shrugged. "It's not like I have a calendar on my wall. But I'd say she's been here for decades." He looked away. "She cries all night, always asking for her mother. Pepta screams at her to shut up, which only makes the kid cry harder." He paused. "All I know is that she's not one of us."

Lili's stomach cramped at his words. She knew he didn't just mean the little girl wasn't a demon.

"She's a mundane somehow pulled here," she whispered.

"There's nothing else she could be." He nodded. He lifted his arms over his head and stretched them toward the ceiling. The thin fabric of his ragged T-shirt grew taut over his muscular arms.

It wasn't easy, but she managed not to ogle too much or allow any drool to slip past her lips.

Dirty, smelly, and still gorgeous. Cleo was right. She needed to get herself a social life. It took her a moment to remind herself she was a doctor. A professional who shouldn't be fantasizing about a patient even if he was... Another mental slap upside the head.

"Why did you wipe out that vampire bloodline?"

She kept her doctor's face on. Watched every nuance in his expression as he stared upward while she waited for his response.

She was nothing if not patient.

It turned out so was Jared.

Silence grew by the minute until he smiled briefly.

"Do you know Dr. Mortimer asks me that exact same question every time he sees me," he said, matter-of-factly. "But he doesn't ask like a doctor wanting to find out what's going on inside the inmate's head. It's more like he wants to know what it takes to create such a heinous act." It was clear he was quoting the doctor.

"What is your name?"

He hadn't expected that. No one else around here cared. "Why?"

"Because calling you Patient 1172 just flat out sounds dumb, that's why," Lili said lightly. "Don't worry. I won't use it to mess with your power."

"Wouldn't happen even if you tried." He pulled down his shirt's neckline.

Lili frowned at an oddly shaped brand that scarred his shoulder. It wasn't the one next to it that denoted him as a mental patient, but something else that glimmered with dark power.

What in Hades is going on here?

"What is that?"

His smile wasn't the least bit pleasant. "You might say I've been neutered. While every patient here is branded to show what they are, my decoration is demon-made and meant to keep my powers in check. It also warns anyone coming in contact with me that I'm a danger to polite society," he drawled with deliberate malice.

"It doesn't seem to work very well if you're able to get out. Or is there more that goes on with you?" Although she already had an idea of what he'd say.

Jared smiled slowly. "Before I lost my mind, my gift was used to bring death to those who deserved it. And my name is Jared."

She returned his smile. "It's nice to meet you, Jared."

Lili wasn't surprised when the door almost fell down from the pounding on the other side.

"Asshole's time is up!" Turtifo bellowed.

She released the lock and waited for the ogre to enter.

"Door's not supposed to be locked." He scowled at her as he roughly pulled Jared to his feet in a grip that could have easily dislocated his shoulder.

"Just make sure that Patient 1172 is returned to his cell in the same condition he's in right now," she ordered, tacking on a snarl of her own.

Turtifo bared his teeth at her. "Won't matter, since you won't be here all that long." He pushed Jared in front of him.

Lili watched them leave, noticing Jared didn't look back. She didn't think he would, but it would have been nice. But then she knew he couldn't show any weakness in front of the ogres. Just as she couldn't, either.

"That's me. Making friends everywhere I go," she murmured to herself, tucking her computer tablet in her lab coat pocket as she wound her way back down the hallways. She stopped where she'd first seen the spirit and turned in a slow circle. She cast her senses out in search of her quarry.

"Little girl," she whispered. "Can you come to me? I want to talk to you."

The words barely left her lips when the pink smoke spun around and the tiny girl appeared at the end of the hallway. She still held the battered teddy bear in her arms.

Lili smiled as she crouched down to the wraith's level.

"Do you remember your name?" She knew many spirits forgot so much of their corporeal life that it was difficult for them to move on. Especially if this little girl had been down here a long time.

I'm Amy. Do you know my mommy? I really miss her. She looked hopeful.

Lili wished she could reach out and hug Amy, but she knew she'd only encounter an icy breeze. "I'm sorry, honey, I don't. Did someone who's called a Guide talk to you?" Why was the little girl still here? Even more puzzling was why she was down here and not upstairs. She didn't even want to imagine Amy in one of those horrible cells.

Amy's little face screwed up in a frown that slowly dissipated as her energy started to fade a little.

Lili started to worry, since that meant Amy wouldn't

go where she belonged if she wasn't Guided over soon. Instead, she'd eventually fade to nothingness. She'd have to talk to Deisphe about the Guides on-site.

"Were you a patient in the hospital upstairs?" She wondered why she couldn't figure out exactly what Amy was. She couldn't have lost so much of her life essence that it wasn't possible. Lili wondered why the girl's mother hadn't been here when she died. She could have helped her cross over.

Amy shook her head. *I wasn't sick. The big black bird came and took me to a dark and scary place.* She buried her face in her toy's plump stomach then looked up. *Mommy screamed and asked the bird to give me back, but he wouldn't. I was so scared, then I fell asleep and when I woke up the black bird was gone and nobody would talk to me or see me.* She pointed her finger at Lili's legs. *Why do you wear men's breeches?*

Lili felt sick to her stomach for more than one reason. She had a feeling the little girl had been frightened so badly she died. But why would a bird steal her? Not to mention how she ended up here. And her question about the witch's clothing meant she wasn't used to seeing a woman in pants.

Her need to make things right reared up big-time. She carefully studied the little girl's gown and realized what she first thought was a nightgown was actually a dress that was almost two centuries old. Frayed and patched, but even in death, the fabric appeared clean. The girl kept a tight hold on her teddy bear.

"Amy, do you know what year you were born?" She spoke slowly, making sure to keep any sign of worry from her voice.

Her head bobbed up and down. *I was born in 1842.*

Lili felt cramps begin deep in her body. Jared was right. The little girl was a mundane who didn't belong here. She could hear a soft drawl to the girl's voice that resonated inside her head. "Do you know where you were born?"

Natchez. Mommy said she was a Sutton, but her mommy and daddy didn't like me. A tear slowly rolled down her cheek.

Lili heard footsteps coming and quickly straightened up. "I'll be back," she promised in a low voice. "Don't worry, no one can hurt you. I'm going to find a way to take you somewhere else."

Amy's hopeful expression tore at her heart. *To my mommy?*

Lili nodded. "To your mommy." She had no doubt the little girl's mother was on a death plane. It was just a question of finding where she was so mother and daughter could be reunited.

"I have to go now, but I will be back soon and I'm going to find a way to get you away from here," she promised, hoping it was a vow she could keep.

They're mean down here. They want to hurt me.

"Not all of them," Lili soothed. "Do you know who Jared is?" She waited for the tiny ghost to nod. She easily read the fear on Amy's face. It seemed the little spirit only knew what she overheard Dr. Mortimer and the ogres saying. "Don't worry, he won't hurt you. If you feel frightened, I want you to go to Jared. I bet you could even slip into his room and I know he'll protect you."

She knew her suggestion would irritate the grumpy demon, but too bad. Jared might not appreciate having company, but deep down, she was confident he'd make sure Amy wouldn't be afraid of anyone or anything. Plus, she felt it would be a good thing for him.

After swearing to the tiny wraith she'd be back, Lili went upstairs to her office.

"That smelly dragon was in here," Cleo announced when she stepped inside. "She wasn't happy you weren't here and even more unhappy that I was." The cat uncoiled her fluffy body from her silk pillow and stretched, making sure her claws dug into the sofa and not her beloved bed.

Lili winced at the snags on the fabric. Cleo knew just how to exact punishment when she was in a snit. She also didn't miss the hint of sulfur dragons tended to leave in their wake. She hadn't met one yet that exuded Calvin Klein or DKNY.

"Did she leave a note?" She noticed her desk surface was as pristine as it had been when she left it.

Cleo opened her mouth wide and perfectly mimicked the Director of Nursing's harsh voice. "Please have Dr. Carter report to my office at two o'clock sharp. I do not tolerate tardiness."

"Who needs a parrot when I have you," she muttered, digging in her tote bag for a protein bar. She considered them on a level with cardboard, but she didn't feel like going down to the cafeteria to pick up something or conjuring something up.

I should have witched something up for myself when I did his.

Cleo lifted her head even higher, her nose twitching madly. She started coughing as if she was ready to hack up a hair ball. "You smell like demon." She paused.

"And wraith. What in the name of Anubis is down there that causes so many stinks?"

"Something no one should ever see." Lili pulled off the wrapper and bit off a piece. "For something boasting chocolate and caramel contents, it tastes more like paper chocolate and fake caramel." She finished off the bar then looked through the file folders in her desk until she found one labeled requisition forms. She quickly filled one out asking for a small refrigerator for her office.

"Why not just create something more edible?" Cleo curled back up on her pillow.

"I'm too lazy." Lili flopped back in her chair and swung her legs up on her desk, crossing them at the ankles.

"Now that you've made yourself comfortable, do you think you can tell me why you smell like demon and wraith?" the cat asked.

"In case you forgot, I was hired to treat patients here." Lili threw the discarded wrapper up into the air and snapped her fingers, turning the paper to ash. She soon discovered she wasn't too lazy to conjure up a mug of coffee, the lifeblood of every member of the medical world. The rich aroma of hazelnut teased her nostrils.

"Ghosts don't hang around hospitals. It's much too depressing." The feline opened her mouth wide in a yawn, displaying tiny needle-sharp teeth and a pink tongue. "Besides, that's what Guides are for. A child, especially, wouldn't be abandoned like that."

"This isn't your typical ghost. It seems she was kidnapped." Her stomach tightened as she recalled Amy's tale.

"Or ghostnapped." Cleo chuckled.

"This is much worse. She wasn't a spirit when she was taken." Lili frowned in thought as she sipped her coffee. "It's something else I'd like to investigate. She's a mundane little girl born in the 1800s. She said she was brought here by a big black bird. My medical diagnosis is that she was frightened to death and now she's trapped down there."

"Are griffins black?" Cleo mentioned.

"It depends on the flock, but I don't think that was what took her. Even after all these years, she's still very frightened and can't understand why she can't return to her mother. I need to see if I can reunite them."

"And the demon?"

"He's not at all what he appears." Lili chose not to tell Cleo that Jared was who they'd glimpsed in Inderman. Cleo would immediately switch her "You need a sex life," to "Okay, let's cross the homicidal maniac off the list." "Dr. Mortimer said the Demon Council signed Jared's care over to him instead of having him destroyed for heinous crimes. I think there's more going on than the miniscule notations in his file. Plus, Dr. Mortimer never refers to him by name. Only by his intake number. Jared's treated like a wild animal."

"You look flushed." Cleo peered at her closely with more than a hint of suspicion.

"There's no elevator to take me below, and I hurried up the stairs." Lili thought of the intense way Jared looked at her. She was positive that had something to do with it too.

At any other time, she would have been interested in seeing where it would go. He was obviously intelligent, seemed way too normal for someone with a grossly damaged brain, not to mention he was damn sexy for a homicidal maniac.

Not that she was considering any kind of interaction with him, even if he stood before her all cleaned up.

Nope. Not at all.

As she drank her coffee she automatically touched the tip of her nose with her fingertip.

Luckily, it hadn't grown.

The cat stared at her, her mouth widened in a smile that would have done the Cheshire cat proud. "You're thinking about the sexy guy we saw in Inderman, aren't you?"

Lili was once again relieved the feline didn't know that Jared had shown up at the house. She never would have heard the end of it. "There's been too much going on," she said, knowing she had to be careful with her words. Cleo had a built-in lie detector.

"I'd rather you drool over him than decide to set your sights on Dr. Mortimer." She wrinkled her nose. "He smells like the unaired interior of a very old armoire. Why can't the heads of hospitals be young and hot instead of ancient?"

"Dr. Ferdinand smelled like snuff and loved silk knee breeches," Lili reminded her, speaking of the sorcerer who was in charge of the hospital in Chicago that she had just come from.

"Nasty thing, snuff. And it was so bad for my allergies too." She stood up on all fours and fluffed out her tail. "All right. While you're facing the dragon, I'll be down the hall making nice kitty with the clerk. I already know I got the better deal."

Lili thought of the fierce-featured dragon-shifter. "I'm sure you do."

Ten minutes later, the witch wasn't sure whether to thank the Fates or curse them when she was paged to go immediately to the ER.

"Bridge Trolls," she muttered, diving into the fray that was quickly turning the area into a war zone. "For once, I thank you for creating trouble."

Chapter 4

"YOU'RE SUPPOSED TO BE A CALMING INFLUENCE there, not stirring up trouble!" Lili scolded as she and Cleo entered her small house through the kitchen.

"I didn't stir up anything," the cat snapped as she prowled the kitchen before settling her furry butt on the floor next to her dish. She tapped her front paw in a *time to feed me* staccato. "You have no idea what atrocities that clerk wanted to do to me! No self-respecting cat should endure such indignities."

Lili was ready to accuse the cat of acting like a drama queen, but that would only extend the argument. Then the cat's reply would be the same, along with a larger measure of disdain until she yowled with ear-splitting displeasure.

She pulled out the container of gourmet kitty food from the refrigerator. A brief nuke in the microwave brought it up to the proper temperature. No cold food for the sovereign kitty.

"Do you know that clerk used baby talk on me? Baby talk, for Fate's sake! She even wanted to put a pink bow on me!" The cat looked disgusted as she nibbled her dinner. "She's lucky I didn't do worse than inflict a few scratches on her." She sniffed her food. "Are you sure this is king salmon? That fishmonger in Inderman didn't look entirely reliable."

"He's been there for four hundred years. He's very

trustworthy." Lili ducked into her bathroom for a quick shower and then changed her clothes. Her light flannel pajama pants and tank top were perfect for an evening of relaxation.

Cleo called out from the kitchen. "We have company."

"Who—?" Lili thought of the bottle of wine she had planned to crack open to accompany whatever she pulled out for her meal.

"Friends," Cleo said brightly as the doorbell chimed.

Lili hurried to the door and squealed with delight to see two old friends on her doorstep.

"We come bearing dinner." The lovely blond and her male companion held up white Chinese take-out cartons.

"Love the outfit, babe." The man grinned and winked at Lili.

"Rea, Adam!" She hugged them both and stepped back. "I am so glad to see you." The empath and witch were the two friends she'd missed the most after she had left San Francisco.

"You look good, Lili." Adam carried the containers into the kitchen. "Hey, Cleo. We brought something for you too."

"Ooh, I love you." The cat purred her pleasure.

"You've got the place looking great," Rea said, looking around the family room furnished with comfortable-looking pieces meant for lounging, not just for looks.

Lili loved the one-story cottage she had purchased back in the 1930s when she returned to San Francisco for a visit. Over the years, she had allowed friends to use her house when they needed a refuge. It had been updated over time, and now it was time for her to add personal touches to her space.

This time she arranged the living and dining rooms into one large family area and updated the kitchen with modern appliances but kept the vintage touches that melded seamlessly with the contemporary.

She pulled out a bottle of wine and filled three glasses.

"I love the colors you've chosen," Rea said, unerringly finding plates and flatware and carrying them to the nook that held a small table and chairs. Twinkling lights on the patio gave the backyard a faery garden feel.

"I wanted a touch of home." Lili enjoyed the deep blues, the bright yellows, and the splashes of coral that surrounded her.

"Can we eat?" Adam begged, transporting the cartons to the table. "Hungry witch here."

They dug their chopsticks into the Kung Pao chicken, clams in black bean sauce, and lobster Cantonese, along with barbecued pork, fried rice and bacon-wrapped shrimp.

"What did you get Cleo?" She frowned at the cat's now loaded dish.

"Peking duck," Adam replied, using his chopsticks to snare a spring roll.

"Tastier than that cheap king salmon you picked up." Cleo narrowed her eyes at Lili.

"And very fattening." The witch bared her teeth.

"How does it feel being back at the hospital?" Rea asked. She refused to use her empath skills to read a friend unless expressly asked to. She usually joked she was off duty.

Adam, as a water witch, was happiest when at the beach, where he felt more in tune with the tides, than he was living further inland. Rea teased him that it was a shame he wasn't born a selkie.

Lili knew a lot of surfers liked visiting Adam's magick shop, since his charms could keep them safe while riding the waves, and fishermen also availed themselves of his skills. The two witches had dated briefly, years ago, but then decided they were better off as friends. Now Adam and Rea were a happy couple, and Lili was pleased she had been able to match them up.

Like her, they chose to live on the outskirts of Inderman, settling on a lovely Victorian Painted Lady home built in 1882 across from Alamo Square.

"It feels the same, yet it's not, since there's not that many staff members who were there the last time I worked at the hospital," she replied. "The doctor in charge is very old-world medicine, and the Director of Nursing is a dragon-shifter."

Rea wrinkled her nose. "Dragons always have way too much attitude. We had one running our counseling center for a while. We held a party the day she left."

"Do you really think you can discover the truth about Sera and the others?" Adam asked.

Lili had contacted her friends before she returned to San Francisco and confided her plan, asking for their help. Both tried to dissuade her from her task, but she refused to back down. She was glad they were available as backup.

"I can try," she admitted. "But there's so much else going on there that's odd." She related her time below in the asylum and described its inhabitants. She glossed over Jared, since she still wasn't sure about him. She also brought up her meeting with Amy in the dungeon space and what she learned about the ghost.

Rea's eyes darkened with tears. "That poor baby,

trapped in such a place. Why would some creature kidnap her and bring her across time?" She shook her head, clearly hating the idea of a frightened child dropped into a foreign situation.

"I don't know. I need to talk to one of the Guides at the hospital about helping her cross over, hopefully to join with her mother. But I'm afraid I'll need someone special. If the right person isn't at the hospital, can you help me find someone?"

"Of course," the empath said without hesitation.

"She said a big black bird took her?" Adam asked, pulling a small leather-bound notebook out of his shirt pocket.

Lili nodded.

"I'll see if I can find anything out for you." He jotted down a few sentences in his notebook before he returned it to his pocket.

"Thanks, Adam." Lili sighed. "The hospital has changed quite a bit since the last time I worked there. Now it's as if the place exists in two opposite worlds. Upstairs is up-to-date, light, airy, and filled with so much healing magick, you feel energized just by being there. But if you go below, it's like being transported backward to a dark, ugly past, where mundanes viewed insanity as a sign of evil and locked their family members away in attics, cellars, or worse. If they had the money, they'd put them in an asylum where the patients were treated no better than something you'd scrape off your shoe," she said grimly. "No wonder I preferred treating the usual diseases of the supes. Just being down there for a short time was draining." She emptied her wineglass and refilled it. She didn't believe in finding courage in alcohol, but there were times it pacified the agitation that made her feel so antsy. This was one of those moments.

Over the next two hours, the three friends ate and talked and laughed. For the first time in the past week, Lili felt well and truly relaxed.

She looked at the couple and saw a relationship that weathered storms and only grew stronger from their trials. She knew that Maura, Adam's mother, hadn't liked Rea in the beginning, thinking the gentle-hearted empath wouldn't be a good match for determined, rigorous-thinking Adam. She was glad they proved the old witch wrong. What Lili saw was a love that only grew over time.

After her friends helped her clean the kitchen and left, Lili settled in bed with her Nook, as Cleo stretched out on the other pillow.

However, the book she'd begun with such anticipation didn't hold her interest. Visions of the demon Jared kept her attention wandering. She finally set her e-reader on the bedside table and snuggled down under the covers.

Even after all these years, was Jared still as dangerous as Dr. Mortimer claimed he was—or was there something else going on?

The world was wild and desolate, and the village was quiet save for a few restless dogs housed near the living quarters.

He'd been at this place once before, when earlier generations had played and lived here. The girl he took at that time had been tasty and provided him with his sustenance. But, over time, his hunger had increased, and he moved among the world and all its planes more often.

Magick was strong here. He could feel his pores taking it in the way dry skin soaked up water. The strongest came from one house, where a young girl radiated it like the sun.

He stole through the cottage entrance and made sure that everyone inside would sleep soundly while he took what he required.

Perhaps he would use the shadows, so he could remain for the days he needed to view their death rites, to send the girl into the next world.

It was always sad when a young one perished, but she also had much power in her blood. Power he needed. The way he saw it, her demise was really for the greater good.

─────〰〰─────

"I'm glad we're finally able to have time for a chat, Dr. Carter." Director of Nursing Arimentha Garrish occupied the large chair behind her desk in the same way that the queen of the universe commanded her royal throne. "It has seemed that every time I've requested your presence, you have managed to find something to occupy your time."

"Well, as you know, it's been very busy lately. Full moon and all."

Lili mustered up a brief smile while wishing for mega air-conditioning. Due to the head nurse being a dragon-shifter, she preferred keeping her personal space at a toasty 110 degrees, unconcerned if her visitors roasted in the process.

The dragon-shifter fingered the file folder in front of her. "I like to have some time to chat, Dr. Carter—a chance to get to know our doctors here." Her dark eyes glimmered.

Ah, there's that royal we. Lili kept a brief smile on her lips. *Never let them see you sweat, even if the room is like a damn sauna.* "Of course, and I'm always happy to help in any way I can. As you know, we've been very busy in the ER, not to mention my work below, treating the emotionally troubled patients."

Miss Garrish's nose wrinkled. "While I realize such a ward is needed, even among our kind, I do not consider it a suitable work place for females." She eyed Lili sharply. "Even if they think of themselves as powerful witches."

Lili swallowed her sigh. She had fought prejudice about her sex, even among the preternatural communities, for so many years that she should have been immune to the bias. *Not gonna happen if the speaker's a know-it-all megareptile.* She was relieved that, at least, the shifter wasn't a T. rex.

"Miss Garrish, I am a healer first and foremost, whether the damage is physical or mental," she spoke in her firm, no-nonsense doctor voice, one that had left more than a few nurses in tears. "It doesn't matter that I have a vagina instead of a penis. I would think that you, being a female, would also see it that way. I know that you wouldn't have this position unless you worked very hard for it and had the knowledge to back it up. Just like you, I have labored hard to be the best healer I can be. I am here to treat the suffering of our patients, no matter what they are or what they're going through. It doesn't matter what my sex is or what I am. All that matters is that I have the power to ease their pain."

The Director of Nursing didn't even blink, and Lili could swear she didn't even take a breath.

Damn.

"How accustomed are you to getting your way?" The elder's eyes shot black-and-gold sparks, revealing a mere hint of her temper.

"Not as much as I'd like," Lili freely admitted, knowing the shifter would sniff out if she said even one word that wasn't true. "And I only truly battle for what I feel is right."

Miss Garrish tapped her long, silver-tipped nails on her desktop. Lili wondered how many victims knew those claws intimately and how many survived.

"I like to think I can offer some hope to the patients housed below," Lili said. She knew she was taking a chance, since she wasn't sure what kind of relationship Miss Garrish had with Dr. Mortimer. *Don't go there, Lili. You'll only sear your brain if you think the worst.* "You have to admit no one should have to look on those ugly ogres every day if they can look at a smiling face."

"They do have their uses," Miss Garrish murmured, with a hint of distaste in her tone proving she wasn't all that fond of Turtifo and Coing either. "Just because you have the title doctor in front of your name does not mean you aren't subject to my rules."

"Of course." Lili really needed to remain on this female's good side—if the Director of Nursing had one, that is.

"One other thing." The elder speared the healer with

a dark eye. "Your familiar." She sniffed as if she just used an odious word.

Good thing Cleo wasn't here. The cat would be having a royal hissy fit. "Cleo isn't my familiar. She merely lives with me," Lili corrected. "Many of us don't have familiars. I'm one of them."

Miss Garrish waved her hand in dismissal. "Whether or not it's a familiar, it still should not be wandering the halls of this establishment. Perhaps we do not follow the same health codes as the mundanes, but we do have our standards."

Oh yes, a very good thing Cleo wasn't here.

Lili reached into her pocket and pulled out a small scroll. "Cleo is a certified therapy cat, warranted free of any disease," she stated, placing the parchment on the desk. "She is also excellent working with traumatized young. She makes them forget their illnesses. And even if she is a long-haired feline, she doesn't shed."

Miss Garrish edged the scroll open and read the contents. There was no denying that the elaborate seals which decorated the bottom gave the cat a lot of immunity within the medical context. Her thin lips narrowed even more. "If there is one speck of trouble from that creature, she will be barred from the hospital. And now I suggest you return to your work, Dr. Carter."

Lili patted herself all over after she left the office.

"What's wrong?" Deisphe asked as the witch passed her.

"I'm just making sure I'm not missing any body parts." She relayed the head nurse's edict.

"Yeah, she tends to do that." The Wereleopard yawned. "Hey, want to go out for a drink with a bunch of us after our shift?"

"Sounds good. Let me know where. Also, you can work with me downstairs tomorrow." Lili sketched a wave and headed for the stairs.

She had already consulted her computer to see which patient she'd be seeing first. Dr. Mortimer had left a written schedule on her desk, which she wasted no time inputting into her tablet. She noted that all the patients but Jared were referred to by name.

"Old fogy," she muttered, sending a ball of witch-flame ahead of her to better illuminate the dimly lit stone stairs. Before she passed through the large iron door, she stopped to check herself in a small mirror and applied fresh lip gloss. "Vain witch." She rolled her eyes at herself and her need to look her best.

"Doctor." The word rolled off Turtifo's black-veined tongue with rich sarcasm. "Who do you want to see first?" His dark eyes mirrored the disdain in his voice.

"Bring Pepta to my office," she said, recalling the list on her tablet. "And, Turtifo, I better not see any bruises on her," she warned him.

He growled under his breath as he lumbered off.

Lili released a soft snarl in his direction as she headed for the small room she'd claimed as her own.

After setting out cups of chamomile tea and a small plate of special cookies, she waited for her patient.

She heard the ogre's rumbling voice before he walked in with a small slender female before him, one of his meaty hands wrapped around the nape of her delicate neck, although his grip on her was lighter than he had used on Jared—probably because of the strong pheromones Pepta was exuding. The nymph's lips were curved in a smile that was pure seduction.

"Hello, Pepta. Come sit." Her gaze flicked over Turtifo. "Return in an hour." She was pleased to see he didn't argue with her this time.

Pepta was a vision, with her porcelain skin that glowed under the lights like a pearl, silver hair hanging loose to her waist, eyes that were a mesmerizing copper, and lips that invited a man to partake of them. What should have been an ankle-length gown of rough cotton had been ripped in strategic places to reveal her rounded breasts and a hint of silver pubic hair and creamy thighs. The nymph walked with the sultry grace of her kind and dropped onto the cushy chair Lili indicated. She deliberately spread her legs as if inviting anyone to have a snack.

"Is Morty afraid of still seeing me?" Pepta asked, with a smile that would have made a succubus proud. She arched her lithe body in a sensuous curve.

"As you know, Dr. Mortimer has asked me to work with some of his patients. I was especially looking forward to our talking together," Lili replied, nudging the tea in her patient's direction. She was pleased to see the nymph had been allowed to wash herself and was wearing clean clothing, even if it was obviously well-worn. She could see the brand on her shoulder, announcing to all she was a mental patient. Lili's fingers itched to hex it off, even as she knew there was no way she could do that. Plus, for all she knew, her effort could only cause pain to the nymph. She made a note to see about arranging suitable wearing apparel for the patients, perhaps even a form of scrubs, in different colors than the staff wore upstairs. She couldn't believe that Dr. Mortimer hadn't taken better care of his charges' needs.

"Sorry, darling, I like cock—although you dress more male than female." She gave Lili's blue scrubs and white lab coat a disparaging sniff. She plucked at one of the tears that revealed the side of her breast. Shrugging when Lili ignored her efforts, she picked up the cup and sipped the hot tea. "You wouldn't have a mug of dark ale up your sleeve, would you?"

"Try the tea instead." Lili watched her pick up a cookie and bite into it. She knew her recipe had additional calming properties. She didn't believe in using even magickal drugs if herbs could do the same thing. She kept her computer tablet in her lap where she could make notes as the two spoke. Lili listened to Pepta's erotic fantasies, some of which she hoped were just that, and others that had to be true.

The nymph had seduced a leader's son and then killed him in a fit of rage. Her punishment had been to be locked away in an underground cave for two hundred years. However, no one had arrived to free her until she was discovered, eighty years ago, when she was finally released from her prison. Her sanity wasn't even hanging by a thread. All she cared about was fulfilling her hungers for food and sex. Lili read, in Dr. Mortimer's notes, that he hoped to help the nymph balance her life in a healthy way, but it had been a slow-going affair. She wondered if that wasn't due to the doctor not wanting to look deeper into Pepta's problems.

Freud would have a field day with this one.

"Why can't the demon be with us?" Pepta asked, choosing another cookie.

"Private sessions," Lili reminded her as she picked up her teacup. "Plus, wouldn't you prefer some girl talk?"

"With someone who wants to dissect my brain?" The nymph sipped her tea. "When will you bring out the tentacles?"

The witch lifted her hands and wiggled her fingers. "Not my style."

Pepta chose another cookie.

Lili could see that the bespelled treats were making her patient a lot calmer. She was pleased that something she'd learned from another doctor who treated the mentally ill was so effective.

"You want to fuck the demon, don't you?" Pepta said suddenly. A sly smile crossed her lips. "You want him to take you hard and dirty."

Lili had spoken briefly to Pepta a few days ago, so she knew it would be a struggle to keep the nymph on track. In looking over her records, it was easy to see the female hurt a great deal inside and lashed out at others in hopes of keeping her own pain under control.

The witch just had to find a way to persuade Pepta to release the agony and face what she'd done before the healing could truly begin.

"And what do you want, Pepta? Do you want to remain a prisoner in a stone cell while the world spins around you, leaving you behind? Don't you want to return to your family? Feel whole again?"

Aha. She watched the nymph's vivid purple eyes darken and a hint of a crystal tear appear in one corner, but just as quickly it was gone, and she showed her true self.

"You're too soft to work down here, Dr. Carter. You should leave before something happens to you."

Lili's headache grew to massive proportions by the

time she had Pepta returned to her cell. She dropped a headache powder in her tea and sorted through her files.

"I'll see Patient 1172 next," she told Turtifo.

The ogre opened his mouth then closed it when he caught the warning look in her eyes.

"And no shackles!" she called after him.

Fifteen minutes later, Jared was pushed into the room, his wrists and ankles manacled in iron chains that obviously pained him. She admired his restraint in not wanting to cause some serious hurt toward the ogre. But she could understand why, after seeing his previous wounds.

"I said no shackles," she snapped, feeling her headache returning.

"Dr. Mortimer's orders, and he's the boss down here. You're just the hired help." He fastened the fetters to the table and left without a backward glance.

It took all of Lili's willpower not to order the door to slam after the orderly. Instead, she shot her fingers at the manacles. She swore under her breath when the iron bands didn't fall loose. Lili had to settle for adding thick layers of soft wool lining to the inside of the restraints. She didn't miss Jared's soft sigh of relief. She conjured up coffee and a thick juicy burger and fries.

"Gotta say, I like your service, Doc." He munched away happily. "Or is this the carrot-and-stick method? You have me all sated with good food, then you bring in the electrodes or fire whips?"

"Fire whips were outlawed in 1822 when many strove to improve the lot of the afflicted."

Jared snorted. "Saying so isn't the same as being on the receiving end. You've been here, what, a week? Maybe a little longer? You only see what you want to see, Doc. Not what really goes on around here. How old are you? How long have you been practicing healing?"

"Old enough to know better, and I was *born* a healer," she told him, tamping down hurtful memories of long ago.

She shouldn't have abandoned her mother to suffer a horrific death alone.

Jared froze as his loaded cheeseburger hovered near his lips. He slowly set the food down and stared at her across the table.

"What's wrong?"

"Shouldn't I be the one asking that?" She threw up shields. She didn't think he could rummage around inside her mind. She hadn't seen signs of it before, but she wasn't taking any chances. Not with her lack of knowledge about shadow demons.

"You look devastated." Shadows crawled from the corners of the room toward Jared's chair. They started to wrap around his ankles, stealthily making their way up his legs.

"Tell them to back off." Her voice was sharp, filled with command, as she glared at the darkness. Her head shot up when he didn't respond. "*Now.*" Lili held up her forefinger, the tip glowing red. She didn't indicate she was in any pain from the flame that engulfed her skin.

Jared's smile was filled with malice. "Make me."

It wasn't the shadows that caused his world to suddenly go black.

———

Jared's eyes popped open at the same time that a blinding pain tortured the inside of his head.

"What the fuck?" He found himself sprawled on the floor while Lili looked on as if there weren't anything unusual about sending a patient into la-la land with the snap of the fingers. "What did you do to me?" he rasped as he finally managed to crawl back into his chair. He swore his shackles had easily gained a thousand pounds since the ogre slapped them on him. He reached for the coffee cup and found his hands trembling from the violent shocks still racing through his body. A glance at the clock on the wall said he'd been unconscious for at least a half hour, yet his drink and food were still hot.

Terrific. She zaps me but thinks enough to keep my lunch warm. Not that he thought he could handle solid foods just now.

"Any reason for what you just did?" He winced as the coffee burned his tongue. Damn, he must have bit his tongue when she zapped him.

"I told you to force your shadows to back off," she told him with a shrug of her shoulders. "You didn't comply, so I did it for you."

Jared's arms felt as heavy as his shackles as he lifted his hands to rub his aching head. No wonder it all hurt. The room was as bright as the noonday sun. She'd not only managed to knock him out but destroyed his shadows too. He felt suddenly bereft.

"You witches pack quite a wallop." He rubbed his hand over the back of his neck.

"Be grateful I didn't use full power. You would have been lucky if you could even drool by now. Speech wouldn't have returned for at least forty-eight hours." She smiled cheerfully.

"And I thought Dumb and Dumber were bad enough." He started to scowl at her but discovered even that hurt. "Does Dr. Mortimer know about that trick of yours?"

"Does he know you have a way to leave the hospital when you want to?" Lili countered.

"Point taken." He took an experimental bite of food and discovered his head was no longer trying to squeeze his brain out through his eye sockets. "First you protect my skin from the irons, provide me with decent food, and then you hex my lights out. Are you sure you're not really an inmate down here?" He felt warm inside as her soft laughter washed over him.

"I wanted to prove I back up what I say."

"I haven't met all that many witches, but you definitely take first page in my memory book." He polished off his burger and worked on the fries. He didn't notice Lili's sharp look of interest.

"Did other witches work down here?"

He missed her all-too-casual tone. "Not on a regular basis, unless more medical care was needed than Dumb and Dumber could provide. They were usually the ones to provide minor medical treatment, even if their bedside manners frankly sucked. Dr. Mortimer handled the bad injuries." His voice tightened. "A Were nurse was down once. Shingleg mangled her pretty badly. You're going to want to keep the two ogres in with you when you talk to him." He started to push away his plate with half the fries still on it but changed his mind. Who knew when he'd get a good meal again? He didn't have enough power to sneak out for the next few nights. He wondered if his shadows could track the lovely doctor down like that night in her house. He wouldn't mind running into her in Inderman again. He'd like to see her in a place of light and laughter instead of down here in darkness and sorrow.

He looked up and found her staring at him intently. "Are we getting to the treatment part now?"

"I don't know if therapy would help you," she said frankly.

Her candid statement left him feeling unsettled. Did this mean she wouldn't come down to see him again? He didn't want to believe that would happen. Seeing the witch was the only bright spot in his existence. While he was able to venture outside the walls, his time away was limited and only at night when the shadows were the strongest.

"What are you thinking?"

Jared wanted to laugh at Lili's typical question. "You head docs need to come up with better questions," he said. "It seems you always want to know what we're feeling and thinking." He was relieved to see his hands were completely steady now and his head felt as if it would stay in one piece. "Wouldn't you rather know why I killed that vampire nest?"

"I asked you that already, and you didn't answer. I thought I'd sneak that question in again later on."

Jared inhaled her scent, wanting to imprint it in his memory banks. Her female scent was mixed with something woodsy and exotic. He'd sensed her fertility cycle that first time but couldn't catch any hint of it now. Obviously, her protective runes didn't shield her from any unwanted male attention, such as his.

"Why do you want to be here?" he asked. "You're nothing like Dr. Mortimer. You're not looking to see if pain will drive the devils from us." He laughed without any form of mirth. "You're not set in your ways." He nodded his head toward her computer tablet. "I may have been locked down for centuries, but I try to keep up with all those newfangled gadgets out in the world." He explained his slight knowledge of modern electronics. "Although Twitter is still strange to me. And I guess Turtifo and Coing have Facebook pages. No idea why, since their faces would break any computer. I bet the only friends they have are each other."

Lili's lips twitched as she fought back her smile. "Why do you persist in acting as if you want nothing more than to kill someone?"

Something dark and dangerous filtered through his mind. Judging by the expression on her face, he was revealing way too much.

Lean bodies, faces contorted with uncontrollable hunger as bloodred eyes fastened on him. He was the creamy center in a vampire sandwich, except there was only one of him and too many of them.

"You defile us by your presence, demon." The voice hissed in his ear as the stench of old blood and something in a state of decay caused his stomach to roll over. Not that it mattered how sick he got. They intended to kill him anyway.

"And you stink like Yeti at the end of winter." He flashed his own pearly whites even though he didn't have the fancy-dancy fangs.

If there was anything vamps hated more than a smartass, it was a smart-ass demon.

Pain everywhere. He thought his throat had been torn out. Screaming. Wasn't sure if the sound came from him or them. He was betting it was him.

"Jared!"

This time, when he opened his eyes and found himself on the floor, he didn't feel as if he had been run through a hex blender. No, more like fear that rendered him boneless.

His stomach roiled when he saw a trickle of blood on her chin. "No," he whispered, starting to reach up to wipe it away, but she moved away, using a cloth to clean her face then torch the fabric.

Jared closed his eyes, willing the images to retreat and the long-ago pain to disappear. Too bad neither happened.

"You had a flashback." Lili spoke softly, as if she sensed how badly his head was hurting and how any loud sound would just tear him apart.

"You went to medical school to figure that one out?" he growled, glaring at the mug pushed in front of him. "What the fuck is that?"

"Just drink it."

He picked it up and sniffed the contents. He reared back as his nose turned numb. "Do you really want to know what this smells like?"

"It doesn't matter. It will help. Trust me."

I don't trust anyone.

Except she smelled good and fed him. She didn't treat him like an animal.

Jared almost gagged as the putrid liquid slid down his throat, but he noticed his head felt a lot clearer and his insides didn't feel torn up any longer.

"You're just one witchy pharmacy, aren't you?"

Lili reached into her pocket and held out small sacks filled with herbs. "A friend makes them up for me."

"You take good care of me." He pushed his hand through his hair, cringing a bit at the feel of the dirty strands. He wished he looked better for her. Maybe not the way he was centuries ago, but the way he looked when he escaped here. Even better, he wanted to be someone who was completely free to pursue the female that he was attracted to. Instead, he had been branded insane and locked in a stinking cell for too many hours of the day. He swore he was being used as some kind of mad medical experiment, even if his memories were so scrambled that there were days he wasn't sure what was real and what wasn't.

"You know what? I think I've had enough mind probing for today," he muttered. He tore his hand out of her grasp so abruptly that he heard her gasp softly as his chains scraped her skin. He pushed himself to his feet, the iron chains clanking against the table. He limped his way to the door.

"Jared."

He paused and looked over his shoulder. "The ogres are right," he said quietly. "You shouldn't be down here. Do us all a favor and worry about the ones upstairs, the ones who have a chance to experience a real life. We were abandoned on a dung heap for a reason." He paused then walked back to her.

Before Lili could ask him what he was doing, he pulled her out of her chair and into his arms. He captured her mouth, kissing her so deeply, the action was as intimate as sex. It blistered her down to her toes, and she could only hang on for the ride as his tongue invaded her mouth without even a thought of protest from her. Lili gripped his arms, feeling the hard muscles ripple under her touch. She kept her eyes closed, losing herself in the sensual clouds that moved around her. She felt wrapped in something that seeped into her bones, a heat that was untamed and had her wondering if the images that flared behind her closed eyelids were his or hers. Sheets flowed around them while their naked bodies writhed in ecstasy, a wild magick that set the room afire as they sought something on a far higher sensual plane than most could attain. The pairing was so perfect that her senses cried at the beauty that flooded her mind. Now she knew he shared the same images.

Lili swallowed her whimper when he stepped back, the loss of his body heat like a cold shower on her senses. His eyes were almost black, and his face portrayed stark lines of passion. There was no doubt what they just shared had knocked them back for a loop.

Jared's jerky movements showed none of his usual animal grace as he turned back to the door. He paused and looked over his shoulder before he pulled the door open.

"Thanks for the food, Doc," he said quietly. The forceful gleam in his eye told her the attraction wasn't all that one-sided. But then all she had to do was look south to see that his pants were a great deal tighter than they were when he first came in.

She barely recovered from their kiss in time to deactivate the lock before he turned the knob.

Coing straightened up from his position across the hall and stared at Jared as he exited the door. He leered at Lili before grabbing Jared's arm and pulling him away in a painful grip.

She slowly put her computer tablet away and took the time to heal the scrapes on her chin. She could hear the sounds of Jared's cell door opening and then being slammed shut along with the metallic clink of the lock engaging. But it was the cell's occupant that ran riot through her thoughts.

Her body was still humming merrily along, reminding her just how long it had been since she'd had sex, although she doubted anything she'd experienced in the past compared to what it would be like with Jared.

"He's a patient," she reminded herself. "Off-limits." She didn't bother mentally bringing up that he was not just a demon but a demon who was classified as homicidally insane. The most dangerous creature of all.

Oh yes, off-limits in so many ways that she shouldn't even look at him that way. Her thoughts didn't border on just unethical, it was slam-dunk illegal. She wouldn't just lose her job, she'd lose her healer status and would be shunned by all.

—⁓—

"You stink, demon." Coing flung Jared into his cell, not caring that he did a somersault along the way.

"Yeah, like you're any better," he muttered, wincing when his head connected with the stone wall.

The ogre grinned. "'Cept I don't reek of witch too." His yellow eyes flared with maniacal glee. "Tell me something, asswipe, What's the bitch like? All slippery and tight inside? Did you taste her?"

Jared didn't think. He roared and lunged at Coing, reaching out to tear his captor to pieces. The ogre wasted no time holding up his medallion. Before the demon could reach him, protective magick kicked in and Jared bounced off an invisible wall. Electric shocks traveled through his body, sending him into convulsions.

"Try it again, and I'll amp it up until you're nothing but a pile of drool." Coing slammed the door shut and set the lock.

It took Jared awhile before he could control his muscles enough to crawl to what was laughingly called his bed. He finally collapsed and closed his eyes against the red dots dancing in front of him. He'd been zapped before, but Coing had gone for a higher voltage this time, leaving his body feeling like something wet and worn-out. He kissed her, and even though he couldn't even move his little finger, he wanted to kiss her again, to experience the incredible magick that had swarmed around them like an iridescent bubble.

"Stupid," he muttered, then winced as he realized even his teeth hurt. The protective charm Coing unleashed on him was something new and nasty. *What the fuck was in that?*

He wanted to close his eyes and lose himself in sleep, even if it brought bad dreams, but he didn't think he could still control his body. He feared that he might never be the same again.

His lips twitched. Still, it had been worth it. He'd carry the scent of her skin and taste of her mouth in his memory. Maybe they'd be enough to keep the pain and nightmares away.

Why are you sad?

He opened his eyes to find the little spirit standing just inside his cell. She looked uncertain as she lingered near the wall with her ratty teddy bear in her arms. Due to her presence, the already cold interior dropped in temperature.

"I'm not sad. How did you get in here?"

She looked as if she'd bolt if Jared even looked at her wrong.

He mustered up a smile in hopes of calming her fears. "What's your name?"

Amy. Feeling emboldened, she stepped forward and looked around. *Dr. Lili said I could come in here if I was scared. That you'd keep me safe.*

"Dr. Lili's a smart witch," he said softly, surprised that Lili put so much faith in the idea that he'd look after the little girl. But then there wasn't much harm that could be done to a wraith. And he didn't want to frighten her. He looked around, "Sorry I don't have somewhere for you to sit."

Amy offered a tentative smile and perched on what had to be an invisible stool.

"Who knew I'd be ghost-sitting today?" Jared said to himself while racking his brain for something suitable to say to a little girl that wouldn't scare her into the next century. "So, does your teddy bear have a name?"

Amy's bright smile told him he asked just the right question.

Demons don't know how to tell the truth. You already know his real name isn't Jared and that there is so much more you need to know about him.

Lili wasn't surprised to find a summons to Dr. Mortimer's office waiting for her when she returned to her own personal space.

"He smells like an old couch," Cleo informed her from her silken cushion. "And he ignored me." She sulked. There was nothing she hated more than being ignored.

The witch didn't miss the sight of a few more snags on her couch cushions while the cat kept her own elegant pillow in pristine condition. She had a feeling that her arrogant feline, as if there were any other, took out her frustration on the furniture.

Note to self. Bring in a scratching post for her highness before she shreds the entire couch.

Lili paused for a quick visual to make sure her hair was still neatly twisted on top of her head. She wore little makeup while working, so she only needed to refresh her lip gloss and add a touch of blush.

"A hint of perfume wouldn't hurt," Cleo suggested.

"He's my boss."

"And he's also an old-fashioned male who's not dead even if he's got to be close to a thousand years old. Don't use enough scent to seduce him, the way I bet you want to with that demon, but a little to soften the old fogy up is a good idea."

Lili knew better than to argue with the former Egyptian seductress. Anyone who had been the lover of both Julius Caesar and Marc Antony knew what she was talking about!

Lili had a habit of pretending deafness when Cleo indulged in too much catnip wine and burbled on happily about her extensive sex life. To this day, she didn't know how the former queen of Egypt ended up as a cat, and that was one thing Cleo had remained close-lipped about.

"Much better," the feline pronounced after Lili presented herself for her approval. She sat up and stretched. "I believe I will visit the children's ward. Younglings always need cheering up."

"No begging treats from them," Lili warned, knowing her words were in vain. Cleo was shameless when it came to begging for adoration and nummies. But she couldn't scold her, since the cat was wonderful at distracting the young from their ills.

Lili made her way to Dr. Mortimer's office and was instantly admitted to the antique-laden room. He directed her to a heavily embroidered chair that she was positive was stuffed with horsehair. She tried not to wrinkle her nose at the strong scent of his tobacco that hung in the air. A carved pipe sat in a nearby ashtray.

After accepting his offer of tea, she took a covert look at her surroundings. Lili was used to a wizard doctor's office being of the stuffy variety. Usually there was too much furniture, books, and scrolls from various eras and frequently a collection of personal keepsakes. She saw books her fingers itched to peruse and pieces of jade and ivory. She narrowed her eyes a bit, sensing a haze over the shelves covering the walls, but discovered it only gave her a sense of disorientation. She swallowed the hint of nausea and returned her gaze to the desk.

"They're lovely pieces," she commented when she noticed he was watching her.

"Thank you. I spent some time in China in the 1700s studying under a revered healer and later moved to Africa where I heard of a tribal medicine man who was successful with herbs. There are gifts from both of them on that table." His demeanor relaxed a little. "According to your personnel records, your mother was a very talented healer."

She tamped down the sharp prick of pain in her heart.

"Yes, she was. I learned a great deal from her before I entered the Witches Academy." She tried not to shift around on the prickly chair as she leaned forward for her teacup in hopes it would help the slight sense of imbalance. Luckily, a few sips seemed to make her feel better. She smiled and waited for her superior's reason for requesting her presence.

"I will be frank with you, Dr. Carter." The wizard sipped his Earl Grey. "The more I think about it, the more I realize just how uncomfortable I am with you treating Patient 1172. Especially with your insistence you not have the aides in the room with you." He nodded at her look of surprise. "Yes, I was informed you ordered them out of the treatment room. Considering his deranged mind, that is not advisable."

"All patients are allowed their privacy," she said, knowing it was a reminder he might not want to hear. "And I will be honest, Dr. Mortimer, I don't feel Turtifo and Coing always consider a patient's welfare. They tend to be a little rough in their handling of some of them. That bothers me a great deal."

"I understand your concerns, Doctor, but you must remember that all the patients down there are labeled dangerous," he pointed out. His expression turned grim, sending a slight chill through her body. "My aides' credentials are impeccable, Dr. Carter. I would like to remind you they are there for your protection. Do not ignore their uses." He picked up a sheet of paper and made a few notations.

Lili felt the tightness in her jaw increase until pain shot around the base of her neck. She didn't miss the darkness in Dr. Mortimer's eyes nor the grim set to his face. She didn't think she dared try a little push of power again. If he realized what she did, she would be immediately dismissed, and no hospital would hire her.

The kindly, somewhat eccentric, wizard doctor was gone and something else took his place. He left her in no doubt who was in charge.

"You may treat the others below, but Patient 1172 will be left to me. He is much too dangerous for you. That is all, Dr. Carter." His dismissal was abrupt.

"Dr. Mortimer," she murmured around her clenched jaw. She pushed herself out of her chair and headed for the door.

"Doctor." The wizard's voice stopped her. "You must realize I am doing this for your own good. You are new to treating the emotionally damaged. In time, I am certain you will have the knowledge to be an asset in this field. After all, even I was under strict restraints in the beginning." He offered her a brief smile. "You young people can be too eager at times when patience is sorely needed. I promise you that this will be the only change."

She nodded and murmured, "Thank you."

Lili left the office with all the speed she could muster and made a quick detour to the ER.

"What's wrong?" Deisphe asked, noting her heightened color.

Lili rummaged in the drug cabinet and pulled out a small linen sack. The scent of lavender filled the room. She instantly pressed it against her forehead while uttering words meant to calm her aching head.

"Dragon lady or Dr. Mortimer?" the nurse asked, leaning a hip against the counter.

"Dr. Mortimer," she muttered, waiting for her headache to subside. She wanted coffee or even a cup of water to wash the aftertaste of tea out of her mouth. She never did like Earl Grey.

"Then aren't you in luck we get off duty in a little bit. You need to get out there and relax." Deisphe grinned. "Put on some sexy clothes and meet us at Crieze at seven. We'll find some hot guys, and we'll drink, dance, and have fun." She wiggled her eyebrows.

Knowing Weres, Lili had no doubt about that. She opened her mouth to decline but changed her mind at the last instant.

"It sounds like just what I need."

The witch stopped in her office long enough to pick up her bag before she headed upstairs to the children's ward. She'd barely stepped off the elevator when she heard the sounds of laughter and loud voices. And knew the source.

"Hello, Dr. Carter," Jana the pediatric nurse greeted her with a smile. "Your cat is making quite an impression with our young here," she told her. "You'll find them in the solarium."

"Cleo does love getting attention," Lili admitted. "Please, always feel free to tell her if she ever becomes too much trouble."

The faery nurse named Zia shook her head. Her pearlescent wings fluttered back and forth with the soothing scent of vanilla. Waist-length hair the shade of a rare pearl was coiled on top of her head in a neat twist. "I doubt the younglings would allow it. Many have parents who can't visit them as often as they'd like, so it's good when they have diversions."

"Cleo's good at that, all right." Lili chuckled, admiring the brightly colored walls and large windows that allowed abundant light to enter the room. A mural of gnomes, leprechauns, and brownies was painted on the walls. She noticed several wraiths, dressed in vintage nursing uniforms, drifting through the halls, stopping in a room and smiling at the occupant. "She's your typical furry drama queen."

"We also have some Wuzzies here for the children who are well enough to play," Zia told her. "But I think Cleo is now the more popular guest."

"What kind of illnesses do you see up here?" Lili asked curiously. "I haven't worked with pediatrics very much except for children who show up in the ER."

"Some of the same common ailments for any child. Broken bones that refuse to knit with traditional magick, some diseases that affect various supe races," the nurse replied. "We have a few Selkie young here who have had trouble with their pelts. A brownie that was exposed to an odd herb that created a horrible skin disorder."

Lili nodded. "I should collect Cleo. I'd like to return here, if I may?"

"Anytime." Zia smiled warmly. "Just follow the noise, and you'll easily find the solarium."

Lili discovered Zia was right. Especially when she could hear Cleo.

"Puss in Boots is nothing like that hunky cat in *Shrek*," she could hear Cleo saying. "More's the pity."

Lili stood in the entryway and watched a young male elf pop up from the semicircle.

"Will you tell us another story?" he asked.

Cleo spied Lili. "It appears I'm being collected." She

arched her furry body and shook her head at the shouted "No!" from her audience.

"I'll be back," she promised with a comforting purr in her voice.

Lili smiled, knowing her feline was also purring to keep the children calm. There might not be IV bags among the young patients, but she could see the charms and medallions they wore and the runes woven into their hospital gowns. No matter the race, they were well protected and everything was being done to restore them to perfect health.

So much magick in the world, and there are still some things we can't protect the young from.

The cat walked regally by Lili's side as they returned downstairs.

"You're very good with them," Lili said, feeling guilty she hadn't praised her friend more often for the tireless work she did to cheer up children.

Cleo sniffed. "I was a mother once."

"And seduced your share of men," the witch muttered.

"Not as many as the movies claim. And the actresses they've used in the past? Puleeze!"

Lili couldn't help it. She had to laugh.

"As if you know what a sex life is like." Cleo got in her parting shot before she picked up the pace and preceded Lili out of the building.

"There is nothing worse than a smart-ass cat."

Chapter 5

IT WASN'T THE BRIGHT LIGHTS THAT SURROUNDED Crieze's large entrance and the sign above it that Lili saw first when she slotted her car into the parking spot. Her attention zeroed in on the tall shadows gathered nearby that looked very familiar and man-shaped. She climbed out of her SUV and started toward the dark tendrils then halted when the silhouette seemed to morph into a tiny ball until it was gone.

A demon does it better, something whispered in her ear.

"Just my imagination, nothing more," she told herself, taking an abrupt turn in the other direction and heading for the club. She ignored the tingles running across her shoulders as she walked swiftly across the parking lot. "Damn him."

Once inside, Lili thought about leaving immediately. She winced as the musical and vocal assault punished her ears. She quickly conjured up a bit of a noise-dampening spell to make it easier and looked around the club until she saw Deisphe waving at her.

"You made it! Cute outfit, by the way." The Were handed her a glass with contents the color of spearmint that fizzed merrily. "You need to catch up with us." She introduced Lili to the two nurses and doctor who shared the table.

Lili looked at her companions' club wear and was glad she'd taken the time to shower and change into a short black silk skirt and hot pink sequined tank top with a black knit shrug that sported iridescent threads. She had flatironed her curly hair and twisted it up into an intricate ponytail.

"How do you stand the noise?" She was grateful she didn't have to shout at Deisphe, since the Were's hearing could easily pick up her words.

The lovely Were grinned and pointed to her ears. "Music protectors. Believe me, this noise is nothing. The music in a Were club can be loud enough to demolish a building."

"Our Deisphe gives a whole new meaning to the name party animal. Always a pleasure to see you, Lili," Heron, the gnome doctor, smiled at her, revealing short stubby teeth that went along with his short stubby body. While he wasn't Lili's type, she noticed more than a few gnome ladies were giving him an appreciative eye, while bubbly Deisphe received her own share of attention — not just because the barely present silver dress outlining her slender body shimmered under the club lights.

"What is this?" Lili asked, giving an experimental sniff of her drink, identifying strong alcohol — even if she wasn't sure which one — and a scent that had her thinking of liquid happiness.

"Something that makes us blissful." Deisphe nudged the glass upward. "Nothing harmful, and even better, it doesn't give you a headache in the morning."

"Deisphe said you're from Chicago and that you'd worked at Crying Souls years ago," commented Fiona, a nurse who worked in one of the main healing rooms.

"That's right." Lili nodded, sipping her drink and finding it everything Deisphe said it was.

"Didn't Sera come from Chicago?" Fiona turned to the others.

Lili snapped to attention. "Sera Rainier?"

The nurse blinked at her sharp tone. "Yes. I worked with her in the ER before she moved upstairs to one of the critical care wards."

"I've tried to get hold of Sera since I got here," the witch explained, keeping her tone as casual as she could. "She worked at the same hospital I did. She has wonderful healing skills." She refused to think of her friend in the past tense.

Deisphe shrugged. "We worked different shifts, so I didn't know Sera as well as Fiona did. Strange thing, though. She just up and quit. Dragon Lady was really pissed about it, since we were shorthanded at the time, and we were seeing a lot of cases of that Mage Flu that was going around."

"It didn't make sense, since Sera was never late for a shift and always did more than her share of the work," Fiona brought up. "You could always count on her." She shook her head, refusing to believe what many would judge as careless and unprofessional behavior.

"And especially when the Mage Flu was so prevalent at the time," Deisphe said. "We were all working double shifts then."

"I don't know why they call it Mage Flu when it doesn't affect the mages." Fiona accepted another deep aqua drink with ingredients that shimmered temptingly.

"Perhaps because a mage's arrogance is enough to make us all sick," Heron joked. "It was a shame that Sera left, though. She was an excellent nurse, and so sweet too. Does anyone know where she went?"

The others shook their heads. Lili was tempted to ask what they might know about her friend, but she didn't think this was the time. After all, she didn't know who she could trust.

She sipped her drink and found the taste as sparkly as it looked. She vowed that tonight was a time for relaxation and laughter, which she hadn't indulged in for some time, feeling that work was always more important.

If you wish to be a true healer, you cannot think just of yourself. You cannot say "I'm tired, therefore, I will see to the ill on the 'morrow." To keep your gift, you must honor it.

"Perhaps I've taken my mother's words too much to heart," she murmured to herself, accepting a third drink.

"I'm glad you came," the Were said with warmth and sincerity.

"I am too." Lili tapped her glass against Deisphe's. Her gaze happened to lift, and she looked beyond her companions to a tall dark-haired man standing at the bar. He stood sideways so that he was facing her, one elbow braced on the surface while a small glass filled with a black opalescent liquid sat by his arm. His gaze wandered over her face then downward until he reached her feet encased in a pair of pink leather heels. She could feel the warmth of the gold of her ankle bracelet. It had a broomstick charm, dotted with a sapphire. Her moonstone pendant gave off a soft glow and warmed her skin as if lighting up a welcome sign.

"Ooh, look at the lovely eye candy," Deisphe whispered in Lili's ear as she realized what had distracted her new friend. "Think he'll come over and join us?"

"Let's find out." Lili downed her drink in one

swallow and stood up. Her world tilted for a second before it righted herself.

He still stood there when she reached the bar.

"I was right. It was you I saw outside, when you should be *somewhere else*." She didn't care if her words sounded like an accusation. Even if she had to admit she didn't want anyone to be incarcerated in such a place.

Jared lifted his glass and raised it in a toast. "Hello, Dr. Carter, good to see you." His cobalt eyes blazed a trail over the expanse of bare skin, lingering on her legs. "Nice outfit, by the way. I like it much better than those scrubs and lab coat you wear at the hospital. They cover up too much."

"How do you speak inside my mind?" she demanded, feeling the tingle of angry magick coat her fingertips. She might be a healer, but she could also lay someone flat with her power if she so wanted it. And right now, she wanted it a great deal.

He leaned over, his breath tickling her ear. "You, of all people, should know. It's magick, Doc."

Lili felt another kind of heat swarm over her body as the warmth of his body wrapped around her, and his deep blue eyes bored through her as if he could see the color of her underwear. She wasn't looking at the un- kempt patient she talked to at the hospital. She was look- ing at a male demon who called to her in an elemental way. Very dangerous to her senses.

She still couldn't understand how Jared spoke to her when she always kept her internal wards running strong.

Just as it was every time she'd seen him outside of the asylum, Jared's shaggy dark hair was clean and brushed against his ears, rather than the filthy strands that touched his shoulders when he was in his cell. His dark gray shirt, open at his throat, was tucked into light-weight charcoal wool trousers. There wasn't even any sign of the sarcastic anger she saw back at the hospital. It was as if he was a totally different person. But then he was, wasn't he?

He smells so good.

Even with the varied perfumes and men's cologne in the immediate area that teased her nostrils, it was Jared she could still detect most distinctly. She sensed a hint of leather and woods, something clean and fresh. There was nothing there to indicate he was a demon, much less what kind he was. *How did he do that?*

She wasn't good at reading auras. Not that it mattered, since she couldn't even see anything resembling one around him. All she saw were hints of darkness.

"No wonder you can leave there so easily, since you manipulate the shadows to escape," she blurted out. She made it sound like a curse. In a way it was, since shadow demons could also be imprisoned by the same shadowy tendrils that helped them.

His head snapped around as he turned back to her, circling her wrist with his fingers. "Would you mind keeping it down? It's not something I tend to advertise."

"No wonder. They're extremely rare and not popular with anyone, not even their own kind," she whispered fiercely, although she doubted anyone could hear them. She was positive the live band could easily be heard in Japan—another reason why she didn't go clubbing all that often. "What in Hades is going on?" She tried to tug her wrist free from his firm grip, but he merely gently tightened his hold. She felt the scorching touch of his skin against hers.

He dipped his head to murmur in her ear. Anyone looking at them would have thought they were lovers desiring a private conversation. "That's what I'm hoping you can tell me. But not here." He released her wrist. He looked over her head. "Your friends look a little too interested. I'm sure we'll run into each other again, Doc." His smile appeared more of a threat than a promise, but it didn't frighten her.

Lili resisted the urge to look over her shoulder. "Yes, I'm sure we will." She spun on her heels and walked away, refusing to look back to see if he was still there. It didn't matter. She could feel the molten touch of his gaze with every step she took.

"Who was that?" Deisphe pounced before she barely reclaimed her chair.

"Someone I saw in Inderman a few days ago," Lili said, taking a quick look this time and seeing the spot at the bar was now vacant. She felt a tug of emptiness in her stomach.

What did you think he'd do? Come over here? Ask you to dance? Suggest we meet for dinner some evening? Introduce himself to the others as a maniacal escapee from the hospital?

"Why can't I meet hot guys like that?" Deisphe moaned, signaling to the waitress for another round of drinks. "There are way too many macho cubs out there who don't understand a female's needs one bit. The last one I dated thought females were good for nothing more than spitting out litters. Good thing my Alpha doesn't agree with that mind-set."

"You know, we haven't met a decent guy here in the past six months," Fiona pointed out, picking up her glass now filled with a liquid the color of butterscotch. "We might have to look for a new club."

Deisphe laughed. "Or lower our standards."

"The last thing I need in my life is a man," Lili stated, laughing as her new friends did their best to argue she was very wrong, even if the women admitted they hadn't gone out on a decent date in months.

For the balance of the evening, Lili smiled and knew she said the right things, since no one looked at her strangely. She even accepted a few dance invitations, including one from a vampire who showed too much interest in her neck. A tiny snap of flame that caught his attention and didn't harm him kept his fangs where they belonged. Even then her attention still wandered around the club, looking for the face she knew she wouldn't find.

By the time she left the club, she felt the bubbles from her drinks coursing through her veins and was more lighthearted than she'd felt in a while.

But she had also learned something new about Sera.

Fiona may have thought that the witch left willingly, but Lili refused to see it that way. No, she was positive her friend didn't leave of her own accord. She meant to find out just what happened.

Burning pain. His veins were on fire, and Jared opened his mouth to release his agony in sound, but he found his mouth covered. The bindings were so tight that dark blood dripped onto the floor. He breathed heavily through his nose, trying to rise above the throbbing.

"I am sorry it has to be done this way, but what we are doing will help." The voice in his ear was like glass digging into open wounds. "Your pain enriches your blood, you see."

Fuck "we"! You're the one doing it, and I'm just the victim.

Jared opened his eyes wide and glared at his tormenter, who bestowed a bland smile on him as he drew his blood. A second later, he lost consciousness.

The soft whoosh of flame coming from her living room prodded Lili awake.

"Isn't it a little early for company?" Cleo said unnecessarily, standing up on her pillow. She lifted her head, sniffed the air, then stretched.

"Friend or foe?" asked Lili, although she doubted just anyone could break into her cottage. Not with the wards she had in place. She pressed her hands against her aching forehead. "No headache," she said. "No, just the head falling off," she whispered to herself, desperate for a headache powder.

The rich scent of Chanel No. 5 floated into the room, a less-than-subtle warning of just who had invaded Lili's private space.

"I know you're awake, Lilianna. Come join me." The memorable contralto voice had Lili mouthing a variety of curses in ancient Greek. "And no profanity, if you please."

Lili stumbled out of bed and reached for her robe. She wrapped herself in the aquamarine fleece and tied it closed, even though she couldn't detect a chill in the air. No surprise there. Her visitor wouldn't have allowed it. She left her bedroom and headed for the living room. Candles were scattered throughout the room, lending a warm and cozy atmosphere for her uninvited visitor.

Eurydice sat in an easy chair, her tall figure elegant in a green tweed Chanel suit and her hair coiled in a neat French twist. With her pearl-and-diamond earrings and accompanying necklace, she looked more like a society matron preparing to chair one of her many Councils than a witch whose age was unknown and whose power fairly radiated around her.

Lili had long suspected that the witch headmistress had been good friends with Coco Chanel. Her wardrobe of the eternally classic styles she wore when she entered the mundane world was proof of that.

A silver teapot and elegant china teacups were arranged on the coffee table along with a silver serving tray holding a variety of tiny cakes and sandwiches and an engraved silver bowl filled with caviar and toast points.

"Thank you, but I'm not really hungry at this hour. Besides, I have a morning shift," she said, feeling her stomach lurch just from looking at the repast. She really had to find out what was in those drinks she had!

"Your schedule has been changed so you do not return to the hospital until the following day." Eurydice picked up the teapot and filled the cups, handing one to her. "That way you will have plenty of time to recover from your night out. Drink this. I am sure it will help your headache."

Lili shouldn't feel surprise that her visitor knew about her hangover. She doubted there was anything that the elder witch couldn't do if she had a mind to. She took a deep breath. "I haven't been there long enough to give you any kind of report," she said, accepting the cup, savoring the warmth against her hands as she curled up on the nearby couch.

"That's all right. I thought we could chat." The Head Witch smiled at her former pupil. She lifted her cup and sipped the contents. Her emerald ring, which mirrored her vivid green eyes, winked in the candlelight as the stone sparked power of its own.

Lili didn't know very much about Eurydice, but one thing she did know was that the powerful witch didn't chat. Not at—she glanced at the clock on the mantel— three sixteen in the morning.

Why is she really here? Her senses weren't telling her anything. Not that she expected much. The elder knew how to keep secrets.

Cleo sauntered into the room and hopped up onto the couch.

"Cleopatra." Eurydice inclined her head at the feline.

Who needs a thousand-pound gorilla in the room when you've got two magickal divas?

"Ooh, Almas," Cleo purred, spying what was known as the most expensive caviar in the world. She flowed off the couch and headed to her new BFF.

"Don't let her have any," Lili said, ignoring the cat's snarl of outrage. "She has enough delusions of grandeur as it is."

Eurydice ignored her former witchling student and allowed the feline a taste. "An occasional indulgence should be allowed." She speared Lili with a sharp green gaze. "Such as my allowing you to play amateur investigator in something that could prove to be dangerous. Yes, I know." She held up an elegant hand to forestall Lili's arguments. "While Margit is an accomplished protector, she still couldn't provide enough training in that short period of time. I am aware that she even tried to talk you out of this stunt."

Lili's jaw worked furiously as she fought to keep her temper under control. "It's not a stunt. Sera came here, and she's missing. I want to know what happened to her." The young witch knew she was losing her perspective. It was easy to do when she worried about the fate of her good friend. "We spoke every day, either by wallmail or by phone. Then one day, there was nothing. I even called the hospital, and they only said she didn't work there any longer."

She ignored the memory of Deisphe telling her nurse turnover there was high. Sera wouldn't have left without telling Lili. It was as if she'd gone into the ether, never to return. Lili's stomach clenched at the idea of her friend being well and truly gone. "Something's wrong, Eurydice, and I need to find out what it is. Crying Souls isn't the institution I remember from years ago. It's as if there are two buildings in one. I see two very different personalities there."

"Secrets have been a part of our existence for thousands of years," the elder witch reminded her. "Some meant to be revealed over time, many kept in the dark for infinity."

"Then let's work on unraveling those secrets." Lili held up her cup in a toast, deciding it was best not to argue with someone who could put her down with just a twitch of her pinky. She sipped her tea, tasting flowers and herbs. Eurydice was right. The warm liquid was just what she needed.

Eurydice smiled and lifted her cup.

"You told me I could do this my way," Lili jogged her superior's memory. "That means when I discover something important, I will tell you. So far that hasn't happened. All I've been coming up with are more questions than answers."

"You are a clever witch, Lilianna," her elder said. "I am certain you are very careful, because I do not want to think what could happen if you are not. All the races have lost loved ones in that hospital. Too many deaths have been deemed suspicious, even though no one could find proof of any kind of wrongdoing. I understand your need to discover what happened to Sera and the more recent disappearances." Her emerald eyes glinted with understanding. "I only agreed for you to come here and see what you could learn as long as you were careful and kept in touch with me. Except you did not follow my instructions. Since you did not, I felt I had to come to you." She speared her former pupil with her intense gaze.

So *not* a good thing to hear. Lili had done the unthinkable. She'd ignored Eurydice's orders, and now the Head Witch was here to let her know she wasn't happy. Lili momentarily touched her moonstone pendant for a hint of comfort, but the stone remained cold under her fingertips. *No one's home. The phone's off the hook. Dead air.*

She'd whimper, but even that didn't seem possible.

She'd always been intimidated by the Head Witch, but then, who wasn't? Eurydice ruled the witches overall and the Witches Academy with an iron wand. She tolerated no fools, and anyone who thought they could best her soon learned a very painful lesson. And never, ever, should anyone lie to her.

In 1313, Eurydice banished Lili and her classmates from the Witches Academy when one of the students cast an illegal spell on a local nobleman's son. No one confessed and the class stuck together, refusing to give up the wrongdoer.

Eurydice told the witchlings at that time if they behaved themselves, they could return to the academy after a hundred years in the real world.

So far, not one witch had returned to the academy.

"As far as anyone's concerned, Sera left there of her own accord," Lili said abruptly. "And they're not too happy about it, since she left during a Mage Flu epidemic."

"And you do not agree."

Lili knew Eurydice said this as a devil's advocate.

"No, I don't. Sera is one of the most professional healers I know. She wouldn't just up and leave," she argued.

Eurydice nodded. "I admire your loyalty, Lilianna. Few would go to these lengths to discover the truth."

"Anyone in my class would," she said with a strong certainty.

The elder witch's nose wrinkled in memory. "Yes, well, you witchlings created a problem back then that was not easy to handle."

"And you never thought of a loss of memory spell?" Lili murmured. "Sorry." She didn't wince when her fingertips suddenly turned hot.

"Enough damage had already been done," Eurydice said sharply as she poured more tea for herself. "Lilianna,

I do not have a good feeling about this path you have taken. Our Seers have only Seen shadows for you."

Lili froze at that, then quickly relaxed, hoping her visitor didn't see her reaction.

"San Francisco is known for its fog."

Eurydice's eyes blazed with a burnished fire. "Impertinence is not necessary."

Lili decided stuffing her mouth with an iced petit four might be a good idea. She even took the time to dab a bit of caviar on a toast point and hand it to the waiting Cleo.

"I did not come here assuming you would know anything by now," Eurydice said. "I came because of what the Seers Saw and didn't See." Her regal features displayed concern.

"The shadows." Lili nodded. "Why hasn't anyone investigated the hospital before? Looked into Dr. Mortimer's work? The asylum is more like a dank dungeon. The patients are treated as if they were feral animals, not any kind of sentient being. Conditions there are filthy and sickening."

"And that is not what any of the inspectors have seen when they visit there," Eurydice said. "All asylums are regularly visited by a Council."

"Then why doesn't anyone see the truth? You can't tell me a really strong illusion spell could continue to be undetectable." She chose another iced cake to go with her tea. "Look what happened in Florence in 1768 when the healing center's illusion spell hid the horrors inside?" She had been one of the healers who had gone in to help the afflicted. A great many creatures had been mistreated by a sorceress who performed horrific experiments in the name of healing. Lili still had nightmares from that time. "What I don't understand is why Dr. Mortimer would do such a thing. He doesn't seem the type." She waved her hand. "Yes, I know the tales of witches who gave the false impression they wouldn't hurt a soul and eventually were proven to use the darkest of magicks. Of others who did that and worse. Sometimes I feel as if he's stuck in another century and unwilling to leave it. I've read his notes. He seems to want to see his patients cured, but at the same time there's one charge he prefers to keep at a distance. As if he knows there's no hope and only does as little as possible."

"You cannot save them all, child," Eurydice said gently. "Just as you need to remember you could not save your mother. Hieronymus Mortimer is well-known for his excellent work with the afflicted." She finished her tea and stood up. She stopped by Lili and placed a hand on her head, her touch warm and comforting. "Contact me immediately if you discover any magickal wrongdoing. Do not confront anyone yourself," she said sternly. "And if you have need of me, you know what to do. I do not wish to lose such a talented healer as yourself." The elder witch turned away and walked to a portal of shimmering golden light. She walked through it and disappeared.

"Consider the tea set a housewarming gift, my dear." Her words drifted in the air. "No household should be without a proper tea service for entertaining."

"Thank you." Lili wasn't sure whether to laugh or sigh in relief that she was alone again. She opted for grasping Cleo by the scruff of the neck when the cat ventured too close to the silver bowl. "You've had enough."

"Oh no," Cleo mourned as the tea set, bowl, and serving dish disappeared. Witch and cat heard water running and cabinets opening and closing in the kitchen. She hopped off the couch and ran into the kitchen, returning in a few minutes. "Her cleaning service is even better than the brownies you use."

"Don't let them hear you say that," Lili warned, abandoning her chair. "They're difficult enough to deal with."

Any energy she felt while Eurydice was there had now gone by the wayside, and Lili wanted nothing more than to crawl into her bed and sleep for the next twelve hours.

Thanks to the Head Witch's rearranging her work schedule, she could do just that.

Nonetheless, she flopped back and forth on her pillows, disturbing Cleo so much that the cat sniffed her disdain and stalked into the other room.

"Look at this, a *Nancy Drew* movie marathon is on cable," Cleo called out. "Maybe you should come out here and watch it. You might pick up some tips. Or I could see if that doctor detective is on right now."

"Go suck an asp," Lili muttered, burying her head under her pillow and finally falling asleep to the soft sounds of the TV playing in the family room.

———⁘———

Some things never change. The acrid stench of unwashed bodies, decomposing food, shit lying along the side of the road. He could hear the clip-clop sounds of a dray horse pulling a wagon, the sounds of drunken laughter coming from a nearby gin house, and the prostitutes calling out to prospective customers as they strolled down the wooden sidewalk.

Soot hung heavy in the air, masking the sky and stars overhead.

How long had it been since he'd been here? Almost 130 years. It was a dark and dangerous world, where even a man's clothing could be the motive for his death. Life meant nothing here. Small boys and girls trained as pickpockets or were sold to brothels.

He felt inside the deep pocket of his frock coat, caressing the cold steel implement he kept there. He walked down the sidewalk, glancing inside the gin houses, keeping to the shadows.

This time he would be more cautious with his endeavors.

Chapter 6

LILI STOOD WITH DR. HERON AS HE TREATED A GNOME for allergies.

"It's a prevalent problem among my kind," he explained to her as he wrote out the list of ingredients his patient would take to the apothecary. "Many spells don't work, so we've learned that certain infusions help with the rashes. What is that?" He frowned, his head snapping upward as a loud voice intruded the ER, which for once was fairly quiet.

"How did you get in? You don't belong here. Leave!"

Lili walked swiftly toward the entrance to find the nine-foot-plus receptionist towering over the petite teenager holding a small boy, who wrapped his arms tighter around her shoulders.

"Please," the girl whispered, clearly frightened but refusing to back down from the threatening presence before her. "My son said he had to come here. That you could make him better."

"This hospital isn't meant for mundanes." The receptionist raised her hands, magick causing them to glow a dark gold. "Go to the ones that will help you," she sneered.

"What's going on here?" Lili demanded, instantly waving a hand to dampen the receptionist's power before the girl and the boy were harmed.

The giant snarled. "I don't even know how she got

in. There are plenty of wards on the perimeter to keep her kind out of here." The receptionist growled at the teenager, who sobbed and took a step back, starting to turn back toward the entrance.

"No!" The little boy screamed, then turned and held his arms out to Lili. "I sick," he implored. "Make it go away." He glared at the receptionist with a bravery that would have had Lili laugh if the situation wasn't so serious.

She didn't hesitate. She stepped forward and braced herself as the boy launched himself into her arms. She wrapped them around his small body as he clung to her like a tiny animal.

"Come with me," she told the mother, offering her a reassuring smile.

"Dr. Carter, you can't—" the receptionist's anger sent sparks flying.

Lili's expression caused her to shut up just in time. "Oh yes, I can," she said softly, but with a large bite to her tone that let the giant know just who was in charge here. Her coffee-brown eyes snapped fire. "This child is in pain and will be treated. Right now, I wouldn't care if he was from Mars. We are here to heal the sick. We all took a vow never to refuse treatment to anyone, magickal or mundane. You best remember that." With a jerk of her head, she gestured for the mother to follow her as she strode toward the ER. She didn't bother to look back to see if the girl would follow. For now all that mattered to her was easing the little boy's pain.

"Bring them in here," Deisphe directed, moving gracefully toward the first examination room once the trio entered ER.

Lili silently agreed, aware the room was set up with special wards for any mundane that might stumble in requiring treatment. This way the nonmagickal occupants wouldn't be harmed by anything that might get loose on the other side. They had this setup in every hospital she'd worked in, but this was the first time she'd seen someone try to turn a mundane away. She knew it would be the last time.

The little boy reached out and smiled as he patted the nurse's cheek. "Kitty. Big pretty kitty."

Deisphe couldn't stop the purr that briefly left her throat. "Aw, honey, I love you already." She smiled and wrinkled her nose at him.

"I'm sorry I caused you trouble. I didn't know what to do," the girl said, her voice thick with tears. "Kevin started screaming the minute we passed here and wouldn't stop. He said he wanted the doctor here to see him. That they would know what to do for him." She moved to the gurney as Lili carefully set the little boy down. "His father—" She shuddered and shook her head. "I've lived nearby all my life. I know this hospital isn't really for humans, but if I take him to a regular hospital, they might say he should be taken away from me. That I did something horrible to him." She swallowed a loud sob. "I didn't hurt him. I swear to you, I didn't. It's just that something's wrong with my baby, and I don't know what to do."

"I know you didn't," Lili soothed her, noting the stress on the girl's face and the tears that filled her eyes. "Now let's see what's going on with Master Kevin." She smiled at the boy.

She performed a quick check of his vitals and found

them a little elevated, but that was no surprise, considering his anxiety. The scent of fear rolled off his skin, and she did what she could to calm him. Then she took a longer look at the mother and grasped her hand, sending calming power over her. She was pleased to sense the girl's respiration slowing, and she seemed more at ease. "How old are you?"

She emitted a watery smile when Deisphe offered her a tissue. "Nineteen."

Closer to seventeen, Deisphe mouthed.

"What's your name?" the witch asked. She didn't doubt Deisphe's calculations. The Were would have scented the girl's age as easily as she would have scented everything else about her.

"Cassie."

Lili and Deisphe didn't miss that she didn't offer a last name, and they didn't ask for one. They both knew that their priority was the frightened little boy sitting there.

Lili offered a small nod and turned back to her new patient. "Why did you want your mommy to bring you here, Kevin?" she asked quietly as she kept her fingers loosely linked around his wrist while she peered into his antique-brown eyes. She frowned as she saw glints of gold and silver in the irises.

"I'm sick, and you can make me better," he said matter-of-factly. "You have pretty magick. It sparkles all around you."

She couldn't help but smile at him. "So do you." She combed her fingers through his dark-blond hair. "I need to talk to your mommy, okay?"

"Can kitty stay with me?" He looked past her toward

Deisphe with a hopeful expression on his tiny face. He cast a quick glance at the door, and fear skittered across his eyes.

"If this ever gets out that I let a kid call me kitty," the nurse muttered, using a hip to nudge Lili out of the way. "Break room should be empty."

"Everything will be fine." Lili didn't miss the panic on the young mother's face at the idea of leaving her son. "No one's going to bother him with Deisphe on guard. Trust me, Cassie." She pushed another hint of calming power into her touch as she took her arm.

She slowly nodded. "Kevin trusted you, so I will too."

Lili sensed it took a strong force of will for the young woman not to flinch at the sight of the various creatures inhabiting the ER. One snaggletoothed Gorman growled at her, and she only moved closer to Lili for protection.

Luckily, Cassie remained quiet until they entered the break room where Lili gestured for her to take a chair. She filled two mugs with coffee and set one in front of Cassie along with packets of sugar and artificial sweetener and flavored creamers.

"Was today the first time Kevin has acted like this? Demanding that he come here?" Lili asked after sipping the hot brew and waiting for Cassie to drink.

Cassie was quiet for a few moments as she cradled the mug between her hands, seeming to savor the comforting warmth it offered.

Lili's therapeutic wisdom sensed the girl's weariness and the raw scent of fear overlaying her exhaustion.

"The changes in Kevin's behavior are recent. He's had trouble sleeping lately, and he's been cranky. This isn't like him at all. I took him out for pizza about a week ago," she whispered, staring into her coffee as if the contents held the answers she hoped for. "I like to give him a special night out on my payday. We get something to eat, sometimes see a movie, or we play miniature golf. I want him to have something to look forward to. I have to work so much that I don't want him to think I don't have time for him." She looked up to see Lili nodding that she understood.

"We usually sit on the arcade side at the pizza place, so he can play some of the games and I can keep a close eye on him." She paused and took a deep breath. Her fingers shook as she lifted her mug to her lips. She used a napkin to dab at the coffee that spilled on her chin. "I don't know how it started. Kevin was playing a car game he enjoys, then he suddenly looked over his shoulder. He looked so scared that I started toward him. Then he just started screaming that the monster was there. The staff knows us, and they thought maybe someone had touched him." Her trembling moved to cover her body. "I had to pick him up and take him home. It took several hours to calm him down." She blinked rapidly. "He didn't even want to go to sleep that night. He said he was afraid the monster would get him," she whispered.

Lili reached across the table and covered her hand with her own, sending some calming power to Cassie. "Did he tell you what he saw?"

Cassie shook her head. "Just that a monster was there, and he knew it wanted him. He refused to go to day care the next morning. He said the monster could get him there. I couldn't afford to stay home with him." Guilt

covered her delicate face. "My neighbor is like a grand-
mother to him, and she looked after him for me. Then
he woke up screaming the next night. It was so bad my
landlord showed up and threatened to call the police.
He said if it happens again he will. He told me he knows
I'd never hurt Kevin, but he wasn't going to take any
chances." Her fragile features were pinched with the
exhaustion Lili sensed. "I didn't know what to do, then
this morning Kevin said he wanted to come here. He
insisted on it." A faint smile touched her lips. "He might
be four, but he's very stubborn. I told him no one here
would see him, but he said they would. And you did."
Gratitude lightened her face. "Thank you."

"He's a smart little boy, then," Lili smiled back. "Did
he tell you what the monster looked like?"

Cassie reached down inside the battered canvas tote
on the floor and pulled out a sheaf of papers. "Kevin
drew them this morning." She placed them on the table,
her fingers quickly drawing away as if she didn't want
to touch them any more than she had to. A tear trickled
down her cheek.

Lili conjured up a tissue and handed it to Cassie
before picking up the papers. She could feel the fear
quivering on the surface.

Shades of black, gray, and brown dominated the
white paper, but they weren't the erratic scrawls of a
little boy. Each page displayed a ghastly face with mul-
tiple mouths filled with brown jagged teeth dotted with
stark black circles. She deliberately kept her fingers
from tracing the lines of the creature and the stick figure of a little boy that cowered under the monster that
loomed over him.

She lifted her head to look at Cassie. "Did he say what kind of sounds this thing made?"

Cassie shook her head. "I think drawing those pictures took so much out of him that he only talks about being scared. Do you know what it is? What's wrong with him? Is he... is something wrong with his brain?"

"No, nothing like that," Lili quickly assured her. "Does Kevin's father see him?" She only had to look at Cassie's red cheeks to know the answer.

"It was just the one night. Six weeks later, I discovered I was pregnant, and my parents kicked me out because I didn't want to give my baby up for adoption," she admitted in a soft voice. "What happened isn't his fault. I wasn't going to give him away as if he didn't matter. It means I work a lot, but he's worth it." She offered up a watery smile.

"For Fate's sake, Cassie, you were barely thirteen at the time!" It wasn't a story she hadn't heard before, but that didn't mean she liked it.

"And I looked older. I lied about my age, found a job as a waitress, and even managed to get my GED," Cassie said matter-of-factly, not bothering to try to lie about her age again. "But it's Kevin I'm worrying about now, and something tells me this place doesn't take my HMO."

"That you don't have to worry about." Lili got up and topped off their mugs. "Cassie, what do you remember about Kevin's father?"

"He was hot, he told me how pretty I was, and the rest of the night was a blur. Not like I was drugged blurred, but..." The girl suddenly looked horrified. "Was Kevin's dad the monster he's seeing now? What did I do?" Her wail revealed her inner pain. "I was stupid back then, okay? I thought I knew what magick was all about. I snuck out of the house and went to clubs I shouldn't. Drank and smoked and…" she shuddered at memories she obviously preferred not to revisit. "But I never took any drugs. I swear it! What have I done to Kevin?" she sobbed.

"I don't think it has to do with drugs, Cassie. At the same time, you were still nothing more than a child. You didn't do anything wrong." Lili was quick to comfort her. "And Kevin won't turn into anything bad. He just has a few extra chromosomes."

"How do you know that?"

"I'm a witch, gifted with a strong healing power," she explained. "I sense pain and illness, and what I feel that's inside Kevin is a frightened little boy who's starting to experience changes he can't understand."

"Those changes are hurting him!"

"And I can help him with that." She conjured up a card and quickly wrote across the back. "This has the hospital number along with my cell. And this is a name and number of someone who I'm sure can also work with Kevin and help him deal with those changes. I want you to call him right away. Asmeth is unconventional," she smiled, thinking of the portly wizard, "but he will help you. Just tell him I sent you."

Cassie reared back at that. "Changes? More will happen to Kevin?"

"Yes, but I don't know exactly what," Lili said honestly. "I can offer you potions and charms." She paused, waiting for the girl to scoff at her suggestion, but Cassie remained silent, merely nodding her head. Lili studied the dark circles under her eyes and the pale cast to her skin. No amount of makeup would conceal her fatigue. There was no doubt the girl was tottering on the edge. She knew Cassie needed much more than her assurance that her son wouldn't end up in an institution.

Lili thought of the dank dark cells below. Of the mentally ill creatures they held and the horrors most of them had performed.

Her resolve to help Kevin and Cassie grew by the second.

She used her fingertip to trace a rune on the tabletop. "You're a very strong young woman, Cassie," she said softly. "You're the kind of mother every child deserves. You didn't run from Kevin when you feared the worst but ran *to* a place and those who can help him." Her brown eyes delved into Cassie's darker ones. She used that same fingertip to smudge the rune before it took a life of its own, then stood up. "Let's make Kevin start to feel better."

"Dr. Carter." Cassie held out her hand, brushing her fingers against Lili's arm. "What is Kevin? He's not completely human, is he? Whatever his father is…"

"Kevin is an empath," Lili said quickly, not wanting Cassie to think about what she might have had sex with that night five years ago.

Cassie shook her head. "I thought empaths detected emotions."

"They do, but there are some who can see beyond a creature's illusions if they're in hiding. Or sense what they are. Deisphe is a Wereleopard, and Kevin saw that. Whatever he saw in the pizza restaurant was probably in hiding. I would guess he saw its true self, and it frightened him. I can show Kevin's drawings to someone who might be able to identify the creature. We're not all monsters, Cassie."

She nodded jerkily. "If you can help Kevin, I will be forever grateful. I'll do anything you want."

"No!" Lili quickly softened her voice and grip on Cassie's shoulder. "Never make a promise or vow to any magickal being," she warned. "For many it's considered unbreakable, and you could land in a lot of trouble. If you want to say thank-you, fine, but nothing more. Crying Souls is here to help, and that's what we'll do."

Relieved she was able to get some information from Cassie, Lili guided her back to the examination room where they could hear Deisphe entertaining Kevin with stories of her childhood. Both women smiled at the boy's laughter. He looked up and smiled happily to see his mother, holding his arms out for her.

"No green skin," He looked at Lili. "Not a mean witch. A pretty witch."

"See why I love him?" Deisphe grinned.

Lili smiled at Kevin as she pulled a pad out of her pocket and began writing. She tore the paper off the pad and handed it to the nurse. Deisphe glanced at it and nodded.

"Back in a jiff."

Lili rechecked Kevin's vitals, relieved to find him a lot calmer and even smiling. She knew she had the Were to thank for that. While she wanted to ask him questions about what frightened him so badly that night, she knew it was best not to.

"Kevin, do you know what witches are?" she asked quietly, placing herself on the stool by the gurney.

His eyes widened. "They're not like you. They're ugly, and they cook little boys in an oven."

No way was she going to tell him that some fairy tales were based on fact.

"And there are witches like me who make little boys feel better. We have special drinks and special things you can carry." She looked up when Deisphe returned carrying a tray. A small squat bottle filled with a pale blue liquid glimmered under the light. Lili picked it up and poured the contents into a glass. "What's your favorite thing to drink?"

He squirmed, glancing at his mother. "I like Coke, but Mom doesn't like me drinking it."

"This will taste just like Coke then." She handed him the glass. She glanced up at Cassie. "It will help dampen his abilities for a while," she explained as she picked up a small medal on a leather cord that she then placed around his neck. The bronze metal glowed slightly when it touched his skin. "This is a protection charm. Between the two, no one will be able to detect Kevin or his abilities, but it's not a permanent solution. He needs to be trained. That's where Asmeth can come in handy."

"How do you know he'll be willing to help us?"

"It's what he does best."

Cassie shifted uneasily from one foot to the other. "I don't make very much money," she said softly.

"He won't ask you for payment." She knew her old friend well enough that the softhearted wizard would take the girl and her son under his wing without expecting anything in return.

Lili waited until the boy drank the entire potion down. She allowed her senses to flare and noticed the change immediately. She still made them wait a bit while she checked on other patients and returned to make sure the potion still worked.

Cassie promised to call Asmeth as soon as she returned to her apartment. As she left the hospital with Kevin in her arms, she looked at Lili and smiled broadly, looking more relaxed than she had since she first arrived.

"Thank you."

Lili smiled back. "You're welcome, and if you need anything, call me any time of day or night. I'm serious about it, Cassie."

Cassie nodded.

"We do great work, don't we?" Deisphe asked, standing at the entrance with Lili and watching Cassie buckle Kevin into the backseat of a battered blue Honda.

"That we do."

The two exchanged high fives and returned to the ER.

Lili was a witch on a mission. A mission to find out just what Kevin's monster was.

And she knew just who to ask when she got a chance.

She wasn't surprised to hear from Asmeth not long after.

"Such gifts you send me, my pet," he boomed in her ear when he called her later that day. "What am I to do with the children? One a mere babe, no less. I am not a nasty witch living in a gingerbread cottage," he laughed heartily.

"If anyone can help Kevin, it's you," she praised the wizard. She ducked into an alcove where she could have a bit of privacy. "I know Cassie told you what happened, and you'll recognize what I did for Kevin. She's scared to death, Asmeth. I think she's afraid whatever Kevin saw will come back for him. Or perhaps even his father will track them down." She wished she knew what Kevin's father was and hoped Asmeth would find out.

"I asked Cassie and her son to come see me this afternoon," he replied. "Not to my shop, of course, but to my other residence. Come for dinner this evening. Hopefully, I can relate something to you by then. I will be back in my shop by then."

Lili had a feeling the invitation was for much more than a meal and idle chatter. The last time she'd seen her old friend, she asked him to keep an ear open about the hospital. Luckily, he hadn't asked any questions, merely looked at her with a sharp gaze and promised to report anything he heard.

"I would love that. I get off duty at three."

"I will see you at six." With that he clicked off.

Lili tucked her phone away and headed for the stairs. She was hoping she might find some answers below.

Of course, she should have known it wouldn't be easy when it wasn't one of her days to be down there. Not to mention that Dr. Mortimer told her she wasn't to have anything to do with Jared. Luckily, she knew the doctor was off today, so she didn't have to worry about running into him.

"Dr. Mortimer didn't say this was one of your days to work down here," Coing growled, his huge arms crossed in front of his massive chest.

"This won't take long," she told him, already determined to throw a massive amnesia spell on the ogre and his cohort before she left. "Just bring Patient 1172 to my office." She used enough persuasion on him that he had no choice but to obey her command. She brushed past him, wrinkling her nose at the rank smell that came from his unwashed body, and headed for her office, hoping her ballsy attitude would be enough.

She paused at the door and looked down the hallway that looked never ending. One large door on the right glistened with power. She looked over her shoulder, wondering if she had enough time to check out the door. Hearing the ogre's voices made her mind up for her. It would have to wait.

She frowned at the fresh bruises marring Jared's face and his split lip.

"What happened here?" she demanded, rounding on his keepers.

"He fell." Turtifo smirked.

"Get out." She held up her hands and used her magick to push them out and slam the door after them.

"You're going to be in trouble after we tell Dr. Mortimer!" Coing yelled.

"That's what you think," she muttered, hexing up coffee and food for Jared as he stumbled into a chair.

"They're better than the ogres Mortimer used to have here," he said, wincing at the hot liquid burned his tender lip.

"Here." She cupped his chin in her hands and lightly brushed her free hand over his face. His bruises soon disappeared, and his lip healed. "How quickly do you normally heal?" She felt the heat of his skin against hers and was tempted to further explore his sharply-defined body. She stepped back before she gave in to the temptation to touch him further.

"Always right away, but they have something down

here that doesn't allow us to heal too quickly. My broken ribs took almost a week to heal."

"That would be a miracle for a mundane," she commented, taking the seat across from him.

"And an eternity for supes. So why the surprise visit, Doc?"

"You left here without anyone the wiser."

"And you didn't tell anyone," he replied.

"I have my reasons, and as long as you don't attack anyone on the outside, I'll keep it to myself," she told him. "But now I need your help."

Jared picked up his sandwich and investigated the contents. "Looks good." He bit into it. "You're asking for my help? I'm supposed to be begging for your help, Doc."

"Stop calling me Doc!" Lili snapped. She took a calming breath. "A new patient came into the ER today. A mundane teenage mother and her little boy…"

"Who's not," he guessed and laughed at her expression. "Why else would you be down here unless something's off."

"I think it's demon-related. Something I haven't encountered before. Demon clans are notorious for keeping things to themselves."

Jared looked puzzled. "So what do you want me to do?"

Lili knew she'd already broken a lot of rules in the hospital, and she was getting ready to break a whopper. She took a deep breath and spoke before she could think twice of what she was about to do.

"I want you to go with me tonight to a friend's house for dinner."

Chapter 7

"WHY ARE YOU SO WORRIED ABOUT WHAT TO WEAR to Asmeth's house?" Cleo asked from her pillow on Lili's bed.

"Because I rarely get to wear more than scrubs at the hospital or my pj's at home," Lili argued as she rummaged in her closet. When was the last time she'd done any serious clothes shopping? Racking her brain only gave her a headache, so she stopped. She finally settled for a pair of charcoal wool pants and a deep red silk top with a draped neckline that left one arm bare, along with a favorite pair of red peep-toe stilettos. She already knew her moonstone pendant would easily nestle among the fabric.

Instead of using a flatiron on her curls, she bundled them up on top of her head in a loose knot.

"I want to go," Cleo insisted, her silver chinchilla fur ruffled in agitation.

"And I want a three-week vacation in Bali. We can't always get what we want." She added a glossy red lip color.

Not that she was doing this because Jared promised to be there. She merely wanted to look nice for Asmeth, who always enjoyed seeing a woman looking her best.

That's right, Lili. You keep on saying that.

"The only reason you want to go is because you know Asmeth will feed you a lot of exotic treats." She reached for the perfume bottle she had picked up at the scent shop.

She stepped out of the bathroom and froze. She noticed that Cleo stared at the bedroom doorway with a fascinated expression on her face.

"Why does everyone feel they can just pop in without warning?" the cat asked, ruffling her fur even more. "No one has manners anymore."

Lili sniffed the air. "I don't think Eurydice smokes cigars. That's it. I'm setting up megawards tonight when I get back."

She followed her nose finding Jared in the family room smoking a cigar, channel-surfing, and sitting in *her favorite chair*.

"Make yourself at home, why don't you?" She glared at the glass of wine he held in one hand.

"I am, thanks. Nice wine." He held up his glass. "Do you want some?"

"Since it's my wine, yes." She stomped into the kitchen and poured herself a glass. "And get rid of that *thing*." She snapped her fingers, gratified to see the cigar wink out of sight. Another flick of her fingers had the lingering smoke following the cigar and a hint of citrus filling the air instead.

"You really know how to ruin a guy's fun, Doc." Jared smiled lazily.

"How exactly do you get in here?" She took a hefty swallow of her wine as she glanced at the clock. Almost time to leave.

Just as the other times she'd seen him away from the hospital, Jared was cleaned up. All signs of his injuries were gone.

"How do you do it?" she asked curiously. "You can't tell me that wrapping yourself in shadows also provides a bath, shave, haircut, and decent clothing." She had to admit he looked damn good in dark stone-washed jeans and a forest-green, long-sleeved polo shirt that showed off a nicely sculpted body.

He settled back in *her chair*, resting one booted leg across his opposite knee.

"Nice place you have here. How come you don't live in Inderman like most of the witches do?"

"Not as many live there as you think. Living units aren't all that plentiful in Inderman," she corrected him. "And the witches I know live in various parts of the city and even in the 'burbs. Housing on that plane is meant more for those who own businesses there. Do you understand why Inderman is here? After all, it's not known for attracting demon businesses except for a tavern on the edge."

Jared shook his head. "I don't know much about the place. I've only visited there a few times because I feel…" he paused, "safe. I stay away from any place where I'd run into too many demons. It's just better for me in case it's someone I know."

"I don't understand it. If you can wrap yourself in shadows and leave the hospital, why don't you just make the ultimate escape? Personally, I can't see Dr. Mortimer sounding an alarm because that would mean he'd have to admit he couldn't hold you. That wouldn't look good for him."

He absently rubbed the edge of his wineglass against his lower lip. "My shadows only allow me to go a short distance. So far Inderman is the furthest I've been able to go," he said finally. "My strength also diminishes when I leave the hospital for too long a period. I can only be gone for so many hours before I'm pulled back there, and then I can't leave for several days while my power recharges."

"What do you hope to accomplish by leaving, even for a short while?" she asked, even though she already had a pretty good idea what his answer would be.

His smile was tinged with sorrow. "A chance to breathe air that's not tainted with sickness. To feel free."

Lili was hungry to know more, but she saw that time was racing. And Asmeth didn't appreciate less-than-punctual guests.

"While I'd love to find out more, we need to go to Asmeth's. Luckily, he doesn't live far from Inderman, so you should be fine." She set her glass down and stood up.

"I wouldn't have all that much more to tell you anyway." He did the same.

Cleo strolled out of the bedroom and sniffed. "Oh, you'll take *him* but not me?"

"He's invited and you are not." Lili went into the closet and pulled out a soft wrap, woven of dark purple wool, and draped it around her shoulders. She led the way through the house and into the small attached garage. "I'll suppose you have no demon macho attitude about a female driving?" She didn't wait for his reply as she opened the driver's side door.

"Not at all. I like being waited on. Plus, I haven't seen the need to get a driver's license." His teeth flashed white in the darkness.

Lili always enjoyed her SUV and the room it offered,

but it suddenly shrunk to the size of a toy car when Jared filled the passenger seat. She was grateful the drive wouldn't be a long one.

"You're pretty calm about all this," he commented as she drove toward the freeway.

"Why shouldn't I be?" She caught his nod out of the corner of her eye. "I've seen strange things over the years. A shadow demon isn't all that unusual for someone in my line of work."

"As compared to what?" He twisted in the seat, resting his arm across the back of her seat.

"A forest druid suffering from termites is one of my favorites." She shifted in her seat, recalling the days she was ready to claw her skin raw after treating the itching patient. "We're talking oozing rashes and bites all over, especially in sensitive spots." Her gaze flickered southward while the tiniest of evil smiles touched her lips.

"Damn, you are one wicked witch," he muttered, shifting in the seat.

"I'm surprised it took you this long to figure it out." She sped up, managing to breeze past traffic lights that always stayed green.

Lili found a parking space near the entrance to Inderman. She frowned when she noticed faint shadows surrounding Jared.

"Are you all right?"

He nodded. "Protective coloring in case someone who might recognize me is around. No one will notice me walking with you, so act as if you're alone."

As they walked toward Asmeth's shop, Lili noticed that Jared not only kept darkness around him, but he also managed to change his appearance. Nothing overt, but enough that if she looked quickly, she wouldn't think she was with the same man.

She walked toward a narrow alley next to Asmeth's place of business and knocked on a bright turquoise-painted door.

"There you are!" Asmeth opened the door and hugged her tightly. He looked past her and smiled broadly. "Welcome!" He rapidly spoke in the guttural sounds Lili first heard Jared make.

Jared smiled back and replied in the same language.

"But I am rude to my beautiful Lili," Asmeth said, ushering them inside. "We must speak so she can understand us."

She stepped in and inhaled the rich spices of food that made her mouth water. She wasn't able to snatch more than a quick lunch that day, so by now she was starving.

Asmeth wasn't just a wizard with clothing but also with delectable foods that tempted her palate. They sat in a room filled with sumptuous silk cushions, low, highly polished black lacquer tables, and elegant bowls filled with a variety of foods.

"I have dragon egg soup, roasted griffin breast, seasoned greens, pickled frog legs, sugared almonds, and many other treats," the wizard continued, naming the foods arrayed before them.

"How many guests are you expecting, Asmeth?" Jared laughed. "There's a feast here."

"Asmeth never does anything by half measure," Lili said, accepting Asmeth's hand as she arranged herself on a cobalt blue silk cushion.

"And one of my special wines." The wizard poured

a golden liquid into three goblets. "To a meal that befits us." He toasted them.

"How did you two meet?" Lili asked curiously.

"The boy needed sanctuary," Asmeth said as he met Jared's frown with a smile. "You cannot tell me that Lili does not know all about you."

"Not everything," he muttered, reaching over to refill his goblet.

"Their calling you dangerous is a travesty," the wizard huffed. "The only danger you cause is to the females who lust after you." His portly belly rolled with his laughter, which gradually subsided. "First, we will speak of the children you sent me." He speared a look at Lili.

"Cassie grew up very quickly when she became Kevin's mother," she reminded him.

"Yes, I saw her maturity and that she is different. Oh, not a preternatural." He waved his hand, smiling as red-and-gold sparks floated off his fingertips. "More as a..." he looked upward as he searched for the right word, "a receiver. She is someone who would easily attract someone from our world. And her son shows great promise as one who sees past illusions. Sees us for what we truly are." His fingers hovered over the bowls until he chose a sugared almond, popping it into his mouth. He spooned dragon egg soup into three bowls and passed two to Lili and Jared. "Of course, I could only perform a few cursory tests on the boy." He clucked under his tongue. "They have very little in their lives," he informed her.

"That was easy to assume," she said, sensing what was coming next.

"I invited Cassandra to stay in my other residence and

told her she was not to worry about any form of rental payment. I assured her she and her son would be perfectly safe there. That I would not be living there, and it would be solely for her own use." He chuckled. "Kevin told her I spoke the truth, and if they stayed there, he could have a puppy or kitten. They will move in this weekend. The girl needs more schooling, but she is too proud to accept much help. She requires a higher-paying position than where she is now. And I will look into Kevin receiving proper education. He is a very intelligent boy, and I know he will learn quickly."

Lili felt her entire body warm. She also knew the little boy would have a pet before the week was out. "I knew I could count on you, Asmeth, and I thank you for all your kindness. After talking to Kevin, do you have any idea what his father is?"

"Besides his obviously being a demon?" He shook his head. "I am not certain, but I will be doing some sleuthing. You might also want to contact your friend Margit. Perhaps she can provide you some additional protection charms for the young man. We must do what we can, so Cassandra will not have to fear that the sire might return to steal the boy away. I am sure his full powers will flourish once he has reached puberty. He needs to learn shielding as soon as possible." He glanced at Jared. "I feel you could assist me with that."

"If there's a way I can, I'm happy to help," Jared promised, realizing as he looked at Lili that he would do anything to receive the bright smile he just received.

He couldn't remember the last time someone looked at him as if he wasn't a rabid animal or treated him even worse. Lili was the first in a long time who showed him any form of kindness. He looked her way, staring into her coffee-brown eyes. Her olive skin, wildly curling hair, and dark eyes gave her a wild, striking look and revealed her Mediterranean heritage.

He knew little about her magickal heritage other than she was a witch talented in the healing arts and had obviously been a doctor for many years. He overheard the other inmates—there wasn't any way he could think of any of them as patients when they sure weren't treated like such—discussing her, their surprise at how compassionate she was. Nothing like Dr. Mortimer, who preferred to deal with a more painful way of *treatment*. He wasn't sure what the doctor wanted from them, but he was at the point where he intended to find out one way or another.

"I knew I did the right thing to send them to you, Asmeth," Lili said, accepting more wine and a slice of griffin breast, along with some seasoned greens. "For all I knew, someone could try to steal Kevin away from her, or he would end up in a mundane institution where no one would understand how to help him. I want to show you something." She dug through her bag and pulled out the drawings Kevin made. She fanned them out and moved aside some of the serving dishes so she could set them down.

Asmeth looked distressed as he leaned over the table to better study the pictures. He shuddered as he carefully examined each one, barely touching the paper with his fingertips.

Jared moved in closer, looking from one to the other until he picked one up. He settled back on his cushion and held the drawing up.

"Dark demon," he pronounced. "Pure predator. They like their meat young and soft."

Lili grimaced. "And they impregnate them?"

"They will when they feel the need for young," he replied. "This probably isn't a picture of the kid's sire. Just another one he saw. Looks like he can see past their glamours now." He dropped the paper back on the table. A flick of his fingers turned the picture to ash. Another twitch, and they were all reduced to powder. "Not a good idea to keep them around. Even these pictures can allow the subject to backtrack."

Asmeth steepled his fingers in front of his chin. "I have heard gossip that there has been an increase in demon activity in the past few years. That they wish to encroach in our territories."

"That kind of info I can't help you with," Jared said, looking at Lili with a regretful expression. "I haven't had a letter from home in years."

"The boy and his mother will be protected," Asmeth vowed.

"You can do it?" Lili asked.

"Of course I can." He laughed as if there was never any doubt. "I have many contacts, dear Lilianna, just as I know you do with your friend in the Hellion Guard."

Jared swiveled around to stare at her. "You have friends in the Hellions? Wow, Doc, you're just full of surprises, aren't you? I may have been out of the mainstream for a while, but I have heard of the Hellions and what they can do."

"It always pays to stay on the right side of the law," she quipped.

"Or at least allow them to think you are," Asmeth joked.

"And here I thought you only bothered with outfitting us with proper robes," Jared teased the wizard.

"That is a very large concern with me." He waved his hand, a ruby ring glinting vividly in the candlelight. "Some magick folk have no idea what they should wear for formal functions."

"How long have you two known each other?" Jared asked, looking from Lili to Asmeth.

"I first met Lilianna in the spring of 1573," the wizard replied. "At the time, she worked for a vile apothecary in Athens. I was there to purchase some fine lamb's wool from a merchant I'd known for many years. Eccentric fellow, but he always provided a wonderful repast." He patted his belly. "I was taken ill, and Lili arrived with the apothecary. The latter was drunk and could do nothing, while she silently mixed a potion that fixed me right up." His lip curled. "Naturally the apothecary took the credit for my return to good health and slapped Lili for insolence."

Jared felt his neck bones crack as he swiftly turned in Lili's direction. "I gather he's been dead too many years to exact vengeance," he growled.

She didn't look up as she nibbled her food.

"Lili was too softhearted when he mistreated her," Asmeth also growled. "I was not."

"Asmeth doesn't believe any female should be abused." She reached over and touched his hand. "Diokles wasn't the best employer in the world, but he gave me a chance to do what I loved. And he especially enjoyed utilizing my skills in stirring up healing potions and growing herbs when he couldn't. But he didn't appreciate being shown up or having his customers start asking me for my help, since women weren't considered all that useful in the medicinal arts. And it wasn't safe for witches to advertise their skills," she said. "Diokles's son took over the apothecary shop, and I was out of work, since his son's wife didn't appreciate my working so closely with her husband, even if he looked like the back end of a goat." She wrinkled her nose.

"What happened to Diokles?" Jared inquired, curious to know everything he could about her.

"Never spoken of again." Asmeth shot him a telling look that meant that if Jared knew what was good for him, he wouldn't press the issue.

"Enough said." Jared busied himself with a few pickled frog legs. And here he thought the wizard was a mild sort. He was quickly learning different.

Asmeth refilled their goblets with more wine and collapsed on his cushion. His expression toward the demon was that of a kindly father. "You should not be in that place." He glanced at Jared's shoulder where he must have known the brand identifying him as deranged had been placed. "You should allow me to speak to Sinsia regarding this travesty of justice. Surely you have suffered enough."

Jared felt an icy spear slide its way through his body. This was information he hadn't expected to hear. "You know my mother?"

"Naturally, my boy. With all of my travels on every plane you can imagine I would, of course, know everyone," he said without any trace of arrogance. "I am very popular."

Jared laughed harshly under his breath.

"But that is not why I befriended you," the wizard

went on. "You are not as dark as you would like to believe you are." He looked from Jared to Lili with a beaming smile.

Jared glanced at Lili and noticed the way she stared at him as if she wanted to dissect him. Not the way Dr. Mortimer might desire to, but as if she wanted to know the deep dark truth about him. But even he didn't know what that was. There were so many blanks in his memory that he felt lucky he could still remember his name.

Name.

His head snapped up, and he stared at Asmeth.

The sly wizard didn't just speak in my birth tongue. He addressed me by my true name.

Asmeth met his gaze with a bland one.

"I know everyone," came to mind. And the garrulous wizard knew his mother. As best he remembered, she wasn't all that kind to any nondemon.

It seemed Asmeth was a great deal more than he first appeared.

"Now as to the hospital," Asmeth began after the main meal was cleared away and a variety of pastries had been set out.

Lili scented chocolate mixed with almonds and unerringly zeroed in on the treat.

"Witches and chocolate." Asmeth chuckled, pushing the porcelain platter closer to her before he poured thick rich coffee into tiny cups and handed them out.

"The hospital," she reminded him. "What have you heard, and what do you know to be true?"

He shook his head. "So much gossip in the air about

the place. More than there has been in decades." His expression turned somber. "Especially since Hieronymus Mortimer took over the hospital."

"He has excellent credentials and is well respected in the medical community," Lili said. "I admit in a way he gives me the creeps, but even if he has some very old-fashioned ideas, I can't say he's given me any idea he's a threat."

"Yes, but have you truly looked at him?" The wizard asked. "There is something not quite right about him." He frowned in thought.

"Does he visit Inderman very much?" she asked.

He nodded. "He was in my shop looking for ceremonial robes. He asked that they be embroidered with healing sigils. While his day wear resembles the inside of a musty armoire," he wrinkled his nose, "he does have excellent taste in robes."

Lili chuckled at the same description she'd placed on the doctor.

"Do you feel he is any kind of threat?" she asked.

Asmeth considered her question and shook his head. "I see no deception in him. But something bothers him. Perhaps it is the type of work he does." He glanced briefly at Jared. "From what little Hieronymus said, he spends much of his time with the troubled patients. Yet it doesn't seem they are truly healed." He looked troubled at that thought. "I do not like you to be down there, Lili."

"I need to be." She took a deep breath and finally confessed her reason for returning to San Francisco and especially to Crying Souls.

Asmeth was outraged at her plan and loudly said so.

Jared frowned in thought. "Did this Sera have dark blond hair and very pale blue eyes? Spoke with a Southern drawl?"

"Yes." She touched his arm. "You saw Sera? When?"

He closed his eyes, trying to focus on her question instead of the feel of her fingers against his sleeve. He only wished they were bare skin to bare skin. He finally opened them and shook his head. "You forget. I don't exactly have a clock or calendar in my cell. But she was below, taking care of Pepta, when Dr. Mortimer was away from the hospital. She stopped at my door and said something nice to me." He shifted uneasily. "I wasn't exactly in the mood for kind words from anyone that day."

Lili felt her frustration level rise up. "I feel as if the answer is just beyond my fingertips. That Director of Nursing Garrish or Dr. Mortimer knows something about her disappearance."

Asmeth wrinkled his brow. "There was that healing center in Prague that absorbed the recalcitrant employees," he brought up. "I believe most of them were used as the foundation for a new wing."

"Dr. Mortimer is..." Jared suddenly felt as if someone had tied his tongue up in knots.

"Is what?" Lili couldn't miss his look of distress.

He stared down at his hands knotted in his lap and shook his head. "I don't know," he said slowly. He shut his eyes tightly then opened them. "It's like there's a barrier inside my head." He paused then shook his head. "I don't know."

Lili and Asmeth shared a telling look. The wizard mouthed *mind wall*, and she nodded.

"Dr. Mortimer will be in next week to pick up his new robes," Asmeth said. "I doubt he will be forthcoming with any information, but I will ask him to have some tea with me, and we'll chat."

Lili reached out and covered his hand with hers. "Thank you, my friend," she murmured, feeling her load had become a bit lighter.

Then she looked at Jared and saw confusion and darkness chasing across his face.

Perhaps it wasn't so light after all.

Chapter 8

"I ALWAYS FEEL AS IF I'VE BEEN STUFFED LIKE A Thanksgiving turkey after I've had one of Asmeth's meals," Lili confessed with a laugh after she and Jared left the wizard's private quarters. They walked through the still-crowded lane. She pulled her shawl more closely around her to combat the chilly damp air. She looked up and smiled at Jared as he lightly grasped her arm to pull her closer to him to avoid being run over by one of the messenger ferrets, who raced along at the speed of light. "Going to his house for dinner is like attending a feast of old." She looked up, admiring the balls of faery light that drifted around, giving off a soft glow in various shades of pink, blue, green, and lilac. No need of electricity in Inderman when magick could do a much better job. She noticed his expression of yearning as he glanced around while they walked toward the parking lot. "Do you think you have time to just wander around here?" she asked, gifting him with a smile.

"I guess so."

"Good, because I'm really not in the mood to return home to a pissed-off cat." She took his arm and made a 180-degree turn so they could head to the heart of the community. "How much of Inderman have you seen?"

"Not much," Jared confessed. "I usually stay in the shadows and the outskirts."

"Ah, then you haven't seen the true area." She looped

her other arm through his and squeezed him tightly. "Let me be your guide."

He looked down, a wild heat visible in his eyes that quickly transferred to her blood. "I'm in your hands."

Her eyes danced with laughter. "Even if a demon does it better?"

~~~

It didn't take long for Jared to realize that even with all the visits he'd made to the magick neighborhood, he'd only seen a bare fraction of what was here.

Lili explained she had made a few visits back when she lived elsewhere, but that little changed here. Businesses remained in family hands over the centuries, and the only new ones that popped up were usually restaurants or taverns.

None of it mattered to him, only the woman walking beside him with her magick so unfettered, she glowed with it. The warm light she exuded revealed her talent was in healing, so it came as no surprise that some strollers stopped her to ask for advice. Each time she was pleasant and answered their questions along with the suggestion they visit the hospital if their ailments continued.

"Just like with mundanes, who corner doctors at a party, preternaturals think we'll happily dispense medical advice," she said with a soft chuckle.

"And why you tell them to visit the hospital."

Lili nodded. "There's a clinic set up there for non-emergencies. So many don't want to part with their coin, even if they need more than what I can suggest. And I won't give out a spell or charm anyway." She pulled him to a stop in front of a brightly lit shop that carried witch balls in translucent glass of all colors, intricately carved boxes, candle holders, and tarot cards and bags. They could see a witch, wearing elegant velvet robes of amethyst, standing behind a waist-high counter. She looked up and smiled at them. Lili smiled back but moved on.

"Lili!"

Jared stiffened just as his companion did, but she quickly masked her emotion with a bright grin as she turned around.

"Rea, Adam." She exchanged hugs with the two and quickly made introductions.

Jared noticed she didn't bother to mention he was a patient at the asylum. In fact, she didn't say a word where she'd met him. He also didn't miss the empath's and witch's inquisitive looks his way. Or that Rea shot her friend a look that probably said, *we will talk about this later*. Not to mention Adam was giving him an all-too-intense look, as if he could see right through to his bones.

"We just left Asmeth's," Lili explained. "What are you two up to?"

"We needed to do some shopping for new moon supplies. We took longer than expected and thought we'd stop at Edwig's for a drink. Why don't you join us?" Rea invited, looking from one to the other.

Jared was surprised when Lili looked up at him in silent question. Normally, he would have said a flat no. There was always the fear his time would shorten and he'd be pulled back to the hospital. There was no way he wanted to do that with an audience. But the need to feel *normal* was strong within him. The witch standing beside him gave him that illusion, and the idea of sitting down, having a drink, and talking with others would strengthen the fantasy.

Obviously she sensed his answer and said, "Perhaps just one. We're still pretty filled from Asmeth's dinner."

"Good." Rea led the way to an ancient-looking hostelry that seemed to have been plucked out of the Dark Ages.

Jared felt a strong prickling sensation along his nerve endings as they entered the building. The interior was acrid with the stench of tobacco and other things. It was obviously a popular spot, filled with witches, wizards, a few gnomes, and some goblins. He even spied a table filled with brownies, drinking something that was wiggling suspiciously in the large jug.

Ghosts floated around the room, pausing here and there to enjoy whatever the table occupants were drinking. Another group of spirits was clustered in a corner playing darts. Considering that many of them had wild aim, he was surprised there weren't more accidents.

Adam led the way to a table in the rear.

"So Jared, are you new to San Francisco?" he asked after they gave their drink orders.

"Not really," he replied, hoping he wouldn't be expected to explain anything. He was an excellent liar. All demons were. But that didn't mean he liked doing it.

"Where did you live before? Jobs aren't always easy to find, even among we supes. What do you do?" the male witch inquired.

"Adam." Lili's voice held a warning. "I don't need a brother looking out for me."

"It's okay," Jared assured her. "I work at the hospital, helping Lili with some of her patients."

"And you're a demon," Rea said softly with no hint of censure.

"It's a tough job, but someone's got to do it." He relaxed a bit when he realized they weren't going to hold it against him.

"There's not a lot of demons in Inderman," Adam said. "Not that they aren't welcome," he added hastily.

"Too bad they're not willing to give it a try. It's a nice place." He leaned back a bit when the nymph waitress left their drinks. "Although like others of my kind, I don't tend to play well with others. Maybe that's why I come here." He grinned.

"Or for the company," the male witch said, watching him with knowing eyes.

Jared decided he liked the straight-talking Adam. He could tell the witch always let a person know where he stood with him. Who knew—in another life, he could have even been a friend. At least he didn't hold Jared's birth against him, as many witches did. He also didn't feel as if he had to choose his words carefully. He sat back and let their chatter wash over him.

Adam glanced briefly at Lili and Rea who chattered away then leaned toward Jared.

"If you hurt her, I will tear you apart," he said in a voice meant only for Jared's ears. "With the power of the sea, I will turn you into chum and dump you out there for the sharks and flesh-eating selkies." While a smile drifted on his lips, his eyes were dark with his intent. There was no doubt he would do that and quite possibly more.

Jared didn't smile back. He knew better than to bait a water witch. "If such a thing happened, I would let you." He left Adam in no doubt he also meant his words.

Adam sat back in his chair, content with Jared's response.

Lili shot them a curious look but didn't ask what transpired between them. Jared figured she knew.

After an hour, she pressed her hand against Jared's and told the couple they had to go. Adam waved away any offer to pay for the drinks, telling Jared he could catch it next time. Jared found himself hoping there would be a next time.

"I can't wait to hear more about him," Rea whispered in Lili's ear as she hugged her. "I haven't forgotten about your request for a Guide, either. However, the one who would work the best is, sadly, very busy, so it may take awhile for her to get in touch with you. I gave her your number."

"Thanks."

"I like him," Adam murmured in her ear as he not only hugged her but let a brief comforting breath of magick wash over her skin.

"So do I." She hugged him back, then took Jared's hand.

"Thank you," Jared said once they were back among the magick folk who populated the area.

"For what?"

"For giving me a sense of normalcy back there." He squeezed her hand.

"But you've come here before."

"Only in the shadows or skirting the edges," he explained. "I didn't venture too far into Inderman or talk to many others. I was always leery that someone might realize I didn't belong."

"Until Asmeth showed you that you belong here as much as any of us," Lili said.

Jared nodded. "He was the first one to notice me when I stumbled into Inderman," He chuckled. "Asmeth said that there was no reason for me to hide. Before I knew it, I was in a room drinking wine and eating those sticky pastries he loves so much. I try to see him every couple of weeks. Not for the wine and pastries, but the conversation where I'm treated as if I'm someone ordinary."

"Ordinary you're not," she argued.

"But I wanted to feel that way." He looked at his companion. He knew she wore a clean and delicate scent at the hospital. Tonight he noticed her fragrance was the sensual one he stroked on her skin at the scent shop. He wanted to bury his nose against her throat to better inhale the aroma and add it to his memory for those times she wasn't with him. He wanted the recollection for the times gloom intruded upon his existence, especially when he was hauled back from his "treatment" where pain was his best friend.

And now he wondered about the holes in his memory. Try as he might, anything he might have considered important about Dr. Mortimer was tucked away in a part of his brain he couldn't access. He hadn't thought about it before, but now he wondered why it was so cloudy in those recesses—and why.

"Come on." She pulled on his hand and walked swiftly toward a brightly lit park that held a Ferris wheel that was so tall it seemed to split the sky.

"Uh, what are you doing?" He watched her hand coins to the Wererat guarding the gate.

"We're taking a ride."

Jared tipped his head back so far, he thought he'd fall backward. "On *that*?"

Lili looked surprised. "Jared, are you afraid of heights?"

"Of course not," he said too quickly.

"You are!" Her eyes widened in astonishment.

"Hey, big bad demon here," he muttered, shifting uneasily from one foot to the other. No way he was going to admit that even stepping into one of the bubbles was enough to make him upchuck dinner. And once it started moving upward, well, not a good thing.

"Except demons prefer their feet firmly planted on earth or under it," she said, realizing why it bothered him. "And why you use portals for travel. Yet members of some demon clans have wings."

"Not mine." He swallowed the rock that was taking up room in his throat as they joined the line to ride the wheel. Maybe he'd be lucky, and it would break down. Oh wait, magick doesn't break down, it fixes itself automatically. And it didn't help when he saw younglings bouncing up and down, excited at the idea of touching the sky. Didn't they realize what went up could easily come down? Sometimes faster than a body could handle?

Lili stepped up on her tiptoes, her lips brushing against his ear. "I won't give away your secret," she said softly. "And you don't have to worry. It's perfectly safe and you will enjoy it. I promise."

All he had to do was look into her beautiful brown eyes, and he knew he would believe anything she said. He kept looking into her eyes as the line slowly snaked along, until they were assisted into a semitransparent bubble with wide covered benches on each side. Instead of sitting across from him, Lili sat next to him, her thigh warmly resting against his.

The rock in his throat quickly enlarged to the size of a boulder, one that didn't allow him to swallow. As he turned his head, he could see beyond the multicolored lines of magick that protected Inderman. Foamy waves crashed against the rocks, and the sound of the sea reached his ears while lights from ships blazed in the distance. Above, stars twinkled like brilliant gemstones in the sky.

For a moment, he thought of his home. All shades of gray with accents of bloodred. His mother wasn't exactly the nurturing type, but she always had his well-being in mind. And she was the only reason he hadn't been destroyed after he'd returned from the vampire nest.

He still recalled the fury in his nature then. The ferocity he'd felt toward others, and his urge to kill anyone who dared come too close to him. His world was the color of blood, and even when he'd been dragged away, he wanted nothing more than to kill his captors.

He looked at Lili. His fingers didn't twitch with the need to wrap them around her neck and squeeze. He didn't want to see her life extinguished by his hand. The blood thirst he'd felt for so many years seemed... gone.

What had changed?

"Are you all right?" Lili asked, keeping her fingers on his arm, her touch warm and soothing.

His lips twitched. Ever the healer. He didn't even notice the rocking movement as the wheel started to turn, lifting them to the sky.

"I am." He wondered what she'd say if he related his thoughts. He wanted to confide in her, but he also wanted to think it through first. He threaded his fingers through hers, capturing her hand to rest on his thigh.

Lili's presence was more than just a comfort for him. She ignited something deep inside him. The need for his other half.

She completed him.

He almost jumped at the jolt to his system. That was what had changed—the witch in his life. She showed him compassion, but he didn't miss the desire that darkened her eyes when she looked at him. Maybe she wasn't sure about it, but she did feel the same attraction he did toward her.

He looked at her face, highlighted by the soft faery light that illuminated the bubble. Privacy spells obviously allowed the occupants of each sphere to indulge in whatever they wished, since the lifting motion was slow and steady. Especially the slow part.

He leaned forward, gratified she didn't move away. His fingertips brushed the silken surface of her face before they buried themselves in her hair, feeling the thick strands curl around them.

"Your hair is like a living thing," he whispered, even though they were the only ones there. "Medusa, but without turning men to stone."

"We might share the same ancestry, but I've never thought of my hair as snakes," she said.

"Good thing." Jared knew he couldn't wait any longer. He needed to know if he could trust his feelings. If she truly wasn't afraid of him. He took that extra inch and covered her mouth with his. Her mouth tasted sweet from the wine she had drunk at the tavern. She didn't turn away but leaned into the kiss instead, parting her lips as his tongue asked for entrance. Needing more, he pulled her onto his lap, feeling her legs settle over his thigh as she rested against his chest, her flat palm finding its way under the hem of his shirt to encounter bare skin.

Lili's touch was like a fiery brand against his skin, but not one placed there as a punishment. He felt as if her contact claimed him as hers.

He pulled away abruptly, staring at her through dazed eyes. Her gaze appeared as stunned as he felt.

"Jared?" she questioned, stroking the side of his face.

He lifted his hand and covered hers. "Mine," he rumbled softly, feeling the tingle racing over the surface of his skin and reaching for hers.

Now he knew that all his solitary, pain-filled years were meant to lead up to this. To meeting a witch whose power would not only heal him, but offer him something he'd never had before. True love.

And here he thought something like this only happened in movies and in books.

He shook his head, not daring to believe what he felt. "How?"

"I—" Lili didn't look as if she knew any better than he did. "Maggie said it could be like this," she said more to herself.

"Who's Maggie?"

"A good friend, a witch who's mated to a half fire demon. This doesn't make any sense."

He started to move away, but Lili refused to release him.

"We can't argue with Fate, Jared. Maybe I was meant to come here for more than finding Sera," she said. "Perhaps it was to find you too."

A subtle rocking motion brought his attention to their surroundings. Their sphere-shaped car had reached the top and had now stopped.

They turned their heads and looked out, seeing the sea far below them and the stars and sky seeming to surround them.

Jared turned back to Lili. "Funny thing. I'm not afraid of heights any longer." He placed a kiss at the corner of her mouth, then rested his forehead against hers. "I want to be alone with you."

He could feel her smile. "We are alone."

"You know what I mean." He couldn't remember the last time anyone had ever teased him the way Lili did, if anyone had ever dared. He looked past her shoulder at a faint light shining in the distance.

She turned around to see what caught his interest. Lili rolled her eyes. "Only a man would be fascinated with Coit Tower," she grumbled good-naturedly.

Jared couldn't help but grin. The witch seemed to bring that side out in him. "Good reason too."

She held up a hand. "Don't tell me. Demons do it better." She broke into laughter that he shared with her.

Jared sensed the slight rocking motion as the wheel started to lower them. And while his fear of heights might have been muted, he was still happy to plant his feet back on solid ground.

"My brave guy." She hugged him tightly before they returned to the main lane that led to the parking lot.

Jared felt her tension as she stopped abruptly in her tracks.

"What is it?" He looked in the direction of her gaze and felt ice invade his veins.

Turtifo walked in their direction with the expression and manner of a being who thought he owned the place.

Jared felt his fists clench against his sides.

"No," Lili ordered, giving him a push to one side where a dark alley invited shadows. "Go before he sees you. I can feel your anger, and with the way you feel toward him, you won't be able to hold a good illusion."

"I won't hide," he growled.

"You will." She pushed him again, this time harder. "I can take care of him. Don't worry."

Jared knew he had no choice and moved toward the alley and its welcoming shadows. In seconds he was invisible, even to anyone walking right past him.

Lili quickly conjured up a few bags and placed a bored expression on her face.

"Hey, Doc." Turtifo leered at her as he waddled up, unsteady on his feet. "What're you doing here all by yourself?"

"Just shopping." She let the bags she held tell the rest of the story.

"Must have made you thirsty," he said, his words a bit slurred. "I'm heading to Fazo's. Why don't ya come with me?"

Lili knew that Fazo's was a bar meant for the less-desirable citizens and visitors to Inderman. A perfect setting for the lecherous ogre with, if she wasn't mistaken, blood on his scarred knuckles. It appeared he'd already had some *fun* this evening.

"No, thank you. I'm on my way home." She started to brush past him, careful not to touch him.

"It wouldn't hurt you to be nice to me, ya know." He grabbed her arm in a bruising grip. "You think I don't know you're down there fuckin' that demon?" His foul breath blasted her face. "That's why you lock us out and make us think you're just talking in there. Even now I can smell him on you." He kept a tight hold of her arm, and she was smart enough not to try to pull away.

Lili felt Jared's fury and feared Turtifo would sense it too. The last thing she wanted was Jared exploding out of the alley and attacking the ogre. She kept one hand behind her, gesturing for him to remain where he was.

"If you don't let me go this instant, either I will make sure you do or I will call out for a Warden," she said in a low voice. "Do you really want that happening?" Her eyes flickered toward a dark, cloaked figure nearby, who was already watching them with growing interest. Inderman's protectors insured no one was accosted, and their methods were well-known to be painful.

Turtifo looked up and released her so quickly, she had to think fast to keep her balance. She felt Jared start to move toward her again and mentally pushed him back to the shadows.

The ogre flashed a nasty grin, revealing brown jagged teeth.

"Your day is coming, bitch doc," he said, moving past her and deliberately pushing her to one side.

Lili covertly watched the ogre until he was out of sight. The Warden had moved on once he saw there was no trouble. "Okay," she said softly.

Jared's face was dark with anger. "I'll kill him," he muttered, reaching her side and gently touching the arm Turtifo manhandled.

"No, you won't. You need to act as if you don't know about this," she told him, taking his arm and pasting a smile on her lips. The shopping bags disappeared as quickly as they had appeared. "We won't let him ruin the evening."

Jared remained quiet during the drive back to Lili's house, but his temper still simmered. Watching Turtifo put his hands on her had him ready to tear the ogre apart. He knew Lili was right. The shadows couldn't have protected him if he'd launched himself at him. Even his mother couldn't have protected him from a death sentence for escaping the asylum and attacking a hospital aide. For all he knew, they'd probably try to accuse him of kidnapping Lili and ignoring anything she'd say.

He breathed deeply, inhaling the rich scent of her skin mixed with her perfume. It ultimately calmed him, and he hoped that once they were in the security of her house they could continue what started on the Ferris wheel. The idea of peeling her clothes off and discovering what lay beneath brought a smile to his face.

Jared took hold of Lili's hand as she led him into the darkened house.

"Don't disappear on me," she whispered with a hint of longing in her voice.

"I won't," he vowed, reaching out to hold her hand in both of his.

Lili held a finger to her lips as they crept past the basket that held a sleeping Cleo. Along the way she pulled off her shawl and dropped it on the couch.

She slapped a privacy spell on her bedroom door once it was closed and snapped her fingers, lighting the candles around the room in a steady succession. Light scents of vanilla and cinnamon filled the air.

"I wonder if this is what they mean by sneaking your boyfriend past your parents to get up to your room," she said softly with a laugh.

Jared looked around the room, admiring the cream-colored silk comforter accented by variously shaped pillows in teal, burgundy, and sapphire, stacked against the headboard. Instead of appearing cold and austere, her surroundings felt warm and intimate. But then, probably anything was warmer than the stone-walled cell he was housed in. A small painting of a modest hut set among olive groves, hung on one wall, and a faint glow seemed to illuminate the frame.

"My home," Lili said softly, seeing the direction of his interest.

"Did you paint it?"

She shook her head. "A friend of mine is not only a gifted artist but can read memories. She created it just as I remembered."

Jared moved back to her and cupped her face with his hands. "Beautiful."

She smiled. "You're not looking at the painting."

"Because that's not what I'm talking about, although it is very nice." He mentally mapped her face, committing it all to his memory. He knew he wanted to keep this time where he could later access them when they would matter the most. "Do we really want to talk about the painting, no matter how sentimental you are about it?"

"No." Her lips barely mouthed the word.

"So we won't play music or watch TV?"

"Not unless you want to." Her deep brown eyes danced with laughter.

He glanced at the windows—the teal sheers were pulled back. "You don't worry about anyone peeking in?"

Lili shook her head. "There are wards around the property. Plus, no neighbor with windows that look this way."

Jared fingered her neckline, the backs of his fingers savoring the soft surface of her skin.

"Why do you trust me?" His lips whispered over her temple.

Her eyelids dropped to half-mast. "I don't know."

"Anything else that attracts me to you other than liking to feed me?" His mouth moved down to the curve of her cheek. "Or kissing me on a Ferris wheel?" He brushed a light kiss against a corner of her lips.

She smiled. "I am a doctor, you know. I believe in doing what it takes to keep my patients in optimum health."

"Mmm, you smell so good." He breathed in the rich scent coming off her skin as he ran his fingertips down the arm left bare by her blouse. "Taste even better." He nuzzled the soft area where her neck met her shoulder. "You're wearing too many clothes." He blew a puff of warm air on her exposed skin.

"So are you." Lili angled her head to one side, allowing further exploration as her fingers moved toward his belt. It didn't take her long to release the buckle and work on his fly and the button at the waistband before pulling his shirt up and over his head. For someone locked away for so many years, he was muscular, and his smooth skin was a dark bronze.

She paused for a moment, stroking her fingertips over his shoulder where she knew the brand marred his skin. Even now she sensed the sharp tingle of demon magick lurking underneath. *Masked, but still there, like the deep burn it was*. She placed the flat of her hand there, keeping her power flared over it like a healing blanket, except she felt something dark backlash against her. She swallowed the whimper that crawled up her throat.

"No." Jared covered her hand with his and pulled it away. "If you try too long, it will only make you sick." He kissed each fingertip.

She edged her fingers under his waistband and pushed his pants down.

"What? No using your magick to strip me of my clothes?" he teased softly as his nose nudged a stray stand of hair back.

"Oh please, that's so last year." She couldn't stop smiling as she looked at the dark and dangerous demon who just made her want to beam—although tearing his clothes off wouldn't be such a bad idea, either. She felt a raw need for Jared sinking deep inside her bones.

"Oh, Jared." She breathed his name, drawing the scent of his skin deep into her lungs, committing it to her memory, the way she knew he did with hers as he buried his nose in her hair.

Jared was agonizingly slow as he peeled each piece of her clothing off her, dropping them by their feet.

"Beautiful," he murmured.

"I bet you say that to all the witches."

"Just one very special witch." He nudged her back to the bed until they both fell onto it. "I can't even say you've bespelled me."

"It goes both ways." She glanced down, seeing his erection nudge her hip. She was already melting inside, and he hadn't even touched her yet the way she wanted him to touch her.

Lili pushed the pillows off the bed and wrapped her legs around his hips as he dipped his head, pulling her nipple into his mouth. His tongue wrapped around the dark, rose-colored nub, moistening the skin before he blew gently on it.

She felt the action all the way to her bones and whispered his name as she nibbled on his neck, grazing her teeth over the taut skin.

Jared shuddered, tightening his embrace. He moved up, capturing her mouth, kissing her with a hint of the ferocity of his kind. Instead of the angry sex demons were known for, she felt a sense of him holding back, as if he wanted to give her something more tempered. In the flick of a second, his kiss sizzled with heat. She met him with the same intensity.

He slid his fingers into her, finding her wet and receptive. She rotated her hips, arching up as she wrapped her fingers around his cock.

"Purr for me, witch," he whispered with a dark edge in his voice. "Show me how much you like it." He growled in her ear as he closed his other hand over hers, increasing the pressure. At the same time he moved his body slowly up and down over hers in the sensual dance of what he intended to do.

Lili closed her eyes, feeling his magick weave a path around her body. It prickled like tiny electric shocks darting across the surface.

"Now, Jared," she gasped, tightening her hold on him.

Not needing any further invitation, he shifted and thrust deeply into her. Lili's cry of satisfaction was smothered by his mouth as he kissed her with the same ferocity his body demanded of hers.

At first he feared he was hurting her, since she was tight, but she quickly assured him that wasn't the case. Her inner muscles clenched around him.

He knew this wasn't just sex. This was something more. A sense of belonging.

"*Mine*," he said between tight lips.

Lili's eyes widened at his one-word declaration that vibrated with demon power the way it hadn't when he said the word on the Ferris wheel. While she didn't know a lot about demons, she did know what had just happened.

Jared claimed her as his.

And all she had to do was say the same back to him.

There was no bond stronger.

She looked up at Jared, seeing the bare need in his eyes, the barely disguised raw desire. She framed his face with her hands, knowing there was gentleness inside and so much more.

"Mine." She said the word without hesitation, without looking away from his dark gaze. "Always mine."

That was all he needed. His rhythm increased as he brought her legs up over his hips, tipping her upward.

Jared felt his balls tighten to the point of pain before he fell over the edge, plummeting into an abyss of sensation that took his breath away. He was vaguely aware of her saying his name over and over again as her orgasm took over.

It was some time before Jared felt as if he could breathe normally again. He closed his eyes, concentrating on the scent of Lili's skin and hair, the silk of her skin, and her husky voice bringing further images to mind. He wanted so much for her. To be with her as a whole male. Not just when the shadows could protect him. He was ready to tell her that and more, but sleep overtook him like a drug, and he felt her boneless body mold itself against him and do the same.

------~~~------

Lili was warm and content. If she hadn't known better, she'd have thought she had turned into a cat. She lay in a haze of partial slumber, aware of the hard, warm body next to her. She sleepily ran her hand down Jared's bare chest and below. Husky laughter rumbled under her ear as he caught her wandering hand.

"Someone's awake," she murmured.

"No wonder, with you teasing him like that." He started to roll over and continue the play when they both became aware of muted sounds beyond the bedroom door.

Lili's smile of bliss disappeared. She sat up, uttering a few choice curses. "What in Hades is going on out there?" she grumbled, staring at the door.

Jared twisted to follow her gaze, seeing bright lights gleaming under the door.

"The privacy spell mutes the sound out there," she said, nodding at the door. "Peace and quiet no more. Tell me what's beyond the door." She winced as ear-piercing yowling invaded the room.

Jared covered his ears. "What is that?"

Lili looked fit to kill. "That's it. That damned cat is going to be turned into tennis racquet strings," she said grimly, waving her hand to retrieve their clothes.

They dressed quickly. A cacophony of sound blasted them the second they stepped out of the bedroom.

"No!" Lili stared at the dark blue glass bottles littering the carpet. "That damn cat!" She charged into the family room.

Jared almost ran into her back when she skidded to a stop.

Cleo lay in the middle of the floor, sprawled on her back, staring intently at her frothy plume of a tail as it waved back and forth. She hummed a snake charmer's tune as the tail danced in circles before her twitching nose.

The feline twisted her head around and stared at the witch and the demon with glazed eyes.

"What do you do with a drunken kitty? What do you do with a drunken kitty? What do you do with a drunken kitty, *early in the morning*?" Cleo howled loud enough to shatter glass.

"If I didn't know better, I'd think she was drunk," Jared choked back a laugh. He hastily erased his grin when the witch turned to spear him with a look fit to hex.

"She is," Lili said grimly. "That furry twit was unhappy because she couldn't go to Asmeth's, so she managed to get hold of catnip wine. How did you get all those bottles?" she demanded of the cat. "I never keep more than one bottle in the house. *Do you know what each bottle costs?*" Her shriek rang through the house, rattling the paintings on the wall, and a vase on the mantel started to teeter back and forth before settling back in its original spot.

Cleo laughed boisterously as she waved a paw in a wide circle. "Did you know they deliver and all you have to do is give them your credit card number? And for an extra fee, they'll even magick express it?" She purred. "So that's what I did. I gave them your Visa." She started waving both paws in the air. "They're even willing to set up an auto-delivery, so I said yes." The cat cackled with glee.

Jared looked down at the clattering sound on the floor. He watched in amazement as the many bottles rolled into the kitchen and tossed themselves into the recycling container.

"You're the one who'll have to suffer the hangover in the morning," Lili snarled, standing over the intoxicated cat. "And it won't be pretty. Remember 1936? You were sick for days." She threw up her hands. "I should make you sleep outside."

Jared turned away to hide the grin that was stretching his mouth to the limit.

"And here I thought I'd seen it all," he muttered, struggling not to laugh and quickly losing the battle.

"Don't even think about it," she warned him. "You'll only encourage her."

"I'm only a puss in a gilded cage," Cleo warbled, rolling from one side to the other.

Jared shook his head and walked into the kitchen. He dropped onto one of the chairs and buried his face in his hands, his shoulders shaking with the laughter he could no longer hold back. The sound sounded foreign and rusty to his ears. When was the last time he'd laughed in true amusement?

"It's not funny!" Lili stormed in, her magick flying around her in erratic flutters. "Cleo can be out of control when she's sober, but you have no idea how bad she is when she's drunk on catnip wine. One time she even snuck into a zoo and tried to seduce a lion!"

He shook his head, unable to form any coherent words. His mouth worked. "My stomach hurts," he finally gasped. He lifted his head when he felt the beginning of the pull that would return him to the hospital. He knew his time was ending before he was ready to leave her.

Jared stood up and turned to Lili.

"I have to go," he said simply.

"Oh." She managed a brief smile, her rant abruptly forgotten. She gulped. "I—" She held out her hand, looking to say more but unsure what it should be.

"I know," he said with sincerity, even as he felt the painful tug growing stronger and knew he'd be gone very soon. "There's just one more thing."

"If you want to take Cleo with you, I'll just warn you she snores," she joked.

"No, this." He pulled her into his arms before he could think twice and lowered his mouth to hers.

Nothing that happened that night had been in his imagination. She was as responsive as she'd been before. She made him forget the murk in his life, and she claimed him as he had claimed her.

Soft sounds traveled up Lili's throat as her hands rested on his shoulders, her nails digging into the soft fabric of his shirt.

He rubbed his mouth against hers, tempting her lips to part.

"So good," he whispered, sliding his tongue past her lips and once again tasting bliss. "You make me feel as if my life isn't such a waste after all." He groaned and deepened his kiss, drawing her even closer against him. He wanted nothing more than to rip her clothes from her and lay her down on the table. No woman compared to Lili—the way she fit so perfectly against him, the way her breast fit so neatly in his palm, her nipple springing up at his touch.

He tightened his hold on her, fighting the wrenching awareness on his spirit. The insistence he had to go, whether he wanted to or not.

He wanted to stay with her!

"No!" He growled, pulling away. He stared at her with stark eyes, raw with emotional pain. A second later, the shadows wrapped around him and he was gone, leaving only a bare hint of sulfur behind.

Lili grabbed hold of the table as her knees turned to pudding.

She refused to believe Jared could leave her that quickly and looked around the room, even as she knew she was alone. She blindly groped for a chair and dropped into it.

"You're in trouble now," she whispered to herself then winced as Cleo continued singing, further off-key than before. Her body still tingled from his embrace and her mouth hungered for more.

Jared had her experiencing so much that she'd never felt with any other man.

She knew he wasn't the insane creature Dr. Mortimer and his own kind said he was. Now she just had to find a way to prove it so that Jared could be released from the hospital.

She smiled, reliving the kiss, when reality thumped her on the head as Cleo's crazy idea of music kept falling from her mouth.

"Bubble of silence, come to me. Give me some

blessed peace, that's the key." She flicked her fingers toward the family room and waited for the slightly audible pop that told her the bubble was in place. A tiny silver key dropped onto the table in front of her. Lili picked it up and turned it over in her fingers. The lock keeping the bubble in place would remain intact until she used the key to release her drunken kitty. She slowly rose to her feet and walked past the cat rolling around on the carpet and singing at the top of her lungs. Luckily, Lili now couldn't hear a thing.

"Good night, you cat from Hades," she told Cleo in Greek.

Lili returned to her bed, burrowing her face in the pillow Jared had used, reveling in his musky scent mixed with her own. She didn't think she'd sleep all that easily. Not when images of their lovemaking still danced in her mind.

After tossing and turning in bed, she thought of releasing Cleo from the bubble just to have company. She even went so far as to go to the family room to check on her feline. One look at the cat spread out on her back, looking as if she was snoring loudly, made her mind up for her.

"Don't come crying to me when you have the ultimate hangover from Hades," she muttered, making her way back to her bed and curling up with Jared's pillow again.

⸺⁓⁓⸺

Lili woke with a smile on her lips, thanks to erotic dreams that brought back her time with Jared. But she also felt a bit unsettled and worried about Jared still locked away at the hospital's asylum. She decided to take her troubled mind to the shore at dawn. Her cotton skirt whipped around her ankles as she walked barefoot on the wet sand. She lifted her face, inhaling the tangy air and listening to the sound of waves crashing against the rocks plus the hoarse barking sounds from the sea lions. They all made an appropriate background music for her somber mood.

When she found the spot that felt right to her, she knelt on the sand and looked out over the gray-green ocean waves and hint of fog hovering over the water. She closed her eyes and drew in the salt air.

"Listen to my plea, Panacea," she beseeched the Greek goddess of healing. "Show me how to soothe minds of the troubled ones and take away the blackness that surrounds their lives." She fingered her moonstone pendant, feeling the warmth of the stone pulsing against her skin. "Hecate, keep my gift strong so that I can protect the weak from those who choose to deliberately hurt them," she begged the goddess of witchcraft. "Help me find my friend and those who were taken, as she was. I know you haven't abandoned Sera, and I refuse to believe she has left this world for good. Wherever she is, please keep her safe and help me find a way to return her to her friends." She held tightly to her moonstone pendant, allowing the warmth of the stone to leach into her bones.

All the witches from the class of 1313 at the Witches Academy wore moonstone pendants, and, later on, they added to their bling with gold ankle bracelets bearing a gold broomstick charm, each one topped with the gemstone that spoke most powerfully to the individual student. For Lili, it was the deep blue sapphire that winked against her skin.

Lili stayed on the beach for some time, ignoring the biting wind pelting her face. She thought of the village she grew up in, the warmth of the Mediterranean sun that used to bathe her skin, the many plants her mother gathered for her herbal remedies, and how collecting them turned into lessons for the girl as soon as she could walk. Her smile at the memories dimmed when they changed to mental pictures of that last day. The vision of what had happened to her mother the night when she was killed was a dark image she kept in a tiny compartment of her mind. It would never be forgotten—because there was no way she could—but she knew her mother wouldn't want her dwelling on her senseless death, either.

She told herself that the salty liquid streaming down her cheeks was from the sea spray and not tears.

"Lili?"

She started at the sound of the familiar male voice, one she shouldn't have heard again so soon. She opened her eyes and looked to her right. Jared didn't look the way he did only hours ago. He stood by her, dirty, with a bruise purpling on his jaw.

"How are you here?" Her voice came out raspy as she got to her feet and reached out, touching his face, allowing her power to heal the bruise. A second later, the mark was gone. "You must have used all of your power last night." She stroked his cheek, feeling a weakness that hadn't been there before. "You need to rest."

Jared smiled and shrugged. "I don't know. I had this strong feeling that you needed me, and the shadows took over from there. It was like that first time I showed up at your house." He touched her face with his fingertips, pulling them away, and staring at the dampness on his skin. "Don't cry for us, love. We've all been demented for so long, we don't know anything else. Heal the ones above and leave us to our punishment."

It was then she realized that he somehow heard her plea to Panacea.

"You all deserve to be healed, Jared, not tormented like wild animals," she whispered. "I don't care that Dr. Mortimer feels you're too dangerous and that he says I can't treat you. I intend to get back down there for you."

His smile warmed her. "My stubborn little witch. No one can stop you, can they?" He brushed his fingers over her hair, allowing a curl to wrap itself around his forefinger. "You want to find out what happened to your friend, and you want to help us in the asylum. Don't take on too much, Lili. I don't want anything to happen to you. You're too precious to me." His cobalt eyes showed his worry.

"My friend Maggie made sure I'm very protected when I'm at the hospital," she assured him.

He nodded his understanding. "Hence the runes and sigils woven into your clothing."

"The Hellion Guards know everything there is to know about protection charms. Maggie has resources I don't have access to. Even she didn't want me to do this."

"I agree with her," he stated. His lips twisted in a brief smile. "But if you weren't the stubborn witch you are, I wouldn't have met you."

"It was easy to convince her I was a better choice

than a Hellion Guard. After all, I have past history here. It was much easier for me to get accepted into the hospital, and besides, Sera is my friend." She refused to think of her in the past tense. "I need to know what happened to her. Maybe I can even find her and bring her back from wherever she is."

He thought for a moment. "If you can get them to make any sense, talk to Panabell or Pepta. I'm sure Sera would have treated them too. And there's always Amy. No one would notice her. She might know something, even if she doesn't think she does. She's always hanging around down there."

Lili felt guilt at the reminder of the little spirit who needed to find her mother. Even with so much going on, she had no excuse for not doing the right thing for the ghostling who desperately needed her mother. She knew she couldn't ask Amy about Sera. The tiny wraith was confused enough.

She looked down and noticed dark gray tendrils of shadows snaking their way around Jared's legs. "You have to go," she said sadly, wishing she could reach out and protect him against the gloom's hold on him. She claimed him last night, damn it! She wanted to insist he was hers, not theirs. The desire to drive him to a restaurant, where they could sit and have breakfast, laugh, and talk, raged strong within her. She hated the idea of his being pulled back to the hospital again, where he'd only suffer again.

He winced as the darkness grew tight enough on his legs to cause pain. "I'm being warned that someone's coming to my cell." He leaned toward her and brushed his lips across her forehead. He whispered something in his language that didn't sound as harsh on her ears as it had been before.

"What did you say?" She stared into his face, feeling the pain as he started to melt into the gloom that surrounded him.

He smiled and shook his head even as he winked out of sight. *See ya, Doc*.

Lili was alone again. The cold damp air enveloped her, chilling her skin. She slowly walked back up the beach toward the parking lot.

Cleo, wearing extra-dark sunglasses, was spread out on the hood.

"You better not have left any claw marks on my baby." Lili reached inside her SUV and pulled out her coffee tumbler. The liquid was still hot and bracing on her tongue.

"Talk to the paw." She held up an appendage, offering the witch a wicked smile as long, razor-sharp claws shot out. She lowered it to the metal and etched her name with that painful nails-on-a-chalkboard screech. Lili snarled and covered her ears with her hands. The witch shot an array of sparks toward Cleo that had her jumping up in the air as the scratches disappeared.

"I hate you," the cat sneered when she landed all feet down. "There was no reason to drag me out here just because you needed to get in touch with your inner witch. I could have stayed home deliberately shedding all over your bed."

"Not when you'd probably projectile vomit all over my silk comforter. Besides, I wasn't the one who overindulged on catnip wine last night and maxed out my Visa." She waited until Cleo crawled her way into the passenger seat.

"Just kill me now or give me a hangover remedy," the feline moaned, curling up on the seat with her nose tucked into her tail.

"The potion doesn't work on catnip wine, and you know it. You'll just have to suck it up and suffer the consequences of your wild night." She glanced at the clock on the dashboard. She gauged she had just enough time to make it home and get dressed for work.

"I smell the demon on you." Cleo wrinkled her nose. Her lush fur ruffled. "How come he gets around so much and can't leave the hospital for good? If I had to smell that musty wizard all the time, I'd be outta there like a puss on a mouse."

"There are wards in place to ensure he can't permanently escape. He's lucky he can use his shadows to leave as he does." She turned on the heater controls, directing the warm air in her direction as she pulled out of the parking lot.

Cleo curled her lip as she batted her paw at one of the vents, fixing it so the air would flow in her direction.

"Should I have been more specific when I told you that you needed a love life? Call me crazy—on second thought, don't—but something tells me that a demon inmate in the asylum comes across as more than a little desperate on your part. Oh come on! You think I didn't know what you two were doing in there last night, even if you slapped a privacy spell on the door?" The cat smirked. "Listen to Auntie Cleo. Get out and meet a nice witch who's got a halfway normal job. I bet Adam knows some suitable guys. Sure, Jared is hot enough to make me think about lifting my tail, but he's still a demon with a scary medical record. You need someone dependable instead of a guy who can disappear when you least expect it. I bet he doesn't even have a decent credit rating."

Who cares about anything else when he kisses you into insensibility and makes incredible love to you and claims you that very first night? Not that she was going to mention that to Cleo. The cat would have a field day with that piece of information.

Lili reached over and twisted the heater control to a lower temp. No reason for it when she was growing warm all on her own. "Don't." She held up a warning hand when Cleo glanced at her action and opened her mouth. "Just don't."

For once, the feline did the right thing and kept quiet. Good thing. If she said one more wrong word, Lili wouldn't have thought twice of making the smart-mouthed cat walk home. And the witch would have made sure it rained on the kitty every step of the way.

Chapter 9

"HOUSTON, WE HAVE A PROBLEM." DEISPHE GRABBED Lili's arm and pulled her into the hallway before she stepped out of her office.

The witch was almost overbalanced on her heels due to the Were's strength.

"Okay, I'm here. What's the trouble?" She had to run to keep up. After looking at the concern on the nurse's face, she had an idea it had to be something wrong with a capital *W*.

"An earth witch was brought in about an hour ago. She's screaming with serious pain that's twisting her body into a pretzel. I can't find any signs of trauma, the scanner shows no spells on her, so whatever it is lies so well hidden that our equipment can't find it. All her stats are off the chart," Deisphe reported, heading swiftly into the depths of the ER.

Lili skidded to a stop as her head started to spin like an old-fashioned top. She felt the protective runes on her lab coat suddenly kick into high gear, allowing her dizziness to disappear. She knew it had to be due to their new patient.

"Are you okay?" Deisphe grabbed her arm to steady her. She looked into Lili's eyes, and quickly grasped her wrist, checking her pulse.

"I'm fine now." She ran her hands down the starched fabric that prickled her palms with magick. "I have a bad feeling that what I'm experiencing is coming from our new patient."

Lili knew she was right the minute she entered the curtained cubicle shielding the witch.

Just as Deisphe described, the young woman's body was racked in agony. Her face was mottled red and white with pain while her eyes were wild with agony.

"Her name is Vonnie," Deisphe said softly. "Neighbors heard her screaming and found her this way. Luckily, they wasted no time calling us. They're mundanes, but they know what she is, so they knew who to contact."

"Hey, Vonnie," Lili said softly. She rested her hand on the woman's wrist and almost reared back at the amount of heat flowing off her skin, along with something that sparked off her palm. "I'm Dr. Carter. Can you tell me exactly what you're feeling?"

Vonnie worked her mouth in what looked like painful contortions, but no words escaped her lips.

Lili continued staring into her face. "Move her into one of the closed rooms," she ordered.

"There are no signs of any contagion," Deisphe murmured in Lili's ear.

"That doesn't mean she isn't. It could be something we can't easily detect. Get her moved now. I'll be right back." She wasted no time heading for her office.

"I need you now," she told Cleo, who was curled up on her pillow, her dark glasses still in place.

The cat looked up, ready to say something nasty but the look at the witch's face told her it was important. She magicked away her dark glasses, and flowed off the small couch.

Lili didn't say anything as the cat followed her into the room. Lili closed the door behind them. She was glad to see that Deisphe had wasted no time getting her new patient moved and set up.

She knew the closed room's strong wards would ensure nothing dangerous would have a chance to escape. Looking at Vonnie, she was positive there was something very bad going on. Now the problem was finding out what.

"Oh my." Cleo hopped onto a chair and stared at the young witch. "She's very sick."

"What do you see that I can't?" Lili knew her furry companion could pick up on things she might not notice.

The feline's eyes glowed a dark green as her gaze swept over the gurney. "Very olde magick. A strong binding spell has been used that allows the spellcaster to leach her power from her. It is like a treacherous drug. Once you start doing this, you can't stop. If you can break the first level of this spell, you'll be able to see the bonds wrapped around her." She shook her head. "She's very sick. It's weakened her a great deal."

"Whoa," Deisphe breathed, looking as if she wanted to step out of range. "I've heard of binding spells, but one that drains off a witch's power is new to me."

Lili searched her memory banks, finally understanding what was said. "Whoever did this was powerful enough to hide his or her handiwork. As Cleo said, it's very olde and dangerous, since it's addictive to the caster. It's like a strong drug. The more you receive, the more you want." She closed her eyes and willed her magick into her hands until the skin glowed with a strong light. "For now, I just want to ease her agony in hopes she'll be able to tell us who did this to her."

"And if she doesn't know?" the nurse asked.

"Then we'll play detective."

Her body received a strong jolt as she placed her palms on her patient.

"Be careful," Cleo warned a second too late, pointing with her paw. "And stay away from those areas." She shot dots of multicolored lights to hover over Vonnie. "Don't touch them at all."

Lili nodded and continued to work her own magick. She wasn't vain about her gifts. She knew she was strong, but she soon learned that what she was facing had little to do with her skills. She was thankful she asked Panacea for strength. It looked like she was going to need it.

The witch was drenched in sweat by the time Vonnie started to breathe easier and a hint of normal color had returned to her face.

"Who bound you?" Cleo asked.

"Who's the doctor here?" Lili glared at the cat. She looked down at Vonnie. "Vonnie, you were bound with a powerful spell that's been leaching your magick. Do you know who did this to you?"

"No," Vonnie said weakly, looking as exhausted as Lili felt. "Why would someone bind me? I don't have any enemies."

"And steal her power," Cleo muttered.

"Shush."

"Oh sure, you drag me in here to figure out what's going on and now you want me quiet." The fluffy feline sulked.

Lili sat down and moved closer to the gurney. She

still made sure her fingertips didn't touch the areas that Cleo had highlighted. The cat was arrogant and a pain in the ass, but she knew her ancient magick.

A voice in the back of her mind suggested she bring in Dr. Mortimer, or one of the other wizard doctors on staff, but years working in supe hospitals had taught her that a lot of the wizards didn't like treating witches and usually shunted their care off to her anyway.

Besides, this was a challenge, and if she could solve it herself without any harm to Vonnie, she'd know she did the right thing keeping it to herself. If it turned out she couldn't, then she'd waste no time seeking assistance.

"Are you mated, Vonnie?" Deisphe asked. She already knew that Lili didn't mind if she asked questions.

Vonnie closed her eyes, breathing deeply. "No. But I do share an apartment with my boyfriend. Zane's a mage second class. He's very talented and should be a lot further along. All of his teachers are so against him." She winced as she moved her body a fraction. "It never hurt like this before."

"How long has this been going on?" Lili inquired, not liking to hear that this wasn't something new.

"Almost three years. But it's never been like this." She bit her bottom lip against the pain punishing her body. "Before it was just some mild headaches or muscle aches that a tisane could handle."

"How long have you been with Zane?" Cleo chimed in.

"Almost three years." Vonnie continued to struggle for a breath. "He's tried to help me, but it doesn't work. I had to stop working because it got so bad, so he takes care of me."

All the gears in Lili's head clicked into place. "I'm sure he does," she murmured, sharing a telling look with Deisphe and Cleo. She rested her palm just above Vonnie's forehead. "Peace to you. Sleep like a child. Rest deep in slumber's arms as I wish it." She waited until Vonnie's eyes drifted closed. Her body truly relaxed for the first time.

"Now what?" Deisphe asked softly. "Do you think the boyfriend had something to do with it?"

Lili stood back, idly chewing on a fingernail. "I'd know better if I saw this Zane. Is there a number for him on the intake paperwork?"

Deisphe picked up the computer tablet and viewed the contents. "Luckily, she'd been here before, and we have his cell and wallmail for contact info."

"Get hold of him and let him know about Vonnie. Ask if he can come in, but don't let him anywhere near her," she instructed. "In fact, let's have her moved up to one of the seclusion rooms. Let me know when he shows up." She turned her attention to Cleo. "Are you willing to stay with her?" She knew that between the Wereleopard and the cat, her charge would be well protected.

"Of course." Cleo was arrogant, but she also had a tender heart. "And if this Zane proves to be a problem…" She unsheathed her needle-sharp claws that Lili knew were tipped with a paralyzing poison.

"Remind me not to get into a catfight with you." Deisphe grinned. "I'll get Vonnie moved upstairs and then I'll call the boyfriend. I'll let you know when he shows up." She carefully covered up their patient.

Lili was barely out of the ER when Director of Nursing Garrish cornered her.

"I do not know how it was in other hospitals you worked, Dr. Carter, but here at Crying Souls, a nurse is not considered a doctor's private property," she snapped. "Deisphe is an important employee of the hospital and as such, needs to be used where she is most required."

"And for now that is with me," Lili countered. "I need her assistance with an important patient."

"Yes, the young witch that was delivered here." The dragon-shifter's eyes turned a dark purple that would match her scales if she were in her other form. "No patient needs private nursing or your cat's assistance," she sniffed.

Lili thought of acting like the total bitch medical professional she could, but she knew she needed the shifter on her side.

"My diagnosis is that her scum mage of a boyfriend wrapped a potent binding spell on her that also manages to transfer her power to him. I think it started out small, but she's been under its control for so long that it's now slowly destroying her. If I can't banish that spell, she'll be dead within a few days," she confided.

Miss Garrish straightened up, crossing her arms in front of her chest. "And what are you doing about it?"

"I've ordered her transferred to a seclusion room and cast a peaceful sleep spell on her. I also asked Deisphe to contact the boyfriend and ask him to come in. I intend to have him properly taken care of if it turns out I'm right and he is behind the spell."

The Director stared at her so hard that Lili felt as if her gaze could see right down to her bone marrow. It wasn't a good feeling at all.

"I do not appreciate anyone casting illegal spells," she said in her rusty voice, "especially arrogant young mages who view themselves as above the law. Inform nurse Deisphe I will require a full accounting once your patient is stable. Naturally, if that mage has done such a thing, you will have him turned over to the authorities."

Lili released an internal breath of relief as she inclined her head. "No worries there. Thank you." She started to turn away.

"Dr. Carter." Lili froze. "Of course, you thought of having lavender scattered in the seclusion room to help with the discomfort."

Damn! She hadn't. "No, I hadn't, Nurse Garrish. Thank you for reminding me."

"Then I shall pass the suggestion on to Deisphe." The shifter nodded her dismissal.

Lili made a quick retreat for the lower floor. "Sure, Lili, you're the big bad doctor in charge and she's still a nurse who's supposed to obey you. A nurse who could easily have you for a late-night snack." She hurried down the stairs and headed down the hallway in the direction of Jared's cell.

She noted there were a few more lights in the hallway and the air didn't seem as dank as before.

"It's not your time for down here," Turtifo greeted her with a nasty growl as he emerged from the small break room.

Lili noticed there were tiny wiggling things on his shirt front. She didn't even want to think what the ogre ate for lunch.

"I won't need your assistance," she told him, ignoring his comment.

His bushy unibrow creased. "And the doc said you can't see an inmate without one of us with you."

"I just said *I don't need your assistance.*" Lili pushed enough power at him to cause him to fall back a couple steps.

Turtifo scowled at her. He lost the staring contest and retreated to the room, mumbling it wasn't anything off his ass if something happened to her. Don't expect him to pick up the pieces.

Lili kept a vigilant awareness of her surroundings as she headed for Jared's quarters. She smiled as she heard the sound of a tiny voice from inside.

Do you have any twos?

"Go fish." Jared's laughter warmed Lili's ears and had her smiling.

She pressed her palm against the special lock and waited for it to click. A faint popping sound alerted her that Amy had left the cell.

"It's all right, it's just me," she said softly, waiting as the door swung open. She stepped inside and watched it close behind her. Her gaze settled on the tiny ghostly figure as Amy reappeared. Her eyes alighted on a deck of spectral cards lying on Jared's mattress.

"I don't think it was a good idea to teach her poker. She's killing me here," he explained. His dark eyes glowed as he looked at her. "Long time no see, Doc." He grinned.

She grinned back. "How true."

"How's the cat?"

"Hungover, but she'll survive." She hesitated, glancing in Amy's direction.

"Amy, would you mind leaving Dr. Lili and me alone for a little while?" he asked. "We can continue our game later."

Amy ghosted out of sight.

"What brings you down here?" He settled back on the mattress, stretching his legs out in front of him.

"I wanted to run something by you." She hexed up a chair and sat down.

Jared cocked an eyebrow as he unleashed his devastating smile on her. "As in?"

It took a moment for her to remember why she was there. He might be grungy-looking, but he was still sexy enough to make her mouth water. Memories of his kisses didn't help with her peace of mind, either. "Let's talk binding spells on a witch, spells that might be demon magick in origin."

Jared shook his head. "Not possible. Any binding spell my kind use can only be used among us, not on others. It's a death offense to even consider targeting a member of another race."

She clenched her teeth against the frustration building up. "Fine, then what about a binding spell that can transfer a witch's magick to another? That it comes to the point where it's creating intolerable pain to the victim." She remained silent, allowing him to think over what she said. "That sounds like demon magick to me."

Jared was so quiet she wouldn't have been surprised if he'd fallen asleep.

"Was the witch hot to the touch?"

"Hot and I was almost thrown back on my butt when I touched her. Cleo pointed out spots where I shouldn't touch her."

He used his hands to sketch in the air. "Ankles, thighs, waist, shoulders, and face?"

Lili thought back to where the dots of light had

hovered over Vonnie. "Yes. I managed to use a sleep spell on her, but I don't know how long it will last. So I'm right? It is a demon-based curse?"

He nodded. "And a nasty one. I've only heard of it in theory. Do you know who was stupid enough to use it on her?"

Her expression darkened. "My first guess is her asshole boyfriend who's a mage second class."

Jared shook his head. "No mage second class should have access to something like that. If he has that knowledge, then he had help. I'm sorry, Lili, it's not good."

She shook her head, refusing to give in. "Do you have any idea what I can use to help her?"

"The boyfriend should have what you require, and he'd need to carry it on him at all times if he wants to keep the magick flowing at a fairly steady rate. The charm will be something innocuous like a piece of jewelry or even a button." He looked grim. "You have to find out where he obtained it. The demon who'd sell a spell like that has to be brought to justice."

"Justice as in destroyed."

"Got it in one."

"I want you to look at her," Lili said.

Jared looked down at his filthy and smelly self. "I don't have a lot of power left after my little trip this morning," he warned her.

"If need be, I can help with an illusion spell. I need a demon to look at her before Zane shows up. Please?"

"You're right—he won't waste any time if he's afraid he'll be found out. What he's done has made him an addict for her magick. The withdrawal from this is bad." Jared stood up and gathered the shadows around him while leaving a piece of himself behind to look as if he was sleeping.

Lili returned to the main part of the hospital with her obscure companion on her heels.

"Just don't talk to me or look at me," Jared instructed in a low voice.

Once on the main floor, Lili entered the ancient elevator to travel to the top floor where patients were housed in the seclusion rooms. Once there she found Deisphe walking out of the room on the end.

"Dragon lady came by and ordered up lavender in Vonnie's room. I've got it scattered around, and it seems to be helping to ease her distress."

"I'm sorry I didn't think of it," Lili said, aware of Jared nearby.

"Same here. I got hold of good ole Zane, and he's very worried about his beloved Vonnie, since she wasn't at their apartment when he got back after his classes," she confided in Lili with a roll of her eyes. "He should be here in about an hour."

"Wow, you only spoke to him on the phone and you don't like him already?" Lili was amused.

"I'm sure I'll not stand him at all once I see him in person. Vonnie's still resting quietly," the nurse told her.

"Thanks. Do me a favor and let reception know that Zane isn't to be allowed up here. He can wait in the lobby until I'm ready to see him." She grasped Deisphe's arm before she moved away. "Could you come to dinner tonight?"

The Were smiled. "I'd love to." Her smile disappeared just as fast. "Lili, is something wrong?"

"No, I'd just like us to have some time to talk," she

assured her. By now she felt she could trust Deisphe, and she hoped the Were could help her with more information about Sera. "About six?" She added her address.

"I'll be there with dessert in hand." She gifted her with a bright smile.

Lili moved toward the seclusion room, sensing Jared's presence close by. She paused once, quickly typing a text message on her cell phone. She smiled when a reply appeared seconds later. *It's good to have friends in the right places*.

Magickal wards covered the glass chamber, ensuring that no harm could come to the inhabitant and preventing Vonnie from causing injury to anyone who entered the room.

Lili stopped in front of the heavily warded glass and looked in. She thought Vonnie looked smaller than before. A soft blue blanket covered her, and golden sigils scrolled on the fabric while more power softly pulsed throughout the room.

"Could Zane break into the room?" Jared asked softly.

"Not without enduring some excruciating pain," Lili said with satisfaction. She briefly savored the idea of the young mage trying to break into Vonnie's haven and ending up on the floor, crying like a baby.

Jared moved around her and stared through the glass.

She didn't understand the words that fell from his lips, but she guessed that they were some pretty hefty swear words.

"Don't you see them?" he demanded, his jaw tight with fury.

"See what?" She followed his gaze but only saw the quietly sleeping witch.

"The bonds. You're right, Lili. That fucking mage has her bound so tightly, it's killing her," he bit out the words. His hands tightened into fists that looked as if they were ready to pound someone.

Lili guessed the intended prey would be a mage second class.

Jared hunkered down on his heels. "Give me something to draw with." He didn't look up as he held up his hand.

Lili handed him a black marker and watched him draw a woman's figure on the tile floor then slashed dark lines across her body in the areas he mentioned before.

"The bonds are on these parts of her body," he stated. "Demon magick means you need a demon to remove them. And it's going to hurt like Hades when you do release them. They've been attached to her so long, they've actually grown into her body."

She absorbed his words. "Will it kill her?"

Jared shook his head. "Not if it's done right. But it will be a long recovery for her. Witch magick and demon magick aren't a good mix. That's why you need to know where he got the charm. Both of them need to be taken care of."

"Tell me what I need to save her." She stared at the witch, sensing her pain and wishing she could just snap her fingers and it would be gone. What good was her healing magick if she was thwarted at times?

"Me."

She shook her head. "No way. That I can't do. I'd have enough problems if Dr. Mortimer found you out of your cell, but if he knew you were helping with me with a patient, I'd be shipped back to Chicago in seconds.

Then I'd be brought up on charges. You'll have to tell me what to do."

"He won't know," he said confidently. "As I said, this is olde demon magick. I bet there isn't anyone else in this building who can help that witch. Something tells me I'm the only demon around." His voice softened to a growling purr. "You asked for my help, Lili. You have it."

Lili straightened up, releasing a healthy dose of her power to give Jared a good push. "Crying Souls is one of the most revered hospitals for the preternaturals, alongside Darkside Manor in England and *Cura para Todos*, near Madrid," she said, allowing her ferocity to show. "Not to mention others in the Pacific area. I have been fortunate to work at many of them and have learned something new wherever I went. Maybe we don't have as many healing centers as we need, but we do our best. Over the centuries, new curses have increased and qualified healers haven't."

Jared shook his head. "Knock off the defensive attitude. Demons always keep to themselves and make sure their magick isn't used by anyone outside their clans. So tell me, *Dr. Carter*, do you know of anyone here, other than me, who can handle a demon-created binding spell guaranteed to kill that witch in there if something isn't done fast?" He crossed his arms in front of his chest, impatiently waiting for her reply.

Lili considered a good bout of primal scream therapy or maybe just zapping him with a good dose of mylethian parasites. The cure was just as disgusting as the disease. She allowed a tiny smile to slip as she imagined the parasites burrowing into his skin.

Jared narrowed his eyes. "I don't like what you're thinking."

"What am I thinking?" She was all innocence now.

"I'd say something not good that happens to involve me, and I'm talking not in a fun way." He pulled in a deep breath and exhaled noisily. "I'm not being arrogant here, Lili. She needs my help."

"Yes, you are being arrogant. All demons are arrogant. It's part of your DNA, or whatever in Hades you want to call it." Lili turned her head to stare at Vonnie. Her heart clenched as she saw agitation move over the witch's body in rolling waves. Then she smiled as Cleo carefully climbed onto the end of the bed and gently touched Vonnie's leg with her paw. A moment later, she returned to natural slumber while Cleo reclined next to her.

"I never saw a cat do that," Jared commented.

"Cleo's constantly full of surprises." She felt her cell phone vibrate and pulled it out of her pocket. "Hmm, seems Zane has arrived early."

"And is probably very worried about the love of his life," Jared said sardonically.

"Of course he is." She quickly typed in a text. "I was going to make him wait in the lobby, but I think I'd like to have a chat with him instead. I asked Deisphe to take him to my office. I'm sure we'll need some privacy for this particular conversation." She looked at Jared and arched an eyebrow. "Are you ready to terrorize what's probably an arrogant little pissant of a mage?"

Jared flashed a grin while his eyes sparked fires. "Nothing I'd like better."

Chapter 10

As she returned downstairs and walked briskly to her office, she ignored Jared's presence, as she had earlier.

Deisphe stood by the door while her charge sat by Lili's desk. Lili didn't miss that the young mage sat there blatantly flirting with the Were. The gorgeous cat looked ready to take a nasty bite out of him.

"Hello, Zane, I'm Dr. Carter." She entered her office and held out her hand. The minute she touched him, she felt a sense of imbalance in his power and noted the flickers of lack of control in his eyes. *Jared's right. He needs a fix. Good thing there's no way he can get to Vonnie.*

She stared at the blond-haired mage with the winning smile and boyish good looks. A bronze pin tucked in his shirt collar indicated his status as a mage second class. She wondered how many exams he had cheated his way through to get that pin.

"How is Vonnie?" he asked, masking his earlier flirtation with concern.

"She's very ill." She gestured for him to be seated and walked around to sit behind her desk. She sensed Jared had taken possession of a shadowed corner. Deisphe straightened up as she felt an odd shift of power in the room, but not even by a flicker of her eyelash did she indicate she knew something was different.

"What's wrong with her?"

"We're not sure. I'm still running tests," Lili said with her best doctor's smile meant to reassure a patient's next of kin.

He leaned forward in his chair, his fingers tapping the arm of the chair. "I want to see her."

Lili looked up at Deisphe and gestured for her to leave the office. The nurse frowned but finally slipped away. The witch still gave no indication Jared was present.

"I'm afraid that isn't possible," she informed the young mage. "Since we don't know what's wrong with Vonnie, I've had to place her in a seclusion room. For all we know, she could have been exposed to something highly contagious. We can't take that chance," she said blandly.

"I want to see her," he demanded.

Lili placed her linked hands on top of her desk. "I'm sorry, only family members will be allowed inside the room."

"*I'm* her family. Vonnie only has me!" Zane shouted, showing a loss of control.

Jared started to push away from the shadows, but an incline of Lili's head stopped him.

"You're not mated, therefore, you're not a family member," she stated. The charm had to be on him. She didn't want to think about finding a way to strip him down to find it. But she would if she had to.

Then she noticed a jagged piece of metal decorating a leather band wrapped around his left wrist. *Near his heart. Power base.*

"I love Vonnie. I need to be with her," Zane insisted, his white-knuckled grip almost breaking the chair arms. "Take me to her now."

"I don't think so." Lili ignored his attempt to compel her to follow his demand. She wanted to slap the youngling down, big-time.

"You're hurting, aren't you, asshole?" Jared stepped out of the shadows. "It's like a drug. Once you're hooked, you can't stop. Your body is demanding a fix."

Zane's eyes widened. The smell of fear flowed off his skin like an acrid stench. "Who… what are you?"

"I'm your worst nightmare, you son of a bitch." He reached down and tore the leather band off the mage's wrist, leaving a painful welt behind.

"You're a demon." Zane almost crawled up the back of his chair. "You're supposed to help me keep what I rightfully paid for."

"I had nothing to do with this transaction." Jared held up the band, the metal glinting dark glimmers in the room. "Why don't you tell me about your talisman?"

The mage couldn't take his eyes off the leather bracelet. His fingers twitched with the need to snatch it back. "That's nothing. Just something I wear for luck."

"Why wear *nothing* for luck?" Jared countered in a silken tone that sent shivers along Lili's spine.

She stood up and braced her hands on her desk. "Luck as in keeping it close to you so you can drain the woman you claim to love of her magick," she accused. "You've almost killed her by using that illegal charm."

"Not to mention getting yourself in a shitload of trouble for dealing with the wrong kind of demons," Jared hitched a hip onto the corner of her desk. "What did you give the demon for this charm?" He dangled it in front of Zane. "And don't tell me it's not a charm," he warned when the mage opened his mouth.

"I'm able to smell and feel a demon binding charm miles away."

"I was told no one could sense it." Zane knew his mistake the moment he spoke.

Jared loomed over him, resting his hands on the chair arms. "I've got news for you, sport. *Demons lie*," he said softly, the words like razor blades across the skin.

Lili ratchetted up her personal protections as she stared at a new scary side of Jared. This creature could easily twist Zane's head off his neck and hand it to him without breaking a sweat.

"He'll be taken care of, Jared," she murmured. "I've already arranged for him to be held accountable for his crime."

"And I will let you do just that, right after he gives me the name." He leaned down until he was nose to nose with a heavily sweating Zane.

"I can't," he stammered, now refusing to look at the band Jared held. "He said I'd die the minute I say his name."

"And you'll die if you don't." He bared his teeth. "So let's try this again. Name and clan. In order for you to have procured this," he dangled the band in front of Zane's frightened eyes, "you'd have to know both."

Lili's nose wrinkled at the acrid sulfuric scent drifting in the air. She couldn't miss the shadows crawling across her office floor, heading for Zane's chair. "Jared, don't take the law into your own hands," she warned. "Get them to back off now."

"Only if he tells me what I want to know." He refused to move as his gaze bored into Zane's eyes. "Don't you have something to tell me?"

Zane looked as if he was going to swallow his tongue. "Fearce," he choked. "Fearce of the Moutanni clan. He sold it to me. He vowed no one, not even a demon, could tell what it was."

Jared pushed himself away and stepped back. "Yeah, well, like I told you. We all lie."

"Is this a private party, or can anyone join in?"

Lili looked at the doorway and smiled at her visitor. "Maggie! I think your new little friend will be very happy to see you."

Maggie O'Malley, a high-ranking member of the Hellion Guard, protectors of all supernatural creatures, sauntered into the room. She looked totally badass in a pair of black skinny jeans and a silk tank top the color of ripe watermelon. A diamond-encrusted black widow spider tattooed on her bicep completed the look.

"Please tell me we won't be here for long," the spider said in a French accent. "I have an important date tonight."

"Hi, Elle," Lili greeted Maggie's sidekick with a broad smile. "You look as beautiful as ever."

"Thank you, *ma chérie*. I must say, you give us the most interesting toys, Lili," the spider told her, eyeing Zane as if he were a tasty treat. He looked more uncertain by the minute.

Maggie was engrossed in her new prisoner, who slouched deep in his chair. Her eyes flicked over the charm Jared dangled from his fingers. "In my professional opinion, I'd say your new jewelry is demon-crafted and very nasty to witches," she stated. "My, my, someone's been a naughty boy." She transferred her attention to Zane.

"Good eye," Jared complimented her.

"My boyfriend's a half fire demon, and I tend to keep up on the bad toys you all come up with," she said, pushing back a lock of pale blond hair. She looked down at Zane. "So you're the nasty little troublemaker I'm here to collect." She shook her head and made strange sounds with her tongue. "I swear, you mages get stupider all the time. Don't you learn anything at those schools you magick users pretend to attend? There are some things you just don't fool around with. Any kind of demon spell tops the list."

Zane looked as if he wasn't sure whether Maggie was his savior or a new enemy. No wonder, since the badass Hellion looked ready to turn him into something a lot nastier than a toad.

"If you're a member of the Hellion Guard, you have to protect me against this demon," he insisted with a defiance that grated on everyone else's nerves. "Plus, this bitch won't let me see my girlfriend who's really sick. I know my rights! I am a mage second class." He puffed up, not realizing he looked even more ridiculous.

"Sorry, sweetheart, just now you have no rights." Maggie snapped her fingers. Manacles clicked tightly around Zane's wrists. "Using demon olde magick on a witch is a very bad offense. A Class A felony, in fact. Now let's go quietly. I have to attend parent-teacher night tonight, and I can't be late, since I'm supposed to bring lemon bars for the get-together. And I'm sure I'm going to hear that my kid's been stirring up trouble again."

"How is Courtney doing?" Lili asked, referring to the teenager Maggie and her demon lover, Declan, adopted.

"She wants a tattoo, she's flunking world history, and for some insane reason, she adores The Librarian, and he's actually nice to her. How twisted is that? In other words, she's your typical teenager." She walked over to Lili and grasped her arms, staring into her eyes. Whatever she saw there had her smiling. "Look at you," she said softly. "Trust me; it's an e-ticket ride, but more than worth it." She dropped a kiss on her friend's forehead. "And if you need me, you know you just have to call," she whispered, hugging Lili tightly. "You're not alone in this."

Lili's smile wobbled a bit. "I know, and thank you."

Maggie's focus then shifted to Jared. She flashed him the sunny smile that most men would consider sexy, but her friend knew exactly what it meant. And it wasn't always good.

"And you, you cute li'l ole demon, you," she practically purred. "If you do anything to hurt my friend, I will turn you into sushi and feed you to the cat."

Maggie stepped back and took a deep breath. "Okay, junior, up and at 'em." She gripped Zane by his collar and hauled him to his feet as easily as if he were a rag doll.

"Wait a minute," he started to say, stumbling, but Maggie held up a warning hand.

"There's no 'wait a minute.' No asking for a lawyer. No insisting you know your rights. There's just me, and I'm not all that nice," she told him in a voice that practically sprouted razor blades. "You violated a witch with an illegal demon-crafted charm. Do you understand the penalty for such a crime?" She smiled at the fear flowing across his face. "Ah, I see you do. You better hope Vonnie doesn't die from what you did. There's a whole new death penalty for that. Time to go, sport. Since I'm short on time, we're using a portal that will get us back to my Compound at supersonic speed, even if it tends to turn your stomach upside down. Do not even think about puking on my boots once we arrive, or you'll discover what real pain is." She hauled him out of the office, easily ignoring Zane's entreaties, then his screaming threats, along with his insistence he hadn't done anything wrong. A moment later there was a popping sound and then silence.

"You have some interesting friends, Lili," Jared commented once they were alone.

"Maggie was in my class at the Witches Academy. With her skills, there was no doubt that the Hellion Guard wouldn't waste any time snapping her up," Lili replied. She eyed the charm the way she'd look at an ugly insect. And she really hated insects. "Do you honestly know what to do to destroy the spell?"

He nodded. He pocketed the leather band and held out his hand. She slipped her hand in his as he gently pulled her toward him.

"I've got to say, you liven up my days," he murmured, brushing his lips across her brow, then trailing them down to the corner of her lips. He smiled as he stepped back. "I know. You have a patient to treat."

"And get you back below before someone discovers you're gone," she said, her eyes shadowed with sorrow. She didn't want him to leave. She would rather they went somewhere, even if only to have coffee.

Jared's eyes darkened as he leaned toward her. His fingers captured a stray curl, and allowed the strands to wrap around them. Lili held her breath as he leaned over and inhaled the scent of her hair then lightly brushed a kiss by her temple.

"I think we should leave before I think about something else," he whispered.

She didn't want to agree, but knew this wasn't the time.

Lili tensed a couple times when they encountered one of the doctors and a nurse, but no one noticed her companion as Jared remained cloaked in the shadows.

She breathed a sigh of relief to find Vonnie's room empty save for Cleo.

"She's been restless," the cat told them as they entered the seclusion chamber. She narrowed her eyes and hissed at Jared. When he hissed back, she arched her tail like a graceful plume and left the room.

"Now she'll be in a snit for the rest of the day," Lili warned him.

"She'll recover. Just as your patient will." Jared pulled out the leather band and ripped the charm from it. He held it up in his palm and muttered a few guttural words in his tongue.

Lili stood back, watching in horrified fascination as the demon-crafted metal started to smoke and turn black. Just as ink-colored flames erupted from it, Jared dropped it to the floor and stomped on it. When he lifted his foot, the charm disappeared, leaving only a hint of brimstone in the air.

"Look!"

Lili gasped in shock.

She stared as wet-looking black leather bonds suddenly appeared. They were wrapped across Vonnie's body in the exact spots Cleo had warned her not to touch. There was no doubt the magickal restraints were causing their victim great pain.

"Wow, very S&M," she said. The witch shot him a warning. "Don't get any ideas."

Jared grinned. "Too late."

They both turned as Vonnie's eyes popped open and she opened her mouth to scream.

"No." He pushed Lili away and rested his hands an inch above Vonnie's body as he chanted in a low voice.

Lili, the healer, watched in fascination as dark gray tendrils of mist left his palms and floated over the young witch's body. They curled in the air, finally settling on her like a lightweight blanket. Minutes passed as the mist slowly dissolved the restraints. The moment they vanished, Vonnie instantly breathed easier and the pain left her face. She blinked slowly and turned her head.

"What happened?" she rasped.

"Welcome back." Jared smiled down at her. He glanced up and caught Lili's attention. "I'll let Dr. Carter explain. You know where I'll be." He smiled as he leaned in to whisper in Lili's ear, "As I told you, a demon does it better." He left the room.

She smiled after him then turned back to her patient. She quickly checked Vonnie over. Her healing gift sensed the tears in the witch's power and the harm done to her body. Jared was right. She'd have a long recovery ahead of her.

Lili briefly thought of contacting Maggie and asking her to drag Zane through the portal several times. Then she remembered that the Hellion witch had her own methods to make her prisoners suffer.

Zane should have stayed a mage second class without

wanting more. She knew the Hellion Guard would ensure he'd be in a world of hurt before his execution. Even then it wouldn't be enough payback for what she did to the young witch.

"What happened?" Vonnie asked, bringing Lili back to her task at hand.

While she would have preferred waiting until she was stronger, Lili knew that the truth needed to be told now. She pulled up a chair and related the story as gently as possible. Even then, she saw shock, horror, and sorrow cross Vonnie's face.

"Why would Zane do that?" she whispered in a raw voice. "I thought he loved me." Her slender fingers plucked the covers.

"I'm afraid he loved power more. You have a strong gift, Vonnie, and he knew drawing on that would increase his own. He didn't admit it, but I'd say he was hoping he would be able to make mage first class without truly working at it. But what he did was slowly killing you. You would have been nothing more than an empty husk in a short time." She knew her blunt words were hurting Vonnie emotionally, but she also refused to hold back the truth. It was the only way she could move on with her life and fully heal. Lili mentally noted to send a counselor in to talk to Vonnie and help her deal with the love of her life's betrayal.

Vonnie took a deep breath. She turned her head away, staring at the wall. Lili remained quiet, but she kept her hand resting lightly on the witch's arm to let her know she wasn't truly alone. She knew there was a lot for her to process. Treachery by a so-called loved one was never easy to understand.

"He was the first man I ever loved," Vonnie said softly. "I thought we'd spend our lives together. I knew he was ambitious. I just didn't know his aspirations would go this far." She pulled in another cleansing breath. "I hope he suffers greatly before they kill him." She turned back to Lili. "Will I recover?"

"Of course." She smiled. "It will take time, but you'll regain your full power. For now, you're to rest." She checked her stats again and jotted them down on the computer tablet hanging on the end of the bed. "I'd like you to stay here until tomorrow, then we'll move you to another room. I just want to make sure you're all right."

"Thank you, Doctor." Vonnie's smile was wan and still held pain, emotional and physical. Her lips trembled with the tears she appeared not to want to fall.

Lili smiled back and stroked her arm. "The pain of betrayal is never easy to get past," she murmured. "But the time will come when the agony will lessen." She brushed her fingertips across the young witch's forehead and left her sleeping again.

Lili knew Vonnie would brood over Zane and his deception. Being seven hundred-plus years old meant that Lili didn't sweat the small stuff. Instead she called on her hexy friend Blair to craft an appropriate revenge spell.

"Note to self," she murmured as she stepped into the elevator car. "Ask Blair about renewing that scab spell on Larkin's ass. He really hasn't been punished long enough for cheating on me." She was still smiling when she arrived at the main floor.

—∿∿—

"What, no Fancy Feast?" Cleo asked in a snarky tone as she watched Lili check the roast and tuck it back into the oven. "You better not share my catnip wine, either."

"Did you know some cats are locked away in crates when company comes?" Lili sang out as she opened a nice bottle of Bordeaux and allowed it to breathe.

"Ha! As if that would work for me." The feline deliberately coughed up a hair ball. "Oopsie, my bad." She offered a toothy smile devoid of any apology.

Lili zapped the hair ball and returned to her kitchen work.

"I thought there was a one-cat rule."

"You're not a familiar. Maybe I should send you down to Jazz's for a visit. I'm sure Fluff and Puff would love having a playmate for a while."

Cleo shuddered. "Not after the last time, thank you very much. My tail was in tatters, no thanks to those insane bunny slippers!"

"Yes, quite a battle you started." She looked up at the sound of the doorbell.

"Oh sure, believe them. Their credibility is in the toilet."

"Just behave tonight," Lili told her as she headed for the front door.

"Cute house!" Deisphe told her as she walked in carrying a large pink bakery box. "A chocolate champagne torte to die for." She handed her the box.

"Thanks." She guided her back to the kitchen. "I thought you'd be happy with a roast."

"Carnivore, that's me." She grinned at Cleo, who bared her teeth back. "Don't worry, kitty, I'm not here to tread on any paws."

"I'll be in your bed," Cleo told Lili while ignoring

their guest. She sauntered out of the kitchen with her tail held high.

"Ignore her. She's usually in a snit when someone doesn't acknowledge she's queen of the universe." Lili handed Deisphe a glass of wine.

"More than just the Nile, huh?"

Lili nodded. "She's popular in the pediatrics ward—proof she's not all bad."

"I heard that!"

Witch and Were shared a soft laugh.

Lili wanted desperately to start asking Deisphe how well she knew Sera, but she tamped down her frustration and concentrated on serving the meal. She liked the Were and didn't want her to feel she had only invited her in hopes of pumping her for information.

Instead of her usual paper plates and her frequent practice of eating at the breakfast bar, Lili set the small table in the tiny dining room and kept the music on low. Dinner was eaten at a leisurely pace where the two laughed and talked.

"We've sure had some excitement at the hospital lately," Deisphe said, lifting her wineglass in a toast, as Lili insisted she remain seated while the witch cleared the table. "And here I thought we'd have a quiet spell for a while." She wrinkled her nose.

"No such thing." Lili brought the torte back into the room along with plates and silverware. By unspoken agreement, they moved to the family room with their dessert and refilled their glasses of wine.

Lili forked up a bite of the torte and moaned as the rich chocolate exploded in her mouth.

"Tell me about it." Deisphe grinned, doing the same.

"This bakery is a killer and so good. The owner is a witch. If I didn't have the metabolism I do, I'd probably weigh a thousand pounds."

"So true."

"So what do you need to know?" Deisphe took another bite. "You want to know something you couldn't ask at the hospital, true?"

Lili's laugh escaped her lips. "I do." She knew honesty was always the best policy, even if she didn't constantly follow it. But she felt the need to find someone she could trust at the hospital, especially since she couldn't rely on Jared's assistance. "I mentioned my friend Sera to you before."

The Were nodded. She paused and sipped her wine, then studied Lili.

"Sera didn't just take off, did she?"

Lili shook her head. "I don't believe so. It's not Sera's nature. She has the same work ethic you do. She never left anyone hanging and was always ready to help out during emergencies, even if her shift was over. And she was truly gifted with healing charms. We talked every day after she moved here. Then she said something odd about the hospital, and before I knew it, I hadn't heard from her for a few days. I contacted some friends living here, and they checked up on her. Her apartment was cleared out, and word at the hospital was that she'd left without notice."

"You don't believe any of it." The Were cradled her wineglass between her hands.

"Not at all."

Deisphe was quiet for several moments. "Like the others," she murmured.

Lili nodded. She got to her feet and went into the kitchen. She returned to the family room with the wine bottle and topped off both glasses.

"How many unexplained absences of hospital staff have you noticed since you started working there?" she asked, settling back in her crimson chair with her bare feet up on the matching footrest.

Deisphe blew out a breath and looked upward in thought. Her lips moved silently as if she said names. She sighed. "If you don't count screwups who left before they were fired, I'd say between eight and ten."

Lili felt a chill travel down her spine. "The same way Sera did?"

"They just didn't show up at work one day, calls to them weren't returned, and they were never heard from again." Deisphe slipped off her flats and curled up on the couch with her legs tucked up beneath her. "Lots of gossip about what happened, but no one really followed up on it." She frowned in further thought. "Although…"

"Although what?" Lili leaned forward.

"I could be wrong, but I'd say every one of them was fairly new to the hospital. I don't think any of them had been working there any longer than six months or so." Her golden eyes darkened. "This isn't good, is it?"

Lili agreed. "It's not. I would think even the authorities would feel that number was a bit high."

"There was no reason for an investigation. It's not like anything was stolen. The Dragon Lady just bitched about how she'd have to rework schedules and went on how it wouldn't hurt for them to call in and say they were outta there." Deisphe took another bite of the rich torte. "You have no idea about your friend? Is that why you came out here?"

"None at all, and yes, that was one of the important reasons for my coming back, but I also felt another need to return to San Francisco." Deep inside she felt that Sera was the catalyst for her meeting Jared and, she hoped, finding a way to have him released from Dr. Mortimer's antiquated idea of medical care.

The Were nodded. "Count me in. If there's anything I can do for you, I'm there, okay?

Lili felt the warmth expand inside her. "I was hoping you'd say that."

"So, on to fun topics. Did you see that new medic handling the portals for the badly wounded?" Deisphe fanned her hand in front of her face. "Talk about smokin'! Plus, he's a Wereleopard. I'd lift my tail for him anytime."

The witch laughed so hard she almost choked. "Why do I get the idea it won't be safe to go into the portal area for a while?" she said once she regained her breath.

"At least have some style while you're at it!" could be heard from Lili's bedroom. "You cubs have no idea how to properly seduce a male."

Deisphe grinned at Lili. "She does hate to be left out of things, doesn't she?"

She nodded. "When you consider her history, you have to admit she knows all about the opposite sex."

"Then maybe we both need her expertise. You with your sexy demon and me with my hot snow leopard." She raised her eyebrows.

"I'm considered sexy now?"

Lili choked on her wine while Deisphe almost dropped her glass. She turned to Lili, accusation running hot.

"He's been here the whole time?"

Lili almost fell over as Jared helpfully slapped her on the back.

"No," she rasped. She glared at him.

"A simple thank-you is enough." He plucked her wineglass out of her hand and drank as he perched on the chair's arm. "Hello."

Deisphe nodded. "Teleportation?"

"Shadows," he replied.

She nodded as she looked at Lili then back at Jared. "I've heard of shadow demons. I only saw you once below. You clean up very well. So which is the real you? What I see here or the animal in a cell?"

Lili tensed at the Were's blunt language.

"A little of both." He leaned forward and refilled the wineglass, returning it to Lili.

Deisphe looked at her friend. "Have you ever done anything the easy way?"

"Yes, but it didn't offer as much satisfaction." She enjoyed the heat of Jared's body close to hers. She didn't know why he was here, but her hormones were happy to see him.

Deisphe continued eyeing him closely. "You were at Crieze."

He nodded.

She looked from one to the other. "You know I'll do whatever I can to help. So, Jared, why don't you tell me what goes on with you."

Lili broke into a broad smile, and she felt the tension leave Jared's body.

"You going to share any of that torte?" he asked, staring at Lili's plate.

The evening ended differently than Lili expected, but she judged it a success. She knew she had a new friend and a willing accomplice in Deisphe. As for Jared, she knew time alone would tell.

She didn't know if Jared was meant to belong in her life or if she would ever learn what happened to Sera. Right now, she felt she was on the right path to both.

—⁂—

The chamber was dimly lit with candles that produced uneasy yellow and orange flames. The acrid stench of chemicals was strong in the air, but the room's occupant was oblivious to the smell.

He sat on a wooden stool, hunched over a long table filled with beakers and burners. Stained fingers trembled as he lifted one of the beakers and carefully poured the coppery red contents into a potion bottle that already contained a thick, bubbling liquid. As he gently sloshed the contents back and forth to blend them, he softly chanted the words that danced around his head. His hair lifted in the charged air that grew stronger the further he reached into his spell.

He smiled at the ear-piercing shriek that rent the air, indicating to him the spell was complete.

The bottle's contents were pulled up into a hypodermic, and he swiftly injected it into his forearm.

He slumped on the stool and closed his eyes as the cold rush of the drug he'd concocted raced through his blood, filling him with the sensation that midnight lived within him.

He stared at the portal that glittered invitingly. Smiling with anticipation, he stood up and walked toward the opening that would lead him to another place and time, where he felt free to utilize his darker skills.

Chapter 11

LILI SAT IN THE SAME UNCOMFORTABLE CHAIR SHE'D been given each time she had been bidden to Dr. Mortimer's office. She noticed the fusty atmosphere along with a nose-prickling scent that sent an odd sensation under the surface of her skin.

She knew some doctors used odd concoctions in their own peculiar way of treating themselves. Many of the potions were so old, only the imbiber knew what was in them. The witch wondered what the wizard took to cause the odd aroma in the air.

"I hope you like ginger tea," Dr. Mortimer said, pouring the liquid into two delicate china cups and handing one to her. "I find it a nice treat in the afternoons."

"Yes, thank you," she lied. She knew ginger was excellent for upset stomachs, but since, luckily, she never suffered that particular malady, she didn't touch the stuff. She hid her reaction as she carefully sipped the hot drink.

"I have studied your notes regarding Pepta and Panabell, and I am pleased with what I read," he said with a broad smile. "Pepta has always been a..." he paused as his drank his tea. "Well, a bit of a trial."

Lili couldn't help smiling at the subtle phrase that didn't speak the truth about the abrasive nymph. "Thank you, although I don't feel I've done enough for her. It was a shame she had been so badly mistreated before she came here, because it means we can't use any kind of gentle treatment with her. She would only scoff at that. She needs someone tough to stand up to her. It seems so many suffer when they've been exposed to any form of tainted blood. Just as the mundanes can suffer that type of sickness, so can the preternaturals." She took another sip of her tea. "I wish we could find a true cure for them, but there are so many forms of contaminated blood, it's not easy to do."

"So much power in one's blood," the doctor murmured almost to himself. "It can heal, it can destroy, and it can bring about so much power in the right spell."

"A blood spell is always dangerous." Lili wondered where this conversation was leading. If Dr. Mortimer was going to suggest using any form of blood spell, she'd have to flatly refuse. She always protected her patients by ensuring that any bloody cloths were hexed into ash.

"Yes, Dr. Carter, but you must remember that it can also be helpful." His faded eyes gleamed as he leaned across his desk. "Sometimes you must think outside the box. To look at all the good something unusual can accomplish."

I'm staring at a wizard wearing clothes straight out of the Victorian era, and he's talking about coloring outside the lines. What's wrong with this picture?

"I'm sorry, Dr. Mortimer, but I must disagree with you," she said, feeling as if she was stepping through a minefield. And wondering where this was heading. "Any charm or spell that's powered by blood can harm the practitioner as much as the victim."

"But there are no victims," he argued, seemingly caught up in the subject. "By using such a strong spell, we could find a way to cure the truly ill ones, such as Patient 1172."

Lili set her cup down. The ginger tea churned around her stomach like a tsunami while bitterness rested on her tongue. She took a deep breath, aware she would have to carefully choose her words because Jared's existence could depend on it.

"Panabell has responded very well with the new treatment," she spoke slowly. "And Pepta's had fewer manic episodes lately."

"But…" His keen eyes didn't miss that she had a lot more to say. By his expression, she was already warned he might not like it.

"I'm really thinking of Patient 1172," she continued. "Personally, Dr. Mortimer, I don't feel he's as dangerous as he first was. What I've observed of him is a male who's healed. I don't see any signs of insanity in his manner."

The wizard clucked under his tongue as he gifted her with a benign smile. "My dear Dr. Carter, you must always remember that Patient 1172 is a demon. Of all creatures, they know best how to hide their true selves. They lie, cheat, steal, they will cut out your heart without thinking twice, and when they reach their darker selves, they are able to do more. I am afraid Patient 1172 has managed to deceive you into thinking he has changed for the better." He shook his head, looking the image of a concerned mentor. "No, he is not ready. But I feel he can be made a bit better, once I begin the new therapy by using a special blend of blood."

Ice traveled down her spine. She saw something wild flickering in his eyes. Something that shouldn't be in the mild wizard's manner. "I don't consider myself unintelligent, Dr. Mortimer, but I'm afraid I don't understand what you're getting at." *Or why you're talking about the base of the most dangerous spells of all, in the way someone else would talk about blending coffee.*

He continued to smile at her as if she were the dull-witted child even she was starting to think she was.

And why was he bringing up something this unsafe to her? It was a forbidden subject for anyone in the healing field. The kind no one even wanted to whisper for fear they'd be overheard and brought up before the Physics Council. If you were caught using a blood spell, you wouldn't just lose your healing powers. You'd lose your life.

Lili could tell it was obvious this was something he'd either given great thought to or worse. She feared it was the latter.

"Over the years, I have studied many ancient scrolls written by healers who detailed a wide variety of primeval healing practices," he explained with the same fervent gleam in his eyes. "Do you know many of them used blood enchantments with great success? They proved that using the life source also gave the charms greater strength for those who required it. You are a gifted healer, Dr. Carter. I knew you would understand what I hope to accomplish here."

"But we don't think that way any longer," she said, doing her best not to sound as if she was arguing. She wondered why he brought the subject up, except that he must have had a good reason and felt he could trust her. A horrifying thought took root in her mind. Why was the doctor considering utilizing blood spells to help their healing process? She knew she wasn't going to allow him to try it on Panabell and Pepta. Not just because the spells were banned, but because they could also go very wrong.

She spoke slowly and continued to tread carefully as she strove to say what she felt he wanted to hear. "I admit I'm not well versed in that area, Dr. Mortimer. Would it be possible for me to borrow some of your scrolls and read about these processes, so that I could understand them better?" She offered him a gentle smile. Suddenly, she was the student again, someone eager to learn from a master, as the wizard would surely see himself. She didn't know a wizard yet that didn't have a mega-ego.

Dr. Mortimer picked up a pipe and tamped the tobacco down. A flick of his fingers had it burning, and the scent of cherry filled the air.

She remained silent, allowing him to ruminate on her words and, hopefully, decide she wasn't any threat to whatever plan he was hatching.

There was no way this idea is a spur of the moment thing for him. He must have experimented with blood spells before. Oh my Fates, what if he's behind Sera's disappearance? Knots tightened in the pit of her stomach as terrifying thoughts raced through her head.

Lili had the unsettling suspicion that Dr. Mortimer might be dabbling in things he shouldn't, but the idea he was looking to blood spells was unsettling. She knew a majority of the wizard doctors were very conservative. The idea of making use of blood in any kind of healing spell was anathema to their natures.

She also questioned why he brought this up now.

What inspired him to dare mention a practice that could have drawn the wrath, not only of the Wizard and Ruling Councils, but even the Physics Council that oversaw all healers? The latter was enough to put fear into the heart of any medical professional.

She felt that the minefield was still out there. Her need to discover just what he was doing grew by the second. By rights she should report him to the Physics Council for just mentioning the use of blood spells, but she didn't feel she had enough facts to back up an accusation that was an automatic death sentence.

By the time Lili felt ready to scream with frustration, the elderly wizard smiled and gestured with his pipe. "I am pleased you are willing to keep an open mind about my work, Dr. Carter. I am sure you realize there are few of us who understand that there are so many unused avenues to explore in healing the mentally infirm. You may read the scrolls," he replied. "But I do ask that you not share their contents with anyone else or even mention their being here. You can understand how dangerous that would be."

Why did she feel as if that danger would be directed more at her, by him, than because of the contents? "Of course." She kept her tone casual as she carefully inched the scrolls toward her. The paper was heavy to the touch and gave off an odd sensation, as if she were touching something unpleasant and long dead.

"And I ask that you only read them on the premises and not take them home with you," he requested. "It's best if they're kept in as controlled an environment as possible."

She nodded. "I'll read them in my office and return them to you as soon as possible." Lili already knew they weren't something she wanted in her possession any longer than necessary. She wondered if she'd be able to scan the contents or if there was a spell on the heavy paper that wouldn't allow it. That was something she'd check out as soon as she could. She stood up, holding the scrolls in one hand. "Thank you for your trust, Dr. Mortimer. I vow to keep the scrolls protected until they're back in your hands." She smiled at him.

"I know you will." He rose at the same time she did. "I have kept you from your duties long enough. And think about what I have said. I do believe we can go a great way if I have your assistance in my research."

"I will," she promised, even as she knew there was no way in Hades she'd even consider it.

Lili didn't waste any time taking the scrolls to her office and locking them in her desk, overlaying the drawer with a major "keep out—or else" spell. Once she finished, she cleansed her hands in salt water then used a lotion on her skin. She collapsed into her chair, feeling exhausted.

"How do I get mixed up in these things?" she muttered to herself.

"Because getting involved is strong in your aura. I don't know what you put in your desk, but whatever it is, it's not good for any of us," Cleo warned her, sitting up tall on her pillow. She lifted a paw and delicately licked it then started hacking. "Damn hair balls," she muttered in a raspy voice, pointing a paw at the hair ball and torching it. "I don't know which is worse, them or the ability to lick my ass. Although I must admit, I do have a lovely butt," she mused, admiring said body part.

"Self-absorbed. Party of one." Lili pulled her hair up into a ponytail, allowing the curls to drop down to her shoulders.

"What did Dr. Musty want, other than to give you something that smells worse than a month-old dead rat and holds nasty magick?" The cat stared at the desk, wrinkling her nose in distaste. "You shouldn't have that around you, you know."

Lili sniffed, but she already knew her sense of smell wasn't like her diva feline's olfactory senses. "All I noticed was an old paper smell, although it does feel nasty. What did you detect?"

"I can tell it's something bad. Like magick that's gone to a bad place." She curled back up on her pillow, her plush tail wrapped around her body. "What's on those scrolls he gave you?"

"I haven't read them yet. Why, do you want to look at them?" She doubted Dr. Mortimer would expect her cat to read them.

"I'll stick to my erotica, thank you very much. It's much more enjoyable than whatever those scrolls hold. I don't think you should read them, either. They wouldn't be good for you, just as I bet they weren't good for him. They changed him, and they'd do that to you too." Her blue eyes rimmed with gold blazed with fire, a sure sign her magick was flaring. Now she stared at the desk as if it held something deadly.

Lili felt the sickness in her stomach flare up. She already had a pretty good idea what was on the scrolls, while Cleo had to rely on her magick to ferret out the contents. And the cat would absolutely do that. Curiosity couldn't kill her for doing it, either.

"Anything else your senses tell you?" she asked. "Do you think I can scan them to my computer?"

Cleo thought for a moment. "I'd have to touch them to tell you that and, personally, I don't care to do so." She groaned when she caught Lili's expression. "But you expect me to."

"You got it." Lili knew just how stubborn the cat was, but she wasn't about to back down. If she could transfer the contents to her computer, she could return the scrolls to Dr. Mortimer and then read them at her leisure.

Cleo continued staring at the desk drawer as if she had X-ray vision. She suddenly hissed and arched her back, her fur standing on end.

"What have you done, you foolish witch?" she spat, spearing her with a fluffy glare. "Those are bad!"

"You already told me that!" Lili batted her hands to indicate the feline keep her voice down.

"Oh no, I first just sensed bad magick," Cleo told her. "But further examination shows we're talking so bad, it could get you into a lot of trouble. Honestly, did you think I spent all these years training you to lose you now?" She leaped off the couch and stalked toward the witch, who had dropped into her chair.

Lili lifted her hands, setting the privacy spell in place. "There's no reason to have a hissy fit."

"There is if you've accepted dangerous materials."

"Dangerous in what way?" She had her own idea, but she badly wanted that second opinion.

Cleo hunkered down, her butt up in the air, her claws unsheathed. "The spells written on those scrolls used the wrong kind of blood. If you aren't careful, something bad will happen to you."

Lili's stomach took a nosedive. She already knew blood spells had to have been mentioned there, or Dr. Mortimer wouldn't have referred to them. Still, she had hoped this was one of those times she was wrong, and the parchments held nothing more than the ramblings of a delusional writer. She knew there was a lot of it out there. Too bad this wasn't one of those times.

She sighed heavily. "You know, just once I wish things would go halfway normally."

Chapter 12

CLEO FLAT-OUT ORDERED LILI NOT TO EVEN CONSIDER scanning the scrolls, either using her computer or even magickally. Lili agreed. Her cat had never been wrong before—something the snarky feline loved pointing out too.

In the end she came into work a couple of hours early the next day so she could catch up on her paperwork and take a peek at the scrolls. By now, she wished she hadn't even asked for them.

She settled in to her office and lit a vanilla-infused candle while she spent her time updating her present cases, then went in search of the offices that held Special Services. It didn't take her long to realize the two Guides there weren't what she needed for Amy. She put a quick call in to Rea, who passed along a pair of phone numbers. In no time Lili had spoken with both Guides, and by conversation alone knew that Rissa would interact the best with little Amy. The Guide promised to be there later that day, and Lili was free to return to the paperwork piled on her desk.

"You'd think we'd be beyond all this," she muttered, flicking her finger over the papers as a way to scrawl her signature. "It's the twenty-first century! At least in Chicago, computers handled it all, because Dr. Hamish loved gadgets."

"Boring," Cleo sang out, hopping off her pillow. "I'm going up to pediatrics."

"Have fun." Lili's attention wandered in the direction of the scrolls that silently wailed her name. The temptation to pull them out and study the contents grew stronger by the minute, but she silenced that voice in a hurry. A glance at the clock warned her that her free time here was waning. She waved her hand to pull up the staff schedule on a blank wall. Names and times clicked into place, showing who was on duty and who wasn't, along with when they'd be in next. She noticed that the space next to Dr. Mortimer's name was blank, with no indication when he would next be on duty.

"Where do you go, Dr. Mortimer?" she murmured, frowning at the schedule. She leaned back in her chair, resting her head against the back. "Most heads of hospitals practically have to be carried out of a hospital, while it seems you're gone more than you are here. No contact information there, either."

"Hey." Deisphe popped in, carrying two cups of coffee, and set one on Lili's desk before she dropped into the guest chair. She inclined her head at the schedule. "What's up with that?" She watched as Lili changed the dates and went backward.

"Just checking out something. Do you notice how often Dr. Mortimer isn't here?" She nodded toward the schedule as she picked up the cup, holding it up in a silent thank-you.

"Dragon lady loves it when he's not. It means she's in charge." Deisphe sipped her coffee. "His main job is down in the asylum, so I guess he doesn't think he needs to be here every day. Or he's holed up in his office or laboratory."

Lili straightened up at that piece of information. "Laboratory?"

The Were nodded. "He doesn't like anyone near it, so it's one of the last rooms before the hall dead-ends, and the door's heavily warded. I only know about it because one of the orderlies was down there and opened the door by mistake. He only put his hand on the handle and was practically zapped back to his birth. He couldn't speak for a month."

"What excuse did Dr. Mortimer give for that happening?"

"That a faulty spell must have been triggered, because there was no reason for it to happen. I should have filched some pastries from the break room."

Lili grinned. "Sugar, chocolate, good fruit. Bring us goodies, nothing healthy, and more coffee to boot." She snapped her fingers.

Deisphe squealed with delight when a platter of doughnuts and pastries appeared on the table next to a tall coffee carafe.

"Did I ever tell you you're my very best friend?" She studied the array and finally chose a lemon-filled doughnut.

Lili picked up a cream-filled doughnut frosted with chocolate and bit down, relishing the thick custard filling.

"Do you really feel he had something to do with Sera's and the others' disappearances?" the Were asked, licking lemon filling off her fingers before choosing another pastry.

Lili didn't hesitate when she nodded. "But I have no proof, only a gut feeling."

"The same gut feeling that tells you Jared isn't really insane?"

"The same one," she said softly.

"So why can't you get him sprung? State that in your professional medical opinion, he's no longer bonkers and is safe to be released?" Deisphe asked.

"That decision is up to Dr. Mortimer, not me, and he doesn't agree." She felt the familiar pain deep within her, the one that she'd come to associate with Jared and her inability to do much to help him. She lived in fear she'd go down one day and be told that she couldn't even talk to him. At least the ogres hadn't figured out she'd used amnesia spells on them when she went down there on days she wasn't supposed to be there.

"What will you do, Lili?" Her golden eyes were warm with concern.

She shook her head. "Figure something out. Maybe approach the Physics Council, although that can be a career-ender unless I can provide a lot of hard evidence to back me up. It's the same reason I can't say anything about Sera and the others. It's all hunches, and if he is behind them, why did he do it? How did it benefit him?"

"Sure wasn't any kind of longevity or good-looks spell," Deisphe muttered. She straightened up as she refilled her coffee cup. "Maybe he has a beautiful wife hidden away somewhere and he needs their life forces to keep her young and gorgeous. Or he's repairing horrible scars on her face and body. Or..."

Lili laughed so hard she almost snorted her coffee out her nose. "Don't tell me. There was a horror movie marathon last night."

"You'd be amazed how many of those movies were based on real life," Deisphe countered, eying her nails that suddenly looked razor-sharp before she retracted her claws. "I wouldn't mind getting my paws on Bradley Cooper. He's just so darn cute."

"Come on, you know you want dark and dangerous," she teased.

"Dark and dangerous means Shemar Moore." Deisphe mentioned one of the profilers on *Criminal Minds* in a sultry purr. "He can handcuff me anytime. I've always tried to figure out if he's one of us, but I don't get the furry vibe. What a waste." She sighed then turned pragmatic again. "What will you do about Jared?"

"Protect him any way I can."

"Dr. Mortimer's in charge here, babe. He may look all sweet and befuddled most of the time, but he's got that steely side too," she advised. "I wouldn't cross him, Lili."

"I got that feeling too," she admitted.

They both glanced at the clock.

"Off to clock in." Deisphe snatched another Danish. "For the road." She grinned. Her smile dialed down a few degrees. "You'll be careful, won't you? I hate losing good friends."

Lili nodded. "I promise." She held her hand up to further strengthen the vow.

After the Wereleopard left the office, Lili first thought of heading below to see Jared but decided to hold off, since she would be going down when Rissa arrived. She alerted Reception that she would have a visitor and to page her the moment the Guide showed up.

She remained in her office for a few moments, mentally cataloging all she knew so far, even if she still had more questions than answers.

She knew one thing. She needed to find out just what

was in that heavily warded room of Dr. Mortimer's. She'd just have to find a way to break in there without leaving any evidence of her presence.

—⁓—

Since the ER proved to be busy, thanks to an influx of Ashbury rash at one of the local magick prep schools, Lili didn't have much time to think before Rissa arrived.

It only took her a few minutes to sense that the young witch was perfect for the job.

"I'll admit I'm surprised you called me, since I know the hospital has some very excellent Guides already working here." The petite blond witch had an edge to her, thanks to her battered brown leather jacket that Lili was positive had a designer label attached to it and her leg-hugging jeans. Her high-heeled boots didn't slip once on the stone steps. Lili had already warned her of the surroundings she'd find there, but Rissa assured her she had worked in stranger places and not to worry.

"As I explained on the phone, Amy is a special case. A mundane who was somehow brought here a couple of centuries ago," she explained. "Considering how long it's been, I guess we can't even hope you can connect her with her mother."

"There's nothing stronger than a mother's love," Rissa replied. "Admittedly, crossing state and time lines isn't easy, but if her mother never forgot her, she might be in the ether, somewhere she and Amy can reconnect. Do you have any clue how it happened?"

Lili shook her head. "Amy only said a large black bird took her. She's at an age where she can't give strong answers."

"Something else you shouldn't discount—kids sometimes can be more articulate than adults. Perhaps it was a large bird." Rissa frowned as she took in their surroundings. "It's very barbaric," she said in a whisper.

"What the fuck are you doing here?" Turtifo appeared so quickly, both witches squeaked.

Lili quickly regained her composure and glared at the ogre. "We have business here." She really hated having to explain herself!

"This ain't no amusement park where you give guided tours," he growled while his gaze swarmed over Rissa, lingering on her breasts. She curled her upper lip but didn't pull her jacket over her silk tee.

Lili gave her points for guts.

"Why don't you go back to your *duties*," she suggested with a decided frostiness in her voice. "We won't be down here long."

He narrowed his already beady eyes at her. "What are you doing down here?"

"None of your concern." She brushed past him, holding her breath so she wouldn't inhale the nasty stench of his skin and clothing. She wondered when he'd last bathed, if ever. She smothered her smile when she heard the sound of an electronic shock and Turtifo's angry yelp.

"Ah, ah, ah, mustn't touch," Rissa said lightly.

He shot them both a glare fit to kill and stumbled off.

"He should be the one in a cell," Rissa muttered as she followed Lili.

"No kidding." Lili opened to the door to the room she used, and they walked inside. "Should I call Amy right away?"

"No, let me set things up." The Guide dug into the leather bag she carried and pulled out pillar candles in soft shades of blue and green. Lili didn't recognize some of the scents but just inhaling them felt comforting.

After Rissa set out the candles, she touched each wick with her fingertips, watching as they flared to life.

Lili helped her move the table and chairs so she could chalk a circle, leaving one end open for now.

"Do you think she's ready to leave?" Rissa asked her. "When a spirit has been in one place for too long, it's difficult for them to do that."

"No matter what, she's still a frightened little girl. She needs to go to a place where she'll be safer. I think she's willing to go."

"Have you talked to Amy about this?"

"I have. She's a little confused, but I know she doesn't want to be here any longer."

Rissa nodded. She examined the rings that adorned several of her fingers and turned them around.

"This will be handled differently, since I'm not Guiding her over but rather trying to bring her mother here to help her leave," she said. "I'll be honest; I haven't done this before, but I don't know why it can't happen. All we have to do is find her mother in the ether."

"I trust you," Lili said simply. She thought of something and headed for the door. "We need someone else here. I'll just be a moment."

"Dr. Carter! This isn't a party," Rissa warned.

"I need to bring in someone who also cares for Amy." She wasted no time heading for Jared's cell and unlocking the door. She found him on his mattress with Amy sitting cross-legged across from him.

Do you really think a kiss can make someone better, the way it did Sleeping Beauty? She asked Jared.

He looked past her at Lili who stood in the doorway. His dark eyes warmed.

"Absolutely."

"Amy," Lili said softly, so as not to startle the ghost. "Would you like to come with me?" She held out her hand, even though Amy wouldn't be able to touch her. She looked at Jared. "And you too."

You found a Guide? He mouthed.

She nodded.

Jared followed them out. "Did you tell the Guide about me?" he asked in a low voice.

"No, but I don't think it will be a problem."

Lili learned she was right when Rissa didn't bat at an eye at Jared's less-than-clean appearance. She merely smiled at him and at Amy, who stood close to the demon, hanging tightly to her teddy bear with one hand.

"Hello, Amy." Rissa crouched down to the little spirit's height and spoke softly to her in a voice that was soothing and musical to the ear. "My name is Rissa, and I'm a friend of Lili and Jared. I heard that you're looking for your mommy."

Yes. Amy watched her wide-eyed.

"What if I can help you find her?"

You know where my mommy is? The wraith was wide-eyed with excitement.

"Not exactly, but I think with your help I might be able to figure out where she is so you can be with her," Rissa said gently. She sat back, cross-legged. She smiled when Amy plopped down and did the same.

Lili took a nearby chair while Jared stood behind her,

his hand resting lightly on her shoulder. She watched as Rissa held out her hands and Amy placed hers in the Guide's palms. There was no sign of discomfort from the extreme cold a ghost generated when touching warm flesh, and her insubstantial flesh actually rested in Rissa's hands.

"I want you to close your eyes and picture your mother," Rissa whispered. "Think of her the way she was the last time you saw her. Then I want you to say her name."

Her name is Mommy. Will my mommy know it's me? I ask her to come get me all the time, but she doesn't.

She nodded. "She'll know."

Amy closed her eyes tightly. *Mommy, I'm lost. Can you come get me? I like Miss Lili and Mr. Jared, and they're really nice to me, but I miss you and our farm. Can I come home now?*

Lili swallowed the sob that started to travel up her throat. "No child should have to go through this," she said softly.

"She's not in pain," Jared murmured in a soothing tone.

Rissa shot them a warning look. Lili looked guilty and mimed zipping her lips closed.

Lili felt the calming warmth of Jared's presence as they watched the Guide weave her magick around Amy. Rissa's lips moved silently. Lili couldn't figure out what she said, but she could feel the power fill the room like a cascading wave.

Then she saw it. She reached up and covered Jared's hand with her own, gripping his fingers tightly as she saw an indistinct form seep into the room then slowly take shape.

The figure was silver-haired, plump, and matronly looking with eyes so sad they tore at Lili's heart. Then she saw the tiny girl across from Rissa and her sorrow disappeared.

Amy?

The tiny wraith opened her eyes and jumped to her feet. *Mama?*

Just that fast, the years fell away from the spirit and she looked as she must have the day Amy was taken. Her smile split her face as she held out her arms.

The mother looked at Rissa as she held on to her child. Tears ran down her face. *Thank you.*

"You're free, Amy," Rissa announced. "Be happy with your mother." She waved her hand, and the two disappeared.

Lili hexed up a handkerchief to catch her tears. She stood up. "Thank you," she choked.

Even Rissa's eyes shone with tears. "You're very welcome, Dr. Carter. I think their love for each other and need to be together gave my power a boost." She snuffed her candles and soon had everything back in her bag. She glanced at Jared then at Lili. "I know my way out." She held up a hand. "And don't worry about the gorillas out there. I tend to be very forgettable."

"I can't believe that." Jared smiled at her. "You're more than just a Guide, aren't you?"

She wrinkled her nose in an impish manner. "It depends on you who talk to." She closed the door after her.

"I'll miss her," Jared admitted, watching Lili move the table and chairs back in place.

"You could have helped," she told him.

"Yes, but you do it with a flick of the finger." He

took a chair and lifted an inquiring eyebrow until she conjured up two cups of coffee. "Thanks."

Instead of sitting across from him, Lili took the chair next to him. She warmed her hands with the cup as she stared into the dark contents.

"I told Dr. Mortimer that I felt you should be released," she said in a low voice.

Jared froze. "Why would you do that?"

Like him she studied her coffee cup. "Because there is no way you have any mental instability in you." She looked up when she felt the table tremble. "Jared!"

If he were a mundane, Lili would have known he was having a seizure, but this wasn't like any seizure she'd seen in mundanes or preternaturals.

Black foam rimmed his mouth, and he fell from the chair, flailing around. Lili winced at the sound of a gong ringing outside the room. She fell to her knees carefully as she wrapped a protection spell around him so he couldn't hurt himself.

And regretted the door wasn't secured when Turtifo and Coing barged in.

"What the fuck have you done now?" the former snarled, reaching down and grabbing Jared's shoulders in a rough hold while Coing took his legs.

"Don't touch him!" she ordered.

"No way Dr. M. won't find out about this," Turtifo told her as they carried Jared out. "You're in big trouble now."

"I need to treat him!" She followed them out.

"No treatment. He just needs to sleep it off." Turtifo grinned at her, revealing his blackened teeth. "And you need to get out of here."

Lili deliberately waited until she heard the clang of Jared's cell door, then waited another fifteen minutes before she left the room. She could hear the two ogres laughing heartily in their private break room.

"Probably downloading porn," she muttered, reaching Jared's cell door.

She looked through the bars and saw Jared sprawled on the mattress with her protective spell gone. His skin was gray, his eyes wild.

When she touched the lock to deactivate it, she was shocked so badly, she was thrown backward and fell on her ass.

She stared at the lock that sparked black.

Jared was not only locked in. She was locked out.

Chapter 13

"I'LL TURN THEM INTO SLIMY TOADS," LILI FUMED, pacing the small confines of her office. "Or go further and send them back as amoeba. Algae to be skimmed off a pond. Hedgehogs. No, forget that, I like hedgehogs."

"Wow, what has your witchy dander up?" Deisphe braved the hex of a tantrum and dropped gracefully into a chair. She ignored the suffocating power in the air.

"The ogres finally did it," Cleo announced from her spot on the couch. "They set a trap on Jared's door so Lili was zapped when she tried to open it. I bet Dr. Musty had something to do with it." She stretched her mouth in a wide yawn, revealing finely honed fangs.

Lili held up her hands to show her badly blistered palms.

"Oh no!" Deisphe was out of her chair immediately and grasped her hands to examine the burns. "Why didn't you heal these?" she demanded with a hint of a growl, while her eyes glittered a dark gold.

"I can't," she said tightly, closing her eyes. "Magick won't work on them."

"Stay here." She was out of the office and returned before Lili had time to blink. Deisphe gently pushed her back into her chair and set a small tray on the desk. After setting Lili's injured hands palm up on a towel, she picked up a tube and started slathering the ingredients on the scorched skin.

Lili hissed as the cream hit the raw spots.

"This will help ensure there will be no scarring or infection since, as you know, some curses can do that," the Were assured her. "Not strictly magick and meant for burns." After she carefully slathered the cream on, she wrapped the witch's hands with gauze. "No instant healing, but they should feel better in about an hour or so. We use it on injuries that magick doesn't heal. And this is for being a good girl." She unwrapped a Tootsie Pop and edged it between Lili's lips.

Lili didn't know whether to laugh or cry. She settled for doing both.

"No, don't," Deisphe purred, putting her arms around her shoulders.

"I don't care that Dr. Mortimer will fire me for disobeying his orders," she sobbed. "It's that Jared is now even more of a prisoner down there. They'll tell Dr. Mortimer what I did."

"No, they won't." There was a grim set to her mouth.

"They can't." Cleo chimed in.

Lili looked at the two cats in her office. "No, you can't kill them."

"As much as the idea appeals to me after what Turtifo and Coing did, I think there are other ways to handle them." Deisphe grinned, displaying her own impressive set of fangs. "Just leave them to me." She put her tools back on the tray. "It's quiet in the ER, so stay here and let that cream work. If things get bad, I'll give a shout." She picked up the tray and headed for the door.

"Deisphe." The nurse looked over her shoulder. "Thanks."

"Don't worry about it. I haven't had this much fun in ages." She closed the door after her.

"She's not so bad," Cleo commented. "For a leopard."

"Elitist." Lili wrinkled her nose at the bandages. She could feel a tingling along her wounded palms, indicating that a healing process was already taking place. She closed her mind, but images of Jared caught in a bad place haunted her, so she opened them again.

"Couldn't Jazz help you with that cursed lock?" Cleo asked. "Curses are her specialty."

"Yes, but there's more involved here than just me," she replied. "I refuse to believe he's now a complete prisoner down there."

"Why do you think that seizure happened?" The feline hopped off her silk pillow and moved to the top of Lili's desk.

"I don't know. I wish I did."

"Maybe a side effect of whatever Dr. Mortimer does to him in that locked room. Please don't try that lock," she advised, placing her paw on Lili's arm. "At least not until you have a way to do it without getting badly hurt. That could be even worse than what just happened."

"Why Cleo, are you worried about me?" she teased.

"Of course I am. At least *sometimes* you remember to purchase quality food for me."

"And there goes that warm and fuzzy moment." Lili laughed softly, getting up and moving to the couch. She tossed Cleo's pillow to the end and stretched out. She set her mental alarm clock to wake her in an hour and closed her eyes. Luckily, no images of Jared appeared, but she felt them on the edges of her mind as she drifted into a light sleep.

While Dr. Mortimer didn't appear to reprimand her for being with Jared, Director of Nursing Garrish did arrive in the ER with the news they were short a nurse.

"She didn't call in, and she isn't answering her phone," the dragon-shifter groused. "We will just have to adjust to it for now, because even if Calla shows up, she will discover she doesn't have a job any longer." After delivering her news, she left.

Deisphe and Lili glanced at each other.

Another one? The Were mouthed, wide-eyed.

Lili gave a bare nod of the head.

"Something odd about this," Heron commented. "I talked to Calla a few days ago, and she didn't mention she was going anywhere. In fact, she just got back from vacation a month ago."

"That's true," Vanna, another nurse, added. "She even said she spent so much money, she was hoping to take on extra shifts to pay off her Visa."

Lili jammed her now healed hands into her lab coat's pockets, feeling the reassuring protective runes surround her skin. She suddenly frowned. Why hadn't the sigils in her scrubs and lab coat protected her below? She hadn't worried about anything from the first day she was here, had felt their protections kick into gear anytime they were needed. Yet this time, they'd abandoned her.

While her first thought was to call Maggie and ask her about it, she knew better. The Hellion Guard would pull her out before she could blink, and Eurydice would ensure she couldn't return to the hospital.

"Want to go out for dinner after work?" Deisphe asked in a low voice as the group dispersed.

The idea of going home didn't appeal to her. She'd

only spend the hours worrying about Jared and what could be happening to him. "That sounds good to me. Anything is fine. I'll meet you out in the parking lot."

She nodded and walked off.

Lili looked around, realized there was nothing urgent going on and decided to beard the dragon in her den.

Director of Nursing Garrish was seated at her desk with a cup of tea in one hand and a scone in the other. She wasn't pleased to have any interruptions to her teatime.

"Will you have some tea, Dr. Carter?" she asked politely.

"Yes, thank you." *What is it with tea? Don't they know it's coffee that keeps all of us going?* She took a seat and accepted a delicate teacup that was at odds with the stocky nurse, who was known to actually breathe fire.

"So what brings you to the dragon's den?" Her smile wasn't pleasant, but it held a hint of wryness.

Never underestimate a dragon-shifter. "I came here about Calla." She already knew the head nurse preferred plain speaking, and that was something Lili was very good at doing. "I don't feel she left of her own accord."

"Oh? I didn't realize you were psychic, Dr. Carter." She sipped her tea, then looked at Lili over the rim of her cup. "Have you had a vision where the little gnome went? Perhaps you aren't aware of this, but gnomes in the healthcare field aren't very plentiful. They tend to prefer working in the open air to being stuck in an antiseptic room." Her dark eyes bored into Lili. "Calla was a competent nurse, but I know I can do better."

"Except she left like the others who suddenly dropped out of sight," Lili countered. "No advance warning. Just silence. Don't you find this the least bit unsettling, since she's not the first one to do this?" She drank the tea, barely managing not to wince at the hot liquid scalding her tongue. No surprise; the tea was very strong. She took a bite of her scone, promptly remembering she hated currants but had no way to cough them into a napkin.

"What is your interest in this?"

"One of the missing nurses is a friend of mine," Lili said candidly. "Sera came here because I suggested it. I worked with her, and I know how trustworthy she is. She wouldn't just walk away like that unless there was a very good reason." Her stomach tightened at the idea of what that reason could be.

Nurse Garrish seemed to look off into the distance. Lili sensed a hint of sulfur in the air and managed to keep her seat instead of bolting for the door the way she wanted to.

"You're a very levelheaded witch," the shifter said. "I admire your dedication to your friend, but let's be frank here, Doctor. What do you expect from me? I have no reason to think that Sera, Calla, or anyone else left here other than of their own accord. If you can prove differently, I will help you any way I can, but without proof…" She held up her hands to indicate she couldn't otherwise.

Lili nodded numbly. "I understand." She finished the tea and managed to eat the rest of the scone even though it lay like a stone in her stomach. The day hadn't been a good one, and she was feeling it more by the second.

"Now I have a question for you," Nurse Garrish said when it appeared Lili was ready to leave. "Why are you telling me all of this and not relating your fears to Dr. Mortimer? After all, you're a doctor." Her thin lips stretched in a narrow smile. "Most doctors would seek him before coming to me. Even more so, since Dr. Mortimer is kindhearted and I am... not."

Lili was never as glad as she was then that she could think fast on her feet. "Nurses are your area, not Dr. Mortimer's. I've noticed nurses and doctors leaving without notice. It happens in all hospitals, but not this many in what appears to be a short period of time. I also know you care about your nurses. You don't allow them to be browbeaten by us doctors, and if anyone can help me figure this out, it's you."

Nurse Garrish poured herself a cup of tea and leaned across the desk to refill Lili's cup.

"I gather that was one of the reasons you returned to Crying Souls." She picked up the plate, but Lili refused another scone.

"Yes." She still felt cautious, but she felt it was too late to back away now. Plus, she had an idea that the shifter and Dr. Mortimer weren't bosom buddies. And if they were, well, *eeuwww*!

The shifter turned to her computer and tapped a few keys. "You were listed as one of Sera's references," she said finally. "You even wrote a letter extolling her skills as a more-than-proficient nurse." Granite-colored eyes turned toward her. "There is nothing in the records to say why Sera or any of the others left. No reports of harassment or any type of wrongdoing. I'll be honest with you—I doubt Dr. Mortimer knows, or cares, about this matter. So what do you expect me to do, Dr. Carter?"

Lili opened her mouth then closed it again. "I—I don't know," she admitted reluctantly. "I just refuse to believe Sera is…"

"Dead." She said the word Lili couldn't allow to slip past her lips. "But you feel Sera's disappearance is linked to the hospital."

She nodded. "And now Calla's gone the same way as the others."

"I don't know what I can do for you, but I will take another look at the records of those who left the hospital without notice."

Lili finished her tea and stood up. She knew a dismissal when she heard it, and that it was wise to exit right away. Plus, she had received a lot more than she expected. Nurse Garrish wasn't known for any type of helpful behavior.

"Thank you." She nodded her head as she left the office.

"The only reason I'm willing to do this is because you show respect toward my nurses and you are an excellent healer," Arimentha Garrish said at her back. "Otherwise, I would have escorted you out of my office before you uttered one word."

Lili nodded again. She decided it would be even money if there were ever a smackdown between Eurydice and Nurse Garrish. She silently ordered her shaking knees to remain in the locked upright position and managed to leave in one piece.

It wasn't until she was back in the safe confines of her office that she breathed a sigh of relief.

"Always nice to have the dragons on your side," she said to herself.

―⁘―

"We can help too," Deisphe told Lili over a dinner of Thai food after she described her visit to Nurse Garrish's office. She forked up lime chicken stir-fry. "You were nuts to think you could do all this yourself."

"Asmeth has done what he can," she defended herself. "He picks up the gossip the way we'd pick up makeup."

"But he doesn't have all the inside dirt we nurses and doctors do," the Were reminded her. She waved her fork at her in a mock-threatening manner. "Didn't you trust me?" There was a hint of hurt in her voice.

"I did, but I'm so used to doing things for myself," Lili explained. She felt exhausted, upset, and actually calmer. Deisphe was right. She didn't need to try to do this all herself. She knew she had Maggie and others who'd be here in a heartbeat, but Lili felt guilty that she was the one who had sent Sera to what could have been her destruction. She toyed with her rice, picking it up a grain at a time.

"Stop playing with your food and eat," Deisphe ordered with a growl. "Otherwise, no luscious coconut cake for you, and the one here is to die for."

Lili smiled and returned to her plate of garlic chicken with mushrooms and pineapple fried rice. The food was spicy and actually made her feel better. Especially when the Were kept on tempting her with the promise of dessert.

As promised, the two-layer cake was moist with toasted coconut covering the fluffy frosting. The perfect end to the meal.

Refusing to allow Lili to sink back into worrying, Deisphe dragged her to a few shops where they indulged in some necessary retail therapy.

By the time they left the last shop, Lili felt her credit

cards whimpering, and her arms were weighted down with bags.

"It sucks we have to wear scrubs at work," the Were groused. "Although the alternative isn't all that great, either. So much nasty stuff ends up on my clothes every shift. I don't think I've found one reliable cleaning spell. The last one burned holes."

"You have to be so specific, it's not funny," Lili agreed, feeling more relaxed than she had in a while. She didn't realize that sharing her worries could ease her mind so much. She hugged Deisphe as they stopped by Lili's SUV. "Thank you," she whispered, meaning much more than just the evening out.

"Hey, that's what friends are for." She hugged her back. "See ya tomorrow. You can always wear the sexy undies you bought," she teased.

Lili laughed. "If I'm lucky, Cleo hasn't ordered up more catnip wine and trashed the house." She climbed in and fired up the engine and heater.

Except now she was alone with her thoughts and worries about Jared.

What if he couldn't call on the shadows any longer? Trapped in that cell until... until what? Until he was nothing more than an empty husk who had no conception of his surroundings?

She parked her car in the garage and pulled her purchases out of the back.

Sexy lingerie she didn't need, gorgeous shoes, and clothing designed to have a guy think wild things.

"And here there's no guy around," she muttered, walking into the house. And froze the moment she entered the kitchen.

No empty bottles of catnip wine littering the floor. No cat yowling to Celine Dion.

"That's the wrong page," she could hear Cleo in the family room.

Lili dropped her bags and ran. Then skidded to a stop when she saw the duo seated on her couch.

"Wha—?" She couldn't believe her eyes. And couldn't control the smile that stretched her face.

Jared looked up from his spot on her couch. Her laptop was on her coffee table, and a glass of wine sat nearby. Cleo was perched next to him, staring intently at the monitor.

"More LOLCats," she ordered, pointing her paw at the screen.

He looked up at Lili and smiled. "Hi. Did you have a nice night out? Do you think I should set up a Facebook page?"

Chapter 14

"HOW?" LILI COULDN'T WRAP HER MIND AROUND THE idea that Jared was here.

"The usual way." He stood up, ignoring Cleo's growls of protest at being pushed to one side. He walked over and took his witch into his arms. He crushed her against him, picking her up off her feet. "Sweetheart, even the depths of Hades wouldn't keep me away from you." He buried his face against her hair, inhaling the rich scent of her perfume mixed with her skin.

"They put a lock on your door. I couldn't get in there," she muttered against his shirt front. "It was so heavily warded that I couldn't even talk to you. And now they'll tell Dr. Mortimer. For all I know, he'll fire me. Not that I care, but I can't leave you down there. We have to find a way."

"After you learn what happened to your friend." He kept his arms around her and walked them both toward her bedroom. "How come you're late?" He punctuated each word with a kiss.

"Deisphe and I went out to dinner, then did some shopping." She kissed him back, needing all the contact she could get.

"Anything good?" He finished walking when the back of her knees hit the edge of the bed.

"Some lingerie that will cross your eyes, shoes that make my legs look like a million bucks, clothes, and makeup to finish my gorgeous self." She couldn't stop smiling.

Jared combed his fingers through the dark curls. "You're already gorgeous." His breath hitched in his chest as he stared down at her upturned face. He had no clue how he became so lucky as to find such a woman who had so much warmth in her heart that she could see beyond his exterior to what he was inside. And want him despite his crimes.

"I can't get to the next page!" Cleo yelled from the family room. "Help! Help! Help!" Her yowl raised in pitch.

"I'll take care of that." Without taking her eyes off Jared's face, Lili flicked her fingers at the door that slammed shut and locked with an audible click.

"Hey! Not fair!"

"I like your style, witch." Jared leaned over so far that Lili landed on the bed with him following. "I can't wait," he rumbled, tearing at her clothes, breaking open the zipper, sending buttons flying. Lili didn't seem to care, since she was busy dissolving his clothes with her magick. "I want you." He breathed into her ear as he ran his palm down her belly, into her center, to find her already wet and receptive. "Need you." He angled his hips and thrust forward, groaning at the moist heat that welcomed him even as she curled her legs around his hips, tilting her hips upward for more intense friction. As she did, she reached down and trailed her nails over his cock as he slammed into her.

Jared uttered curses in his language before covering Lili's mouth with his, his tongue mimicking what his body was doing. He could smell her arousal like a fragrant perfume, feel the silk of her skin as he slid over her, and her taste was an addiction he would never get over. Each time he was with her just fed his craving for more.

Lili had healed his spirit.

He dipped his head and gathered her nipple into his mouth, rolling the hard nub with his tongue and pulling gently. The faint salty taste of her skin fed his hunger.

"Jared." She moaned his name, frantically touching him everywhere she could.

He felt her power flow over him like a series of electric shocks that only spurred him on. His sac tightened to the point of pain, and he increased the tempo, pulling her up against him and before he knew it, he spilled himself in her while his breath seemed to leave his body.

It took all of his control not to collapse on top of her. Instead he managed to roll to one side, bringing her with him. Lili purred as she looped a leg over his hips and snuggled up against him. She rested her cheek against his chest and sketched idle words on his skin. He grinned and grabbed her hand.

"Is that position even legal in this state?" he teased.

"I won't tell if you won't." She propped herself up on her elbows and looked into his face. "I'm so glad you're here," she confessed, drawing a line across his jaw.

"I am too." He sat up, pulling her with him until her back was settled against his chest. "The word love isn't in our language," he said slowly, trailing his fingertips down her arm and back up. "We have no concept of the emotion or what it means. Relationships are nothing more than sex for recreation or to procreate, nothing more. There's no such thing as hugging or being together the way we are now." He kissed her temple as he felt her body stiffen a bit. "But with you, I want that and more. I want it all." He took a deep breath. "I love you, Lili. I love you so much that I want to give you the world, except I have nothing to give you."

"No!" She rolled over, bracing herself on his chest. "What I mean is, you have a lot to give. You have yourself. I love you so much, Jared, and I'm going to get you out of there," she vowed with a ferocity he didn't doubt. "And then I'm turning Turtifo and Coing into slimy toads."

But he also knew that while her intentions were true, Dr. Mortimer wasn't going to release him all that easily. He had no idea whether his mother was still among the living or if she'd moved onto the plane of death. He was positive his clan could care less about him. He'd have no home to return to, but that was all right. The idea of making a home with Lili was appealing. He knew there had to be something he could do. It wouldn't matter, as long as he was free and with Lili.

For now, it was nothing more than a dream, but who knew? Maybe this dream could come true.

Content with Lili in his arms, Jared closed his eyes and felt sleep take over.

———

She ran down the twisting narrow hall, almost tripping on her nightgown. The thin fabric offered little protection against the chilly air and the stone walls that scraped her bare arms. Sobs of fear escaped her throat as she stumbled, feeling the rough surface of the floor abrade her feet.

"This is wrong!" she cried, falling against the wall

again. She choked against the reek of dark magick that permeated the air. She pushed away from the damp stones and made her way toward her destination, even though her mind couldn't decide what it was. She only knew she had to keep on going.

He needs me. Only I can save him. *The words raced through her mind.*

The farther she walked down the hall, the stronger the magick grew, until she had to fight even to lift one foot in front of the other. She used her fingers to swipe the tears from her cheeks and almost screamed to find the tips red. Her tears were blood-tinged!

She had to keep going, no matter what. Find him. Save him. Her stomach started to cramp, causing her to double over, but she refused to turn around. She was a healer. She refused to leave anyone in pain.

She skidded to a stop when the door she sought suddenly appeared in front of her, its surface shining dark purple with a strong shadowy power that left a metallic taste in her mouth.

While she was reluctant even to touch the door's surface, the screams from inside the room compelled her to pull it open.

The scent of blood was strong, and more magick filled the air. But what caught her attention was the male chained to the far wall. He was naked with blood streaking his skin. His head hung down, and his chest heaved in and out as he struggled to breathe. A counter along one wall was covered with burners and various beakers bubbling away.

"No!" She started to move forward, but something kept her in place.

"Ah, my dear, I see you've arrived." The sorcerer who faced her wore a stained lab coat and looked like a mad scientist straight out of an old black-and-white movie.

Wait a minute.

She looked at her surroundings and realized it was just that. There was no color in the room, only shades of black, gray, and dirty white.

"Let him go!" she ordered.

Her tormentor smiled at her as if she was nothing more than a child. "I can't do that. Just as you have no power here." His eyes lingered on her shoulder but not in a lascivious way.

She looked down, stunned to see a raised mark on her skin. The brand was a familiar one. The same as on the demon manacled to the wall. One that declared to the world she was insane and was to be avoided at all cost.

"This is wrong," she insisted.

"No, my dear, it's not." The sorcerer took her by the arm and led her over to a long table. "I am so pleased you have come to me, so I did not have to have someone bring you." He pulled out a pocket watch and studied the time before tucking it back in his pocket. With a sudden show of strength, he pushed her onto the table and quickly attached shackles to her wrists. She cried out and tried to pull away, but it was already too late.

"The blood of a demon is very strong, filled with so much power," the sorcerer told her in a conversational tone. "Ah, but the blood of a witch mixed with a demon." He kissed his fingertips as if he just complimented a chef for a gourmet meal. "I tried before to add that very special touch, but sadly, her blood wasn't strong enough. Now you, you have the power I require." He headed for

*the counter and rummaged among the instruments set
on a tray.*

*Her breath caught in her throat as she realized his
intent. Then she looked at her lover, saw the sorrow in
his eyes and the white lines of pain tightening his mouth.
She rattled her chains to no avail.*

*I love you. She mouthed the words, refusing to allow
their tormenter to hear her admission.*

*His lips lifted in the briefest of smiles that disap-
peared as the sorcerer approached him with a large
vial containing charcoal powder and an equally large
needle that he promptly plunged into the demon's chest.
He threw back his head, screaming with pain that she
couldn't help but echo.*

"Stop it! You're killing him!"

*"It's all for the greater good, my dear." He filled the
syringe then expelled the contents into the vial.*

*She stared with horror at the blood that bubbled the
moment it dripped onto the fine particles. As the mad
scientist turned toward her, she knew that not only
would her blood be added to the mixture but that both
of them would die as a result.*

*She looked past the sorcerer's shoulder at her lover
whose respiration was barely visible. His skin was a
pasty gray, and his eyes were dull with the realization
their future was very short-lived. Yet he managed to
convey how he felt for her, that they wouldn't be parted
in death.*

*She was so caught up in gazing at him she didn't feel
the needle sliding into her vein or the essence of her life
trickling out. The haze that covered her eyes deepened
as she felt her flesh grow weak.*

"Now I shall have it all," the sorcerer chortled, obviously pleased with himself. "More power than anyone. The two of you have given me exactly what I need! The two are now one." He stared at the vial's contents with a maniacal raptness.

She wanted to lift her arms and twist her chains around his neck, taking his life just as he took hers, but her strength was gone, just as her lover's life force was diminishing. It wouldn't be long before they both were dead.

The spell was blood. Blood was the spell.

"No! Jared!"

"Lili. It's all right. Wake up."

"We're dying!" she screamed, flailing her arms around, striking hard flesh.

The arms around her were warm and familiar along with the scent of a protective male. She still refused to open her eyes to her black-and-white surroundings, but the hand stroking her face encouraged her to.

She finally did, noticing the bedside lamp glowed with a warm light and the walls were the familiar coral with soft turquoise accents. Cleo was perched on the end of the bed, her back arched and claws dug deeply into her comforter.

"I warned you about doing that," she whispered between dry lips. Her body shook, and her teeth chattered as if she suffered from hypothermia. Lili didn't notice the blanket that Jared draped around her as he kept her close to his body to share his personal heat. "How did you get in here?"

"You screamed. I zapped the lock open," the cat told her, looking as freaked as Lili felt.

"You had a nightmare," Jared said, kissing her temple.

She shook her head. "No, it was something much worse. My dream showed what could happen to us if we aren't careful. It was all about a blood spell. Two are one, and we'll die." She glanced down at her chest, fearing she'd find the brand on her shoulder, but it was mercifully bare. She also couldn't find any needle marks on her arm. Just that her skin was slick with sweat and the stink of her fear tainted the air.

Jared brushed the sweaty strands of hair away from her face and kept on stroking her as if she was a frightened small animal. "It's only a nightmare, love," he crooned.

"Dreams show what can happen."

"That's your Greek blood talking."

Lili wondered if she'd ever become warm. "It's a warning," she insisted. "The room I haven't been able to get into. The one at the end of the hallway."

Jared's caresses stilled. "What did you see?" Tension colored his voice.

"Counters with burners, beakers, and vials. Iron shackles set in the wall, a long table with more manacles." She shivered, hating to even remember the place of nightmares. "You were imprisoned against the wall, and he chained me to the table." She touched her shoulder. "I was branded like you."

He tightened his hold on her. "Who chained you, Lili?"

But no matter how hard she concentrated, she could only see a sharp image of the body. The face was nothing more than a haze in her memory.

"I don't know." She huddled against him, allowing him to pull her onto his lap and wrap the sheet and blankets around them. He kept kissing her temple and rubbing his hands up and down her arms.

"How about some tea?" he asked.

Lili shook her head, grabbing hold of his arms. "Don't leave me." Her eyes turned wild with fear.

"Okay, I won't."

Cleo made her way up the bed and stretched out along Lili's hip. She purred loudly, the rough sound strangely soothing.

"I don't want to go back to sleep."

"We don't need to," Jared said softly while he shot the cat a thank-you smile. "We'll just sit here and cuddle."

Lili looked toward the window. Since there weren't any neighbor's windows on that side, she could leave the blinds open. She stared at the pink and lilac edges of dawn touching the sky. "But you'll be gone soon." *And I'll be alone with my nightmare as a horrific memory.*

"You know I'll stay as long as I can," he vowed, resting his chin on top of her head while his hands stroked aimless patterns down her arms, leaving a trail of heat wherever they went.

"It's in the blood," she murmured. "He said something about both of our bloods being what he really needed. It doesn't make sense, since demon blood isn't compatible with anyone else's. It's a well-known medical fact. It's even more dangerous than mixing two different blood types. It's like pouring acid on a nuclear reactor." She closed her eyes and rested her cheek against his chest. She could finally feel her respiration slowing, and while she wasn't exactly feeling calm, she did feel a bit more settled. She slid her arms around his waist, as if she could keep him with her, but she felt the pull on his spirit, as if a thick cord had been wrapped about his body and was tugging at him. She gripped him tighter, but she knew even her magick couldn't keep him with her.

"If you were a djinn, I'd bind you to me," she whispered, brushing her lips across his collarbone that was already feeling less substantial to the touch.

"I won't wear a silk turban or those puffy pants," he warned her, but she also heard the hint of pain in his voice.

Lili knew the more Jared resisted, the more painful his departure would be. She slowly edged away from him and sat up, looking at him with dark eyes warm with love that he returned with a smile and a gaze. He grazed her cheek with the back of his fingers that started to turn to mist.

"I love you," he said just before he disappeared.

"I love you too," Lili said to the empty spot where he'd been, then burst into tears.

"Hey, at least you know where he is," Cleo soothed, crawling up into her lap and purring noisily.

That made Lili cry even more. Cleo was well-known for preferring to receive comfort than give it.

"He'll die, and there's nothing I can do about it." She picked up a corner of her sheet and dabbed at her eyes, then blew her nose.

"That's not the witch I'm used to," Cleo said. "What all was said about blood? Not just your chatter about mixing yours and Jared's blood. What else was said?" She waved a paw in the air. "Just because I have fur doesn't mean I don't have a brain, you know. And what you had wasn't just a nightmare, either. You were seeing what could happen if you don't stop it in time. And something tells me it has to do with stale old Dr. Mortimer. He's the one who 'treats,'" she rolled her expressive eyes, "Jared, and he talked to you about blood spells, and then there are those nasty scrolls."

Unwilling to wait for her coffeemaker to perform its own magick, Lili hexed up a large mug of her favorite mocha latte and settled back against her pillows, sipping the hot liquid. The scent of Jared's skin blended with hers and the memory of sex offered her a form of solace.

"I have to do something about this," she said, pulling her knees up while managing to pull the covers up to her chin. Even her coffee and the covers didn't seem to provide enough warmth to combat the early morning-chilled air.

"Just remember, you have backup now. You can't do it alone," Cleo warned her, settling down beside her. "There's no way, after all these years, that I want to break in a new witch."

"I'm so glad you're worried about my well-being." She didn't ask the cat how she knew she'd confided in Deisphe. Cleo tended to know everything. She finished her latte and waved the mug back to the kitchen.

"Do you think it's all that easy to find the right witch to hang out with? At least you're not one of those New Age witches who wear tie-dyed clothing, are drenched in patchouli, and sing all the time. Please, the sixties are over, so let's move on, thank you very much." The fluffy feline stretched out alongside Lili, then rolled over onto her back. "It's bad enough that people do that 'ooh, you're a witch's familiar' when, excuse me, it's not even close. I'm nobody's bitch."

Lili couldn't help smiling as Cleo chattered away. It didn't take a psychic to know her cat was talking to cheer her up. She obliged her furry buddy by flicking her fingers, sending colorful feathers floating in the air. Cleo gurgled happily and batted away at the bits of fluff that drifted around her.

Between the feathers and Cleo's purring, Lili eventually drifted back to sleep and dreamed that Jared held her in his arms.

Chapter 15

JARED LEFT PARADISE FOR THE UNDERWORLD.

He'd barely returned to his cell when Turtifo showed up to drag him off to the treatment room. Not that he was totally aware of what happened there. The ogre dragged him to his feet, slapped a charm on his chest, and it was lights out. When he woke up again, his body was covered with blood and agony racked his body. He felt so weak he doubted he could even lift his little finger. The impulse to roll over and throw up the acid in his system was strong, but he couldn't even do that.

His power was very low after his night with Lili and he usually managed a day or so to get his strength back before he was hauled off for any kind of treatment. He wasn't as lucky this time around. He might not have known what happened, but he had the feeling there was a chance he could have died. He wasn't about to admit to that possibility, since he had Lili to think about and protect in his own limited way.

Now he was sprawled on the ragged mattress, and his pain was drowning out the laughter in the hallway.

"Think he'll last much longer? He was a mess when we dragged him outta there." Coing said. The scent of his cigarette drifted through the bars in the door. "He's always been a strong sonofabitch, but he sure went down fast this time."

Jared wasn't sure what they smoked, but whatever

it was, it smelled like ancient shit. For now, he was too absorbed in blocking out the pain and wishing he could instantly heal the cuts along his arms and legs.

"He better. He's the only thing that keeps us going too. The boss promised we'd always be along for the ride." The stench from Turtifo's unwashed body joined the smell of the cigarettes. "He gives off a lot more power than the others have combined."

"What do you think he does when he uses that portal?"

"No idea, and I don't care. He told us not to think about it, and it's a lot safer not to. Otherwise, we could end up like the others."

Jared frowned but discovered even that hurt. *The others? Could they be talking about Lili's friend and the other missing nurses?* He saw a hint of shadow at the bars and quickly closed his eyes, keeping his breathing even as if he was still unconscious. For some reason, they were talkative, and he needed to listen in, so he could tell Lili what he learned.

"He still out?" Coing asked.

"Yeah, and not waking up any time soon." Turtifo's laughter rumbled. "His last 'treatment' took a lot out of him."

"Too bad we don't have that witch down here." Coing's laughter was lewd. "I bet she'd have a lot to give." His cohort joined him in ideas of what they could do with Lili.

"Fuck it; she's got major protection going on. You see the sigils in her lab coat and scrubs? Somebody's made sure nothing can hurt her," Turtifo snarled. "Wonder who she screwed to get them? I wouldn't mind bending her over a table." He went on to fantasize what it would be like if he had her.

Jared's temper overtook the pain racking his body. He clenched his hands at his sides, imagining popping his captors' heads like melons. After that, it was easy to visualize tearing them apart like a couple of wishbones, but eventually his pain receptors went on overload, and it was lights out all the way around.

~~~

Lili wasn't looking forward to her shift that night. She would be working the ER and not allowed below, although she'd try to sneak in if she could. She wanted to make sure Jared was all right. She'd had a bad feeling all day that something was wrong, but she didn't have any way of finding out.

She sent a wallmail to Maggie, asking for advice while making sure not to mention everything. She didn't want her friend going to Eurydice, who would ensure Lili was out of the hospital ASAP.

Then she did the next best thing by going to Inderman.

"My darling Lili!" Asmeth held out his arms and gathered her in. His smile turned a bit dim as he leaned back and studied her. "You are upset. What is wrong, and how may I help you?"

Lili opened her mouth and then did the unthinkable. She broke into tears, the kind of heartrending sobs that couldn't stop easily.

"No, no." He hustled her through his shop and into the rear, where he sat her down and rapped out sharp orders for tea. "Do not cry," he crooned, bringing forward a handkerchief and pushing it into her hands. "Tell me what troubles you. What I can do. It is Jared, is it not? Is he all right? Well, as all right as he can be in that place?"

Lili gulped, trying to organize her thoughts into a semblance of order. She took a deep breath.

"You can't pass on what I tell you," she whispered, as if afraid of being overheard. "If the wrong people were to find out—well, it would be very bad." She started shaking so hard her teeth chattered.

Asmeth poured the tea and pushed the cup into her hands, making sure her palms enfolded the porcelain object for warmth. He added a lacy cashmere wrap around her shoulders and carefully tucked it around her.

She managed a weak smile and leaned over, pressing her lips against his cheek. "You take such good care of me."

"You are the daughter I couldn't have." He beamed. "And you must tell me what troubles you."

After that, the words tumbled out. She spoke of her further suspicions about Dr. Mortimer, her talks with the wizard, his insistence that Jared could never be discharged, and how, beyond losing her job, she could be banned from the asylum altogether.

"I can't abandon Jared there," she declared. "But I have no way to get the brand off him, since it's demon-bound. His time out of there is limited, and being there drains his power. There's no way I can get him far enough away without him being pulled back there."

Asmeth nodded. "I have conducted some discreet research on shadow demons, along with Jared's history." He held up his hand. "No one knows what I was doing, because I kept it as a broad subject." He inclined a hand, gesturing to scrolls stacked neatly on a delicate teak table. "Did you know that Jared's insanity from the blood ingestion wouldn't be eternal? Like any disease, it can fade away, and from what I have discovered, it must have done so years ago. If there is any damage to him mentally, it is because someone else has caused it."

"Dr. Mortimer," she said to herself.

He nodded. "I have looked into records you would not have access to."

Lili understood he meant anything to do with wizards.

"The Physics Council's database has him listed as a well-qualified doctor and highly revered in his field," she said.

Asmeth poured more tea into her cup as the delicate hint of jasmine wafted through the air.

"As it is said among the wizards," he agreed, flicking an etched gold hookah and picking up the pipe. "But there are things missing there." He raised an eyebrow as he smoked.

"And no way to know what they are," she sighed.

"Not so much words about him but periods of time," Asmeth pointed out. "As in missing."

Lili shook her head, feeling even more confused. "Time? I'm sorry, I don't understand."

He tapped his pudgy bejeweled fingers together. "There have been times when Hieronymus Mortimer seemed to drop out of sight. He has always worked in hospital administration or research and treatment for the mentally unbalanced. But it appears there are times when he isn't visible." He frowned as if trying out the explanation inside his head.

"Do you mean he was just *gone*? As in *poof*?" She held up her hands, magick dancing on her fingertips.

"Yes, that is it." He looked relieved. "Hieronymus

would not be in touch with any his colleagues. He couldn't be found at any of his private establishments."

"As in a wizards' club?" she asked.

He nodded. "Did you honestly think the British started that tradition? There are many private clubs available for us, depending on our interests."

"Of course." Lili couldn't help but smile. She hadn't realized at first that the tea Asmeth served her was meant to relax her. Now she felt more in control. She should have known what he had done, since he taught her the technique years ago, and she used it with troublesome patients.

"Most of us might say something if we decide to visit another plane for a few centuries." He spoke of it as if he merely meant a weekend away. "Hieronymus never discussed his travels. All of a sudden, he would be gone." He looked at Lili. "You feel something is wrong, Lilianna. Please tell me."

Chapter 16

LILI FELT A CHILL SETTLING IN HER BONES. SHE RAISED her hands in defeat.

"I don't know," she whispered. "I feel there's something wrong, and I don't know how to fix it. Jared's in danger, Asmeth, and I can't help him."

"And what of you?" His kind face warmed in a gentle smile. "Do you not worry for yourself? You obviously feel Dr. Mortimer has done something that is considered prohibited. If he has, and you feel at risk, then he could do something to you."

She paused at his question. The memory of her dream still haunted her. What if it wasn't just a dream but a premonition? She licked her dry lips and took another sip of tea, allowing the hot liquid to calm her nerves.

"I had a dream," she said slowly, looking down at her hands, which lay in her lap, moving restlessly.

He leaned over and touched her hand, silently urging her to continue.

Lili spoke in fits and starts. Asmeth only offered her silent comfort, not saying a word to urge her to continue. He allowed her to go at her own pace. By the time she finished, she felt like a piece of overcooked spaghetti. It wasn't until Asmeth handed her a handkerchief that she realized she'd been crying.

"What did Jared say about this? He was with you, wasn't he?"

She nodded, beyond embarrassment that the wizard had figured out her love life. It was no wonder, since her connection with Jared was so strong.

"I have to get him out of there, and I don't know how. I'm afraid," she gulped. "I'm afraid he'll die there. Or disappear the way Sera and the others did." She stared down at her hands, seeing sparks of dark red fly off her fingers. She took several deep breaths to compose her magick.

Asmeth stood up and retreated to a corner of the large room. He opened a carved box, rummaged inside, and returned holding something. He took one of her hands, opened it, and carefully placed a piece of rose quartz in the palm, then closed her hand over the stone.

Lili smiled as she felt the crystal warm from her skin and offer its calming properties.

"You have no proof, do you?" he asked softly.

She shook her head. "Nothing to take to anyone in charge. He's an icon in the medical field. Dr. Mortimer's medical practices are widely known and respected. Who will believe me if I say he's performing dark magick?" She heard her voice take on a high pitch and reminded herself she had to remain in control.

"Have you spoken to Eurydice?"

Another shake of the head. "Again, no evidence. I've sent her a few wallmails, reporting that it's as if Sera and the other nurses disappeared into thin air."

"What of their families or loved ones? No one was worried about them?"

Lili opened her mouth, then closed it again. "Families," she said softly. She swung around, keeping the rose quartz in one hand while gripping his hands with the other. She paused for a second, forcing her breathing to slow down. "Sera had no family. She and her last boyfriend broke up more than a year ago. I think it was another reason why she wanted to leave Chicago." Her mind started to whirl with possibilities. "Could that be one of the reasons why she's gone? There would be no one looking for her. What if it's the same with the others?" Her hold on his hands tightened until his skin turned pale from the pressure. She shot him a look of apology as she realized what she'd done and released his hands. "I need to find out about them, discover if they're also without any family. But I would think they'd have friends who'd matter."

"And perhaps not." He urged her to finish her tea.

"I need to find out," she decided. "I think Deisphe is on duty tonight. Maybe she knows. If she knows nothing, someone else there might. It seems everyone who vanished originally worked in the ER."

"You must be careful," Asmeth cautioned her. "Hieronymus has been around a very long time and gathered much power over the centuries. If he is involved in any wrongdoing, he will not allow you to interfere."

Lili's head bobbed up and down. "I'm glad I told you of my suspicions. That way, if something…" She didn't want to voice the words. "If something goes wrong, someone else will know."

"My dear, you have me and Eurydice, who will tear all the planes apart to find our favorite witch. You are not to worry." He pushed the quartz back at her when she tried to return it. "Keep it with you. And wait." He revisited the wooden chest and came back with another stone, this one red jasper. "Strong protection. You keep it with you at all times. Wear your charmed clothing at the hospital when you are on duty, but you also remain vigilant." He squeezed her hands tightly. "I do not wish to look for a new doctor," he said lightly.

She could feel the power emanating from the stone and knew the wizard had added more magick to the gem.

"Now I shall give you some pleasant news," he said lightly. "Cassie has enrolled in college and Kevin is under the tutelage of a good friend. Both are thriving in their new home and new lives. I crafted protection runes for them both, so they cannot be found by either Kevin's sire or anyone else who means them harm."

Lili smiled, feeling better at hearing his words. "I'm glad to hear that. How did you manage to talk her into attending college?"

"I merely paid the fees and told her she must make use of the opportunity. I can be very persuasive when I'm of a mind to," he assured her with his typical warmth. He touched her chin with two fingers and tipped it up. "Do you love Jared?"

She blinked rapidly to keep her tears back. "Yes."

Asmeth's beard quivered with his broad smile. "I thought so. You two are beautiful together."

"But even if I can find a way to free him from the hospital, the demons will want him back."

He shook his head. "Not once it's proven he hasn't been ill in a long time. I am certain I can help you convince his mother and the Demon Council that Jared was never as deranged as they thought he was. I feel changes in the air, my Lilianna. Good changes for you." He patted her hand. "Everything will turn out all right."

His light kiss on her forehead prickled from his beard but also felt like another charm. For all she knew, it was.

Lili left Asmeth's quarters lighter in heart and calmer. She only hoped she could retain the feeling when she walked into the hospital that night.

—◦◦◦—

"And the mood is gone," Lili muttered, staring at her first patient of the night.

"Icky," he/she moaned, rolling back and forth on the gurney.

"OMG." Deisphe made a *this is totally gross* expression as she skidded into the curtained area.

"Icky," the milky-colored, gelatinous mass of a patient repeated mournfully.

"Where do you feel icky?" Lili asked.

"Tummy. Too many castigats," he confessed, holding what might have been his stomach as he moaned and groaned. Deisphe made a gagging sound. "You actually ate those? They're disgusting!" She drew a picture in the air that Lili picked up on right away.

Lili knew that castigats were a delicacy among some creatures. They were hot pink squirming maggots that squirted a thick fluid. And this Fooz had imbibed enough acid-flavored worms to put him/her in serious stomach distress.

He/she started caterwauling.

"Geranium tea," she prescribed. "It should soothe his stomach."

Lili's patient held out a globby hand. "Make icky go away?" he whined.

"The nurse will bring some tea you need to drink.

And she'll bring a couple more packets of tea you need to drink tonight. Stay away from castigats."

The Fooz nodded. "Good doctor."

She smiled and left him/her to Deisphe.

"We rotate on who treats the Foozes that come in," Dr. Heron told her with a mischievous grin. "It was your lucky day."

"If a Bloater shows up today, I'm not here," she told him. She'd barely started her shift, and she was already desperate for every doctor's lifeblood, also known as coffee.

Her fingers itched to go below and check on Jared. She thought of even using Panabell as an excuse for being there. Not that she cared to make any type of justification to Turtifo and Coing. She knew she'd have to be careful, since they wouldn't mind snitching to Dr. Mortimer.

"Deisphe." She snagged the Were when she moved past her. "Do you know if Dr. Mortimer is on duty tonight?"

She thought for a moment. "I don't think so. He's always more in and out or just down in the dungeon where nobody knows what he does. He never shows up on the staff board. It was never magicked, so your name doesn't automatically appear when you're on the premises. Do you want me to find a way to get the ogres out of there for a while?"

"Are you sure you want to deal with them?"

Deisphe waved a hand. "No prob. Just tell me when."

Lili thought about it. "Maybe in an hour or so?"

"Easy-peasy. Word will get down to the bowels that there's a megacake in the cafeteria. They love to get to it before anyone else does." She made a gagging sound. "That's because they know no one will touch it after they've put their claws into it." Deisphe brightened up. "But this time, I'll ask for a very *special* cake that they'll love to eat, but it won't love them in the long run. I'd say you'll be good to go in about an hour."

Lili studied her friend's face. "You know what, Deisphe? Your mind is very scary. But in a good way."

"All in the name of love." She grinned before loping off.

"There's that word again." But Lili couldn't resist smiling as she returned to the ER.

"Dr. Carter," one of the nurses called out. "That Fooz you just treated had some more castigats tucked away. This time he did some incredible projectile vomiting." She made a face.

"My turn," Dr. Erbe assured her. "Once a night is enough for any of us," the witch told Lili. "I've had it pretty easy so far tonight. Although," she tipped her fashionable glasses down her nose. "If Wattle shows up, he's all yours. That bridge troll is more trouble than a herd of Foozes."

Lili chuckled "Done. Thanks, Sasha." She moved down to the desk to see what else might be waiting for her.

Even though thoughts of Jared remained in the back of her mind, she was able to concentrate on her new patients.

She thought of the dark scrolls still resting in her desk drawer. She needed them out of there and back with their owner. No doubt Dr. Mortimer would ask her how she felt about utilizing the spells detailed in the scrolls, and she'd have to be as tactful and cautious as possible. No doubt if she said one wrong word, he'd completely ban her from the asylum and she couldn't allow that to happen. She not only wanted to protect Jared in any way she could, but the other patients there as well.

"Hey, Lili." Annis, one of the elf nurses, with pale blond hair tucked behind her pointed ears, and an easy smile, slid to a graceful stop. "There's going to be a cake displayed in the cafeteria," she told her. "Warning, don't indulge. It's something the ogres won't pass up." Her eyes sparkled.

"Really?" She pretended innocence.

"They can't control themselves when it comes to sweets," she confided. "So every once in a while, we give them what they want. You'd think after all this time, they'd figure out it's the cake that makes them sick. They end up in the ER as our least favorite patients, but it's always worth it. Deisphe said it was time for them to have dessert again." She was off.

Lili chuckled. "And here I thought Blair knew everything there was to know about revenge."

Chapter 17

"OFF WITH YOU." DEISPHE PUSHED LILI OUT OF THE ER once two groaning and vomit-smelling ogres were wheeled into the area. "Dr. Mortimer is gone for the day," she whispered. "We tend to work slow with them. They're considered low priority, but don't take any chances, okay?"

"I won't. Thanks." She hurried to the back stairs.

Lili realized her plans were subverted the moment she reached the entrance door. It refused to open to her palm print or even any of her spells.

"Damn it!" She slammed her hand against the door, barely wincing as the pain traveled up her arm. She walked in a tight circle, aware time was running out. She snapped her fingers. "Of course!" She ran up the stairs and tagged Deisphe. "Can you lift the medallion from one of them?" she asked. "The door is secured against me. If it's not attuned to them, I can use it."

She barely took a few breaths before the Wereleopard appeared.

"You really owe me for this." She handed the witch the medallion. "I told them they'll need a special shower to get rid of a certain mite that's aggravating their stomach distress. But it's going to cut your time down there."

"An hour?"

"No longer," she warned Lili.

"Thanks." She wasted no time returning downstairs

and breathed a sigh of relief when the medallion allowed her entry.

The first thing Lili noticed was the sorrow and fear thick in the air. Sounds of sobbing and mewls of pain reached her ears.

"Lili." She barely heard Jared's gasp. She ran to his door and looked between the bars. The darkness didn't allow her to see much. "Light, now," she ordered. "Half light," she amended when she saw him throw his arm across his eyes as he winced at the brightness. She flattened her palm against the bolted door and held it there. "Keep in. Keep out. Not done. Not fun. Give me entrance. Give me what I want now." She poured her power into the lock and soon felt it give way. She pulled the door open and ran inside. "Damn." The lover gave way to healer as she examined the many slashes on his skin along with bruises and what she swore was a broken cheekbone.

"Lili, you shouldn't be here." He tried to brush away her hands, but she wasn't about to be deterred.

"Shut up," she said fiercely as she worked on healing his injuries. She blinked back hot tears as she ran her fingers lightly over the damage done to him and worried as she saw that it took longer and more command of her magick to mend him. "Something's wrong." She might be a doctor and aware that one's heart couldn't climb up into their throat, but hers sure felt that way. She draped his arm over her shoulder and helped him back to his filthy excuse for a bed. "You need to get better and get out of here tonight," she told him, even more worried to hear a rattling sound in his lungs.

Jared shook his head and tried to push her away. "Help

Pepta," he rasped. "Something's really wrong with her. I think the ogres did…" he stopped and held his arm across his chest holding the pain, or something broken, back. He hissed a variety of curses as she worked to heal his broken ribs. "Fuck, woman, do you know how much that hurts? Go to Pepta. Please," he begged.

She nodded even as she reluctantly rose to her feet. "I have to lock your door again. I can't let them know I was down here. The only good thing is with it so dark in here, they shouldn't notice you healing until you normally would have healed."

"It's fine." He stopped her action by wrapping his hand around her neck and pulling her down for a deep kiss. "I love you." He rested his forehead against hers.

"I love you so much," she whispered, leaving the cell and hating herself for resetting the lock.

Lili might have known where Pepta was kept, but all she had to do was follow the soft cries.

"Pepta." She did the same with the nymph's lock and moved into the cell. This time she kept her lights on dim. What she saw didn't just take her breath away; she felt her fury rise up until the air thickened with her magick. She dialed back her temper, and the atmosphere immediately eased. "Those bastards," she hissed, moving toward the corner where Pepta lay sprawled like a bag of potatoes.

"Get the fuck away from me!" Pepta spat out the words even as Lili knelt down next to her.

Just as with Jared, she ignored the nymph's words and performed a quick examination.

"Who did this?" she demanded, seeing not just cuts and bruises, signs of broken bones, but also trauma no female should endure. The rips on Pepta's cotton pants and top weren't deliberate designs but random signs of a male's misguided sense of empowerment. And the nymph would never have wounded herself so badly as to cause so many splotches of blood. "Did Turtifo and Coing do this?"

Pepta flinched when she tried to shrug it off. "You're only here a few days a week, Doc," she drawled, but her pain-laced voice told Lili more than enough.

"Come on." It wasn't just Lili's voice that was ice-cold, but her blood too. She only hoped the cake made the ogres suffer for a long time. If not, she was more than willing to help it along. She reached down and carefully helped Pepta to her feet.

"What are you doing?" the nymph cried in anger and pain.

"I'm taking you upstairs for treatment," the witch said grimly, sending some pain-fighting endorphins into her body.

Pepta reared back so sharply that Lili almost fell on top of her.

"I can't go up there." Fear, dark and strong, flashed across her pale face that was also black and purple with bruises and dried blood on her lips.

"Oh yes, you can." Lili was at the stage she would have dragged her upstairs. The nymph was too weak to battle her for long, and the witch managed to get her out into the hallway. She didn't care if she left the cell door open.

"They did it to her," Panabell told her as they made a halting way along the floor.

"Assholes should be turned to dust," Orkey growled.

But it was Jared's face Lili sought as she helped Pepta toward the large entrance door.

"No more," she vowed.

He smiled at her then disappeared into the darkness.

By the time they reached the stairs, Lili was practically carrying Pepta. She tagged Deisphe for help as they made their slow way upward.

"Holy shit," the Wereleopard breathed when she met them halfway down the stairs. She took Pepta's other arm and helped take more of her slight weight. Her gold eyes narrowed with anger. "And I just bet I know who did it. Good thing they're suffering big-time right now."

"Not enough," Lili said fiercely.

"I'm not allowed up here." The normally abrasive nymph tried to pull back, but a determined witch and strong Were proved to be too much for her.

"Dr. Carter." Arimentha Garrish stood at the top of the stairs. The faint scent of sulfur clung to her clothing and, if Lili wasn't mistaken, there was a hint of smoke coming off her well-tailored suit. The dragon-shifter's dark eyes flitted over Pepta. Not a flick of an eyelash revealed her thoughts. "The disturbed are not allowed up here."

"I don't give a damn what's allowed or not allowed," Lili informed her in a hard voice. "This patient was attacked and badly injured. She requires more than superficial treatment. More than I can do down there." She glanced at Deisphe, giving her a less-than-subtle mental nudge.

Director of Nursing Garrish didn't move, still blocking their path.

"Was this the work of the ogres?" she asked Pepta.

The nymph kept her head down. "I just want to go back to my cell," she mumbled.

"You don't have the strength to argue." The shifter snapped her fingers. "Bring a gurney now!"

Lili released a sigh of relief when two trolls ran in with a gurney rolling between them. They gently helped Pepta onto the surface.

"Take her to the trauma room," Nurse Garrish ordered, gesturing that Deisphe follow them. "And make sure Turtifo and Coing don't go anywhere." She turned back to Lili. "You are a very brave witch to do this. Dr. Mortimer's orders that the patients not be up here were set in stone."

"I wasn't going to allow her to stay down there when she was in so much pain," she countered.

"Of course you shouldn't." Her voice softened. "Anyone injured within the confines of the hospital is under my care, not Dr. Mortimer's. That aides he hired inflicted these injuries only makes the situation much worse. The nymph will be protected here, and I promise you that I will arrange it so her state of mind be reevaluated."

Lili's nose wrinkled as the smell of sulfur grew stronger. She was so tempted to take a few steps backward in case the shifter's temper got the better of her and Lili ended up as charbroiled witch.

"You have impressed me with your bravery and inner strength, Dr. Carter," she told her, straightening her suit jacket. "Keep it up."

Lili leaned against the wall as her knees weakened. She took a couple deep breaths, then headed for the ER where she knew her new patient was waiting.

"They're at the other end, and Security is now standing by, per Nurse Garrish's orders. I gave Pepta some valerian to calm her down," Deisphe told her when she entered the room. "What did you do to the dragon lady?" she whispered, as she efficiently and gently cut away Pepta's clothing and carefully spread a soft sheet over her. "She's almost a nice shifter."

"I think she's on my side," Lili whispered back as she worked to assess the nymph's injuries. The more she saw the angrier she grew.

"Uh, Lili," Deisphe's fingers hovered just above Lili's arm. "You're glowing like something ready to go off any second."

She looked down and saw that the Were was right. Her olive skin showed her power glimmering strong on her skin. She took several strong breaths to bring it under control.

"I want them in the Hellion Guard's custody," she said around a jaw tight with fury. "I don't care if they're even cured before they're tossed to the Guard. And I don't care that Dr. Mortimer is in charge of this hospital. I don't want them on the grounds." While her voice fairly vibrated with her temper, her hands were tender as she worked on Pepta who mewled softly.

She thought of the arrogant nymph at their first meeting and the way she fought Lili at every encounter. But the witch had refused to back down, and she saw the faintest hint of softness begin to show in Pepta's harsh nature.

The idea that she lay before her whimpering like a small child was disheartening.

"They really did a number on her, didn't they?" Deisphe's eyes were liquid with concern.

"We can help physically, but some things…"

"Dr. Carter."

Lili turned to see Nurse Garrish at the door. The dragon-shifter walked in and glanced at Pepta. Her demeanor was as emotionless as ever, but Lili knew that rage simmered below her skin, and the smell of brimstone grew stronger until it was pulled back under control.

"She will not see them again," Nurse Garrish said. "Dr. Mortimer has no say in this. He is not on the premises, and I am in charge when he is not. That authority extends everywhere. I contacted the Hellion Guard, and two members will be here shortly to transport them from here." Her thin lips narrowed even more. "I have allowed my sight to remain dim for too long. I will also be sending a report regarding Dr. Mortimer's unorthodox activities to the Physic Council."

Witch and Were exchanged a look.

"We still don't know everything," Lili said.

"We will, and even more, once he's returned." Her eyes softened when she glanced at Pepta. "There is still a great deal of anger inside her, but I feel with your help, that will eventually be gone."

"I want all of them out of that dark place." Lili wasn't going to back down now. "There has to be a ward up here that can be fitted out for them. I refuse to believe any of them are as dangerous as Dr. Mortimer states they are." She kept her gaze on the head nurse.

"Even Patient 1172?" she asked with an arched eyebrow.

Lili managed to unclench her fists that hung at her sides. "His name is Jared, and whatever sickness he had is gone. He's not dangerous."

"Lili!"

Deisphe's panicked cry had her spinning around to see Pepta thrashing so wildly on the gurney she almost slid off. She returned to her patient, barely aware of Nurse Garrish close behind her.

"*Noooooo!*" Pepta screamed, sitting upright, her body a bowed arc of pain that whitened her joints. The brand on her shoulder flared a hot orange color that flashed into a white-hot flare.

Lili, Deisphe, and Nurse Garrish were forced back as the room lit up in an eye-blinding white. They shielded their eyes, and Lili felt the dragon-shifter unhesitatingly threw up a protective ward around them.

By the time she could see again, the gurney was empty save for a nymph-shaped pile of silver-colored ashes and the acrid stench of burned flesh in the air.

"No." The word escaped her lips. "No." She started to touch them then held back. "No." She shook her head, refusing to believe what was in front of her.

"The brand on her skin," Nurse Garrish said, sounding as shocked as Lili felt. "It must have had a tracking spell embedded in it. If a patient was away from below for too long, the brand…"

"Killed her," Lili flatly finished for her. "Burned her like trash." She could hear the sounds of Deisphe crying softly and sense the anger in Nurse Garrish. All she felt was numb.

This could have been Jared lying here in cinders. If it weren't for the shadows protecting him, he would have erupted into flames long ago.

She covered her mouth to hold back the screams that threatened to crawl up her throat. Not in fear but rage that a life was snuffed out as if it meant nothing.

"What has he done to them?" she whispered. "And what can we do to protect the rest of them?" She couldn't remember the last time she felt this helpless. She didn't like it.

"Let me check their records," Nurse Garrish offered. "There has to be something there about the brands, what exactly they do, apart from declaring the wearer a mental patient." She reached out and touched Lili's shoulder. "Pepta will be treated with respect. I promise you that this tragedy will not go unnoticed." She turned to Deisphe, who looked as shell-shocked as they did. "Have her remains handled with care, then have this room thoroughly cleansed. I will also arrange for appropriate help to be sent downstairs." She speared a look at Lili. "I suggest you refrain from returning there this evening. Wait until tomorrow."

Lili watched the dragon walk away and turned to her friend, who sat trembling in a chair.

"I go hunting in the mountains once a month," the Were murmured, staring down at her lap. "I'm a nurse, for Fate's sake. I've seen all forms of death before. More of it horrific than gentle, but this—" she shook her head, her dark hair glinting under the light. "This was just too wrong."

"It was, and that's why we'll make sure it doesn't happen again." She didn't want to think about it happening to Jared, of his flashing into flames before her.

"After you have the aides come in here, I want you to take a long break." Lili rested her hands on Deisphe's shoulders. "I don't care if all Hades breaks loose out there; you are to stay away from here for the next thirty minutes."

She licked her lips and nodded jerkily as she rose to her feet and walked away with the stiff, odd gait of an elder.

Lili turned back to Pepta's remains. "I am so sorry, Pepta," she said softly. "We will avenge you."

Then she went to her office, closed the door, and collapsed on the couch, crying as she hadn't done since the night her mother was killed.

She barely noticed when Cleo crept into the room—as if a closed door could keep the cat out—and curled up in Lili's lap.

And Lili cried even more until there were no more tears left within her.

Chapter 18

"WHAT ARE YOU DOING?" CLEO HOPPED ONTO LILI'S desk, watching as she dug into the bottom desk drawer.

"What does it look like I'm doing?" Her face was set in stark lines as she laid a silk cloth across the desk surface, then carefully piled the scrolls onto the material.

"Giving them back to Dr. Musty?"

Lili shook her head. "Not after what just happened. There had to have been a blood spell cast into that brand for Pepta to die that way." Her body ached to return downstairs and see Jared, but then he'd know what happened to Pepta. She doubted anyone down there would take the news well, and she couldn't blame them. She'd vowed to protect them all as best she could, but instead she had been the cause of one's death. She had to come up with a way to save them from harm.

"He won't like it," the cat warned her. "He could get you barred from working in any hospital or even a healing center."

"Let him try," she said grimly, carefully folding the silk over the scrolls so that she didn't have to touch them. "He knew he was taking a chance in showing them to me. It wasn't like I agreed with his methods to begin with. Besides, I've got Nurse Garrish on my side now." She rummaged in the top drawer and pulled out a stick of sealing wax and a brass seal. She touched the wax with her fingertip, heating it until enough wax dropped onto the folds, effectively closing the packet, then pressing the seal on top of the wax. "Warning to all. Lest you fall. Dark contents to be sent where they belong. Be gone." She pushed the packet that seemed to go up in smoke.

"Eurydice?" Cleo asked.

She nodded. "She'll know what to do with them."

"You really should have strung Dr. Musty for a while longer. Put on one of those Victorian dresses you have in storage and showed him a hint of ankle." Cleo returned to her silk pillow and curled up, her tail draped around her round body.

"I don't think Dr. Mortimer will be surprised that I did this," Lili said with strong conviction. "He knows what my thoughts are about those blood spells."

"And maybe he'll think of a way to use it against you." The feline started to groom her paws.

"He better not, not after what happened to Pepta." She picked up her bag and coat. "We're going home for a quiet dinner."

"And you are hoping the demon will show up."

"He will." *Please, Jared, show up.* She shrugged on her coat and walked out of the office with Cleo following.

Lili stopped in the ER first, relieved to see that Deisphe looked more like herself, even if her eyes were red and puffy.

"I can take that away for you," Lili offered, gesturing toward her eyes.

The Were shook her head. "It's a good way to remember."

Lili nodded her understanding. "I'll see you tomorrow."

She felt uneasy the moment she stepped outside and found the fog lying low on the ground. The moist air clung to her skin the way she imagined shadows wound their way around Jared.

"I don't like this," Cleo grumbled, walking beside her. She looked over her shoulder as they headed for Lili's CX-7.

"The lot is protected," she reminded the cat.

"That doesn't mean anything, and you know it." She started to weave her way around Lili's ankles, careful not to trip the witch.

"What are you doing?"

"They always say not to be an easy target. A zigzag motion is your best bet."

"Yes, well, you're doing it around me, making *me* the target." She clicked the remote for the locks, and they got into the vehicle. Lili turned on the engine and adjusted the heater. She didn't admit she had the same uneasy feelings and still did. She knew even a locked SUV couldn't keep out most creatures, especially when they had fangs and claws meant to tear into metal as if it were paper.

"Can we go out to dinner first? Some nice salmon perhaps?" Cleo peeked out the passenger window.

"Jared might be at the house."

"And he seems to have a way of tracking you down," she reminded her. "You need to be somewhere with others right now. I don't mean you have to laugh and drink and badly sing in a karaoke bar, but it's not too late to go out for a bite to eat." Her stomach rumbled to add credence to her words. Lili's stomach soon followed suit.

"We'll go to Inderman," she said, turning left instead of right and head for the ocean's edge, where the supernatural community thrived.

Cleo was right. She needed to be among others, and at least the Inderman Health Department wouldn't have a fit about a cat dining in the restaurant.

"Well, that was fun. *Not*," Cleo rumbled as she followed Lili into the house. "I thought we were going out to relax and have a nice meal."

"We did." Lili tossed her leather bag on the kitchen table, the keys clattering alongside it.

"You barely ate a bite while you looked around, waiting for the demon to show up." The cat headed for her kitty kibble dish and began crunching down. "The totally cute waiter flirted with you, and you didn't throw him a bone." She threw her head back, laughing hysterically. "Throw him a bone! And he's a Werewolf." Her laughter turned into a sigh. "No one appreciates my humor."

"What humor?" Lili pulled a bottle of her favorite Chardonnay out of the refrigerator and poured herself a glass. She kicked off her shoes, nudging them into a corner, and padded barefoot into the family room while Cleo continued to grouse that witches didn't understand the need for a sense of humor.

Lili stopped short at the sight of a familiar body lying asleep on her couch. She almost dropped her glass as she ran to the couch and knelt down.

"Hey," she said softly, whispering her fingers across Jared's brow.

He opened his eyes halfway and smiled.

"How long have you been here?" She hated the idea she hadn't been in the house when he arrived.

Jared glanced at the clock. "A couple hours." His voice was rusty with sleep. "You weren't here, so I made use of your couch."

"You should have used the bed and been more comfortable." She was pleased to see all of his wounds were fully healed. Even his broken jaw was fine now. She threaded her fingers through his, relishing the warmth of his skin. Then she remembered the afternoon's events. "Pepta's dead." She knew better than to try to sugarcoat the words. Jared would prefer the stark truth.

His eyes darkened to a blue that mimicked the bottom of the ocean. "I was afraid of that. Because of what they did to her?" His lips thinned in anger.

Lili shook her head. "Because of me." She picked up her wineglass and drank deeply. Jared took it from her fingers and finished the contents.

"It's the brand. It has what you'd call a kill switch. I was treating her, and all of a sudden…" she gulped at the memory, "the brand burst into flames, and she was reduced to ashes in seconds. No wonder she was so afraid of leaving the asylum," she finished in a whisper. She lightly traced her fingertips over his shirt front where the brand would be. "I have no idea how you manage to escape such a fate. After seeing what happened to her." She paused. "It was awful."

"Poor Pepta," he murmured. "But maybe she was better off. She hurt inside and out."

"The Hellion Guard took Turtifo and Coing into custody," she told him. "Nurse Garrish wanted them gone as much as I did." She pointed a finger at the wineglass and raised the digit slowly until wine filled the glass again. She took a sip, then handed it to Jared.

He closed his eyes. A few words of his language left his lips before he drank.

"I wanted to take everyone out of there," Lili said, feeling defeat color her words. "To bring them upstairs. I can't do it now. They'd all end up like Pepta. And while you can leave, your time is limited." She inhaled his scent, drawing it deep into her lungs. While she was here, she couldn't smell the rotten stench of the asylum, the reek of unwashed flesh, or the sickness that seemed to permeate the air down there. She saw the male he was before he was thrown into a cage. "I sent Dr. Mortimer's scrolls detailing the blood spells to Eurydice. She'll know what to do with them. With her connections, I'm sure she can help me find a way to safely release all of you." She rested her forehead against his shoulder, feeling the buzzing sensation of magick under his skin.

"I always thought you were one of the less-troublesome students. It appears I was wrong."

Lili jumped to her feet and spun around but kept her body in front of Jared, protecting him. He immediately sat up and pushed her to one side, keeping an arm around her.

The elder witch sat in the same chair she had the last time she visited Lili. The only change was her Chanel suit was now a heavy silk gown the color of fresh blackberries. There was nothing threatening with her manner as she gazed at one of her past students then moved on to Jared.

"I see." Her knowing smile flickered on her lips. "You are Sinsia's firstborn."

He nodded.

"Lovely woman, but she cheats at canasta."

Lili's silver tea service appeared on the table with three filled cups. Eurydice nodded in their direction.

"We all need clear heads."

Lili handed out the cups and sat down next to Jared, savoring the warmth of his thigh resting against hers.

"Is that *witch* back?" Cleo hollered from the kitchen. The cat's yelp was sharp and sudden as a poof of smoke appeared and the bedroom door closed.

"They only get worse as they grow older," Eurydice said by way of explanation. She turned to Lili. "The scrolls you sent me were very illuminating. And dangerous." Her emerald eyes glinted with her strong power. "Did Hieronymus tell you how he obtained them?"

She shook her head. "I gathered that he'd collected them over the years. He tried to tell me that the spells will help the patients, but I can't believe that. I think they somehow work on his behalf. And I wouldn't be surprised if he had something to do with Sera's and the others' disappearances." Her voice broke. "I know there's no way of finding them, but I want to know what happened to them." She sipped the tea, not surprised that the hot liquid was calming. It seemed everyone wanted to use tea as a comforting mixture.

Eurydice nodded before she looked at Jared. "You thought your mother abandoned you, didn't you?"

"I didn't have to think," he bit out the words. "She did."

"No, she made sure you were well protected. Those shadows that allow you to leave also protect you."

"Protect me?" Jared barked a laugh. "She left me in a cage like a wild animal."

"She did what she could to keep you safe," the Head

Witch corrected him. "Her enemies wanted you executed. Her plan ensured you would remain alive until you could be healed. And it appears, my boy, you have been cured." She smiled at Jared then turned to Lili.

"Jared may have been healed emotionally before I saw him, but he has been badly treated physically," the younger witch told her, but her tension rode high, giving her voice a hard edge. "He has been branded, beaten, sliced and diced, bled, and Fates know what else. We preternaturals pride ourselves on being highly evolved, and yet we treat the mentally ill the way they were treated in the Early Days of healing. They're still considered nothing more than animals." She paused, blinking rapidly to keep the tears back, but she could still feel the hot damp drops trickle down her cheeks. "How could this have happened without anyone knowing about it? I have worked in a number of hospitals over the years, and I know the Physics Council keeps a close eye on how care is delivered. That doctors and nurses can even be monitored to show they are giving the proper care. Yet, the ones imprisoned here were… were abandoned," she finished in a breath of air. She blindly reached out, resting her hand on Jared's thigh. His hand covered hers and squeezed tightly. Their "guest" didn't miss the act of comfort and solidarity. "Why are they forgotten?"

"I don't know, but I will do my best to find out." The witch's eyes sharpened with the same anger that boiled in Lili's blood. "We are not perfect, Lilianna."

"And Pepta died because of that neglect," she spat out. She accepted the cup Jared pushed into her hands and urged her to drink.

"Then we ensure it doesn't happen again." Eurydice

finished her tea and set the cup down. "Hieronymus will have to answer for his actions."

"The brands need to be removed," Lili stated.

She nodded. "I will speak to the Council this eve. Is there anything else?" She smiled.

Lili suddenly gulped. She'd just given orders to the Head Witch! And so far, still had her fingers and toes.

"Ummmm... I didn't mean to be so assertive."

"You are thinking of others, not yourself. It is a valuable trait to have. Do you have any idea where Dr. Mortimer is?"

Lili shook her head. "He comes and goes. Unlike other heads of hospitals, he doesn't have a secretary or even an assistant. The staff schedule only shows when he's in the hospital or out of it. Director of Nursing Garrish doesn't appear to be fond of him, and after what happened today, I'd say that dislike has increased."

"Yes, I can imagine Arimentha would despise him," she mused. "Knowing her, I'm certain she has also filed a complaint against him."

"She said she was going to." Lili leaned forward, resting her hands on her knees. "I still feel whatever Dr. Mortimer is up to has to do with Sera and the others. Either they discovered the blood spells and he had to"— she shook her thoughts off—"to get rid of them or send them to a plane they can't return from."

"I only wish I knew how he managed all of this," the elder witch murmured, shaking her head.

"The blood spells," Lili told her. "What else can it be?"

"You still don't know why," Jared said.

"What treatments did you have?" Eurydice asked him. He shook his head. "I can't tell you other than the sense of blood and pain. If I try to think about it, my head feels ready to explode." He winced at the memory.

"A blocking spell," the witches said in unison.

"Have you tried to release him?" Eurydice asked Lili.

"I'm afraid I could make matters worse," she replied. "And after what happened to Pepta…" Her voice drifted off.

"True." She conjured up a silk pouch and handed it to Lili. "A pinch in any liquid you choose to each patient. It won't release any previous charms on them, but it will protect them from anything further. If I can arrange it, Dr. Mortimer will be immediately removed from his duties."

"We can't." Lili grimaced at her protest. "Not until I can find out what he's done."

"And you don't think he won't be furious with you for what's already happened?" Jared asked.

"I'll handle that," she said with a confidence she didn't entirely feel. "I just want one week."

Eurydice considered her request and finally nodded. She turned to Jared. "Your mother has never forgotten you. I am sure she will prove this once things have settled down." With that she was gone, leaving only a faint hint of Chanel No. 5.

"So she's the big boss of witches?" Jared asked, finally breaking the charged silence.

Lili nodded. "I can't believe I gave her an order," she said with wonder. "And I'm still in one piece." She fingered the silk pouch, untying the strings and checking the contents. "I think you should have some tonight."

"Then I'll take it in wine."

Lili and Jared picked up the tea service and carried

everything into the kitchen where she quickly washed everything up.

"You seem more relaxed," he commented.

"Relieved is more like it. Having Eurydice on my side is a very good thing," she replied, putting everything away.

She filled two glasses with wine, adding a pinch of the powder to Jared's glass. She handed him his wine and took his free hand, pulling him toward the back of the house.

"Are you going to have your way with me?" His interest, along with other parts, perked up.

She looked over her shoulder, flashing him a bright smile. "Absolutely."

Chapter 19

"TELL ME ABOUT BLOOD SPELLS," JARED SAID. HE FELT sated from extraordinary sex, Lili whispering how much she loved him, and the idea, which grew stronger by the second, of having a true future with his beautiful witch. He'd claimed her, and he wasn't giving her up.

Now they sat in a bubble-filled tub with Lili resting against Jared's chest. A light citrus scent floated in the air around the bubble bath, and candles hovered around the bathroom.

"I fixed this bath for us to relax," she whined as she reached down to find his cock, which happily twitched under her attention. Fates bless demon recovery time!

"And we are." He created a little diversion of his own as he created a path down her neck with his lips. "But let's talk too."

She tipped her head further to one side to allow his mouth more access, which he happily took advantage of.

"Do you know anything about blood spells, or should I start with Blood Spells 101?" Lili asked, giving him one last light squeeze before she released him.

"I know blood is required."

"Ah, a novice then." She nodded to herself, leaning her head back against the hollow of his shoulder. She'd twisted her hair up into a knot before they got into the tub, and her curls were tightening in the steamy room.

"Yes, first off, it's obvious that blood spells require

blood. Some bloods, such as virgin and demon, are stronger than others," she explained. "They've also been prohibited for centuries, since too many thought the blood should come from a sacrifice. They're used for baneful magick, the darker the better in their eyes. You take a dark spell and twist it even more by using fresh blood. It can be utilized in more uses than you might imagine."

Jared stilled. "How do you think Dr. Mortimer uses it? And would you say he's using my blood for those spells he talked to you about?"

She was so quiet that, if he didn't know better, he'd have sworn she hadn't heard him. But the tension in her body told him differently.

"Yes." She spoke so softly Jared had to strain to hear her answer. "But I have no idea what he uses it for. There's no word about him doing any remarkable healing with anyone below, but he's doing something with it."

His power ratchetted up with a protective vibe as he stroked his fingers down her arms. "And he wants you as a part of his insane plans. What other reason would he want to confide in you? I don't like any of this. Let Eurydice and the others find him and put him away in a cell," he growled.

Lili shrugged. She cupped her hands in the bubbles and blew gently, watching the iridescent balls dance before them. She added a hint of her magick to keep them drifting around the room.

"I don't think it will be that easy. We have no idea how long he's been doing this." She shook her head. "I don't understand why Dr. Mortimer approached me with his ideas. From the beginning, I was very vocal to him that I felt the basement area was too antiquated and the patients should be treated with more modern methods and have better quarters," she admitted. "Yet he called me in and brought out those scrolls." She shuddered at the memory of how the malicious surface felt to even the lightest of touches. The urge to climb out of the tub and gather up the supplies to thoroughly cleanse her hands grew stronger by the moment. And she wasn't thinking of using antibacterial soap, either.

"Would there be a reason why he'd think you'd even consider using a blood spell?" he asked, keeping his touch soothing until she finally relaxed against him again. "Anything in your past?"

She shook her head. "The only thing someone would consider a crime was seven hundred years ago, when my class refused to admit who had cast the illegal spell that expelled us from the Witches Academy. And it really wasn't all that bad. The baron's son deserved what was done to him," she stated.

Jared's smile warmed the top of her head when he rested his lips there. "What did you do, Lili?"

She shook her head again. "We all took a vow that the spellcaster wouldn't be revealed."

"A blood vow?"

"We never needed one. Our word was always enough and still is. We've always been there for each other." She nestled against him, enjoying the slick feel of his body against hers.

Hunger rose up fast and furious. She knew the hours were ticking away for them before the shadows would capture Jared and take him away from her.

"Keep within. Keep us safe," she whispered, stroking the sides of the tub as she twisted around. The water curled upward but went no further than the invisible barrier keeping it in the tub as she straddled his legs and settled on his lap. She smiled at his erection nudging her inner thigh. "Obviously I don't need magick for everything." She wrapped her hand around his penis, caressing the velvety skin while rubbing her thumb over the tiny slit.

Jared's smile held the same wicked intentions that Lili's did. "Do with me as you will." He lay back, his arms draped along the sides of the tub. "Good thing you've got a bathtub more than big enough for the two of us."

Lili switched the Jacuzzi feature on low, laughing as the bubbles tripled without causing an overflow. She made sure not to get too close to his cock as she rocked forward on her knees while palming his chest. Her fingers combed the dark hair that ran in a thin line down his stomach to gather in a thicket around his penis. She felt the magick from the brand try to reach out to her, so she stayed away from that part of his shoulder. She always feared what it might do to Jared if she tried anything with it. Besides, there was so much more of him to explore, and this kind of investigation was something she planned to enjoy tonight.

"You're my prisoner," she whispered, trailing her tongue over the curve of his ear. "That means you just sit here and enjoy it."

He closed his eyes. "Do with me what you will."

"Good answer." Lili combed her fingers through his silky hair, curling and damp from the steamy room. She buried her nose against the curve of his neck, inhaling the scent of his skin that she felt blended so well with hers. She knew that he wouldn't move while she had her way with him.

She turned her head, licking his neck and tasting the salty skin and flavor uniquely known as Jared.

"Umm, you taste so good," she murmured, keeping her hands busy with mapping out the planes of his chest, skimming over his abs, teasing the tip of his cock, then moving upward again to find his nipples and rub her forefingers over them until they turned into hard pebbles. Not content to just touch him, she dipped her head and took one of the coppery circles into her mouth, drawing on it deeply. To add to the sensation, she began to hum, sending vibrations against him that by the trembling in his body was affecting him a great deal. She stopped the second he moved.

"Against the rules, remember." Her lips curved in a knowing manner when he froze. "Good boy."

Once finished, she moved her attention to his other nipple until it stood out in a hard tip. After that, Lili was content to map the rest of him, seeming to memorize every inch of his body. She felt his frustration as she kept away from the part of his body he clearly wanted her interest to focus on.

Lili felt her own desire increase to the point of exquisite pain, where her skin felt so tight, she felt she'd explode and even touching Jared flared a fiery sensation along her body.

She knew she wouldn't be able to keep on for much longer. Plus, she feared their time was growing short. She lifted her head, gazing into his eyes, allowing him to see her thoughts, how she felt. She shifted her body and lowered herself slowly downward, hissing in relief as he filled her.

"Mine." She grazed her teeth across the taut skin of his throat.

Jared gripped her waist, pulling her against him as he thrust upward.

"Mine." He dipped his head, doing the same, leaving a slight bruise that mimicked the one on his skin. "Nothing will separate us." His voice vibrated against her throat. "Not even Hades will keep us apart."

She lifted her head, so she could look down at his face. The stark planes that she'd grown to love so quickly. His name dropped from her lips, the whisper sounding more like a prayer, as she felt their connection as more than physical, but emotional, mental, and even spiritual.

Nothing will happen to you, Jared. I won't allow him *to do anything to you ever again. You're another part of my soul.*

As you are mine. His smile was enough to tip her over the edge of the cliff they teetered on.

The water cooled around them, and the bubbles floated to the floor as they remained in each other's arms.

Lili knew what was to happen the moment she felt the tension tighten Jared's muscles.

She lifted her head, staring at the dark tendrils curling out of the corners and snaking their way toward the tub.

"No." Her voice was raspy while her heart stopped with fear at what she knew was to come. "No. *You can't have him!*" She tightened her embrace. "*You can't take him back there!*"

"Shhh," he soothed her with long strokes down her spine. "It's all right, love. At least you know where I am."

Lili's eyes burned with her tears. "I'm banned from below. And probably even worse now."

Jared's smile wobbled a bit, telling her he wasn't as calm as he pretended to be.

"You're a very talented witch," he whispered. "And I'm an insane demon. What a pair we make."

Lili glared at the shadows as they crawled past her keep-the-water-in spell and enfolded Jared. She felt pushed back until she fell on her butt, the water splashing over the sides as the spell was broken. It didn't matter. All she cared about was feeling so helpless as the darkness enveloped him, and in a matter of seconds, he was gone from her.

She opened her mouth in a parody of a silent scream. No sound escaped her lips. Moving slowly like a very old woman, she pulled the stopper and sat there watching the water drain away.

A push of power dried her off, and she stumbled into the bedroom, crawling into bed and pulling the covers over her.

She was so lost in her misery, she barely felt the comforting touch of a paw on her neck and fur circling her back. The soothing sound of a purr and whispers of *I'm here* and *We'll get him back for good* pacified her into a deep sleep.

"You won't hex me if I tell you you look like shit, will you?" Deisphe stared at Lili as she dragged herself into her office. The Wereleopard was already sitting in the visitor chair, and two mugs of coffee sat on the desk.

"She's looked worse," Cleo announced, nosing the bowl of kitty kibble set in a corner of the room. "Chicken? You put chicken in here?" She shook her head in disgust. "I'm heading for pediatrics. They always have the good stuff up there." She sauntered out of the office.

"Jared?" Deisphe asked as Lili dropped into her chair, took one of the coffee mugs, and drank deeply.

"If I don't do something, he'll die down there. I keep seeing what happened to Pepta…" her voice trailed off.

The nurse looked solemn at the thought. "You know I'll help any way I can. I've been keeping my ears open, but the only gossip about Dr. M. is the staff wondering why he's out of the hospital so much—although no one's all that worried, since he didn't do that much apart from whatever he was working on below."

"I know you'll help, and I appreciate it. I'm out of my depth here, Deisphe," she admitted with a sigh. "I thought I could come here, easily figure out what happened, and either find Sera was sent to another plane or worse. I saw myself as the witchy Nancy Drew."

"And Jared is Ned?" Deisphe smiled at her friend's look of surprise. "I loved those books. Although I'm not sure what that makes me."

Lili finished her coffee, then ran her finger from the bottom to the top of the cup, refilling the steamy liquid. She leaned across the desk and did the same to Deisphe's cup.

"I'm arrogant. But then doctors tend to have that in their genes. Maggie didn't come right out and say I was crazy to even consider this, but I know she was thinking it. And now I know why." She took a deep breath. "I've seen the shadows take Jared before, but last night was…" She shook her head as if she could easily banish visions that she knew would haunt her forever. "They hurt him. I thought they'd protect him. In a way, they do keep him from being detected by others when he's at Inderman or upstairs at the hospital. But last night was more intense. It was as if they were punishing him." She kept her voice low. "If it continues like that, they could eventually kill him."

"Then we get him out for good," Deisphe stated with the usual directness Weres were known for. She glanced at her watch. "Playtime is up, girlfriend. Let's go see what we've got in the ER." She hopped to her feet and walked around the desk, pulling Lili upward and hugging her. "Just remember we have Dragon Lady on our side. What can go wrong?" She grinned, showing a hint of fang. "Come on. Let's see if there's any gossip running around."

Lili started to say they were the absolute worst words to say, but the Were was already out of her office.

Lili felt her nerve endings on fire as she worked in the ER. Every ailment that showed up was the kind she could treat in her sleep.

"Hey, Carter, the big boss wants to see you," one of the elf nurses said, passing by her. "And considering the way Dr. Mortimer was acting, I'd say you better not waste any time."

She touched her stomach, feeling the acid build up at the announcement.

"Thanks, Spips," she told the elf nurse, managing the brief resemblance to a smile.

The door to the wizard's office was open, and she could detect nose-wrinkling smells coming from it. This time there was no hint of age or must; only the strong stench of the wrong kind of magick.

"Dr. Mortimer?" She tapped on the heavy wood door.

"Come in, Dr. Carter."

When Lili stepped inside, she found her superior seated behind his desk. Instead of his usual Victorian garb, he wore fine midnight blue silk robes, edged with silver, and a small cap on top of his head. A small porcelain dish sat on one corner of his desk, and the scent of incense filled the air.

She felt the protections in her lab coat kick into high gear. After seeing the wild darkness in his eyes, she only hoped they were enough.

"Sit down, Dr. Carter," he ordered crisply. He waited until she was seated before saying anything further. "While I realized you and I do not have similar thoughts on treatment for the deranged, I did hope you were willing to keep an open mind." His lips thinned. "It appears you do not."

Couldn't Eurydice have had him removed?

"I do have an open mind, Dr. Mortimer," she kept her voice low and calming. She already knew she couldn't try a push of power without it backfiring on her, especially when something disorienting appeared on the edge of her vision. Yet when she turned her head, nothing was there. "But I also like to think we have evolved, since so many of those early treatments that have shown to be detrimental to patients. For Fate's sake, you talk of blood spells as if they're nothing more than a simple charm! There's an excellent reason why they're considered illegal."

"And an even better reason why we need to use whatever is at our disposal." His anger seemed to fill the room like a thick cloud.

For a moment, she was afraid to breathe. The need to leave the office was growing by the second, but she found herself unable to move.

"I should have followed my first instincts," he growled at her. "I knew upstart doctors such as yourself wouldn't have the vision to look at what must be done. What can be accomplished if you are willing to look beyond the narrow scope of our kind." He shook his head, looking at her with scornful pity.

"What have you done, Dr. Mortimer? What am I missing here?" Lili struggled to keep her voice calm even as horror started to trickle into her bloodstream.

"All of you try to stop what needs to be done. The mentally ill provide a new strength to us. Even the demon in the bowels has a power in his blood I cannot receive from the others," he said.

"Jared has no power."

"You have no idea what kind of strength Patient 1172 has in his life's blood." The look of scorn he directed her way increased. "What he offers is a chance to retreat and view what should have been done."

"Retreat?" Her head started to spin. "Retreat where?"

"To the past, of course," he said impatiently. "Years ago, mundane blood was much purer than it is now. My spells are much stronger when I can blend that with preternatural blood. And some of the rituals in times past…" He closed his eyes, smiling as if thinking of a pleasant memory. One that Lili just knew she would find deplorable.

Help! She didn't expect anyone to hear her mental plea, but it made her feel better.

"Even some of the ones that came to work here had what I needed," he mused, seemingly unaware of her building horror.

Lili's thoughts screeched to a screaming stop. "Worked here? Such as staff members?"

"One nurse, a witch such as yourself, had blood that showed an unusual power when paired with Panabell's blood. I was even able to return to a time in London I found pleasurable. Whitechapel during the late 1800s wasn't known as a pleasant place, but I found the residents fascinating."

Whitechapel. The 1800s. There was always the thought a doctor had been behind the infamous crimes. Lili forced the bile down. "You—you were Jack the Ripper?" It was difficult to force the words between her lips.

"Merely something to titillate the members of the press." He waved it off. "The same with The Mercy Blade. Horror of Madrid. Scourge of Sydney." He sighed. "I never could understand yellow journalists and their love of frightening the people. I really preferred visiting the more isolated areas. Villages no civilized man had ever seen. Peeking in on tribes that many would see as savages… but the power they invoked!" He shivered, almost in ecstasy. He lowered his head and opened his eyes, peering at her. "If only you had kept your mouth shut. We could have done wonderful things together. But now it is not to be."

"What did you do to Sera?" she demanded. "Where is she?"

"Sera. Ah, the nurse. I told you. She allowed me to return to Whitechapel. Of course, I had to leave her there, but a lovely woman like that could find a way to make a living."

"You monster," she hissed, digging her fingers into the desktop. "You have no business pretending to heal anyone." All she knew was that she wanted out of there and to find Nurse Garrish. The dragon-shifter would know exactly what to do. Then Lili could contact Eurydice and relate what she just heard. She even half stood, prepared to do just that.

"You thought to stop me, but I have many friends who believe the same as I do." His words stopped her action. "I know what you've done with Patient 1172, Dr. Carter. And I truly must thank you. The two of you have provided a connection that will give me so much power that no one will be able to stop me." His formerly faded eyes glinted with a mania that flat-out frightened her.

Lili felt what she saw in the asylum wasn't true insanity. What she saw before her was much worse. All she could think about was getting out of there.

Dr. Mortimer tsked under his tongue as he shook his head. "I had so hoped we could work together, my dear. At least I know you will be a great use to me."

"What do you—?" She started to turn when a large figure loomed over her. Before she could throw up any shields, she felt a blinding pain shoot through her head.

Then she felt nothing at all.

Chapter 20

"LILI. *LILI!*"

So much pain. Not just her in her head, but all through her body, as if someone had wrung her out like a wet washcloth.

"Damn it, Lili, open your eyes!"

The familiar male voice pounded all throughout her brain.

After what felt like days, she managed to roll over onto her side and vomit up black bile.

"Oh, baby." Hands stroked the side of her face, and she was nestled against cold skin.

"Jared?" she croaked. She tried a spell to cleanse her mouth, but nothing happened. She looked down and frowned at the scratchy cotton pants and top she wore instead of the scrubs and lab coat she'd had on earlier. She didn't even want to think who undressed her.

"The only magick allowed in here is his." He picked up her hands and rubbed them briskly to warm the ice-cold feeling.

Lili didn't want to open her eyes. But it hurt just as much to keep them closed. She was finally able to keep her eyelids at half-mast.

It was her nightmare come to life.

A long table, covered with burners, potion bottles, and beakers. A wall covered with odd-looking runes that pulsed red with deadly intention. But it was the smell that had her ready to throw up whatever contents were left in her stomach.

Olde magick. Death. Fatal ingredients meant to damage the mind and body beyond repair. The air was noxious with it.

"Why did the shadows do this to you?" Her throat was raw from the bile that had escaped her stomach. "They brought you back only to be tortured again?"

"They brought me back, so I'd be here for you," he assured her with a small smile. He gently brought her onto his lap, stroking her tangled hair.

Lili grimaced as she searched her mind for what happened. "I was in Dr. Mortimer's office. He said he'd hoped I'd feel the same way he did about the blood spells. But he also said that our combined blood held a lot of power. He," she caught her breath, "he did something to Sera and the others. They're in the past. Sera's in Whitechapel in the 1880s. Jared, Dr. Mortimer was Jack the Ripper." She fanned her palm against his bare chest, seeking the comfort of his body against hers. "And so many other serial killers in the past. He used everyone's blood down here, along with others, to return to other eras. He's a healer, yet he has distorted his power to kill." She felt the acid sickness rise up again, but she managed to keep it under control.

"There is nothing distorted about what I did, Dr. Carter."

Jared hissed a curse under his breath and kept her tight against him.

Lili raised her head slowly, wishing she could dial down the pain to a *just kill me now* level.

Dr. Mortimer stood in a doorway she recognized as

a portal. The breeze of the unknown flared his robes around his legs, and she inhaled the rancid reek of the long ago colliding with the present.

The blood spells allowed him to use the portal in ways not allowed.

What chilled her blood were the grinning ogres standing on either side of her.

How had Turtifo and Coing escaped the Hellion Guard? She knew they had been taken into custody.

"No, they are not the ones you think." The wizard easily read her thoughts. "Sismin and Zeno are their brothers. I value loyalty." He bestowed a smile on each before turning a frown in her direction. "And punish those who go against me."

"I didn't go against you," she argued. "I didn't believe in what you're doing."

"No matter." He waved a dismissive hand. "It merely means I have to speed up my plans. Once I have finished here this night, I will go to another time and begin again. You and your demon lover's blood will enable me to go wherever I wish." He smiled benignly up on her as a father would look upon a beloved daughter.

Lili wanted to gag. Her fingers tingled, but she knew she couldn't bring any magick up to help them.

Memories of her mother flooded her mind. Her smile, the way she'd touch Lili's hair and drop a kiss on her brow.

You will always have me with you, my beloved child. Your gifts are strong and will be there for you. Never forget you also have an agile mind that can save you.

Lili tamped down the nausea that kept threatening to erupt.

"Why do you think I kept Patient 1172 for so long?"

the wizard went on. "I knew from the moment I obtained him he was a prime specimen, holding a great deal of demon magick. Persuading his mother was very easy. The few times she visited him showed her nothing more than a disgusting animal."

Jared stiffened. "My mother was here?" he snarled. "You bastard." His eyes started to glow obsidian then suddenly flattened as pain racked his body.

"No!" Lili threw her arms around him as if able to stop the shocks battering him. "Stop it!" she ordered.

"He must learn." But Dr. Mortimer lowered his hand, the sparks slowly disappearing from his fingertips. "I first thought of taking the two of you with me, keeping you alive, and taking your blood only when I required it. But I sense that could prove to be a problem, since I fear it would not be easy to keep the two of you under my control. No, it would be easier to drain you here and once I am in a new place, I will work on finding new patients." He gestured to the two ogres, who moved toward them.

"We can't fight them without magick," Jared whispered in her ear.

She stared at the two tables with straps. She knew if they didn't do something fast, they'd both be restrained there and out of blood in minutes.

"No, but we can slow them down a little." She closed her eyes, calling on an inner calm instead of the shrieking she wanted to do. "We need to create a diversion. Fight them and get to the beakers. Break them, and let loose whatever's inside them."

"It could kill us."

"He plans to do that anyway, but it's better than his

surviving to create more death." She swallowed the rock in her throat. "I love you."

Jared kissed her hard and fast even as one of the ogres dragged him away. He fought the creature as he was hauled over to one of the tables. Lili glared at the other ogre who grabbed her.

"No more!" She bent her head and bit down hard. Never in her wildest dreams had she imagined ogres tasted so bad! *I will* so *need shots for this!*

She broke for freedom the second he roared and twisted away from her. Jared took advantage and leveled his elbow against the ogre's testicles.

Witch and demon ran for the table.

"No!" Dr. Mortimer screamed as Lili reached the table and swept her arm across the top, shattering the glass and sending the contents spilling everywhere. She chose a vial at random and threw it at the wall, watching as the runes that covered it burst into flame as the liquid struck them. She wrinkled her nose as some of the noxious liquids stung her nostrils and danced away from the ogre trying to catch her. She felt her power return once the runes dissolved.

She turned and watched the wizard gather up the scrolls and return to the portal.

"Jared! He can't leave!"

She couldn't concentrate on him and his safety until she put the ogre down. She doubted a simple sleep charm would work on the lumbering creature, but her healing nature wouldn't allow her to destroy him, either.

"Bring a Fooz to me, Bring him fast. Bring him to last. Bring him now!" she shouted, throwing everything she had at the ogre, who was instantly engulfed in a

glob of green jellied Fooz. Sismin—or was it Zeno?—
flailed his fleshy arms around, but he was well and truly
trapped. She spun around and did the same to the other
one. Lili breathed a sigh of relief as Jared managed to
escape the same fate, then felt her heart fall to her feet as
the demon raced toward Dr. Mortimer, who was inching
his way back to the portal. "Jared, no!" She saw that
the dark interior and fetid air coming from the doorway
beckoned to whoever would enter first. She knew if
Jared fell through, she would never find him again. And
she had no way of closing it.

The wizard smiled at her with yellowed teeth as he
grasped Jared's neck as if ready to wring it. Jared clawed
at his hands to no avail as an iron collar suddenly appeared around his neck. He gasped as his air was cut off.

"Good-bye, Dr. Carter." Dr. Mortimer started to drag
him into the portal.

"No!" Lili's mind scrambled with possibilities. "Floor
so slick!" She watched as an oily substance covered the
floor by the portal. Jared wrenched around, in a way
that she knew had to hurt him badly, as the wizard went
one way and he went the other. She ran closer to him to
grab his arm and pull him away, while Dr. Mortimer lost
his balance. They stared as the portal opening suddenly
changed in color to vivid reds and oranges. He twisted
around, obviously seeing something they couldn't, and
released an ear-shattering scream as he fell backward
with arms flailing in hopes of keeping his equilibrium.
Flames whooshed into the room, instantly turning the
tables and ogres to ash.

Lili managed to release the collar from Jared's
throat and hugged him tightly. She shook her head.

"Jared." She suddenly laughed as she ran her hands over his chest. "Look."

He followed her gaze to see his skin unmarked.

Both brands marking him mentally ill and dangerous and demon dangerous to boot were gone.

Lili looked at her demon and smiled that he would forever be free of his cell.

Jared threaded his fingers through her hair and dipped his head until their lips barely touched.

"I always knew you did great work, Doc."

"I gather you didn't need our help after all."

Lili gasped and quickly rearranged her clothing that Jared had been only too happy to disarrange. She almost lost her balance until he steadied her with his hands as he gracefully jumped to his feet.

"Hello." She winced at her inane greeting to Eurydice, Nurse Garrish, Deisphe, and a woman wearing a black pin-striped pantsuit that looked very Armani. Lili was guiltily aware the ragged pants and top they'd dressed her in was spotted with various smelly liquids from the beakers. She gestured back at the portal opening that was now lifeless. "He fell through, and I don't know where he went."

The woman smiled. "I would not worry, Dr. Carter. Hieronymus Mortimer is exactly where he should be."

"Mother?" Jared stepped away from Lili and moved toward the woman.

Lili mouthed the word as she turned to the others. "He thought he could use our combined blood to further his power. That's how he's moved through the ages and killed people." Breath was pushed out of her lungs as Deisphe ran forward and hugged her. "Air. I need to breathe," she gasped with a laugh.

"You smell really bad." The Wereleopard wrinkled her nose.

"That can easily be taken care of." Eurydice told her with a smile. She walked around Lili in a tight circle, sending out magick, and by the time she finished, Lili's hair was in its usual high ponytail and she was garbed in a pair of burgundy silk pants and a lighter burgundy blouse. She paused to admire the gray python peep-toe pumps and was grateful she no longer smelled like bad magick.

"No wonder Jazz and Thea love their shopping. I need to take more lessons from them." She turned to see that Jared's mother had done the same with him. And felt her heart skip a few beats as she watched her lover hug the woman who birthed him. He looked freer than she had ever seen him, even during their intimate moments. She also felt a bit of fear that he might walk away from her and not look back.

"You've made Sinsia very happy by keeping her son safe." Eurydice touched her arm. "She had no idea Hieronymus had lied to her or what he had been doing to him. He is now in the hands of her clan, who will appropriately deal with him."

Lili shivered at the idea of what appropriate handling would be. Knowing demonkind, it wouldn't be a pretty sight.

She still felt a lump in her stomach and the urge to leave. A long hot shower and a good cry seemed like a good idea.

"Thank you," she said quietly. "Thank you for believing in me, for letting me come here, for, well, for everything." She blinked back tears. "I'm only sorry I couldn't do anything for Sera and the others."

"The Hellion Guard is going to do what they can to find them," the elder witch assured her, taking her arm and leading her toward the door.

That was when Lili realized they were down in the asylum. She glanced at the iron doors.

"I want them free and placed in rooms that offer light and staff members who will provide better treatment. With Dr. Mortimer dead, their brands should have disappeared the way Jared's did."

Nurse Garrish and Deisphe shared a look and nodded.

"Already taken care of, babe," the Were told her. "Panabell told us where you were. Cleo had followed you to Dr. Mortimer's office, and once she realized you were taken from there, obviously through a hidden panel in his office, she found me, and I went to Nurse Garrish."

"Hieronymus set strong locks on the door to this room, but many of us are better at magick than he is," the dragon-shifter said without a hint of conceit. "Otherwise, fire can be very satisfying if someone doesn't welcome our presence." She smiled, releasing a hint of sulfur.

Lili looked at the trio and wanted to laugh. "You three are such a welcome sight to me."

"Lili." Jared reached her and grasped her arm, pulling her around to face him. His mother stood just behind him, watching Lili with sharp eyes.

"So you are the witch who captured my son's heart," Sinsia said with a small smile.

Lili knew she was under strong scrutiny and didn't back down. "As he has mine."

The demon looped her arm through her son's. "Yes, I am sure you feel strongly about him now, but things happen. For now, my son returns with me where he belongs." Her teeth showed a sharp edge with her smile.

Lili stared at Jared, who looked as stunned as she felt. She didn't have a chance to say a word as Sinsia circled her hand around her body and Jared's. A moment later, they were gone in a burst of blue fire.

"No!" Lili stepped forward, but Eurydice pulled her back. She rounded on the Head Witch. "How could you let her do that?" She hated the demon for taking away Jared and Eurydice for the sympathy in her dark green eyes.

"It is the way of the demons," she said quietly. "Jared was diagnosed as dangerously ill and taken from her. It was only her intervention that ensured he would not be destroyed back then. She wants time with him."

"She took him from me!" Her voice raised in pitch. "We claimed each other."

Eurydice stilled at the pronouncement. "Just as Maggie and Declan did," she sighed. She draped an arm around Lili's shoulder and guided her to the stairs. "For now, think about what the hospital needs—a new doctor in charge."

Lili's feet lagged as they ascended the stone stairs.

"Sometimes the doctor needs something too," she murmured, wishing for a mega-amnesia spell. But she doubted even that would help her forget about the man she loved with all of her heart.

Epilogue

"ARE YOU SURE ABOUT THIS?" DIRECTOR OF NURSING Garrish faced Lili across the desk.

"Absolutely."

Lili hadn't really wanted the post as head of the hospital, but she knew leadership was needed, and Eurydice impressed upon her that she was their best bet. Lili agreed to her suggestion only as long as she worked in the trenches, so to speak.

She smiled at the dragon-shifter, who had turned out to be a good friend. While Arimentha had a harsh side to her personality, she also had the detail-oriented mind Lili didn't. In other words, she reveled in paperwork and dealing with all the everyday details that Lili had but to look at to develop a nasty rash.

"The head of a hospital and director of nursing normally do not work together," Nurse Garrish told her.

"And that is why they should now. We'll break new ground," Lili told her with sincere enthusiasm. "I don't want to sit behind a desk all day when I can help patients. I even hate this office, so if you want it, it's yours." She looked around Dr. Mortimer's former stronghold. She wasted no time dispensing with the furniture, and while clearing it out, discovered well-crafted illusion spells that hid books and scrolls dealing with dark charms. She handed them over to The Librarian, who vowed to keep them safe. She kept scented stones everywhere to banish the scent of tobacco and the musty aroma that permeated the office. Pulling down the heavy velvet drapes revealed a set of tall windows that allowed in much-needed light.

"Excuse me, cat here who refuses to give up her new space!" Cleo yowled from a corner where a luxurious silk-cushioned couch was set up for her comfort.

Nurse Garrish sighed. "The cat may stay and, thank you, I could use a larger office."

"Decorate it any way you wish. All I ask is that you have it thoroughly cleansed first," Lili advised. She had used a lot of smudge sticks and salt, but she knew the whole room needed more.

"Thank you." She dipped her head in thanks and respect. "You are not at all what I expected. Eurydice said you were a healer to be reckoned with, but she didn't say how devoted you are to those in need. I am impressed."

"Thank you, Arimentha." She poured two cups of tea, handing one over and nodded toward the plate of cookies. Who knew a dragon-shifter would have a sweet tooth?

"Have you heard from him?" She sipped her tea.

Lili didn't require clarification as to whom she spoke of. She looked at the floor, allowing her curls to cover her face as she shook her head. "Nothing," she admitted painfully. "Still, he's been away from his family for centuries." She wrinkled her nose, aware her excuse sounded as bad to her guest as it did to her.

"Males are annoying that way," Arimentha proclaimed, finishing her tea. "Better to have your way with them and move on."

"I'd like to interject here." Cleo held up a paw. "Euwww!"

"Says the cat that had sex with the major league in Ancient Rome," Lili muttered, rubbing eyes that were still puffy and scratchy from the previous night's cry-fest. She had spent too many nights crying herself to sleep, when she could sleep at all, and others roaming the house, remembering the nights Jared had come to her. Even Asmeth did his part in comforting her, with festive meals she pretended to eat for his benefit.

Arimentha excused herself to take a call on her cell phone, then returned to the office.

"We are wanted in the ER." She headed for the door.

"It's not even a full moon," Lili grumbled, walking with her, scuffing her feet along the way. "Dr. Heron and Deisphe are in charge tonight. There's nothing they can't handle."

"Straight back, m'dear," Arimentha said crisply. "A doctor must look as if she is in charge."

Lili heaved a deep sigh, but she straightened her posture.

The first thing she noticed when they neared the emergency room was the babble of voices, all excited.

"Probably a bridge troll with a post stuck up his ass," she muttered, stepping in, not realizing that the dragon-shifter had slowed her pace.

Deisphe looked over her shoulder and flashed her a big grin.

"It's about time you got here," she sang out.

The group parted to reveal a tall man.

Lili blinked because she refused to believe her eyes.

"Jared!" She ran forward and jumped into his arms.

He laughed as he grabbed hold of her before she fell

to the floor. Then he did the right thing and kissed her so deeply, she felt her breath leave her body.

"Hey guys, a lot of jealousy going on here." Deisphe laughed. "Trauma room's empty if you want some privacy."

Lili stepped back but didn't feel a bit of embarrassment. She was too happy to see Jared.

"I didn't think you were coming back," she confessed, running her hands over his shoulders and arms.

"I would have been here sooner, but I had to do something first." He cupped her face with his hands and gently turned her head to one side.

"Sera!" Lili quickly kissed Jared then ran to her friend, hugging her tightly. She looked at the others behind her who were greeted by the nurses and doctors. She turned back to Jared. "But how?"

"That's what took me so long," he told her. "But thanks to some of my mother's associates, we were able to track them down. Luckily, Mortimer only sent them into the past instead of killing them."

"Do you know what London in the 1880s is like?" Sera babbled, hugging her friend again. "I'll never take soap for granted again!" She grinned at her. "Jared said you were here, looking for me. That you never felt I was dead. I owe you big-time for that." Deisphe pulled the witch to one side and gestured for Lili to get back to Jared.

"I can't believe…" Lili shook her head in amazement.

"I'm here to stay, Doc." His lips brushed her forehead. "If you'll have me, that is."

"Just try and get away." She wasn't sure whether to laugh or cry.

Jared grinned at her. His dark eyes sparkled with

laughter and passion. "I'm not going anywhere, Doc. You're stuck with me now." He wrapped his arms around her. "I've been doing a lot of digging while searching for Sera. It seems Mortimer was doing this for years. I can't let those victims stay lost. I'm going to do my best to bring them all back to where and when they belong. I figure I need a base of operations, and there's nowhere better than Inderman for someone with my skills. Asmeth told me I'm needed, and I think I'd make a pretty good private investigator." His dark eyes blazed blue fire. "But what's important is that you need me."

Lili looked at the group around her. Their smiles echoed the one stretching her lips. "Excuse me, everyone. I'm taking the rest of the day off." She grabbed Jared's hand and pulled him out of the hospital.

"You'll all die!" the vulture, still perched on the granite gargoyle, flapped his wings at them.

The witch laughed as she looked up. "Not today," she declared as she turned to the man she loved with all her being. "Need you? I claimed you, my love, and I don't give up easily."

Jared smiled and stole her breath with his kiss. "I guess a witch and a demon as a team do it even better."

Read on to explore the world of Linda Wisdom,
where feisty witches and hot demons
will take you on a magickal ride!

50 Ways to Hex Your Lover

Hex Appeal

Wicked by Any Other Name

Hex in High Heels

DEMONS ARE A GIRL'S BEST FRIEND

50 Ways to Hex Your Lover

Alderley Edge, Cheshire, England
The Year 1313

SOMEONE'S THOUGHTLESS USE OF MAGICK HAS PUT OUR school in great jeopardy."

Emerald velvet robes flew around the reed-thin body of the headmistress as if a storm brewed within her. Red and blue flames flashed from the foot of her staff as she tamped it to punctuate her words with the ring of cold stone. Not one of Eurydice's thirteen students moved a muscle as they stood in line awaiting her judgment.

On their first day at The Academy for Witches, the headmistress had laid down the rules and the consequences of breaking them. She pronounced that there would be no exceptions if any of those rules were broken. Yet today, her cardinal law had been broken—one of the students had gone so far as to cast a curse on a mortal. She walked down the line of girls, spearing each of them with her angry gaze.

"We are sor—" one of the girls sputtered.

"*Silence!*" Eurydice turned on her heel to face down the unlucky witchling. "Whoever cast the spell must step forward and be accountable for her actions."

Not one of the acolytes spoke up. All thirteen stared at the ancient stone floor.

"Your shared silence to protect the guilty one is laudable." Eurydice's dark eyes matched the flames flickering at the end of her staff. Still no one moved. "However this offense was committed against a member of royalty. A man with the power to close this school, do us harm, even destroy us. I am certain some would commend you for not betraying the classmate who cast this spell, but the culprit must step forward and accept her punishment."

The girls looked at each other, linked their fingers together and then, as one, all thirteen stepped forward.

"Very well. As you will have it," Eurydice said. The air around her swirled dark and purple as she pronounced judgment. "Henceforth, all of you are banished from this place and are cast out into the world for one hundred years with only the powers you presently control. If any of you dares to cast a spell not meant for the greater good, your banishment will be extended. At the end of your banishment you will be brought before the Witches' High Council to determine your final fate.

"And I hope—" she made eye contact with each girl who managed to meet her furious gaze "—you will learn just what a merciless mortal world you have been cast into."

Then she tamped her staff against the cold, unforgiving stone floor, and the thirteen acolytes vanished.

The headmistress turned to face the three elder witches standing quietly by the wall.

"Do you think they'll be all right, Eurydice, all alone in the world?" Allene, the softhearted, asked. "Do you think they'll be in danger?"

"Hardly, dear sister," the headmistress chuckled. "I fear more for the world."

Pasadena, California
The Year 2007

How long are we going to sit here?"

"As long as it takes." Jazz Tremaine shifted in the Thunderbird convertible's bench seat. She loved her 1956 aqua and white classic sports car, but there wasn't much legroom for her five-foot-eight-inch frame.

Nice neighborhood for a stakeout though, with its wide, posh swath of multi-million dollar homes set behind high iron fences and ornate gates. Still, Jazz hoped she wouldn't have to wait all night for Martin "The Sleaze Bag" Reynolds to come home. Her left foot was falling asleep, and that large Diet Coke she'd had with her dinner was warning her that bathroom time would be in her near future.

A scraping sound, a flare of sulfur, and a whiff of tobacco smoke from the passenger seat made Jazz's nose twitch. "Irma, put that damn thing out."

Irma clicked open the ashtray and heaved a put-upon sigh. "I'm bored."

"Then leave," Jazz snapped.

"Ha, ha," Irma snorted. "Very funny."

She sat in the passenger seat wearing her Sunday best, a navy floral-print dress with its delicate lace collar and navy buttons marching down the front. A dainty navy and white spring straw hat decorated with tiny flowers sat squarely on her tightly permed iron-gray hair. White gloves and a navy patent leather handbag completed her perfect 1950s ensemble. No surprise there because Irma had died in the passenger seat of the T-Bird on March 12, 1956.

Irma was the bane of the 700-year-young witch's existence and the sole drawback to the snazzy car she dearly loved. Her 100-percent success rate at eliminating curses had fallen to 99 percent when she'd failed, no matter what she tried, to remove the highly irritating Irma from the car. In the end, Jazz's client refused to pay her, and Jazz ended up with the classic sports car instead; with Irma as an accessory.

"I can make that lamppost disappear with a snap of my fingers." Jazz gestured toward a nearby post standing at the corner and did just that. Another snap of the fingers and the post reappeared. "But with you ..." She snapped her fingers in front of Irma, but nothing happened. "With you, nothing. Nada. Zip. No matter how many times I try, you're still here!"

Hex Appeal

"You shall pay, Nick Gregory. This I vow. You shall suffer and scream for a mercy I shall deny you." Jazz's parted lips trailed across Nick's collarbone. She ran the tip of her tongue up the taut lines of his throat while her fingers danced their way down his abs following the line of crisp hair lower still.

"Mercy," Nick whispered as her fingers wrapped around his erection. He lay naked on his bed, legs slightly spread to accommodate Jazz's bare thigh draped over his.

"But we've just begun, darling," she purred, nipping his earlobe just hard enough to cause him to jump in response, then soothed the bite with her tongue. "You must lie there very still while I have my way with you."

"Feel free to do what you will—soon enough it will be my turn." He lowered his voice to a husky growl that made promises she knew he would keep. Her body quivered in anticipation.

But for now, it was her turn and she intended to make the most of it.

Leaning back, she admired the view. Sheer male beauty stretched out beside her. Nick had kept himself in excellent physical condition in life and, as a member of the undead, his well-honed body would never deteriorate. She tangled her fingers in the light dusting of dark brown hair on his chest. She knew many women admired a hair-free chest, but she liked to see a bit there, as long as the man didn't look as if he needed a good chest waxing. No, Nick's was just right. Surrendering to temptation, she lowered her head to nibble on a dark brown nipple that peeked out among the hair. It peaked to a hard nub and brought another groan to his lips.

"Wuss," she teased, dividing her attention between both nipples, alternating with tiny nips of her teeth and soothing licks of her tongue. She glanced up under the cover of her lashes. "Why no nipple rings? So many vamps love them as bling."

Nick made a face. "Not my style. Makes me think it would be too easy to loop a chain through it. Make me a slave."

"Hmmmm," she giggled and hummed as she mouthed her way down to his navel. "The picture that conjures up…"

"Seems like you've already conjured something very much up." His eyes followed as she cupped her hand around his straining cock, slowly stroking from root to tip in a rhythm that had him clenching his teeth when her other hand gently cradled the sac beneath.

"I ask that thee render me that which I deserve. Because I say so, damn it!" She finished with her own version of "so mote it be" on a wave of throaty laughter right before she raised her body up over him and settled on him with perfect ease. She straddled his hips, bending her long legs alongside his.

"What? No foreplay?" He grasped her hips, although

she needed no help in finding a rhythm. It had been written in their blood ages ago.

She leaned forward and brushed her mouth across his, tickling the seam of his lips and teasing the tips of his fangs, darting out before they could prick the tender skin. "We had foreplay at the movies," she breathed against his mouth. "And during the drive home when I unzipped your jeans and…" she deliberately paused for effect, "it's time for the main event, fang boy." She moved in a circular motion, tightening her core to massage him with her inner muscles.

Nick suddenly jackknifed his legs, flipping her onto her back with ease.

"You are so right, m'lady. But I'll be the ringmaster for this show." He dipped his head, kissing her deeply. The scent of arousal grew thick in the room. He reared back until his cock left her folds. As she whimpered the sorrow of her loss, he thrust forward, filling her once again. With each deepening stroke, she arched up, meeting him as his equal.

Jazz looked up, smiling at the dark intensity of his features.

Her smile faltered a bit when she saw the arousal turn to something else, as his expression sharpened and his eyes turned a burning red. The growl that traveled up his throat turned into a feral hiss. Before she could react, his fangs lengthened and he dipped his head. Pain shot through her as his fangs pierced the sensitive skin of her throat.

Why isn't my blood making him sick? Everyone knows a witch's blood will sicken, and can even kill, a vampire! She wanted to shriek, to fight back, but her heavy limbs refused to obey her commands. Lights danced before her eyes and she feared instead of her blood killing Nick, he would kill her.

Jazz's eyes popped open as she shot up in bed, her hand pressed against the side of her neck where pain still radiated. Nick lay slumbering beside her.

Fear, memory of searing pain, and just plain fury warred inside her. She looked down at the source and let her temper—and fist—loose.

"You son of a whore!" She threw a punch to his bare abs that could easily have broken her hand. Not that she would have noticed. "*You bit me!*"

"What? What?" Nick scrambled away from her flying fists and fell out of bed. He grasped the covers and stared at her as if he was positive she'd somehow lost her mind. "What in Hades is wrong with you?"

"You bit me!" She slid off the other side of the bed and hurried around the room, keeping her hand pressed against her neck. Pain and anger translated to red and purple sparks flying around her.

"Bit you?" Confusion mingled with being just plain pissed off at being awakened with a punch to the stomach. "I was *asleep,* damn it!" He hauled himself to his feet and stood there in all his naked glory. For once, Jazz's cold stare warned him that she wasn't admiring the view. He stared at her hand covering her throat but saw no signs of blood or trauma to the skin. He refused to believe he would take her blood without permission, asleep or not. In all their times as lovers he hadn't even given her a hickey. He also kept a close eye on her free hand. The last thing he wanted was witchflame thrown at his favorite part of the body. "Damn it, I didn't bite you!"

Wicked by Any Other Name

"Can you believe this absolute nonsense? I'm being sued!" Stasi stormed into Blast from the Past with the force of a Category 5 hurricane. She held up a sheaf of papers that looked suspiciously like ancient papyrus with lines of gilded lettering streaming across it. The large, embossed seal stamped at the bottom made it official. "And in Wizards' Court, no less!"

"Uh, Stasi, love, I have customers." Blair's gaze darted to the four people prowling her shop, who were now looking at Stasi with fascination. Blair's shop specialized in authentic retro items, from a 1940s Madame Alexander doll to a 1950s chrome table and tie-dyed clothing from the 1960s. It was easy for Blair to keep a varied inventory when her sister witches tended to clean out their closets of personal treasures every so often and were happy to have Blair sell them on consignment.

She quickly held up her hands. "Freeze frame, make it so!" She moved swiftly toward one woman who had frozen in the process of returning a tall Warner Bros. Roadrunner glass to the shelf, grabbing the glass just as it slipped from the woman's fingers. She placed it carefully among the other glasses and turned to Stasi.

Stasi's mid-length sunny brown hair flared around her with a life of its own as she stomped to the rear of the shop. She pulled herself up to sit on the waist-high counter and tossed the papyrus down on the polished surface. "This is insane," she snarled, staring at the parchment so hard Blair was amazed it didn't burst into flames. "Hic!" A perfectly shaped iridescent bubble escaped her lips.

Blair stared at her best friend in amazement. Anastasia Romanov was known for her sweet, romantic temperament and calm, almost placid, demeanor. Right now she looked ready to go off into a major witchy hissy fit, as evidenced by those angry bubbles. This was not the Stasi she'd known for more than seven hundred years! Stasi hiccupped and two more bubbles floated into the room.

"Now isn't the time to get the hiccups! Take a breath," Blair ordered, running a hand through her dark auburn curls. "And tell me what is going on. Slowly!"

Stasi closed her eyes, hiccupped again (three bubbles this time), and pulled in a deep breath, then another. When she opened them, she looked a bit calmer. And when she hiccupped again, only one tiny bubble slipped out. Blair relaxed a little.

"Carrie Anderson is suing me for alienation of affection. She's claiming it's my fault her rotten husband didn't come back." Dark purple sparks shot out over her head.

"Stasi, you need to calm down!" Blair said firmly. She glanced at the front door and promptly set a stay out spell on it. The last thing she needed was someone walking in to find customers playing Statue and Stasi shooting off magickal sparks. "Everyone knows Carrie's totally delusional about things." Blair glanced at the papyrus. "Why would she sue you for alienation of affection?"

Stasi's golden brown eyes glittered with unshed tears that had more to do with fury than sorrow. "She's claiming that I did something to the sachet I tucked into her package that made sure her cheating, lower-than-scum husband wouldn't return to her and that by giving her a charm that harmed her marriage I interfered in mortal affairs. The 'cheating and lower-than-scum' description is mine. She's claiming he's the love of her life and she just knows he would have come back to her if I hadn't done something horrible to make sure he wouldn't return. He's, what, her fourth husband? It's a well-known fact that every man she's been with has been driven to cheat on her! And I've never made a claim that the sachets I put in the bags do anything. I make it sound like a joke that they inspire romance, and the customers love it. And it's not as though I can do much more than that, anyway. If I did, Cupid would be on my butt faster than a flea."

"Oh yeah, he's real protective of his job and doesn't like anyone interfering in his field," Blair agreed.

"Like most of the people in town, Carrie knows I'm a witch and she thinks my romance sachet should have brought Kevin back to her." Stasi crossed her arms in front of her chest, a full pout on her lips. "So now she's mad at me and wants vengeance. To top it off, she somehow persuaded a top wizard lawyer to file suit against me in Wizards' Court!"

"It can't be done. It has to be prosecuted in Witches' Court." Blair wasn't an attorney, but over the centuries she'd learned more than she liked about witch law.

Stasi shook her head. "Obviously it can, if that bottom-feeding wizard lawyer took the case and filed it. It would be bad enough if she'd hired that one that's on the late night paranormal channel. Herve Rovenal will take any case to defend innocent mortals from the ones who prey on them. But she hired Trevor Barnes!" Her lip curled as she glared at the parchment again. This time a thin wisp of smoke curled up from its surface but was quickly snuffed out—not by Stasi, but by the parchment itself.

"We can't discuss it here," Blair said. She checked the black Kit-Kat clock hanging on the wall. "It's almost closing time anyway. I'll herd these people out once I've unfrozen them and we'll see what's going on. Okay?"

Stasi nodded. "They'll have another thing coming if they think I'll put up with this insanity," she muttered, hopping off the counter. "It's not my fault that Carrie's husband left her! Kevin used to be a nice guy, and she treated him like dirt. I'll make her sorry she started this." She marched to the door, which opened and closed behind her without her hand touching it or the brass bell hanging over it making a sound.

Blair quickly unfroze her customers, made a sale to a bewildered woman, and ushered the rest out before they realized what was happening.

"Girlfriend's got a problem," Felix, the black Kit-Kat clock Blair had owned since the 1930s, announced from his spot high up on the wall. His large eyes swept from side to side as his tail swung back and forth above a sign proclaiming him Not for Sale.

"No kidding." Blair emptied the old-fashioned cash register that had once resided in Moonstone Lake's general store back in the mid-1800s and tucked the checks, cash, and coins into a bank bag. With the spell surrounding the bag, no thief would dare try to steal it unless he wanted his hands covered in nasty itching powder that wouldn't disappear for years. Blair Fitzpatrick took her revenge spells seriously and did the utmost to protect her assets. No shoplifter would get away without some serious pain.

"You're going to tell me all in the morning, right?" Felix asked, always eager to learn any new gossip that cropped up out of his range.

"Good night, Felix." Blair blew him a kiss as she headed for the front door. Judging from the sounds overhead, Stasi was upstairs creating havoc.

Hex in High Heels

"YOU TURNED THEM INTO TEENAGERS?" JAKE HARRISON howled, which sounded eerily like his Were–Border Collie self, even though this morning he was deliciously human. He was lounging in a red vinyl and chrome chair by the 1950s diner table on display in the back of the vintage shop, long legs stretched out comfortably. Dressed in his usual faded jeans and flannel shirt, Jake's shaggy black hair was in need of a trim and his black eyes were bright with laughter. One hand rested idly on the Select-O-Matic jukebox on the table, while the other held a paper cup filled with coffee. The rich scent of cinnamon mocha filled the air.

"They were lucky that's all I did to them. And let me tell you, there's nothing scarier than trophy wives suddenly reverting to pimply face, original nose, stringy hair teens. Not one of them was a cute kid, either. All of their so-called natural beauty came from a surgeon's knife, hairdresser's skill, and make-up." Blair Fitzpatrick stood a short distance away, studying with satisfaction the primary colors adorning the walls of her shop, Blast from the Past. She specialized in selling vintage items and liked to make her shop bright and welcoming to tempt customers inside. But what really revved her engines was the way Jake was looking at her, with a dark gaze that held more than a hint of hunger. Yep, Jake was the one who really stirred her hormonal cauldron.

"Some people just don't understand that my gifts are meant for the greater good." She sat down across from him and sipped the caramel latte Jake had brought her that morning.

He grinned at her. "Oh yeah, anyone can see that revenge spells are for the greater good."

"You craft the right spell, and husbands and boy-friends think twice about cheating on their women. A woman who's illegally run up a man's credit card suddenly finds the bill in her name, or worse." She absently touched her curly, dark auburn hair to make sure her '40s updo was still in place. Each week Blair took the time to decorate the shop in a different theme. This week was the 1940s and she was dressed accordingly. "Two small examples."

"It's a good reminder never to piss you off."

Blair rested her chin on her hand and studied his silky black hair and lean, rough-hewn features. In human form, Jake was one hot-looking guy; and even in dog form, any woman would want to adopt him. But she knew she could look into his dark eyes all day and never see all that was within. Jake had kept his Were nature secret for a long time and even now, despite her witchy senses, she couldn't detect a hint of Canis lupus famil-iaris. That didn't stop her from gazing at his mouth and imagining it on hers, or his hands running over her body or… wowza! Was it hot in here or was she having a hot flash? "I have to say, you'd come out pretty good even as a toad or a warthog."

"Blair!" A young woman's voice echoed through the

archway separating Blair's shop from fellow witch Stasi's lingerie boutique, Isn't It Romantic. "It's Horace again."

"'It's only for three days,' she says," Blair grumbled, rising to her feet. "'Trev's taking me away for a romantic long weekend. Ashley will watch the shop, so no worries there,' she assures me. If Stasi wanted no worries, she should have taken Horace with her. But I suppose her wizard boyfriend wouldn't be too keen on that. Not that I blame him." She walked through the archway into the neighboring shop. A moment later a multi-colored spike of light flashed between the shops, and Horace the gargoyle's yelp of pain was heard. Blair returned, rubbing her hands in a gesture of a job well done.

"Stasi only tells me no!" the gargoyle yelled after her.

"Yeah, well, I'm in charge now."

Jake glanced at Felix, the Kit-Kat clock on the wall, and stood up, pulling on his fleece-lined denim jacket. "You're going?" she protested.

"Agnes asked me to replace some boards in their front fence and I promised to do it today."

"And you decided to do it while she's at her hair appointment," she guessed.

He nodded. "Floyd, I can handle," he said, naming the town's mayor. "But Agnes seems to feel she should be out there supervising, when she doesn't know a thing about carpentry. Plus that heavy stuff she calls perfume makes me sneeze. With luck, I'll be done before she gets back. I'll see you later." With a wave of his hand he was gone.

Blair resisted to the urge to let her own inner teenager peek out the window and watch him walk down the street.

While she and Jake had become closer since the dramatic events of last Samhain, they still weren't as close as she'd hoped. She knew the man was interested. He stopped by just to chat a couple of times a week and often brought her favorite latte and muffins with him. Who could resist a man who brought her something that, in her mind, was better than roses?

Every so often Jake still showed up as his Were–Border Collie alter ego, and while Blair complained about the shedding—things could be worse.

She stared at the colorful flyer announcing the upcoming annual Winter Carnival, sponsored by a nearby resort. The town of Moonstone Lake was gearing up for attracting the tourists. Maybe the carnival preparations would provide the opportunity she'd been waiting for to pull Jake closer.

DEMONS
ARE A
GIRL'S BEST
FRIEND

"OH YEAH, JUST ANOTHER SATURDAY NIGHT HITTING the clubs, watching the dancers, feeling blood stream out of my ears." Maggie O'Malley winced as Static-X's "Destroyer" screamed from the state-of-the-art speakers embedded in the club's walls. Still, she couldn't stop her hips from moving to the throbbing music. If she wasn't there on business, she would have been out there dancing. "Why don't you just shoot me now?"

"Any females get naked yet?" the voice of Frebus, one of her team members, rumbled from the mic in her ear. "It's only a matter of time 'til somebody gets caught up in the moment and starts tearing off their clothes. You gotta love shape-shifters cuz they're always the first to get down and dirty."

Maggie played idly with the crystal earring that dangled almost to her bare shoulders. She considered her jewelry a much better look for a mic and earpiece than the usual spy gear. If only she could mute the music for an hour. Or ten.

"Sorry, sweetie, I'm only seeing half naked, but think positive. The evening's still young." She grinned as she heard the low groan in her ear. Frebus and her other backups, Meech and Tita, were strategically placed around the interior, on the lookout for one particular degenerate in the sea of questionable characters.

She made her way through the hordes of glassy-eyed, gyrating dancers, skillfully avoiding the groping hands on her ass and breasts. She muttered a spell against any who returned for another feel. Nothing like a magickal zap to the genitals to spoil the mood. Judging from the yelps that followed her, at least five tried.

Maggie didn't believe in giving anyone a second chance.

She viewed the large, creature-populated under-ground club with an expression of distaste and the desire for her olfactory senses to be on the fritz.

"Haven't some of these guys ever heard of deodor-ant?" she muttered, passing one scaly creature that fell in the "totally gross" category. It peered at her through red-slitted eyes and hissed, its forked tongue flicking toward her. Maggie hissed back and moved on.

The club's name, Damnation Alley, fit the interior with its glossy black walls, black glass bars with the interiors pulsing with ice-blue and black lights casting an unearthly glow on the preternaturals thronging the interior. Any unlucky human who managed to get past the door ran the risk of exiting in a body bag—or some-one's stomach.

She'd planned to spend tonight with a bowl of pop-corn and DVDs at home, but one of her team members got word that a fugitive they'd been after for the past month would be at the club tonight. Maggie and her team were sent here to bring it in.

She locked gazes with a vampire she remembered going up against a year earlier. He flashed fang. She responded with a smile that promised a repeat of what had happened before. The vamp wisely turned away.

At first glance, Maggie looked like a typical party gal

in her barely there black skirt and bandeau top. Shiny silver glitter accents covered the fabric that bared her shoulders and taut midriff, and only she knew of the protective spells woven into the fabric.

A dazzling, diamond-encrusted black widow spider with ruby eyes was tattooed on one bicep. Dangerous bling. Don't leave home without it. She'd slicked back her chin-length pale blonde hair with glittery gel, knowing that it made her features seem sharper than usual tonight. She smiled at one man who focused his attention on her legs and her black stilettos.

Maggie believed in themes, and tonight's was dangerous sexy female on the prowl. *The better to destroy you with, my dear*.

She cast her senses wide, searching for her prey. Her gaze skittered to a halt when it reached a man standing in the doorway leading to the private rooms.

A few inches taller than her almost six feet, he was also dressed in black, but he didn't look like the typical clubgoer. The silk shirt and slacks looked well tailored and suited his tanned skin, dark eyes, and spiked hair. He oozed danger. Judging by the hungry looks women were directing his way, they didn't mind the danger part at all.

Maggie didn't miss that most of the females were much more generously endowed than she was. She normally didn't mind her slender athletic figure, but sometimes she'd like to have enough to fill more than a middling B cup.

No time to play, pretty boy. Maggie's got other creatures to fry. But stick around, and maybe we can fit in a dance later on.

What a concept. Your everyday witch having an evening out where she could flirt with a gorgeous guy, get in some dancing, and just talk. When was the last time she'd had a date? Did she have enough fingers and toes to count back that far?

She purposely looked away until her gaze slammed into an odd-looking creature standing at the rear bar.

"Okay, that thing is butt ugly." Maggie noted the bloated body dressed in rags. She was positive he wouldn't smell all that good, either. Not that the smell seemed to bother those around him.

"Beauty's in the eye of the beholder, blondie," Meech's disembodied voice reminded her. She caught a glimpse of the big, blue-skinned monster on the other side of the room, guarding a side door. He was grinning as his voice continued through the mic. "While some think you're smokin', all I see is that you're damn scrawny, your nose is out of place, and those pearly whites aren't jagged enough. Plus, they're not healthy unless they're gray or yellow."

"Aw, baby, you know just what to say to make a girl feel good about herself." She took a quick glance down to make sure the girls were at their best advantage. Nothing like giving a perp something to look at while she took him down.

Not that anyone around here would notice. They'd just think it was another S and M show. Another thing Damnation Alley was known for. Although at present she wasn't seeing the kind of sex shows that had gone on here when Ratchet owned the club.

"Oh, Frebus, you bring me to the classiest of places," she purred.

"Better than that tavern two months ago. Plus, this one needs to be put down quick before he causes any more trouble. Him being here tonight is pure luck for us."

"Just stay on alert in case I need backup. Bloaters aren't the type to go quietly." Maggie put her hips to work as she glided over to the bar. She could feel the dark-haired man's eyes on her with a searing intensity, but she kept him on the back burner.

"Hi." She flashed her sultriest smile at her quarry.

The creature looked up, revealing a puce-colored fleshy face, round chartreuse eyes, and a dark slit for a mouth.

"You are witch." He looked at her from the top of her head to the tips of her shoes.

"No one's perfect." She rested an arm on the bar top, acting as if the putrid stench emanating from his skin didn't assault her nose. "Buy me a drink?"

"Witches do not drink maiden grog." His gray claws wrapped around a clay goblet.

"The main element in the grog is a virgin's urine," Tita whispered in her earpiece.

Maggie's smile didn't slip even as her brain screamed *euuwwww!*

"You'd be surprised what I drink." She cocked a delicate brow. "They have private rooms here." She ran a scarlet polished nail over his claws while moving forward enough to brush her breasts against his arm.

At the same time that the creature's gaze fastened on her bare skin, she whipped iron-laced restraints out and slapped them on his wrists.

"You bitch!"

"Aw, now you're just sweet talking me."

The Bloater roared, rearing back and striking her with his chained claws, sending her sailing onto the top of the bar.

Maggie didn't have time to react, finding herself thrown down the slippery slab. Drinks scattered everywhere, and earsplitting shrieks rose above the din. As she slid to a stop, she saw her quarry trying to escape, scrambled to her feet, and ran after him while others tried to stop her.

"Hellion Guard!" she shouted, even as she knew there would be those who didn't appreciate the authorities being there.

Before her prey reached an exit door, Maggie launched herself with a leap worthy of a football player and tackled him to the floor.

"You are under arrest," she began even as she realized he was inflating like a Macy's Thanksgiving Day balloon, and it didn't look like he intended stopping any time soon.

"We're on our way!" she heard Frebus shout from her earring.

The second her three team members shouldered their way through the watching crowd, Maggie's prisoner reached the breaking point.

And that's when he blew up, splattering pea-green goo everywhere.

About the Author

Linda Wisdom was born and raised in Huntington Beach, California. She majored in journalism in college, then switched to fashion merchandising when she was told there was no future for her in fiction writing. She held a variety of positions, ranging from retail sales to executive secretary in advertising and office manager for a personnel agency.

Her career began when she sold her first two novels to Silhouette Romance on her wedding anniversary in 1979. Since then, she has sold almost eighty novels and two novellas to five different publishers. Her books have appeared on various romance and mass market bestseller lists and have been nominated for a number of Romantic Times awards. She has been a two-time finalist for the Romance Writers of America RITA Award.

She lives with her husband, one dog, one parrot, and a tortoise in Murrieta, California.

When Linda first moved to Murrieta, there were three romance writers living in the town. At this time, there is just Linda. So far, the police have not suspected her of any wrongdoing.